GIDEON'S TORCH

GIDEON'S TORCH

CHARLES COLSON
& ELLEN VAUGHN

WORD PUBLISHING

DALLAS LONDON VANCOUVER MELBOURNE

PUBLISHED BY WORD PUBLISHING,
DALLAS, TEXAS

Book Design by Mark McGarry
Set in Monotype Bembo

LIBRARY OF CONGRESS CATALOGING-IN-PUBLICATION DATA
Colson, Charles W.
Gideon's Torch / Charles Colson and Ellen Santilli Vaughn.
p. cm.
ISBN 0-8499-1146-X
1. Vaughn, Ellen Santilli. 11. Title.
PS3553.04767G5   1995   95-21744
813´.54—dc20
CIP

PRINTED IN THE UNITED STATES OF AMERICA

56789   BVG   987654321

To the heroes of Eastern Europe, known and unknown: the believers of every confession who defended the Truth, overcame evil with good, and toppled the greatest tyranny of the twentieth century. May their lives both inspire and caution us in the tumultuous times in which we live.

" . . . A Christian must be a sign of contradiction in the world . . . A Christian is one who all his life chooses between good and evil, lies and truth, love and hatred, God and Satan . . . Today more than ever there is a need for our light to shine, so that through us, through our deeds, through our choices, people can see the Father who is in Heaven."

JERZY POPIELUSZKO, 1947–1984

PREFACE

THIS IS A WORK of fiction. Apart from obvious historical references to public figures and events, all characters and incidents in this novel are the products of the authors' imaginations. Any similarities to people living or dead are purely coincidental.

Writing this book has proved to be an eerie experience for us. While it might appear to the reader that a number of the incidents included in *Gideon's Torch* have been taken from real newspaper headlines—including the suicide of White House counsel Vincent Foster, the murders at several abortion clinics, and, most recently, the tragic bombing of the Alfred P. Murrah Federal Building in Oklahoma City—our fictional episodes were conceived and written long before those actual events took place. The truth *is* stranger than fiction.

Charles Colson
Ellen Vaughn
June 1, 1995
Washington, D.C.

Do not repay anyone evil for evil. Be careful to do what is right in the eyes of everybody. If it is possible, as far as it depends on you, live at peace with everyone. . . . Do not be overcome by evil, but overcome evil with good.

ROMANS 12:17–18, 21

1

"ALL CLEAR for your approach, United 6031," said the crisp voice from the control tower. "Runway number thirty-five cleared for visual approach. Come on down, and welcome to Fargo."

As the twin-engine Beechcraft 1900 slowed and bobbled toward landing, the thin, rumpled, dark-haired woman in seat 3-A looked absently out the window, then checked her watch: 8:35. They were coming in about ten minutes early. Unusual, but good. She had a full day of appointments at the clinic.

Hope John is there to meet me, she thought, putting her newspaper back into her leather satchel. She stretched her legs, rubbed her eyes, and flexed her long, narrow hands, then settled back as the plane touched down, braked, and headed toward the terminal.

Dr. Ann Sloan was exhausted. She felt like she had fur on her tongue and grit in her eyelids. For five years now she had been a "circuit rider," shuttling between abortion clinics in three states. Fargo was her busiest stop. The approval last year of RU-486 had slowed early-trimester abortions, but there was still a booming business in later-term procedures. Since no doctor in North Dakota would perform them, Ann and another out-of-state physician took turns servicing the women who traveled for eight and ten hours from all over the state in order to terminate their pregnancies.

Ann earned more than $100,000 a year, but it wasn't easy work. The travel was draining, and then there was the harassment. She had received more death threats and horrifying messages than she cared to remember; as a result, her teenage daughter knew never to listen to their answering machine unless Ann had previewed the tape first. Their home in Minnesota had been the target of routine harassment over the last few years: blood-colored paint on their driveway, grisly photos of aborted fetuses stuffed in their mailbox, "wanted" posters of Ann nailed to trees in the neighborhood.

This had only deepened her resolve. She hated the anti-abortion movement, hated its smug self-righteousness, hated these terroristic fundamentalists who were always trying to intimidate women from exercising their constitutional right to reproductive choice. She hated the songs, the sidewalk prayers, the taunts, the harassment of patients. It made her so angry that she felt the only reasonable response was to continue to supply the needs of North Dakota women, no matter what.

The "no matter what" had escalated over the years. After two doctors and several clinic staffers were shot, the FBI had paid her a formal call. A dispassionate agent, speaking in stiff, bureaucratic language, had let her know that though federal marshals and other officers had stepped up their protection of the clinics and their investigations of anti-abortion groups, the agents were spread too thin to cover every abortion facility all the time. It would be in her best interest, he said, to endure various "inconveniences."

She took his advice.

Now she never took the same route anywhere for two days in a row. She constantly checked her rearview mirrors. Her car phone was programmed to dial both 911 and a special FBI number. And if an unfamiliar car passed her house twice in an evening, she recorded its license plate. The FBI kept a file of those numbers. She had even started checking underneath her car for bombs, using a special mirror the police had given her.

At the airport she always positioned herself near clumps of other commuters, taking comfort in the cluster of the crowd. And though she hated it, she had begun to wear a Kevlar vest. It was hot and bulky, but at least she was doing all she could reasonably do to protect herself. It was up to the government to do the rest.

But come what may, she was not going to let the "antis" win. She was not going to quit her practice. She was not going to be intimidated into abandoning these women who needed her help.

Today, however, she wasn't thinking much about any of this. She was worried about her daughter. Lindsay, a junior in high school, was in love for the first time, and the object of her affections was a freshman at the nearby university. Her daughter's apparent obsession with this young man was pulling her in over her head, but she just would not listen to Ann's warnings to take it slow.

The plane had rolled to a stop near the small commuter terminal, and Ann could see men in bulky parkas, their breath frosty in the cold air, pulling luggage from the plane's underbelly. As the copilot wrestled the cabin door open and positioned the portable stairs, Ann belted her heavy trenchcoat, picked up her satchel, and made her way to the door. The copilot nodded at her.

"Thanks, Greg, good flight," Ann said and headed down the stairs. When she reached the ground, she looked toward the waiting area in the terminal. She could see John, one of the clinic volunteers, waving to her. Good. She'd have time to have a cup of coffee before she began her appointments.

AS THEY NEARED the clinic, a large old house that had been rehabbed, Ann groaned. She always hoped the protesters might take a break one Friday, but it never happened. Today there were at least seventy of them. Their numbers always swelled in January as it got closer to the anniversary of *Roe v. Wade*. Ann had also noticed that there had been more protesters since November's election, probably because President-elect Griswold was aggressively pro-choice. Or else they were venting their frustration with the defeat of Martin Masterson, the anti-choice candidate.

"Why can't these people just march on Washington and leave us alone?" she said to John.

Today there were reporters on the scene as well. *Must be a slow news day*, Ann thought as she noticed a van from Channel 11 parked out front and a smaller white van from Channel 4 at the curb near the side entrance. She could see Channel 11's crew already filming out front. She dreaded the sight of them, too. The media's presence always made the protesters louder and more aggressive. Fortunately, the reporters usually gave the clinic personnel an opportunity to advance their point of view as well.

John gunned the car toward the narrow driveway. Simultaneously, two clinic workers appeared at the door and came down the front steps gripping a large sheet of white canvas, moving quickly toward the car door on Ann's side. She unlocked the door and stepped out, ducking behind the sheet. John slid across the seat and followed her.

The protesters' chants turned into vicious shouts.

"Baby killer!"

"Cursed are the hands that shed innocent blood!"

Ann stumbled up the steps and through the clinic doors. Inside its haven, past the metal detectors, she looked at her watch. Still running a bit ahead of schedule. Great.

"Good morning!" she said to her colleagues, who were folding the canvas as if it were a flag. "I see our friends outside are in full form today. Do we have enough volunteer escorts to handle all of today's appointments?"

"I think so," said Diane Brook, the clinic's administrator. "We've got twenty-four clients scheduled, and the first three are already inside. One of them is a basket case. She got here early, but the antis were already here and harassed her on the way in. She asked if she could talk to the doctor before the procedure, just to ease her mind. We told her she could if you got here in time."

Diane took Ann's coat. "Let me hang that up for you, and I'll get you a mug of coffee. Anyway, this girl is twenty-one. By herself. Boyfriend left, family not supportive. She's been in the bathroom for a while. Said she was nervous."

"I'll talk with her," Ann said. "Just get me that coffee first. I need it bad today."

Ann walked down the narrow hallway toward the small room that served both as her office and as the clinic's file room. Ann took out her keys, but the door was already unlocked. Diane must have been in there for some files; her key was stuck in the dead-bolt on the inside of the door.

ANN HAD JUST dropped her satchel on the desk when Diane came in carrying a big blue mug of coffee and leading a petite girl in jeans and round, dark sunglasses, the kind Ann's daughter favored. Her hair was swept up under a baseball cap, and she was huddled in a too-big leather bomber jacket, her hands jammed in the pockets. Underneath the jacket Ann could see an EarthFirst! T-shirt. *Poor thing*, thought Ann. *That jacket is probably all she has left—that she wants—from her boyfriend.*

"Here's your coffee," said Diane. "I'm going outside and have a word with those antis while the guys from Channel 11 are still filming."

Ann went around to her side of the desk and scanned the open appointment book. She sipped the hot coffee gratefully.

"Please sit down," she said to the girl, gesturing toward a metal folding chair in front of the desk. "I'm Doctor Sloan. I understand you were given a hard time this morning."

The girl perched nervously on the edge of the chair, hands still in her pockets, head down. "It was awful," she said softly. "They said not to murder my baby. They said there was still time to change my mind. They had big bloody posters of tiny babies…"

Ann flushed, the familiar anger rising in her chest. It was one thing to harass the strong, she thought. It was a pain, but she could handle it. But here was this young girl, all alone, vulnerable. It made Ann crazy. This was a medical procedure, for heaven's sake, perfectly legal, affordable, safe… and yet women across the country faced every obstacle these fanatics could think of to keep them from exercising their rights. It infuriated her every time she thought about her own daughter and the future *she* faced...all of the advances feminists had fought for, and women still couldn't freely control their own bodies and lives. It was insane.

"What's your name?" she asked.

"Sherry," the girl said, her head still down.

"Sherry, those people are living in the Dark Ages. They're just trying to impose *their* morality on you. They don't even care about you; all they care about is their own agenda. But this is still America. You have the right to make your own choices."

The girl looked up for the first time, and Ann was struck by how much she reminded her of Lindsay.

"They just made me feel so bad," Sherry said. "It's not like I'm so crazy about having this done. It's just that I don't know what else to do. I'm in school, I don't have much money, I don't have anyone to fall back on."

"I can understand if you're not happy about having an abortion right now," Ann said. "I've dealt with thousands of women over the years, and believe me, what you're feeling is normal. But you do have a right to make this decision. It's your choice—nobody else's. Probably now isn't the right time for you to continue a pregnancy. But it's up to you. Not a bunch of terrorists shoving posters in your face."

Sherry sighed. "You said you've dealt with lots of women," she said hesitantly. "How many of these do you think you've done? Abortions, I mean."

Ann paused for a moment. She had left her gynecology practice during Lindsay's last year in elementary school. Now she served three clinics in three states—about six thousand procedures a year.

"I've done this about thirty thousand times," she said. "And I can't begin to tell you how many of those women told me that it was the best choice they ever made for themselves." She lowered her eyes as she took another big swallow of coffee.

THE GIRL SLID the gun from her pocket. The safety was off; the silencer was on. She kept it and her hands below the edge of the desk.

"Thirty thousand babies," she said slowly, taking a deep breath. "Then your own lips have condemned you."

The doctor looked up, startled.

Both of her gloved hands on the gun, the girl stood, raised the barrel quickly, and aimed at the quarter-sized round of skin between the woman's dark eyebrows.

She gently squeezed the trigger, just as she had been taught. There was a spitting sound and, simultaneously, the doctor's head exploded against the wall behind the desk. A pink mist hung in the air; the coffee cup dropped to the desk, spreading a brown stain across the appointment book. The doctor's body slid down in the chair and to the floor.

The girl turned, as she had practiced, slipped the pistol back in her pocket, and ran the few steps toward the door. She took the key hanging from the deadbolt, closed the office door behind her, and locked it. Hands back in her pockets, she moved quickly down the hall.

The woman who had escorted her into the clinic earlier looked at her questioningly.

"I'm sorry," the girl said. "I just can't go through with it. I've got to get out of here." She moved toward the doors.

The woman shrugged. Sometimes it happened; patients panicked. Well, that made one less on the schedule.

The girl burst through the front doors and pushed through the protesters. They were still trading insults with the woman who had brought the doctor her coffee. The cameras were rolling, and the woman kept talking, jabbing her finger at the pro-lifers.

The girl made her way through the crowd and around the corner. The white van was waiting, its motor running. The side door slid open, she jumped inside, and the van pulled away from the curb, the Channel 4 logo on its side just a bit off-center.

2

I RA LEVITZ SAT at his computer, his fingers darting across
the keyboard. Usually he wrote his newspaper columns at home,
relishing the privacy of his book-strewn office and the silent com-
panionship of his cat, Josephus, who loved to lie in the wide
windowsill adjacent to his desk, flicking his tail, while Ira pondered
and pounded the keys.

Now and then, however, Ira liked to come into the newsroom,
so the *Post* reserved this cubicle for him. As usual, it was cluttered
with Styrofoam cups, books, and unanswered mail. Dozens of his
colleagues milled around in the huge room, phones to their ears,
drinking coffee, arguing with one another, and clattering away at
their computers.

Writing in the midst of this newsroom furor always gave him a
satisfying sense of power: He really could block out the chaos and
force clean, organized thoughts onto the computer screen. And he
loved the energy, the camaraderie, that flowed from the network
of people, all striving toward the same goals: Get the story. Make
the deadline. It reminded him of his early days as a journalist,
before syndication had beckoned.

Now he was nationally known, with regular invitations to give speeches, appear on talk shows, and kibitz with Washington's inside-the-Beltway powerbrokers. All this because he hammered out his blunt, hard-edged opinions twice a week. It never ceased to amaze him. He was forty-eight years old, but he would never lose his childlike delight in his work and the fact that, somehow, he was well-paid and well-regarded just for the privilege of doing what he loved.

Ira Levitz was an anomaly. He was Jewish, liberal, a watchdog on constitutional issues, bombastic, aggressive... and pro-life. His colleagues put up with him because he was a good liberal and exuded an eccentric charm. The pro-life community liked him because he was a straight shooter and had the guts to believe and write about constitutional protection for the unborn. And both sides were drawn to the large, lumpy man because of his unmistakable air of compassion.

Nine years earlier, when his marriage had fallen apart, Ira had fallen into clinical depression. He still went to therapy once a month, but the Prozac his psychiatrist had prescribed kept him on a fairly even keel. His experience with the dark side, however, had given him an aura of empathy that was unusual among journalists. Ira knew the numbness, the helplessness of deep-rooted despair. So in spite of his talent, his privilege, and his sophisticated lifestyle, he had compassion for the weak and helpless. And that fact, paradoxically, made him very attractive to the strong and powerful.

Ira paused in the middle of a paragraph. He ran his hands through his thick mat of unkempt black hair. This particular column—musings on the upcoming Griswold presidency—had been giving him fits. That's why he was working in the newsroom today, hoping that inspiration would seep by osmosis into his work. But he was stuck—not just on ideas, which always came hard, but on words, which usually came easily.

He leaned back in his chair, pressing his palms against his eyebrows. What was another word for "aggravate"? His software thesaurus listed ten perfectly good synonyms, but Ira had an innate distaste for the computer's automatic wordsmithing options. It seemed so lazy. He possessed a perfectly good brain; surely he could come up with the right word.

Besides, choosing a term spat out by software seemed so technical. No heart, no passion, no sweat. He used to feel the same way about writing at a computer, preferring the tactile sense of hand gripping pen, ink mapping paper, words arranged in rows on yellow legal pads. But now here he was, banging his hands on his forehead, driven in desperation to the auto-thesaurus. Maybe he was just getting soft.

As he sat there, thinking that maybe he should go walk around the block or get an early lunch at the deli around the corner—feed the muse—he suddenly heard the soft, urgent tone of two short bells.

The *Post's* satellite dish constantly received news stories, personality profiles, sports information, digitized photographs, and sophisticated graphics of everything from cutaway drawings of the latest space technology to the eldest Supreme Court justice's recent prostate surgery. Hundreds of stories, photos, and graphics streamed from the receiver on top of the building right into the newspaper's computer system, neatly organized by directories.

The computer software was designed to notify writers and editors when the satellite had picked up a story of particular interest. Five bells meant "huge" news: a presidential assassination. Three bells tolled plane crashes and other such disasters. And today's two bells, according to the information just now spilling onto Ira Levitz's computer screen, meant that an abortion doctor had been killed in North Dakota.

10:30 AM Inches: BULLETIN PM-Killing-AbortionDoc 1st
<B>PM-Killing-Abortion Doctor, 1st Ld-Writethru, 4236<D>

FARGO N.D. (AP) — A Minnesota abortion provider who serves North Dakota's only reproductive choice clinic was shot and killed this morning, evidently by a woman posing as a patient.

Ira stared at the screen and took a long swig of coffee. A minute later the first writethru came through with a fuller account of the story.

... Assistants found Dr. Ann Sloan, 47, in her office, dead of a head wound apparently caused by a high-velocity bullet shot at close range. Sloan had been conferring with a patient, who left the scene shortly before the doctor's body was discovered.

"Dr. Sloan was tireless, utterly committed to the needs of women," said Diane Brook, administrator of the Fargo clinic. "She gave her life so that women in North Dakota could have access to reproductive rights."

Sloan, a gynecologist who left private practice five years ago in order to provide abortion services in three states, had been the target of numerous death threats and harassment by anti-abortion forces. She had obtained a standing court order barring protesters from entering her residential neighborhood.

The Fargo clinic is the regular site of demonstrations; anti-abortionists were protesting outside the clinic at the time of the shooting. It is not known if Sloan's attacker was associated with any particular anti-choice group, but many of the clinic protesters, detained at the scene by police, seemed less than sympathetic when told of Dr. Sloan's murder.

"What goes around comes around," said a protester who identified himself as John Smith. "This woman was a cold-blooded baby killer. Maybe it's shocking that somebody went in there and blew her away, but isn't it more shocking that dozens of babies die in there every day and nobody seems to care?"

North Dakota police have launched a full-scale alert for Dr. Sloan's assailant. Fargo detective Mike Boyle said that officers are circulating descriptions of a young woman in her teens or early twenties who may have fled in what appeared to be a local Channel 4 news van. Channel 4 reporters who appeared on the scene in response to reports of the attack informed police that they had no van at the clinic at the time of the shooting.

Clinic personnel informed police that Dr. Sloan had complied with FBI recommendations to purchase a bullet-proof vest in response to threats on her life. She was wearing it at the time of her attack. AP-DS-01-10 1115 CST

Ira Levitz looked at his watch. Given the time difference, it had been about two hours since the shooting. He could imagine the scene: reporters scrambling over each other, screaming their stories into cellular phones so the fragments could go up onto the satellite.

Ira was ideologically opposed to abortion; he also empathized with the pro-life cause. Perhaps his own broken marriage had softened him in this regard. Precious things were so fragile. And the *feelings* of abortion—a stronger being asserting its will over a weaker being…the elimination of the most defenseless—sickened him.

Ira had talked with many in the pro-life movement who articulated their position with wit and grace. Their arguments, he believed, could not effectively be rebutted by the pro-choicers.

Yet he had also seen the crazies at work, the fundamentalists dressed in their Grim Reaper garb shoving pickled fetuses in politicians' faces. Ira knew the minds of the Washington circuit: Such demonstrations only steeled the resolve of even the least committed pro-choicer.

Their cause is just, he thought. *But they ravage their cause by the tactics they use.*

As he stared at the story on the screen, the buzz in the newsroom increased. His colleagues were reading the account, too.

"Mr. Levitz." He looked up. Threading his way between the cubicles, waving a large, thin brown envelope, was one of the earnest journalism students who served as interns at the *Post*. "This came for you, sir. By messenger to the front desk. Marked extremely urgent."

"Thanks," said Ira. He unfolded the fat paper clip he had been playing with and used it to raggedly slit open the envelope. The brown paper tore. He pulled out a single typed sheet, and his stomach tensed as he read:

Ira Levitz,

You have shown yourself to be a responsible journalist on the issue of the human right to life. We ask that you pass this letter on to our president-elect.

AN OPEN LETTER TO J. WHITNEY GRISWOLD

Mr. President-elect,

In a few days you will assume the highest office in what used to be called the civilized world. To whom much is given, much is required. Let the actions of this day serve notice as to what is required of you.

For now you must read the writing on the blood-soaked walls of our nation. An individual who takes the lives of the defenseless has no defense; she brings judgment upon herself. A nation that devours its young digests its own future. A leader who allows lambs to be led to the slaughter *will* be held responsible.

It appears that our nation is no longer content merely to spill the blood of the unborn, to turn human blood into profit, but will now begin, in large numbers, to extract the brains of the near-born. Turn from these evil policies while there is still time.

Perhaps you find it shocking that in Fargo, North Dakota, a woman took the life of a woman. In cold blood. Well, consider that you have helped to create a nation where every day women kill their own young.

Surely you have not forgotten the horror of the millions of Jews and others who lost their lives in the killing centers of the Nazis.

Turn while there is still time, Mr. President-elect. If you do not, no clinic will be spared, no hospital operating room will be immune. We will not stop until the innocents are safe, until this nation has turned from its wicked ways. Otherwise you will find your administration undermined at every turn, thwarted by those who answer to a higher law than your own.

The Holocaust Resistance

In the midst of his reading, Ira had risen to his feet. He reread the sheet quickly as he walked toward the glass-walled office of the A-section editor. He entered without knocking.

"Larry," he said. "Here's something you should see."

3

J. WHITNEY GRISWOLD stood at the window of his temporary offices on the top floor of the New Executive Office
Building. Outside, far below in Lafayette Park, he could see a
ragged man perched on the edge of a bench feeding the pigeons
from a plastic bag he had just dug out of the nearby trash can.
Dozens of the fat, ugly birds clustered around his feet, jabbing
their purple beaks at crumbs of corn chips.

"I don't get it, Bernie," said Griswold. "Why doesn't that
homeless guy eat the Doritos himself? Why isn't he in a shelter
anyway? Why don't they enforce some order around here—we're
across the street from the White House, and we've got a park full
of crazy people and pigeons!"

Bernard O'Keefe, sitting in a leather chair next to the desk and
buried in a pile of documents, didn't even look up. "This is
Washington, Whit. It wouldn't be Washington without homeless
people and pigeons. We'll look into clearing the park once you're
president, but right now we've got a few more important things
on our plate."

Whitney Griswold restlessly returned to the rosewood desk and stood behind its black leather chair. In spite of the thick navy blue carpet, the rich cream-colored walls, and the grouping of bright flags on stands behind the desk, the office seemed cold. The walls were bare, save for an enormous seal of the president of the United States on the wall behind the desk. Whitney looked at it for a moment, then sank into the chair and stretched out his long legs.

Yes, the huge office was sterile, as was the whole New Executive Office Building. Built in the 1960s, its flaming red bricks had been chosen by Jacqueline Kennedy to match the style of the Federal period. Instead, it looked like art deco. Across the street, next to the White House, stood the Old Executive Office Building, a lofty gray edifice that had gained a certain whimsical grandeur over the years, despite the fact that when it was erected there had been so much criticism of its flamboyant designs that its architect had committed suicide.

Whitney Griswold, president-elect, had just moved his transition office from New York to Washington a few days earlier. He had waited this long because he felt much more at home in New York than in this capital city, which seemed so strangely small-town and southern, this place that would be his home—if all went well—for the next eight years.

Griswold was a tall, athletic man in a loose-fitting Brooks Brothers suit—rumpled yet attractive. His clear gray-blue eyes changed according to his circumstances. With his wife or constituents they were usually a serious shade of gray, but with Bernie or other close friends they were often a warm blue. He had longish still-blond hair that started out each day neatly in place but was tousled before his first public appearance was half over. The effect made him look unconcerned with personal image, and that unselfconsciousness, along with his privileged family position and immense personal wealth, had proved a seductive combination with the voters. Here was a man, they believed, who could be independent, above politics as usual.

Bernie O'Keefe, Boston trial lawyer and, in ten more days, counsel to the president, was Whitney Griswold's oldest friend, but the two men could not have been more different. They had, however, three common bonds: law school, their mutual ambition for J. Whitney Griswold, and an old secret, long-buried by the years.

Whitney Griswold had been born to wealth. His father was one of New York's most successful lawyers; his grandfathers and uncles had been establishment pillars and among Connecticut's earliest land owners. Bernie O'Keefe's father, grandson of Irish immigrants, had worked for Boston Edison in the construction division.

Whitney Griswold always noted "Episcopalian" on any form or questionnaire that required a religious affiliation; beyond that, he thought little about it. Bernie's family was devout Roman Catholic. Bernie himself regarded his Catholicism the same way he regarded his rust-red hair: it was simply part of who he was. He had noticed the hair was thinning lately. He hadn't thought much about the religion.

After graduating with honors from Groton, Griswold had been accepted at Harvard, Yale, and Brown. He had chosen Brown, which at the time was considered the most exclusive of the Ivies. O'Keefe, a top honors graduate of Sacred Heart High School, had earned a full scholarship to Boston College, lived at home, and worked thirty-four hours a week at two jobs to help his family.

Griswold, an ardent sailor since he was nine years old, had captained Brown's championship crew team, rowed at Henley, and won the cup. He and his family spent every summer at their nine-bedroom Martha's Vineyard oceanfront home, golfing, sailing, and playing endless, graceful sets of tennis. O'Keefe had never been to Martha's Vineyard until Griswold took him when they were in law school. Bernie was not much of a sailor, but with his fire hydrant build he had been a fierce linebacker for BC.

The two had met at Yale. "It was fate," Griswold would joke later, winking at his friend. Bernie was the brightest new student in the law school, with top scores on his aptitude tests. Griswold's performance had been mediocre, but Yale could not turn down someone named Griswold.

Their relationship in school soon found the pattern that would define it for the next two decades. Bernie was broke most of the time; Griswold always had money. Bernie briefed the cases, Griswold bought the beer, and they both lived the experience to the hilt.

J. Whitney Griswold had first felt political stirrings during his Groton days while staring at the school's photo homages to Franklin Delano Roosevelt. Then at Brown he had studied economics under George Borts, a renowned free marketer. Griswold read and mastered the writings of Frederick Hayek and Milton Friedman. He even subscribed, while an undergraduate, to *The Freeman* and soon became absorbed in classic libertarian arguments.

This fit the Griswold view of life. His great-great-grandfather had helped Andrew Carnegie in many of his bold enterprises, one of which was forging a railroad across Pennsylvania, eventually linking the railroad across the continent. Some historians derided his ancestors as robber barons, but Whitney Griswold was proud of their entrepreneurial spirit, so classically American—the energy that had opened the land from sea to sea and prepared the way for the Industrial Revolution.

While at Brown, he had begun to dream that that same spirit could unleash market forces and bring about yet another revolution. One that would end poverty and usher in an age of peace based on knowledge, education, and true human autonomy. The more he thought about it, the more optimistic he became. And the more he dreamed about his own political future.

At Yale, these views began to gel, and for the very first time, J. Whitney Griswold imagined he might be president of the United States. That thought had initially entered his head when someone boasted that three out of five presidents since the mid-seventies had been Yale men: Jerry Ford, George Bush, and Bill Clinton. It could be fate, thought Griswold.

Then one day, after class, fate took a hand in an unexpected form. It had been a deadly session on civil procedure. He and Bernie had been out late the night before, and Griswold's head kept bobbing down throughout the lecture. Eventually he fell into a deep sleep. The professor let him doze, but called him over after class.

"What do you plan to do, assuming you graduate from here, Mr. Griswold?"

"Practice law, of course," he replied, startled at the question.

"Some branch other than civil law I should imagine, Mr. Griswold, though that rather narrows your choices."

Griswold was flustered. He had done badly on his midterms and hated this course. "I'm sorry, sir," he stammered. "I just didn't get much sleep last night."

The professor jabbed his index finger into Griswold's chest. "Mr. Griswold, for every student we accept, thirty are turned away. If you are not going to apply yourself with diligence, you might at least have the decency to make way for one of the other thirty."

That stung. "I'm sorry," Griswold repeated. "It won't happen again."

The professor continued as if he hadn't heard. "Remember, Mr. Griswold," he said, "to whom much is given, much is required."

Griswold nodded, not sure what to say. He had heard the phrase before; he didn't remember where, but its principle made sense to him. For generations, the Griswolds had lived well. He had much, by anyone's standards, and there was a certain responsibility for him to give it back. He should serve. It was his duty. Perhaps the state legislature, perhaps the governor's office. Or why not, like those other Yale men, the presidency?

When he told Bernie, his friend did not laugh. They were standing in the sun-warmed quadrangle at Yale one afternoon in front of Harkness, the old Gothic stone clock tower.

"It's weird, Whit," said Bernie, "but I've been thinking—you really could go a long way. You've got everything you need. I don't see why you couldn't be president one day. I mean, somebody's got to do it..." Bernie trailed off as the carillon above their heads began to peal, the bells tolling five o'clock.

"Why not you, Whit?" Bernie continued with a grin. "You've got money, looks, charisma, connections, you'll end up with a decent background in law...and you've got an asset that no one else coming up the ladder has. Me!"

THERE WAS A KNOCK at the transition office door, and it swung open. "Robbie," Griswold said, without looking up. His chief of staff was the only person, other than Bernie, who didn't wait for an invitation. Besides, the Secret Service wouldn't let anyone else come in like that.

Harvey Robbins, known to all as Robbie because he hated the name Harvey, was cold, efficient, and brusque to an irritating degree, but his colleagues put up with it. It didn't matter that he rarely smiled, rarely seemed remotely human. After all, in every office someone had to make the trains run on time. And Robbie did.

"Mr. President-elect," he said, even more imperiously than usual. "We have something unexpected on our hands. There's been a shooting in North Dakota. One Dr. Ann Sloan, who performed late-term abortions."

Robbie proceeded in his usual staccato style, information bites designed for Griswold's easy digestion. "Point-blank, one shot to the head, dead at the scene. Suspect is a woman posing as a patient, fled in a fake news truck. Police are all over Fargo and surrounding areas, but no hard leads at the moment. Happened about 10:30 our time. FBI is on the move.

"But here's the wrinkle. Ira Levitz, over at the *Post*, is writing his column at about noon, courier brings him a letter from the anti-abortion terrorists claiming responsibility. Open letter to J. Whitney Griswold. *Post* sent it over here, confidentially—but it's gonna break on the front page tomorrow. Above the fold."

Griswold's face flushed with anger. Bernie sat straight in his chair, his mind already considering and rejecting various courses of action.

"Here's the letter, sir." Robbie placed a copy of the single sheet at precise right angles in front of Griswold's nose.

Griswold read it quickly, then spun it across the polished rosewood toward Bernie.

"Those cockroaches," he said quietly. "They're crawling out of the ground all over the country. Stamp 'em out one place, they breed and come out somewhere else. These anti-abortion bigots break up the party, turn the nation upside down, execute doctors, and smile all the way to the electric chair. I can't stand it, and we are not gonna let them get away with this. This administration is not going to be held hostage to religious terrorists.

"Last November the nation voted for decency. People are sick of this. We have got to root it out once and for all."

Bernie, holding the letter in his hand, shook his head. "I knew things were too easy," he said. "Here I thought all we had to worry about was the economy, the international balance of peace, taxes, education, health care...you know, the basics. But before we're even out of the gate, here come the crazies. Look at this: They're not just going to shoot up clinics, but hospitals too."

"Let me see that," said Griswold.

Bernie handed the paper back and Griswold stood up. "The country's going to be in a panic if this stuff spreads. We've got to get the attorney general on the job at 12:01 on January 20."

"We've got to get her confirmed first," said Bernie. "We need to get her confirmation hearings moved up fast so she can get on this right away."

"Right," said Griswold. "Get hold of the chairman of the Judiciary Committee. We're dealing with extraordinary circumstances here, and we need those hearings immediately."

"I'll take care of it," Bernie said. "But right now, we need to get a statement out, and it's always a good touch to call the victim's family. What was the doctor's name again?"

"Sloan," said Robbie. "Ann Sloan. Divorced. One teenaged daughter."

Griswold jotted the name on a pad with his heavy gold pen. "Well, let's get Caroline in here and work up a statement for the press. And let's get that daughter on the phone. People need to see that their president cares."

4

WHILE HE might think it fate, it was actually a bizarre series of events several years earlier that had catapulted J. Whitney Griswold to power. And, like many historical watersheds, it all began with a small leak: an overheard conversation in a Washington, D.C., office elevator.

Bill Rudnick, gray eminence of the mid-1990s Republican resurgence and respected neo-conservative, was clutching a sheaf of papers and explaining one of them in a whisper to his aide. "If we can just keep the Dillman crowd quiet, I think we've got a deal here. We won't announce it until the convention."

The paper was a compromise pro-life plank, and the Dillman to whom Rudnick referred was Jason Dillman, conservative evangelical radio preacher whose program reached seven million homes a day—a force to be reckoned with by conservative power brokers.

The amended platform just might have slipped by. It was, after all, a ringing affirmation of the GOP as the pro-life party, asserting the party's historic commitment to the defense of the unborn. It also spoke of sparking a renewed moral dialogue leading to change in public attitudes and reforms gained by returning power to the states.

But in the back of the elevator, unnoticed by the bulky Rudnick, was a young writer who had just been hired by the leader of an evangelical ministry located in Washington. He eagerly passed the tidbit on to his new boss, who called Dillman immediately.

It was still almost a year before the Republican Convention. But Rudnick had been working feverishly to come up with a "big tent" platform, one that the pro-choicers in the GOP would tolerate, but one that wouldn't alienate the religious right—what the press saw as the anti-choice wing of the party. The religious conservatives were 20 percent of the party, maybe 10 percent of the electorate. Problem was, the Republicans couldn't win with their platform, and conventional wisdom said the party couldn't win *without* their votes. A major dilemma.

The radio preacher's aides saw immediately what Rudnick was doing. The plank was strong in its defense of the pro-life position, but Rudnick had pulled its teeth by extracting any support for a human life amendment. By relegating it to the states for decision, the party was effectively surrendering the abortion issue.

A few years earlier, in *Casey v. Planned Parenthood*, the Supreme Court had declared the right to an abortion a fundamental constitutional liberty protected under the Fourteenth Amendment. No state law, therefore, could interfere. You could win the moral debate over abortion, change the minds of 90 percent of the voters in a state, and it would make no difference. They couldn't overrule the court. Thus, a constitutional amendment regarding human life was about the only way to stop the widespread practice of abortion.

Dillman wasted no time. In a broadcast heard by millions, he exposed Rudnick's plank as a "covert conspiracy of cynical Republicans who would trade lives of the unborn to get elected."

The evangelical grapevine surged to life. Technology had done for them what the printing press had done five centuries earlier for the Reformers. While secular minds still controlled the major media, by the mid-1990s talk radio, fax machines, and the Internet and other online services had created a whole new world of alternative communication. So even without a mention in the *New York Times*, the *Washington Post, Time* magazine, or the four major networks, within a week, ten million evangelical families were hopping mad.

And the news hit more than the grapevine. Within four days, Phil Calvin, evangelical commentator and widely read syndicated columnist, captured the irony in his column.

The Republican Party, he wrote, had been born out of just such a divisive moral debate. In the 1840s, Democrats advocated non-interference with slavery. The other major party, the Whigs, were too timid to touch it. But by 1852, 20 percent of the delegates to the Whig Convention were outspoken opponents of slavery. The majority turned them back on the grounds that raising the slavery issue would be "dangerous and agitating."

But for the minority, the moral issue was non-negotiable. That 20 percent split away and in 1856 called their first national convention, under the banner "Republicans of the Union." Thus the Republican Party was born—out of a principled defense of unalienable rights, Calvin reminded his twentieth-century readers.

Then, in the 1858 Illinois senate race, Stephen A. Douglas argued that slavery was a state issue. A matter of choice. His opponent, Abraham Lincoln, defended the Republican position that slavery was a moral wrong, that human rights were unalienable. Douglas won the debates and the election. But two years later Abraham Lincoln was elected president, and the Whigs were finished.

"Today's Republicans are selling their birthright for a mess of pottage," Phil Calvin thundered from the pages of 250 major papers.

The ruckus over the Rudnick plank only furthered the already-growing rift between mainstream Republicans and the religious right.

Old-line Republicans had grown accustomed to big government. Some governors boasted that they could be tax-slashing economic conservatives and social liberals at the same time.

The evangelicals countered that social liberalism—more welfare, education, pensions, and the like—inevitably led to more spending and made economic conservatism impossible. The new breed was anti-establishment, disgusted with the failed, big-government, liberal dream.

Several Republican governors courted the gay vote and championed gay rights initiatives, as if openly challenging the religious right.

Fundamentalists and evangelicals were latecomers to the Republican Party. Traditionally, fundamentalists didn't vote, and evangelicals, for the most part from the South, were Democrats. But during the Reagan years, millions had moved into the Republican Party. Yet there was always an uneasy tension in the alliance. The mainstreamers slammed the door on Pat Robertson's 1988 campaign bid, and the Republican establishment battled hard in state after state to keep Christian activists from taking over the party machinery.

Had the evangelicals read their history books, they would have recognized that they were barely tolerated guests at the GOP's big tent party. Historic American conservatism had precious little room for the religious activism of these unsophisticated interlopers. So the Dillman broadcast and the Calvin columns simply accelerated the inevitable.

Bill Rudnick had already figured that the party overlords had had enough. Give the back of the hand to the noisy and demanding activists, and the Republicans could shed the negative image of the 1992 Houston convention and then, with their enormously popular tax-cutting promises, move to the center, scooping up millions of Independents and disaffected Democrats, more than making up for the loss of hardcore evangelicals.

Besides, Rudnick thought, millions of these evangelicals would put pocketbooks ahead of principles. Only the extremists would stamp out of the tent. And good riddance.

It was these events that brought Martin Masterson to center stage.

CENTRAL CASTING couldn't have picked a more perfect candidate for the Religious Right. A former history professor at Furman, in Greenville, South Carolina, Masterson had catapulted into South Carolina state politics by age thirty-eight after he headed a commission to reform welfare. By age forty, he had been elected governor.

Masterson, a tall, energetic man with a shock of prematurely silver-gray hair, blue eyes, and a winsome smile, coupled his personal charisma with populist policies, slashing taxes and downsizing government. He was unabashedly pro-life, uncompromisingly against special rights for homosexuals, and was the darling of the pro-family movement.

His campaign ignited. First, South Carolina conservative activists announced Masterson would be their favorite son as an Independent. Petition campaigns began in neighboring states and then, as with Ross Perot's independent campaign in 1992, organizing groups sprang up across the country. In some states there were six or more state chairmen, and confusion reigned until the Christian Alliance, almost reluctantly, assumed central command. In fact, the Alliance, whose leadership had become more concerned with the overall conservative fiscal agenda than with social issues, had been surprised by the grassroots intensity for Masterson. They had planned to play a kingmaker role in the primaries and at the Republican Convention. Now they were being forced to bypass it.

While the abortion issue was rewriting the American political script, it had also convulsed American life in a more incendiary way. The most passionate pro-lifers concluded, in light of the *Casey* decision, that there was no hope for change through the courts or the political system. Driven to the fringes, all other strategies exhausted, some openly concluded that violence was the only recourse left.

So, as murders of doctors and clinic workers, bombings, harassment, and other threats escalated, abortion rights activists demanded protection, and federal forces began guarding clinics. The Freedom of Access to Clinic Entrances Act measured off justice in inches: Protesters could sing and pray thirty-five feet from a clinic, but do so at thirty-four feet and you were guilty of a federal offense.

As the anti-abortion activists' frustration erupted into further violence, columnists condemned not only the pro-life movement, but all conservative evangelicals and Catholics. Incidents of overt intolerance against believers mounted.

Federal grand juries convened, police powers unleashed. The more moderate elements of the pro-life movement were intimidated and called for an end to protests. Dependable political allies fled. Many moderates lost heart.

Energized by this harsh opposition, however, new cells mutated from the pro-life movement. Some advocated violence. Some proposed blowing up empty clinics. Others simply stepped up their efforts in every creative though illegal way possible, short of violence.

The decentralized nature of the pro-life movement made it impossible for authorities to control it. Just when the government thought it knew all of the threats and had everyone identified, new groups emerged. It was like the French Resistance in World War II: an underground, spidery web of activists spun through every level of society.

THE REPUBLICANS meanwhile, freed from any obligation to the intolerant Religious Right, slid quickly to the center. The party's abortion plank became a placebo: Republicans were officially pro-life—who, after all, was *against* life?—and would work to discourage abortion, while at the same time fully respecting individual liberty, the "bulwark of historic Republicanism." This liberty included the right to make one's own informed decisions about life's most intimate matters. The party moved aggressively on the same reasoning—individual liberty—to court the gay vote. Above all, the GOP concentrated on tax-cutting, welfare reform, downsizing government, and tough crime-fighting policies. Polls showed big gains, particularly among Independents and centrist Democrats disillusioned by their party's identity crisis.

A divided field of candidates emerged from the primaries, and the surprise front-runner was J. Whitney Griswold, governor of Connecticut. In any other year a candidate from the Northeast would be unimaginable, but the emergence of Martin Masterson reduced the South's influence, and the field was generally fractured with five candidates from west of the Mississippi. Moreover, Griswold was very appealing. He had slashed individual taxes by 40 percent in Connecticut, had reduced the size of the bureaucracy in Hartford by over one-third, had a surplus in the treasury, and was presiding over the state's economic renaissance.

On the Republican Convention's fourth ballot, he went over the top. The polls showed him an instant front-runner in the campaign, and the GOP faithful were jubilant.

As Griswold appeared on the platform for his acceptance speech at the convention, the crowd roared. They smelled victory. Balloons dropped; confetti swirled. Griswold stood grinning broadly, clutching his wife's hand, arms raised in the traditional V.

Beside him, Anne Griswold grinned and waved. They would never know how much she hated this whole thing, how tired she was of huge campaign buttons, stupid hats, and even the eager faces of the campaign workers who lined up to shake her hand and fling their arms around her as if she and Whitney were their best friends.

Anne, tall and well-tailored, her short, straight hair framing the planes of her aristocratic face, was, like her husband, from an old New England family. She was more reserved than he but smiled enthusiastically at the milling throng. Behind them stood their son, Robert, and their daughter, Elizabeth.

Gripping Griswold's other hand was vice presidential candidate, Stuart Potter, the conservative senior senator from Virginia, chosen to blunt Masterson's appeal and to hold on to some support in the South.

As the Griswolds and Potters waved to the crowd, Harvey Robbins paced back and forth, just behind the entrance to the platform. Robbie had picked the optimum moment for television coverage of Griswold's speech, and he was worried that the thunderous, endless ovation would upset his timing. Any later and they might start to lose some of the East Coast audience. And, he noted with irritation, Griswold had unbuttoned his suit jacket. Robbie had warned him about that a thousand times; it looked unpresidential. Little things like that made a difference.

As Robbie paced, shaking his watch and peering out through the curtains, Griswold cleared his throat to speak.

"About time!" Robbie muttered. "Let's get on with it."

"My fellow Republicans, my fellow Americans. Tonight we launch a great crusade on behalf of all Americans who want this once again to be the land of liberty, opportunity, and decency…"

On the word "decency," the crowd broke into a frenzy.

"No more bigots!" they began chanting. "No more bigots! No more bigots!"

Griswold took Anne's hand and raised it high. The crowd thundered its approval.

"For America, this has been a long night," Griswold said, "but that means the dawn is much nearer. And it is. A bright, new dawn for America…"

The crowd roared, but he plowed ahead.

"A new dawn with fresh economic opportunities for every American; a new dawn of social enlightenment in which the last vestiges of bigotry and bias are finally rooted out of our midst, and tolerance, respect, and civility restored."

Griswold's jaw was set. He meant it. He was not a great orator, but he understood passion and momentum in a speech. He knew how to pace his words; he knew, intuitively, how to connect with a crowd.

Glancing at the 3 x 5 card in his palm, he continued. "In this past century, we have witnessed a world transformed. My Republican predecessors, Ronald Reagan and George Bush, were unshakable in their commitment to liberty. They faced down the Communist tyrants… and we won. Millions were set free from their ideological chains."

The crowd roared.

"And now, we must finish the job. Ironically, in this era of human freedom, there are those who would use uninformed prejudice to oppress us. But we will unshackle hearts and minds from the blind biases of darker times gone by. We will usher in a new era of enlightenment in which all people—regardless of the color of their skin, their station in life, or the lifestyle they freely choose—can live together with dignity and mutual respect.

"We will celebrate our diversity, the source of true greatness; and we will rise up on the wings of eagles to new heights, and from those heights, we will see the dawn's light from sea to shining sea, a land of true liberty ... Yes, my fellow Americans, that new dawn is coming. I promise it."

THE CAMPAIGN was grueling, but the Republicans gained weekly in the polls. The incumbent president, with only the Democratic ideologues still behind him, slipped badly. Masterson, the Independent, however, was close on Griswold's heels.

The election itself was a cliff-hanger. But by one o'clock in the morning, California made Whitney Griswold president. He had just 40 percent of the popular vote but managed to get 286 electoral votes, sparing an electoral deadlock that would have thrown the election into the House. First the lame-duck president, then Masterson, conceded.

OVERNIGHT, the Griswolds' lives changed. The day after the election, the family was flown to Hobe Sound, Florida, in a back-up presidential jet. The Cabots, in whose guest house the Griswolds had regularly stayed in the past, now moved into the guest quarters themselves, giving the Griswolds the main house. The neighbors on the quiet, exclusive island were not pleased with the Secret Service roadblocks, the helicopters buzzing overhead, and the Coast Guard patrol boats that ignored the "no wake" signs as they crisscrossed the usually tranquil sound.

The sudden change was hardest on the children. Robert, thirteen and already self-conscious because of the miseries of acne and a changing voice, was a middle classman at Groton, an oarsman like his dad. Though his wire-rimmed glasses gave him a bookish appearance, he was only a modest student. Robert had enjoyed the fact that at Groton, being a governor's son was not all that noteworthy. But being the son of the president-elect of the United States now made him the uncomfortable center of attention.

It was even tougher on Elizabeth, a perky eleven-year-old with wide blue eyes, a sprinkling of freckles, and shoulder-length blonde hair. Elizabeth was in the sixth grade, or "form" as it was called at Hotchkiss, another exclusive New England prep school, and two Secret Service agents now followed her everywhere. Some of the older girls teased her about them—"Wish I had a hunk like that following me around"—but Elizabeth, at the age where everything was mortally embarrassing, hated the fact that the men were always with her. She called her mother and asked to come home.

"Griswolds," her mother reminded her, sympathetic but unyielding, "do their duty."

FOR ANNE, the days glided by. She began packing personal items, negotiating with the lieutenant governor's wife for the continued loan to the governor's mansion of Griswold family art treasures, scheduling State Department protocol sessions, and tendering her resignation from the boards she had served as Connecticut's first lady. There were eight, including the Hartford Hospice, the Sierra Club, and, of course, the Junior League. All quite worthy, she thought, satisfied that she had spent her time well. Still, she would have to be more selective in the White House.

Meanwhile, Griswold set up his transition office in New York City, more convenient for his closest advisors and of symbolic importance. New York was, after all, still the financial capital of the world. There, each day, delegations from the National Security Council, the Defense and State Departments, and the CIA briefed him on policies and trouble spots around the world.

He learned much he'd never known before; for example, there were two governments continuing to vie for the sympathies of the Angolan people, and at various times U.S. policy had favored one, then the other. "One policy for Angola," he jotted in his notes.

The Middle East left him utterly perplexed. Israeli intelligence was once again fearful of a secret nuclear capacity in Damascus. China was sending military aid to Iraq in exchange for oil. And the CIA presented a worrisome intelligence analysis indicating that the ultra-right party might make big gains in the Knesset in Israel's upcoming election. That could well precipitate attacks on West Bank Arabs.

Griswold's stomach knotted every time he thought about Middle East policies—and soon it would all be in his lap. He hadn't even mentioned the Middle East on the campaign trail except for the obligatory pledges to the Jewish community of unyielding support for Israel. "The brave people of Israel will have no greater friend in the world than Whitney Griswold in the White House," he had assured the United Jewish Appeal banquet six weeks earlier in New York. It had sounded fine then, but what if the extremists gained control?

After these briefing sessions, Griswold found himself retreating to the men's room, the only place he had any privacy these days. There, besides the essential bodily functions, he would practice the relaxation response a doctor friend at the University Club had recommended: "For sixty seconds, let your mind focus on some desirable thing and take deep breaths, exhaling slowly." He usually thought of his daughter, Elizabeth, or a perfect summer day sailing off Martha's Vineyard. That helped, but still his stomach churned.

On January 3, the Griswold team had moved to Washington and taken up residence in the New Executive Office Building. And there, as in New York, every afternoon at precisely four o'clock—Robbie was ruthless about the schedule—Griswold met with his inner circle. Robbie and Bernie; investment banker Nicholas Berger, a Brown classmate; his personnel chief, J. Stuart Upham, former managing partner of an internationally renowned headhunting firm; his chief domestic advisor from the campaign, Geraldine Klein, on leave from the Hoover Institution at Stanford; Marine General George Maloney, a Pentagon whiz kid and old friend of Bernie's from Boston; and Griswold's long-time press secretary, Caroline Atwater, known by the Hartford press corps to be coolly efficient and unflappable. Caroline was a tall brunette in her early thirties, attractive and unmarried, which had given rise to unsubstantiated rumors of something more than a professional attachment to Griswold.

These meetings would last until seven in the evening, at which point, mercifully from Bernie's perspective, the bar was opened. Discussions were orderly and civil, agreement on policies and appointments almost always unanimous—a sign of orderly minds at work, men and women groomed and chosen for this kind of service.

The new appointments to the Griswold administration had been announced each Friday morning at the New York press center by Atwater or, in the case of cabinet announcements, Griswold himself. This gave the news magazines thirty-six hours before their deadlines and assured Sunday feature articles and some discussions on the weekend talk shows.

The appointments were, to Griswold's delight, received well. His cabinet, after all, was a model of diversity: eight men, five women; one Hispanic, three African Americans, and a secretary of interior-designate who was a Native American. The secretary of health and human services was an avowed lesbian with two adopted children, and the secretary of agriculture, wheelchair-bound, had written a biographical bestseller on how his New Age beliefs had carried him through physical adversity. Griswold had made a note to read it.

HIS ATTORNEY GENERAL designate was the last nomination announced, and now, only ten days before his inauguration, that appointment had become the most crucial.

Lafayette Park looked cold and frosty, but the men in blankets and the perennial protesters of every stripe were still there.

"Bernie," said the president-elect from his place at the window, "we need to start planning now. No time to waste. These people are putting us to the test, and we're not going to let them get away with it. Where is our attorney general anyway—do you know?"

"I think she's still up at Harvard," said Bernie. "We're working on it."

5

Tｈｉｎ ｗｉｎｔｅｒ sunlight dappled the bare trees of Harvard Yard as Emily Gineen took what would be her last stroll there for quite some time. Everything was packed and in order for the move. Emily liked order, demanded it in fact, but this morning she needed to get away from the boxes, the lists, the telephone, the aides, the memoranda already flowing in a fat stream from Washington.

The square was quiet. It was reading period, before exams, and most students were huddled away somewhere reviewing last fall's material. She relished the solitude. The past few weeks had been a frenzied blur of people.

She jammed her gloved hands in her coat pockets. The frosty air stung her cheeks, and she was glad she had grabbed the old wool hat off the top shelf of the hall closet at the last minute. The hat smelled like the dog had been wearing it, but she had pulled it on over her chin-length dark hair, put on a pair of sunglasses, and left the house. Swaddled in a heavy sweater, pants, coat, and a long scarf that belonged to her son, she didn't look like the urbane constitutional law professor her students admired. Nor did she look like the attorney general-designate of the United States.

She exhaled, watching her breath flow out in the cold air. She had wrestled horribly with the decision to accept Whitney Griswold's offer. Her life at Harvard was just about perfect. She loved the detached, peaceful life of academia, and between her law professorship, board memberships, consulting fees, and the occasional constitutional case she carefully selected, she was earning $800,000 a year. She was devoted to her family as well: a son and a daughter, twelve and fourteen, in a Cambridge prep school, and her husband, Frederick, also on the Harvard faculty at the Kennedy School of Government.

They took lavish vacations whenever she and Fred could get away at the same time, and their large old Victorian home was a haven of books, dogs, teenagers, and Rosemary, a rather corpulent live-in housekeeper who ruled the roost with a firm hand. Along with all this, she and Fred had made great friends in the Harvard community, spending many a pleasant evening brimming with pasta, red wine, and simmering discussion.

That circle of friends had encouraged Emily to work with Governor Griswold when he had first called her, back during the campaign. "He needs your help, Emily," they had teased. "He's a good guy, about as charismatic as you get these days, but he doesn't have a clue about the tough issues. You can serve a strategic role right now. You're the woman of the hour."

Usually at that point in the dinner discussion she would throw a sourdough roll at someone, but she knew that what they were saying was partially true. She did have something to offer. She had a good brain, good ideas, and good law experience. But she also had a gut sense of how to strip layers of rhetoric, bureaucracy, and spume to get to the essence of an issue. In short, she could discern the heart of a matter. Which was an instinct that J. Whitney Griswold, for all his breeding, charisma, and political clout, didn't have. She had noticed, however, that he surrounded himself with a few good men and women who did, so perhaps he at least realized his own limitations and compensated for them.

After Griswold won the presidential election, however, she figured her association with him was finished. Then had come the formal phone call regarding the attorney general appointment.

Frederick knew how much she loved their comfortable life at Harvard, but he had encouraged her to consider the president-elect's offer. After all, he said, a stint in the new administration would mean a commitment of only a few years, not a lifetime. (Though it would probably seem like a lifetime, he had teased.)

"Besides, you need something new," he had said. "You're comfortable here, but I know you. You get too comfortable, and then you get uncomfortable. You need a new challenge. Think of it as a temporary teaching post. The kids and I will weather it just fine. Do your duty."

That phrase was a mantra for her. During her childhood in Alabama, Emily's father, an attorney, and her mother, a social services counselor, had always stressed duty: One did one's best in order to give one's best to others. So Emily had excelled in academics, won a Princeton scholarship, went on to Harvard Law, edited the *Law Review,* spent her first year out clerking at the First Circuit in Boston, then her second year clerking at the Supreme Court.

She had her father's head, people used to say, and so she had carved out a career even more illustrious than his. But she also had her mother's heart and had grown up visiting the women's shelters where her mother counseled young women toward new lives. Emily had seen how few arrived at those new lives. Too many were drawn back to the men and addictions that eventually destroyed them.

She had also seen her mother drained, her health wasted, by the effort of pouring herself into individual lives, and so Emily had, almost subconsciously, gravitated toward systemic cures. Surely government could do more than the thwarted efforts of the too few committed volunteers like her mother.

She became the U.S. attorney from Alabama, known as a fearless, utterly efficient prosecutor. Then later, while at Harvard, she had filed an amicus brief in *Casey v. Planned Parenthood.* For this and her committed defense of women's issues, Emily Gineen was a heroine to feminist groups; because of her prosecution work, she was a favorite of the law-and-order crowd.

She was proud of her work on *Casey*. But at Harvard she had also taken pride in equipping a new generation of lawyers, feeling it was one of the best means of doing her duty and shaping the future. She thought of the comments she had recently given her students on *Marbury v. Madison*, cornerstone of every constitutional law course.

"The final thought to keep in mind regarding *Marbury*," she told the class on the last day of the term as they capped pens and stuffed books into backpacks, "is also the most basic: *Marbury* establishes the Court's right of judicial review, its authority to rule on the constitutionality of laws enacted by Congress. But the Supreme Court has no enforcing mechanism of its own, no militia or troops to execute those rulings.

"As we have discussed, at certain points in our nation's history, the civil rights movement key among them, when a state refused to comply with a Court ruling, the federal branch of government had to call in troops. Mercifully, those occasions have been rare. The continuing success of our democratic experiment in America today depends on the consent of the governed, the compliance of not only the citizenry but the various branches of government itself, to submit to the checks and balances intrinsic to our system. Otherwise we could well find ourselves, civilized people though we are, on the brink of anarchy, in constitutional crisis. I leave you with that sobering thought."

NOW SHE WOULD have a chance to make it work, she thought, as she pulled her coat tighter around her. The sharp air stung the inside of her nose as she inhaled, and something in the smell of the cold courtyard reminded her of Januaries gone by.

She had always loved January's sense of beginnings: fat new calendars, the smell of new textbooks, fresh snow not yet tracked. But now, as she took a deep breath, there was almost a pang, a hint of melancholy. A sense of something half-remembered, something known but lost.

It's Proust, she thought. The French writer had called it "the remembrance of things past."

Or C.S. Lewis, the British writer whose autobiography she had read after she and Frederick had seen the movie *Shadowlands* some years back. Lewis had called it the intense desire of something never to be described, the near-realization, then loss, of something from another dimension. The longing for Joy.

She kicked a cluster of dead leaves, watching them skitter across the pavement in a flurry of cold wind. Life would never be the same again, she realized. Soon they would be off to Washington, far from the familiar, constrained rhythms of academic life. She hated what she knew of politics, but it was the next challenge.

She looked up and saw a figure running toward her. *I knew this was too nice to last*, she thought. It was Jerry Kirkbride, the aide who was managing her transition to Washington. He had an odd look on his face.

"There's been a shooting," he gasped, coming right beside her and looking around to make sure no one else was close enough to hear. "An abortion doctor at a clinic in North Dakota. Griswold wants you in Washington, wants to get the big guns on this right away. They're pulling some moves to get your confirmation hearings ASAP."

6

W INTER IS usually quiet in Fargo, North Dakota. The
wheat, corn, and sugar beet farms are under snow, and
activity ebbs until spring, when the agricultural cycle begins
again. But within hours of the clinic shooting and the leaked
news of the open letter to President-elect Griswold, Fargo's
Radisson, downtown at the corner of Second Avenue and First
Street, was fully booked. Even the old Holiday Inn out by the mall
at Route 29 was sold out. Avis, Hertz, and Budget had rented
everything in stock. The four-wheel-drive vehicles went first. And
to make matters worse, it began snowing at dusk. The bartenders
in town grinned and replenished their stock.

Reporters weren't the only people milling around. Law
enforcement officials were everywhere, sometimes creating more
confusion than order.

At 10:00 A.M. Chief Walter Larson of the Fargo Police
Department assured Channel 11's live coverage that he and his
men were on top of the investigation.

One hour later, the governor announced that the North
Dakota state police, headed by Colonel Tollefson, had been

ordered to conduct a statewide manhunt for the party or parties involved in the murder.

Thirty minutes after that, the FBI special agent from Minneapolis, Jim Grady, arrived by King Air and held an impromptu news conference in the Radisson lobby. The Freedom of Access to Clinic Entrances Act of 1994 and the RICO statutes, as interpreted by the courts, made the killing of an abortionist a federal crime, and the federal government would assume jurisdiction from the outset. The director of the FBI, Anthony Frizzell, had authorized him to say that the bureau's full resources would be committed to this case. Grady added, however, that the federal government would, of course, welcome and indeed expect the state's full cooperation.

State trooper patrols fanned out to Grand Forks in the north, Jamestown in the west, and Watertown to the south. In the east, Minnesota state police joined in the hunt. Before the snow arrived, the civil air patrol, along with police helicopters, had covered a one-hundred-square-mile area. Though it was easy to see great distances across the wide-open spaces, a white van had the best camouflage possible. Everything was white—roads, rooftops, fields, and the light reflecting off them.

By 5:00 that afternoon, reports came in that a van rented from Hertz in Bismarck, 180 miles away, had not been returned; police, who were checking all car rental agencies, discovered that this van had been rented to Jerome Nordland, 320 Sixth Street South, who had presented a valid North Dakota license and paid cash. But police found no Jerome Nordland at the address on the license. It was clear that the young woman who had shot Dr. Sloan had not acted alone.

Pictures of the missing van were faxed to law enforcement officials in five states as well as to the Royal Canadian Mounted Police along the border.

IN THE FIRST twenty-four hours after the shooting, eighteen agents, including latent-fingerprint experts (those who can, through powder, chemical, and laser, find even fragments of prints), combed every inch of Dr. Sloan's office. They made over seven hundred separate impressions of full or partial prints, each one placed on a small card, then carefully catalogued and boxed. Footprint impressions were made throughout the clinic, along with tire impressions outside.

Another team of forensic experts flown in from Washington worked over Dr. Sloan's body at the morgue and in the clinic office. Hair and blood samples were extracted for DNA analysis. Skin fragments, particularly around the wound area, were carefully put in plastic bags, all marked. Every piece of clothing was carefully examined by agents wearing plastic gloves, marked and individually wrapped.

The ballistic experts found the spent round, dug out the bullet, and did elaborate calculations about direction and velocity of the bullet fired.

Other agents visited Channel 11 and obtained a copy of all the footage shot that day. Very likely the killer would have been caught on camera either entering or leaving the clinic.

It snowed heavily the second day. Though the roads stayed open, thanks to the heroic efforts of removal crews, air operations had to be suspended. Out-of-state federal agents spent more of their day digging their vehicles out of snowbanks than they did patrolling. The reporters congregating in the Radisson and Holiday Inn bars took it all in stride.

EVERY SCRAP of potential evidence was assembled, catalogued, boxed, and loaded aboard a small FBI jet, which got airborne as soon as the runways were cleared from the latest storm.

The fingerprints were taken to the bureau's facility in Clarksburg, West Virginia, where over two hundred million fingerprint cards are in the center's fingerprint identification services. When the boxes arrived from Fargo, they were instantly entered on an encoding terminal, and technicians began a high-speed search. Laser readers scanned the impressions and, by computer, compared them to the millions of fingerprints in the agency's information banks.

By the end of the third day, the prints of Dr. Sloan and every clinic employee had been identified and eliminated. Sixty-two prints were unidentified, and these were encoded; one of them could possibly belong to the suspect.

Meanwhile, Dr. Sloan's clothing, hair samples, blood, and skin fragments had been delivered to the FBI laboratory, which occupies 145,000 square feet on the first basement level and the third floor of the J. Edgar Hoover Building, the gargantuan FBI headquarters complex at the corner of Pennsylvania Avenue and Ninth Street Northwest in Washington.

Each year this lab handled 20,000 cases with 170,000 pieces of evidence and 900,000 examinations. But the evidence from Fargo, on Frizzell's direct orders, was moved to the head of the list.

The blood, hair, and skin samples were taken to a laboratory inner sanctum, the DNA analysis unit. The chances of one person having the same deoxyribonucleic acid analysis as another is one in one hundred million. Since there had been no signs of a struggle, there was little chance that the killer's blood would show up, but the possibility had to be eliminated. Hair samples, on the other hand, offered more promise, and every speck of human hair found in that office had been scooped up and catalogued. The agent in charge of that detail speculated that no one had vacuumed the floor in months.

Ballistics experts had the easiest time. Within hours, they identified the weapon as a Smith and Wesson service .38, but the bullet fired from six feet away and from slightly above the victim's head was a soft-nosed, hollow point. That's why it had virtually ripped off the back half of Dr. Sloan's skull.

Agents had also figured out how the killer had gotten the gun past the clinic's metal detectors and security. In the rest room across the hall from Dr. Sloan's office they found traces of electricians' tape, and a waterproof bag was recovered from the trashcan. Evidently the killer had retrieved the gun from the toilet tank, where it had been placed earlier, the agents surmised, by some accomplice—possibly a supplier or even a member of the cleaning crew. The custodians were interrogated first.

A team of handwriting and document analysis experts was

hard at work on the letter delivered to Ira Levitz. With computer analysis and laser, they identified the machine on which it had been printed, but it yielded no fingerprints other than those of Levitz and *Post* personnel.

Meanwhile, from across North Dakota and, indeed, across the country, written reports by agents were being faxed to the Minneapolis field office, distilled, and in turn sent to the situation room on the seventh floor of the Hoover Building.

ON THE FIFTH day they found the van, buried in a snow drift behind a deserted barn in the tiny town of Hamilton, approximately ten miles from the Canadian border. With so much fresh snow, it was impossible to check tire tracks or footprints, but agents descended on the vehicle, dusting every piece of metal and plastic for fingerprints. Not one good print was found inside; in the North Dakota winter, everyone wears gloves.

Frizzell called his Canadian counterpart to ask for intensified efforts on the other side of the border, though both men knew the task was next to hopeless. Whoever was in that van had not likely passed through one of the numerous border stations. There were a hundred ways to avoid detection, including snowmobile or private plane. And, of course, the killer and her accomplices could have fled east, south, or west after dumping the van.

A TEAM OF FBI agents, with sketch artists, interviewed clinic personnel trying to get a description, in this case a painfully frustrating process. The killer was young, her hair tucked up under a baseball cap, and she was wearing sunglasses. Nothing distinguishing about her. No visible moles, birthmarks, or scars. No one had noted anything distinctive; One witness said her nose turned up; another said it was straight.

The Channel 11 film had offered some help. In a two-second clip, someone meeting the assailant's description could be seen, side view, exiting the building. Lab technicians did exhaustive enhancement on the individual frames, then fed it into computers used to reconstruct visual images.

The final composite lacked any distinguishing details, but it was the best they could do. The sketch was pumped out all over North America on the law enforcement fax line.

Within minutes, the calls began. One came from a student at Concordia College, a conservative Lutheran school in Moorhead, Minnesota. There was a strong pro-life group on the campus, the anonymous caller claimed, and one of its members looked "exactly like the girl in the poster."

In less than an hour, two agents waiting outside a classroom met nineteen-year-old Dorothy Wilkinson and escorted her into the college administrator's conference room. The picture could fit her, but it also could fit at least 20 percent of the student population.

Wilkinson was chairperson of "Concordians for Life." Her hands shook as she admitted to the G-men that she had picketed that very clinic. "But I was at home in Minneapolis on Friday morning," she quavered. "I h-h-had four wisdom teeth removed." The agents rolled their eyes and called her dentist. It was true.

In the first four days, thirty-two similar young women were investigated, some the result of crank calls, others from people settling a score. There were no serious leads.

Whitney Griswold could do nothing officially, but he did get written reports from Director Frizzell about the progress, or lack thereof, on the shooting. Much of Griswold's frustration with the case came from the fact that apart from the economy, crime had been his biggest campaign issue. He had advocated stiffer sentences, repeal of the Miranda rule, random roadblocks, and other extraordinary measures in the cities, as well as expanded federal police powers. The promises had struck a responsive chord in a public gripped by fear: Violent crime was up 16 percent in just the past twelve months. Some cities were like no-man's lands; random violence was epidemic.

The murder of Dr. Ann Sloan was the worst kind of crime and social disorder and a direct affront to the decency and order Griswold had promised. And thanks to the open letter, published by the *Post*, it was also a direct assault on his administration. On him. So it deserved top priority.

7

J. WHITNEY GRISWOLD didn't actually think about abortion itself very often. And when he did hear the word, it did not evoke mental images of a medical procedure; instead, it immediately conjured up notions of choice, autonomy, freedom, and tolerance. In fact, abortion had gradually, unconsciously, become a metaphor for matters near and dear to what it meant to Griswold to be an American. So when those so-called pro-lifers waved their bloody posters, all he could see were the ugly tactics of sensationalism; when they shouted about life for the unborn, all he could hear was the fanatical clamor of bigots who would trample other Americans' freedoms to advance their own agenda. What Griswold called a "direct threat to the nation's domestic tranquility, an assault on the Constitution itself."

During his campaign he had spoken freely about using "whatever measures are necessary to protect a woman's right to choose, her sacred right of privacy." And he often spoke of wanting young women like his daughter, Elizabeth, to live in a land that enjoyed true liberty so they could experience, unfettered, the "full flower of their personhood."

The president-elect was a champion for all the political messages that "choice" had come to represent. In this, he was not unlike most Americans.

And he, like many, was dismayed and somewhat bemused as to why the abortion issue itself would not just lie down and die. Hadn't the right to choice been affirmed since 1973? Weren't we now living in a society in which diversity and tolerance had become accepted standards of civilized behavior?

For years Griswold, like many progressive Republicans, had ignored the issue as best he could, maintaining a fair degree of uncomfortable silence and hoping it would just go away. But in the early 1990s, angered by the "indecency" of it all, he had begun to speak out, and found his words resonating with many who were sick and tired of the "anti-choice zealots."

But then the tide had turned. After the first abortion doctor was murdered in 1992, a wave of fury swept the nation, and a similar wave of revulsion swept through the pro-life movement. Its leaders condemned any use of violence as a means to advance their cause. The more radical cells of the movement, however, stepped up their harassment, intimidation, and violence.

Then, with FDA approval of the American version of RU-486—"the abortion pill"—there was a lull in the violence. The pill still required a doctor's oversight, of course, but it removed a focal point for pro-life protest. Since any gynecologist could prescribe the drug, there was no way to know which patients were seeing the doctor for a pregnancy checkup, which were there for a pap smear and physical exam, and which were seeking the abortion drug. Even the most aggressive pro-lifers had a hard time identifying appropriate targets for demonstration.

In addition, swallowing the RU-486 tablets was an utterly private act, and revulsion against the invasion of that kind of privacy was an integral part of the American fiber. Many who might have been sympathetic to the pro-life cause revolted at the thought of taking away such personal privilege.

But it wasn't long before the pendulum swung back—for two reasons. First, RU-486 was too complicated to use for second-trimester abortions, so abortion clinics that had done the procedure at eight to twelve weeks were now routinely performing much later abortions. And second, through new technologies and discoveries in fetal tissue research it had become apparent that fetal tissue might hold the key to a cure for the most dreaded epidemic of the century.

AIDS.

Throughout the history of medicine, each new advance in science had been yoked with an accompanying ethical debate. Modern medicine's early history, for example, had been marked by a reluctance to disturb the dignity of the deceased, bringing strict statutes against the dissection of human cadavers. (Some of these remained on the law books longer than most people might suppose. In 1975 four Boston doctors were indicted for performing an experiment to determine if antibiotics to combat fetal syphilis could breach the placenta in therapeutic concentrations. They were charged with "illegal dissection," as defined by an 1814 Massachusetts grave-robbing statute.)

In the 1960s, the ability to actually transplant human organs brought new debates. When the news broke on December 3, 1967, in Cape Town, South Africa, that the heart of a twenty-five-year-old woman killed in a car accident had been sutured into the chest of a fifty-three-year-old grocer named Louis Washkansky, commentators questioned everything from the permission granted by the family of the deceased, to the location of the human soul, to the formal definition of death.

By the 1980s and 1990s organ transplants were routine. But the questions regarding donors had shifted: The ethical debates no longer revolved around how to treat the dead with dignity, but when it was permissible to remove organs from the living.

As medical advances made organ transplants possible even in the tiniest of infants, the lack of organs small enough for that age group could not keep up with demand. That was when medical researchers turned to anencephalic infants. Since these babies were born without most of their brains, they had no hope of survival. Most lived only a few hours or days.

But there was a problem.

Because these infants demonstrated brain-stem activity, they did not meet the legal requirements for total brain death called for by the Uniform Determination of Death Act. Hospitals were therefore legally bound to care for them until brain-stem activity ceased. But by the time they could be declared legally dead, their vital organs had usually undergone irreversible hypoxic injury and were unsuitable for organ donation.

Some advocates of this procedure lobbied for changes in the laws to allow the organs of live-born anencephalic infants to be used without a requirement of total brain death. In California, Senate Bill 2018 was introduced in 1986 but was subsequently withdrawn. Still, there were few who were willing to suggest out loud that organs be taken from anencephalic infants while they were still alive.

But for the pre-born, a different movement was afoot.

Research involving human fetal tissue had become the source of debate almost immediately after the Supreme Court handed down *Roe v. Wade*. In 1974, Congress created the National Commission for the Protection of Human Subjects of Biomedical and Behavioral Research and made the formulation of regulations on fetal research the first item on its agenda.

Some on the commission sidestepped the question of elective abortion by recommending that only tissue from spontaneous abortions be considered. But half of those spontaneously aborted in the first trimester were chromosomally abnormal, and most spontaneous abortions were subject to a variety of microorganisms, including cytomegalovirus, herpes simplex types 1 and 2, rubella, and toxoplasma. Thus, relying on miscarriages for fetal tissue was not a viable option.

For a number of years the ethical dilemma simmered on the back burner, for during the Reagan and Bush administrations, federal monies were blocked from tissue research on fetuses obtained by elective abortion.

Then, in 1993, in one of the first official acts of his presidency, Bill Clinton ended the moratorium on federal funding for research on transplants of fetal tissue. Many researchers breathed a sigh of relief and set to work.

The first grant was awarded to a doctor who had made headlines in 1988 when he used private funding to perform the first fetal tissue transplant on a human in the United States. Now this $4.5 million grant, funded by the National Institute of Health's National Institute of Neurological Disorders and Stroke, afforded him the opportunity to conduct large-scale testing of the effectiveness of fetal tissue as a treatment for Parkinson's disease. Though controversial, the study opened the floodgates.

Fetal tissue offered doctors distinct advantages over adult tissue: It lived longer than adult tissue in a graft, had low immunogenicity, and was still differentiating into mature cells. Now dozens of research teams vied for a piece of the multimillion-dollar grant action, considering proposals for using implanted neurological fetal tissue in diseases from Alzheimer's to diabetes to severe immune deficiencies.

The immune deficiency studies, however, carried the most political clout. By the mid-1990s, researchers had determined that fetal tissue held what might well be the only hope to disarm the AIDS epidemic. Other hopes for a cure or a vaccination had come up short. The fetal proteins held the key. Members of populations at risk for HIV could have government-funded testing every three months; if the virus was present, injections of fetal tissue seemed to stop its spread.

The studies were not fully conclusive, and doctors had been careful not to reveal the extent of the procedures required to extract the tissue. For in the frantic atmosphere created by the urgent search for a cure for AIDS, some of the standard ethical questions about tissue procurement were falling by the wayside.

Doctors had found that the more mature the tissue, the better its immunogenicity; and if any deterioration of the cells set in, its effectiveness was severely affected. Consequently, they were working more and more with second-trimester abortions: fetuses that were more mature than those of an earlier gestation but that could not yet sustain life outside the womb.

Once viability became a factor, the questions about uniform determination of death and legal limits of brain-stem activity became part of the equation. But before viability, doctors had fewer concerns about removing tissue from a living organism.

As word of the tissue's potential effectiveness leaked out to a sympathetic press, there was a tidal wave of euphoric public reaction. Thrilled homosexual groups organized benefits and lobbied Capitol Hill to speed the FDA approvals process. Hollywood entertainers threw lavish fund-raising galas.

The new technology was still in its testing stages, but pressure from the homosexual community was so great that government-funded programs, matched by private funds, were already fueling a series of new centers for harvesting fetal tissue. The umbrella for all this, the Regeneration Foundation, underwrote a series of public service announcements to introduce the notion to the public.

"Life to Life," a thirty-second, slow-motion advertisement, showed children and young men, old people and teenagers, all holding hands and dancing on a grassy mountain meadow while passing flowers to one another.

The focus was fuzzy, and so was the message: These images of dancing people somehow had something to do with the coming "regeneration centers," to be announced later. These centers would be built in six key cities across the nation, and Washington, D.C., would host the first, which was even now under construction on a site across the street from the George Washington University Hospital.

THE REGENERATION CENTERS caught many in the pro-life community unawares. But for those who read medical journals and for those who read between the lines of the exultant news reports, the regeneration centers meant nothing less than a national holocaust of the unborn.

And the pro-life grapevine had it on good authority that the National Institutes of Health were already producing a video for mass distribution in training hospitals: "Correct Procedures for Removing Fetal Cranial Contents."

Now, with this looming threat of fetal tissue transplantation on a broad scale, a new movement appeared on the scene. Calling themselves The Life Network, these Christians, who had long been committed to the pro-life cause, had formed a network of twenty cells across the country, with a total membership of just under four hundred people.

Their goal was twofold: first, to uphold an unwavering policy of nonviolence, and second, to hold an unwavering spotlight on the new reality of abortion in America. To strip away the benign political messages that hid the reality of fetal tissue harvesting and to illuminate the fact that, in modern America, doctors in sterile white lab coats were suctioning brain tissue from the skulls of live, unborn babies.

The Network's organizers purposely kept their network small. Members were chosen on the basis of their ability to infiltrate communities of influence. Pro-life journalists, for example, would quietly try to persuade their colleagues in the press of the patent injustice of the regeneration centers; businessmen and women did the same in their spheres. Each cell was directed by a small executive committee whose members were determined to keep the Network a tight, disciplined, and nonviolent movement.

Members were asked to read a booklet prepared by a senior member, who didn't hesitate to draw chilling parallels between their existence as an "underground" resistance in abortion-plentiful America and the activities of those who, compelled by conscience, resisted the tide of ideology that took the lives of millions of Jews and others during the Nazi reign of terror.

"During the Nazi Holocaust," the booklet asserted, "an entire nation of otherwise civilized people allowed a malevolent insanity to rule them, not by becoming insane themselves, but simply by looking the other way. They refused to recognize the evil for what it was.

"They said nothing when their neighbors disappeared without a trace. When ashes from the crematoria rained on their neighborhoods, soiling their sidewalks, they simply went inside their homes.

"The ugly spectacle of those mass rallies of the Nazis, the banners, those thousands of voices shouting 'Seig hiel!' in the night... that ugliness was far surpassed by the monstrous horror of silence.

"In the same way, if we don't speak out today against this holocaust of the unborn, against this gruesome medical experimentation reminiscent of the worst the death camps had to offer, then we bear the blood of these helpless infants on our hands."

The author of this booklet, leader of the Washington cell of The Life Network, was a cheerful, unassuming pastor named Daniel Seaton.

8

D ANIEL SEATON threw his head back and laughed loudly as his four-year-old daughter shone the flashlight under her bed. They could both hear thumps and yowls as the kitten chased the beam of light, crashing into the legs of the bed and making the ruffled bedskirt twitch.

"Daddy, she's so silly," Abigail giggled, bringing the light out from under the bed and shining its beam on the opposite wall of her bedroom. The little cat flew out from under the bed like a furry rocket, her paws flailing after the circle of light. "Doesn't she know she can't catch the light?"

Daniel laughed again as the yellow kitten circled round and round, chasing the light on its own stubby tail. "No, honey, she thinks she can get it. I don't know what she'd do with it if she could catch it."

He straightened up and kissed his daughter on the top of her head. "Okay, now, you need to settle down. Try not to kill the cat. She's still little, and you're going to wear her out. Why don't you read her a book?"

Abigail snapped off the flashlight, unusually compliant. "Okay,

Daddy. Dan and Mark and me are going to build something with Legos."

"That's great," Daniel said. "We have a lot of people coming over, so you guys need to be quiet. Dan is in charge, okay?"

"Okay," Abigail said, hugging her dad's knees just as the cat pounced on the cuff of his khaki pants. Daniel winced. The little bugger's claws were like tiny needles. He disengaged the kitten from his ankle and tossed it gently on his daughter's bed, where it bounced a few times and started attacking the pillow furiously, obviously hallucinating tiny mice.

Daniel went into the hall bathroom off Abigail's room to brush his teeth. Downstairs he could hear Mary moving chairs around, pushing the dining room table against the wall, getting ready for the buffet dinner. He had wanted to get his colleagues together to talk about the shooting in Fargo, and a potluck supper seemed the best, and most outwardly innocuous, way to do it.

The Reverend Daniel Seaton was about six feet tall, an earthy, stocky man with an easy grin. He wore his bushy, dark-brown hair rather short, lest it sprout out of his head in all directions, but allowed himself the luxury of a lush mustache. When he read late at night, at home, he also allowed himself the luxury of a pipe. Mary told him he looked more like an Oxford don than the pastor of a suburban American church. He rather liked that.

After college graduation, eighteen years earlier, Daniel had toured Europe with a backpack. He had taken odd jobs here and there, eaten vast quantities of pasta in Italy, considered a master's program in English literature at Oxford, and lingered at a Christian study center in Switzerland, partially because he loved the mountains and the courses offered there, but mostly because he had met an engaging, independent young woman named Mary.

Then his money had run out. Reality invaded. He had come home, considered his options, and ended up, with Mary's encouragement, in seminary. They had married after his first year, and she had supported them through her work as a nurse while Daniel took on odd jobs, as his study schedule allowed working as a carpenter.

Now, three children and many years later, the Seatons lived in a modest home in Falls Church, but their rooms were graced by the most intricate wainscotting in the Washington area. And for the past four years Daniel had pastored a small church that had sprung off from a larger congregation in McLean.

Daniel brushed his teeth, splashed water on his face, and combed his hair, then descended the stairs to the living/dining room. When they had bought the old house, it had been cordoned off into a small, dark warren of rooms. Daniel had knocked out walls with abandon, and now the airy great room was a frequent gathering place for people from their church, as well as the twenty or so local members of The Life Network.

Mary looked up and smiled at him as he entered the room. Tonight, Daniel thought, in her trim jeans and faded denim shirt, she looked about eighteen. Her long, heavy, glossy dark hair was clipped back with a tortoise shell barrette, revealing dangling silver earrings.

At the moment, she was talking with Amy O'Neil and Jennifer Barrett, two early arrivals who were helping her set out plates and silverware.

Amy and Mary had been friends for five or six years. Just before they met, Amy had been six months out of college, working as a receptionist for a congressman on Capitol Hill, and eight weeks pregnant. Her boyfriend was in law school at Georgetown, and when she had told him the news, which had coincided with his midterms, his entire demeanor had changed. His face had hardened, and he had told her in a cold voice, as if he were already an attorney dispassionately arguing a rather distasteful case, that their lives were really on separate tracks and the next few months were going to be extremely busy for him in terms of his study schedule.

"Listen," he had concluded. "I care about you. But we've got our own lives to live. It's not fair for you to look to me for something I can't give. I want to do the right thing in this situation, though. I'll split the cost of an abortion with you."

Shaken by both his attitude and the farewell in his voice, Amy had declined his offer.

Alone with her fears in the middle of the night, struggling to concentrate on her work during the day, Amy became more and more panicked. Her family was on the West Coast, she had to support herself, and the only way to do that was to keep working. And besides, a baby would squelch every dream she'd ever had. So she had made an appointment for an abortion.

A friend offered to drive her to the clinic, but she said no; this was not a day she wanted to share with anyone. She took a taxi, thankful for the anonymity provided by the typical Washington cabby, who barely spoke English.

Then, her worst fears were realized. Anti-abortionists were protesting at the clinic, waving signs and shouting slogans, while a group of pro-choicers in yellow T-shirts stood inside the yellow police tape, guarding the clinic and shouting through megaphones at the pro-lifers.

Dazed by the din, Amy hesitantly raised her arm to attract one of the yellow team's attention, and a small group of them burst through the barricades toward her. Surrounding her with their bodies, they escorted her toward the clinic.

The pro-lifers intensified their screaming, pressing toward her, thrusting their signs into the air. "Jesus loves the unborn," read one. "Abortion stops a beating heart" said another.

Then the shouts began.

"Murderer!" some of them shrieked. "Murderer!"

Amy put her head down and hung on to the arms of the women dragging her through the crowd.

"Murderer!"

Finally, they were at the clinic doors. A security guard held them open as Amy half-walked was half-dragged through. As the doors shut, the screams dimmed slightly.

Afterward, she could remember little of the procedure itself. The doctor had offered general anesthesia, and she had taken it, inhaling hungrily through the mask, vaguely afraid that she would never wake up but desperate for the oblivion it offered.

She awoke in a crowded clinic room. All around her were women stretched and huddled on narrow cots. She felt nauseated and groggy from the anesthetic, and powerful cramps rolled through her lower body in waves. She felt like she had to go to the bathroom, but she couldn't get up. The cramps kept coming. With each one, she could hear the echo of the people outside: *Murderer! Murderer!*

After several hours, she was free to go.

The clinic was quiet now; the protesters had left, and so had most of the yellow-shirted pro-choice squad. A woman pressed open the double doors for her, and Amy walked slowly down the steps, still bleeding a little and feeling woozy.

She looked for a cab. There were usually a lot of them here on Sixteenth Street, across from the Capitol Hilton hotel and only about four blocks from the White House. Now there were none in sight.

As she waited, an attractive woman, dressed neatly in a denim skirt and long-sleeved plaid shirt, approached her.

"Hello," she said. "I noticed you when you went into the clinic. I know this must be a very hard day for you. Is there any way I can help you? Do you need a ride home?"

Amy stared at the woman, still groggy. "Are you with the clinic defenders?" she asked.

"No," said the woman. "I was here with the demonstration. I come here every Saturday to pray in front of this clinic. But I'm afraid some of my colleagues allowed their emotions to get out of hand. I saw them shouting at you. I've been waiting for you to come out so I could apologize for their behavior. I'm really sorry they were so hateful.

"My name is Mary," she continued. "And I'd be glad to take you home, or buy you a cup of coffee or something to eat, if you like. I just want you to know that not all Christians are so hurtful."

Amy felt dazed. She looked out at Sixteenth Street again. Still no cab in sight. This woman looked safe enough; and the way she felt, she didn't care if anything bad happened to her anyway. All she wanted to do was go home and go to bed.

"I'm Amy," she said. "If you wouldn't mind, it would be great if you could take me home. I don't live too far from here. And I feel horrible."

Mary had driven Amy to the townhouse she shared with several friends on Capitol Hill. No one else was home, so Mary had walked Amy up the stairs, gotten her into bed, made her drink a cup of hot tea, and left. When Amy woke from her deep, deathlike sleep hours later, she found a note propped on her dresser.

"Hope you feel better soon," it said. "Please give me a call if I can be of any help to you. I'll be thinking of you." She had left her phone number and her name. "Mary Seaton."

A month later, Amy still couldn't shake off the abortion. Maybe it was all in her mind, but she felt hollow. The medical term for the procedure kept running through her mind: dilation and curettage. That was exactly how she felt: swollen, then scraped out. Empty.

Meanwhile, at work, she answered phones, arranged appointments for the congressman, and issued White House tour tickets to eager constituents visiting Washington for the first time. The business of her days exacerbated the emptiness she felt whenever she was alone, but she didn't feel like going out with friends to the usual distractions of movies, restaurants, and parties. Few of her friends knew about the abortion, but all of them knew about Brad's abrupt departure from her life. She hated the feeling that they pitied her.

She found herself watching more television then usual, reading magazines she had read before. Drinking a couple of glasses of wine every evening helped her go to sleep—but then she often woke in the middle of the night, exhausted and terrified, alone with her thoughts.

Finally one evening as she finished up at her office, she pulled Mary Seaton's number from her wallet and dialed.

"Amy!" said Mary. "I'm so glad you called. I've been thinking about you. How are you doing?"

Amy could hear the clamor of a toddler in the background.

"I'm sorry to bother you," she said. "This probably isn't a convenient time, but I was just wondering if you would mind getting together tonight for a cup of coffee or something."

Mary hesitated for only a moment. "That would be great," she said. "I'll have to get my kids' dinner on the table, but my husband will be home any minute, and he can watch them for the evening. I could probably leave here in forty-five minutes or so. Where would you like to meet?"

The two had met for coffee many times after that evening and had become close friends. Amy spilled out her feelings about the abortion—about feeling like she had hurt not only herself, but someone so small and defenseless that she couldn't even begin to think about it, about Brad's desertion, about the empty feeling inside.

For the most part, especially at first, Mary just listened. When she did talk, she spoke of forgiveness and second chances, of grace—a word Amy vaguely remembered from her childhood Sunday school. Mary talked without embarrassment about Jesus, about His love and the fact that He alone could offer new beginnings.

Then, one evening, it all broke through in Amy's mind. She prayed with Mary. She began attending Daniel Seaton's church. She was baptized.

And now, several years later, though she still had sad memories of the ghost-child she had aborted, the awful weight of guilt was gone. She had special empathy for women who felt trapped, women who felt they had no choice *but* abortion. She had a special horror about the procedure itself. And she was one of the most fervent members of The Life Network. As a congressional staffer she was well-positioned to distribute literature to key Capitol Hill offices.

Jennifer Barrett was newer to their group. Daniel didn't know much about her, but now, as he watched her talking with his wife and Amy, he was glad she had come. Physically, she was the opposite of petite, blonde, blue-eyed Amy. Jennifer had a no-nonsense look about her; she was tall, with short-cropped black hair and the healthy, thin-skinned look of a regular runner.

She was also very articulate. In the few conversations they had shared, Daniel had found her to be an utterly confident person. She didn't speak often, but when she did, she was quite insightful. She had just started coming to their church, and though she wasn't yet a full-fledged member of the Network movement, she seemed seriously interested in their cause.

The doorbell rang again and again as others arrived. John Jenkins was a member of Daniel's church, a quiet man with his own printing business, who, for no charge, produced the article reprints the group distributed. Jan James was a public-relations contract writer with good press contacts. Melissa Brett, whose husband owned a chain of successful restaurants, devoted a significant proportion of her wealth and energies to the pro-life cause. Linda Demmers was a nurse; her husband, Mark, was working on his doctorate in genetics. They both had excellent access to the latest in medical developments. Chris Smith was a carpenter who had worked with Daniel on building projects years before. He often spoke to area church groups about their cause.

Many in the group were from Daniel's church; others were members of various evangelical churches in the D.C. area. But none of them were the wild-eyed religious bigots and crazies so derided by the media.

They were a group of ordinary people who paid their taxes, voted, worked in their local PTAs, contributed to the Boy Scouts and disabled veterans, brought Meals on Wheels to homebound sufferers of AIDS and cancer, and gave themselves to dozens of other worthy causes. They just happened to hold uncompromising views about abortion and had been drawn into The Life Network because of their conviction that the abortion battle in America was entering a new, more ominous, phase. They sought to inform and educate opinionmakers, to calmly and reasonably expose the horrors of the coming regeneration centers.

WHILE DANIEL, MARY, and their friends were enjoying lasagna, bread, and salad, Alex Seaton was rounding the last bend in his evening run, his Nikes pounding the cold pavement. The hill before he got home was always the worst; but tired as he was, he always tried to speed up as he ran the final incline.

The streets were quiet; most people were probably inside watching the final play-off game before the Super Bowl. Alex's breath came in deep gasps, but he disregarded the pain in his chest. The chilled air felt fresh on his face as he ran up the long hill, fixing his mind on the goal. Then, finally, he hit the plateau where the street evened out.

He slowed to a walk and glanced at his watch. Not bad. The six miles had taken him a little less than thirty-eight minutes; his pace was consistent, day after day. He hadn't wanted to miss the dinner at Daniel's, but his run came first. No problem. He'd take a quick shower and be there in time for the meeting itself. He didn't need the lasagna anyway.

Alex Seaton was two inches taller, four years younger, and a good deal leaner than his brother. He was dark-haired, like Daniel, but lacked both the lush mustache and the robust good will his brother exuded, although he had always followed his brother's example. Daniel was the first to focus in on the pro-life cause, but Alex, with characteristic intensity, had elevated it to the primary cause in his life.

He had long since run through the inheritance that had come to him and his brother when their parents were killed in a plane crash, and he had bounced between a variety of jobs over the past few years. He borrowed money from Daniel all the time. But, as he had told Daniel rather stiffly, his part-time construction work was perfect; it allowed him the freedom to spend more time on the pro-life movement.

"If you're so pro-life," Daniel had responded cheerfully to his bachelor brother, "you need to get more of a life of your own!"

FORTY-FIVE MINUTES later, Daniel came back downstairs after checking on the kids. While he was talking to Mark Demmers he had heard thumps and scuffling upstairs and had gone up to find all three of them jumping on Abigail's bed and throwing pillows at one another and the kitten, who had then fled under the bed again.

Daniel had separated them, made them put on their pajamas, heard their prayers, and was now ready to get back to adult conversations. Usually Mary refereed bedtimes, but she had seemed so engrossed in conversation—or maybe she was just pretending not to hear the ruckus upstairs—that he had taken care of things himself.

Downstairs again, he saw that Alex and Lance Thompson had arrived. They stood by themselves in a corner, both holding mugs of coffee, looking over the group. Lance, a disciplined, private man who was cordial when approached but always restrained, had been part of The Life Network for some months now.

With his powerful build, his bulky arms, and his wide, thick neck, Lance was the epitome of the Special Forces officer he had been during the Gulf War. Daniel had learned through his brother that Lance had worked with a team of civilian demolitions experts commissioned to defuse the network of mines and booby traps the Iraqis had left in the desert, and had seen fellow team members blown to pieces in the millisecond after a moment of carelessness.

Lance lived in the District and felt more comfortable in the worship style of the all-black church he attended there, though he had visited Daniel's church. He had for years been deeply concerned about what he called the "genocide" of African-Americans because of Planned Parenthood's pervasive presence in the inner cities, and had enlisted many influential black pastors in the Network's cause.

On Saturdays, Lance usually could be found in front of the Women's Reproductive Health Clinic of D.C., simply standing the requisite number of feet from the clinic entrance, holding a placard depicting an aborted fetus and the black-and-white photo of a 1920s-era lynching of a young black man. "Abortion: the new black lynching," read the poster.

Lance kept to himself most of the time, unless he was with Alex. The two had spent a lot of time together in recent months, and to Daniel it seemed they had both grown increasingly paranoid.

Two days ago, when they'd heard of the Fargo shooting, Alex had told Daniel there was a possibility that leaders within various pro-life groups were being monitored by the FBI. Daniel had rolled his eyes.

"You've been listening to Lance too much," he said. "This isn't the mine fields of Kuwait or the back alleys of Baghdad. Leave the cloak-and-dagger stuff for Lance's war stories."

And, Daniel realized, they were both potentially dangerous men. Their commitment to the pro-life cause was linked with their reactions against powerful ideologies. Daniel agreed with Lance that it was clear that Planned Parenthood targeted the poor. But for Lance, slavery was just a few generations in the past, lynching only a few decades removed, and the goals of the civil rights movement still largely unrealized. To him the politics of abortion were simply the most recent threat to true equality for African Americans.

And though Daniel shared his brother's fascination with Nazi Germany and the forces that had allowed Hitler to seize and retain power, it seemed that Alex's interest now bordered on obsession. He often read late into the night, reviewing again and again the details of the Nazis' crimes against humanity, the capitulation of many German Christians, and the underground attempts to assassinate Adolf Hitler. The evil they faced in America was similar. But Alex, without the stabilizing influence of a wife and children, seemed to be more willing to go to extreme lengths to fight it.

Looking around at the group now, Daniel cleared his throat. "Well, why don't we come to order," he said. "I don't have a big agenda here—most of our projects are proceeding well and all of you know what you're to be doing—but I thought it would be good if we got together to talk just a little about recent events and the potential fallout."

People found chairs, settled down, and looked up at him with the same expressions he usually got when he was preaching from the pulpit.

"I'm not preaching tonight, folks!" He smiled. "So let's cut to the chase. This Fargo thing, coming right at the same time as Whitney Griswold's coming into office, means that some ugly forces are on the move. You've seen the news reports. Pro-lifers are going to be blamed for anything and everything. No matter what we say—assuming we're still allowed the right to free speech, which I sometimes wonder—it will be twisted.

"So we have to be absolutely clear about what we're doing here in Network. No violence. No ugly demonstrations. We just need to keep up the pressure of exposing the regeneration centers for what they really are. Through every creative means available."

He paused and looked around. Most were nodding, sipping coffee, tracking with him.

Inside his head, he counted to five. He knew who was going to speak up first.

There was a movement in the corner, and Alex cleared his throat. "Look," he said, "I hear what you're saying. But I don't think you're saying enough. That shooting in Fargo is neither here nor there. One abortion doctor down. Good riddance. But we don't have enough time to shoot every abortionist in the country, though that's not a bad idea. In about six months, those regeneration centers are gonna be up and running.

"How long are we going to sit here? Right now we've got millions of early abortions because of RU-486—and even worse, babies are being killed in the womb, their brains sucked out for research studies. Dilation and extraction. D and X for short. They don't have enough doctors trained in the procedure; it takes a high level of surgical skill. So do you know what they're doing? Producing training videos! Government-funded snuff movies . . . and people don't even care. Now women are being told that they're not only exercising 'reproductive choice'—the most glorious of all human rights—they're at the same time saving human lives. Women who hesitated about abortion before won't waste a minute now."

"I've been there, Alex," Amy O'Neil interrupted quietly as Alex took a breath. "No woman can feel good about getting an abortion. I don't care how much bull you feed her about helping others. It's a death. It's a vacuum. It stays with you."

Alex paused, then continued as if no one had spoken. "I don't think we should exclude any means of action available. If a sniper was shooting people at random on the street, wouldn't we stop him?

"Why are we sitting here, going on with our everyday lives,

when the Auschwitz camps of our day are under construction right now? We ought to bomb every center they build."

"Wait a minute, Alex," interrupted Chris Smith, the carpenter. "Do you hear what you're saying? People just don't realize what these regeneration centers are all about. We need to find ways to expose them for what they are. People aren't so far gone that they won't recognize that it's wrong to suck the brains from a live fetus. Our job is to reveal the truth, however we can. Letters to the editor. Nonviolent protests. Get on the talk shows. Pictures. Be reasonable, so people can see we're not crazy. Our cause is *reasonable*: People in a civilized society do not behave this way."

"But that's just it!" exploded Alex. "*Who* is the epitome of a civilized, utterly sophisticated human being in America today? I'll tell you: It's our new president, J. Whitney Griswold, who talks all the time about 'bringing decency back to America'! Meanwhile he's gonna make sure that every neighborhood in the country has its own private fetus-harvesting center by the end of his administration.

"We can't reason with people anymore," Alex continued. "What we should do is show up at the inauguration and pour buckets of blood on the Capitol steps. Griswold is just another Adolf Hitler."

Mark Demmers sipped his coffee and let Alex's energy dissipate for a moment before he asked, dryly, "So you want us to get out our buckets, Alex?"

Alex raised his eyebrows. "I'm not proposing anything to this group right now except that we don't bury our heads in the sand and think our little tiny efforts here and there are going to accomplish anything. The time has passed for sitting around and having meetings. We've got to do something. We've got to be ready to give our lives for this cause. Millions and millions have already been slaughtered, and more are on the way!"

"Skip the rhetoric," somebody muttered.

Daniel held up his hand. "The main thing I'm concerned about is that we don't get carried away," he said mildly. "When people are frustrated—it sounds like we all are—they don't think clearly. As long as I'm involved with this group, we will not consider any action that involves violence. We cannot use evil means for 'good' ends. That's too easy. We have to do the hard thing. We have to overcome evil with good.

"If I were preaching," he said, "I would say that God ordained government. In America, however dark it seems, we've still got the best thing going. And if the apostle Paul could sit in a jail cell and write that believers were to be in subjection to the governing authorities, who were 'established by God,' when the guy on the throne in *his* day was totally insane Nero, then certainly we can respect Whitney Griswold.

"And we need to pray for him. We're supposed to love our enemies. No matter what. And I'm not trying to be the heavy here, but if I hear of anyone in this group planning anything that has to do with violence, we'll have to disband. Period."

There was a general shift in the room as people moved in their chairs, exhaled, and several stood up to get more coffee. At Daniel's last words, Alex and Lance exchanged a quick look—just a tightening of the mouth and a blink of the eyes that nobody else noticed.

9

Senator Byron Langer leaned back in his old black leather chair and thumbed through the fourteen-inch-thick sheaf of papers on Emily Gineen. The FBI had completed its background check in record time, and as ranking member of the Judiciary Committee, Langer was entitled to the full report, background interviews included.

"Quite a woman," he muttered, as he flipped page after page.

Professor Gineen's record was unblemished. Not so much as a traffic violation, and her finances were beyond reproach. She'd paid Social Security taxes on nannies and household employees. Her own taxes had been audited twice, and in both cases, it turned out the government owed her money.

Her personal life was as flawless as her public record. She had married her first serious boyfriend, a Princeton classmate. The couple had been devoted to one another for eighteen years, with never a hint of indiscretion. She drank wine only with meals. No one remembered her ever making an insensitive or politically incorrect remark or losing her temper.

One former neighbor, whose name had been blocked out on

the report, summed up the general attitude about Emily Gineen: "I didn't think I'd like her when she moved in next door. Here comes this famous Harvard couple with their twin BMWs, the television crews setting up in their front yard now and then, the articles and interviews and the whole bit...I didn't think we'd have much in common. My husband does very well with his software company, but I didn't even finish college. I've devoted my whole life to being a wife and mother.

"But the first night, she came over and introduced herself, wearing jeans and an old sweatshirt. She asked if she could use our phone since hers wasn't hooked up yet. They'd forgotten to get that taken care of. That shocked me. Later, when my son was in the hospital, Emily helped with our younger kids, visited the hospital, cooked casseroles. I've never heard her raise her voice with her own kids. They're great. And she's almost always cheerful too, just about the best person I've ever known. She couldn't do anything wrong if her life depended on it."

Langer sat forward and scribbled some notes on his yellow pad. "Admirable character... probably self-righteous." He knew he would keep his questions to the issues only. With a sigh, he looked at the stack of articles, books, and volumes of the court reports that his aides had piled on the left side of his desk.

Tall, vigorous, and once athletic, Langer was now thirty pounds overweight. Most of it had settled around his middle so that when his coat was open, his bulging, wrinkled shirt obscured his belt; the rest was in his puffy jowls which, along with his large lips and drooping eyelids, cast him as the stereotypical good ol' boy one could find at noontimes eating biscuits and sausage gravy at the Elite Cafe across from the Jackson Courthouse.

Langer was given to quoting Scripture in his deep Mississippi drawl which had somehow deepened since he came to Washington. With his flowing, wavy hair, he looked the part of a filibustering, Bible-quoting, segregationist senator from the South of two generations past.

But appearances were deceiving. His detractors believed that Langer cultivated this image, often shrewdly using it to lure his opponents into his trap. Honors graduate of Ole Miss and former editor of the *Vanderbilt Law Review*, Langer was a formidable intellect with a prodigious memory.

His public record read like an old school politician's: decorated Green Beret officer in Vietnam, distinguished attorney, state supreme court justice, and now in his third term in the U.S. Senate. He and his wife, Lily, along with their four children, always pictured together on Langer's campaign posters, were a tight-knit family. He was untouchable in Mississippi politics, and had he been a little more photogenic and from a larger state, he would have been a national contender.

Langer sighed and shoved away from his desk. It was 7:30, time to go home for dinner with Lily. Then after dinner he'd read cases. There was still time before the hearings, and he wanted to be ready.

He picked up his briefcase, stuck his old leather Bible in the side, and thought about the psalm he'd read that morning. Psalm 139. "You wove me in my mother's womb," the psalmist had said. It was one his favorites, and spoke to the main issue he had to deal with when it came to the appointment of Emily Gineen. The view of human life that he held wasn't politics; it was something he knew deep in his soul. Emily Gineen did not. Nothing personal, but she simply didn't know.

SURROUNDED BY pushing reporters, trailing cords, and popping flashbulbs, Emily Gineen, carrying a large lawyer's file case, made her way slowly to the entrance of the Senate Caucus Room. The Judiciary Committee was in the Dirksen Building, but the demand for seats and press credentials had been so great that the chairman had elected to hold Dr. Gineen's hearing in the most illustrious room in the Capitol, the room where the McCarthy, Watergate, and Iran Contra hearings had been held.

Byron Langer had not been happy with this change. It would put too much attention on Gineen and would give Griswold too big a victory when, as was all but inevitable, she was confirmed.

Dr. Gineen was smiling until the moment she was asked to raise her right hand and repeat the oath. Then her blue eyes were sober as she repeated, "I do, so help me God." Her dark-brown hair was swept back, her makeup understated, just enough to emphasize her clear eyes and even smile, and she wore an unremarkable dark blue suit with a soft cream blouse.

Langer noted her calm manner. He had seen many at that witness table start to come apart even before the questioning began, rattled by the pomp, the press, and the procedures. But the Harvard professor sat easily, even eagerly, as if she looked forward to the session.

The chairman invited her opening statement. Some witnesses took far too long to say far too little, reading slowly from dull documents, their hands trembling. But Dr. Gineen spoke briefly, animatedly, and without notes about her understanding of the role of attorney general, her sense of the historical context in which this administration found itself, and her commitment to discharge her duties faithfully, in accordance with the law and the Constitution.

She finished and smiled at the chairman, who seemed nervous himself, perhaps because he had been roasted some years earlier for his insensitivity in questioning a woman. His counsel handed him a page of typed questions, which were notably timid and quickly dispatched by Dr. Gineen. Predictably, she was asked about the situation in Fargo; if she was confirmed, she said, she would vigorously prosecute the investigation and provide more resources for clinic protection.

Before long, the chairman announced, "I yield to my colleague, the ranking majority member and distinguished senior senator from Mississippi," and leaned back, relieved.

"Professor Gineen," Langer paused, adjusting his dark-rimmed glasses, "let me commend you on a very direct and forthright presentation and for illuminating this committee on the role of attorney general. Let me say also that I find your record admirable, particularly your history of prosecuting criminal offenders.

"But I do have some concern that you have made it sound as if you are just a high-priced functionary, enforcing the law my colleagues enact and the Court interprets. Would you not agree, Professor, that the attorney general has a policy role as head of the department and of course as advisor to the president?"

"Of course that is so, Senator."

"Then, Professor, may I assume you are able and willing to discuss your views on the great policy issues that confront our Republic?"

"Of course, Senator, I am prepared to do so." Emily's grin masked her impatience. *Get to it, Senator, we all know what's coming.*

"To begin, let us turn to your arguments so eloquently advanced in *Casey v. Planned Parenthood.* You wrote, and I quote," he pushed his glasses to the end of his nose, "'The ability of women to share equally in the civic social life of the nation depends on their ability to control their reproductive lives.'"

Gineen nodded.

"You should be complimented that the Court adopted your language almost verbatim in its decision."

"Every lawyer is gratified, Senator, when the high Court endorses his or her arguments," she said softly.

"This is, or I should say was, a rather novel argument. Do I understand this means that abortion is a necessary right in order to assure gender equality for jobs and that sort of thing?"

"Yes, Senator, for 'that sort of thing.' Indeed. A woman's right to control her reproductive life is a matter of her liberty protected under the Fourteenth Amendment. This case, sir, was a very important step in the process of emancipating women."

Hard as she tried not to, Emily allowed a slightly defiant tone to slip into her last sentence, but it was drowned out by the applause from the women who had packed the spectators' seats.

"Order, order," the chairman cracked the gavel. "We will maintain proper decorum here."

Langer resumed. "I am familiar of course with the arguments in *Roe v. Wade,*" he said, "the implied right of privacy. And I am familiar with the Court's application of the Fourteenth Amendment to this issue, distressing though I find it. But what I was getting at was your reasoning. Do we abort children to achieve gender equality? Was that your argument, Professor?"

"No, sir. The argument turned on questions of liberty. Equal rights was a consequence."

"But you advanced it as a reason, Professor, to assure women's economic and social rights. I don't know anyone who argues that abortion is a desirable thing. It is taking a life, or if you prefer, a potential life, and it is offensive to the deepest-held convictions of conscience for millions. But you would advocate it as permissible to help someone get a job? And if so, what other difficult and painful things would you allow in order to secure 'social and economic equality'?"

"I think we may be confused here, Senator. We are talking about liberty." Gineen, for the first time, appeared flustered, repeating her answer.

"The question is not difficult, Professor." Langer paused after "Professor" as if for emphasis. "What else do we offer up to achieve gender equality—the gentle, loving syringe for those burdensome and dying patients whose care prevents us from sharing equally in the economic and social life of our nation?"

"That's inflammatory, Senator. I've never proposed any such thing, and you know that."

"But how far do you go? Would you sterilize welfare mothers who refuse abortions and bear children repeatedly? This disposition on their part denies them full economic equality. Costs us a lot too."

"Many women choose sterilization, Senator."

"Or lose their welfare checks... but my question, Professor, goes much beyond this."

Langer paused, took off his glasses, held them at a distance, and stared through them; then, with what Emily found to be maddening deliberation, he began cleaning them with his handkerchief. Langer's capacity to unsettle witnesses was legendary.

After what seemed like minutes to her, he continued. "It might seem somewhat philosophical, but the question is: What is liberty and who defines it? One person's liberty can be another person's bondage."

"Liberty is well defined in a long series of cases, sir." Emily started to reach for her notebook, but Langer never gave her a chance.

"Let me read what the Court said in *Casey*, again I believe relying on your brief. 'At the heart of liberty is the right to define one's own concept of existence, of meaning, of the universe, and of the mystery of human life.' Do you agree with that?"

"I recall the wording."

"Do you agree?"

"I think I argued it slightly differently. But it does, certainly, define liberty of conscience."

"Ah yes, quite so, Professor. I would defend with my life a person's right to his or her deepest personal convictions. But there is a difference between holding convictions and acting on them. Certainly the state, to preserve order and domestic tranquility, can limit one from acting on his thoughts."

"Of course, Senator."

"Then there are limits on liberty. So I come back to my question. How do we define those limits?"

"The legislature, you and your colleagues, sir, make the laws. The Court interprets and enforces."

"Indeed, Professor. I'm familiar with the process." Langer tried not to be condescending, but he was no more successful than Gineen was in disguising her impatience. Two different cultures were facing each other across the witness table.

"But my question goes to the basis on which our legislatures and courts determine what is liberty and what is to be restrained. It is not a new question, of course. It is the one Plato asked and then attempted to answer in *The Republic*: What is justice?"

"It is the rule of law, sir, which protects liberty, secures the peace, and promotes the greatest good," said Emily. "Law is sustained by the plain language of the Constitution and by the laws and decisions of the courts over the years."

Langer looked up, fixing his gaze on the fresco around the ceiling edge. "Yes, indeed," he said slowly, "the greatest good... Bentham, of course, of course."

There was another of those painful delays, but this time it hit Emily. Suddenly she sensed where he was taking her. *I might have known he'd pull this*, she thought, *the one impossible dilemma*. She braced for his next question, annoyed that she hadn't seen it coming earlier.

"What then do we do, Professor, in the case of a law that benefits the greatest number but is manifestly unjust—might I even say one that is self-evidently unjust?"

"The Court would have to declare it unconstitutional, sir."

"And if it did not?"

She knew the trap was set and there was no way to escape. "Well, sir, we trust our system to work."

"But let me invite your attention to an historical episode that is painful still to some in my region of America, Professor Gineen. The majority in America once believed that slavery was in the best interest of the greatest number. The majority approved slavery when the Kansas Nebraska Act was passed by the Congress. And the Court in the Dred Scott decision then affirmed it on the grounds that the black slave was not a person under the Constitution. Now as you well know, President Lincoln held a very different view."

"It is a good example of an unjust law, sir. And of course it took extreme courage to resist it. But America's heritage is rich in that characteristic, sir." Emily wanted to divert him from this issue in the worst way.

"Courage? Courage indeed, my dear Professor. Courage that ran crimson, draining the life from 600,000 men and boys. The system didn't remedy itself, Professor, did it?"

"Dred Scott was reversed, sir, by the Thirteenth and Fourteenth Amendments."

"Amendments enacted by an army of occupation. This was after a war, Professor, a war that almost destroyed us. So I come back to my question. How do we deal with an unjust law today? Another war?"

"No, Senator, the majority ultimately favored the abolition of slavery. I trust the majority today to see and do what is right."

"Majorities create tyrannies, Professor. You need only look at what the Germans in the thirties thought was just. No, my question is: How do you measure justice? Do you believe, as Lincoln did, that there is a higher law beyond the law?"

"In our social contract, sir, the majority determines the law. We rule by the consent of the governed. Sovereignty is in the people."

"Our founders spoke of certain self-evident truths and unalienable rights that are not given by government and thus cannot be taken away by government but rather are endowed by our Creator," said Langer. "It is a government under God, Professor Gineen . . . or perhaps you prefer Jefferson's formulation that the nation was governed by 'laws of nature and nature's God.' This is what Lincoln relied on. Without that, perhaps I'd own slaves, as my great-granddaddy did."

"I'm glad to have the assurance you do not, sir, though from what I hear, I'm not sure your staff would agree." Emily tried levity, and for a moment it worked.

But Byron Langer knew just where she was headed, and he knew what he wanted on the record. He chuckled, made a half bow in her direction, and resumed.

"Are there no truths by which the state is bound? After all, there are physical laws governing the universe. Are there not also moral laws binding us? Are there not binding truths that limit the state?"

"Truth? I believe truth, sir, is, as the great Justice Oliver Wendell Holmes once wrote, the majority will. In fact, Judge Robert Bork, whom you so enthusiastically supported, once said, 'Truth is what the majority thinks it is at any given moment, precisely because the majority is permitted to govern and to redefine its values constantly.'"

Emily had been on the defensive, but she had him on that one. Her grin gave her away. The crowd chuckled.

The senator showed no emotion but once again removed his glasses and leaned forward.

"Well now, Professor, no one is perfect. Judge Bork was an eminent jurist who was crucified by this very committee—to its shame." He glanced at the Democrats, only one of whom had been sitting when Bork was nominated. "And he was, to his great credit, a strict constructionist, looking at what the framers meant. He clearly would have voted to overturn *Roe v. Wade*. But he was, I will confess, a bit myopic on the broader question of whether the laws of men and nations are judged by a higher law. I think Judge Bork in time would have come to see that."

"Truth, sir," Gineen said, her eyes sparkling, now on the

offensive, "is when a government sees to it that every individual can enjoy his or her full and equal opportunity; when every man and woman, following the dictates of conscience, is not just tolerated but respected in their lifestyle choices; when bigotry is banished from our common life."

There was a sprinkling of applause and the chairman gaveled for quiet. He turned to Langer. "The gentleman from Mississippi has exhausted his time. One more question, sir."

Langer nodded, propped his glasses on the end of his nose, and leaned back in his chair. For several seconds he simply stared at Gineen, without rancor.

"May I simply say, Professor Gineen, that I respect your intellect and ability and your record of public service. But good people, particularly those who are smart and can't imagine that they can do anything wrong, frighten me. For in their zeal and idealism, they can often become the very thing they most deplore. To guarantee your definition of liberty, Professor, will ultimately make us oppressors of liberty."

Emily stared at him, caught in the web of his riddle. Then a photographer knelt in front of the witness table; she smiled, and the web was broken.

Emily remained in command throughout the rest of the hearing. Most of the questions dealt with her views on law enforcement and fighting crime, and she was eloquent, armed with facts, statistics, and studies that she rattled off without looking at a sheet of paper.

Late in the day, however, shortly before the hearing ended, a Langer aide handed her an envelope containing a handwritten note.

"I'd be greatly obliged if you will meet me in my office at the conclusion of the hearings. Byron Langer."

Emily read it twice. Nothing good could come of this, she thought.

DESPITE HIS SENIORITY, Byron Langer chose to remain in the Russell Building, the oldest of the three Senate office buildings. He liked the older architecture, the ten-foot-high, dark-stained doors, the ornate moldings, and the well-worn black-and-white tile corridors.

It was after 6:00 when Emily arrived at room 141, accompanied by Jerry Kirkbride, the young Washington lawyer assigned to her by the presidential transition team. The office was ablaze with lights, people still hard at work at each of the old mahogany desks that lined both walls. The smiling receptionist jumped to her feet, took Emily's coat, nodded Jerry to a waiting-room chair, and immediately escorted Emily through two more crowded offices.

Senator Langer was standing in his office door, putting on his jacket. "Come in, Professor, come in," he said.

As she entered, she gave the senator's crowded office a quick scan. One wall was floor-to-ceiling books; the other three were covered with pictures, plaques, degrees, and certificates. Langer showed off a few favorites.

"This is my family last Christmas. This is my granddaughter, little Eugenia, here." He jabbed a finger at a blonde toddler who was laughing right into the camera. "She's a pistol."

"And over here was my first visit with President Reagan, years ago . . . here's my Green Beret company in Vietnam. The sergeant beside me, what a guy. For forty-one days the unit was behind enemy lines taking a pounding. He got three Bronze Stars for saving men under fire."

"You did too, didn't you Senator?" Emily had read up on her adversary.

"Well, one does one's duty. I was proud to serve my country. Still am."

He pointed to an overstuffed leather chair. "May I offer you a seat?"

"Do you mind if I sit here?" Emily asked, pulling over a black lacquered armchair with the Ole Miss seal on the back. "If I sat there, I'd be too relaxed. And for you, Senator, I need all my faculties."

"Well now, Professor, I wasn't all that rough on you today—at least I hope not." He took the leather chair himself. "Just a friendly exchange between two people who care about the law."

"Of course, Senator, entirely so." She smiled like she always did when she had to lie. She hated politics—one of the reasons she was already regretting that she'd accepted this job. But she couldn't go back now. And she knew she had to get along with the man. Bernie O'Keefe, in one of her briefing sessions, had told her the senator was the key to making her life here bearable or unbearable. He could be a fierce adversary. He could also be eccentric and sometimes talked in enigmas, a throwback to an earlier time. Not an easy man to deal with.

"Ms. Gineen," the senator said, gently twirling his glasses, "I thought we should have this discussion alone simply so that I could be completely forthright with you, as is my habit.

"You are remarkably well-qualified to be attorney general of the United States. Much about your life and professional career I find extraordinary and admirable. The president is indeed fortunate you agreed to serve."

Emily nodded while adjusting her cuffs. "Thank you, Senator," she said, waiting for the other shoe to drop.

"And you will, of course, be confirmed."

She smiled, beginning to relax slightly.

"This means you and I will have to work very closely together, being that I am the ranking member."

"It will be a pleasure, sir. After all, we are both committed to stopping crime and we are both Republicans."

"Yes, ma'am," he said. "But I was a Masterson Republican—and you, of course, were with Griswold."

"The election is over, Senator. We need to bring the party and the country together."

"Of course, of course. The election is over. But there is still a great gulf that divides us, Professor."

"I've not been in politics as long as you, Senator, but I understand it to be the art of the possible. That means compromise and consensus. People have to work to understand each other and arrive at prudential judgments." Emily was annoyed to find that she sounded as if she were pleading.

"That's just it. Political judgments, like anything else, are mere reflections of deeper beliefs. The real issue today is truth. It's not the rot that passes for political discourse in this place." Langer swung his arm as if to embrace the whole Capitol. "I mean the real questions are of life and existence, of meaning, of ultimate things. Truth itself—that's the great issue of our age."

Emily was groping for an answer. Just when she thought she was engaging the man, he'd slip away into philosophical issues. What was his game? She detested abstract discussions. *Just give me the cases, the citations, and the holdings to support your point. I want the law,* she would tell her students at Harvard.

She started to answer, but the senator cut her off. "That's the gulf: We're from two very different cities; we both speak the same language, but the words mean different things.

"It's like driving in England. I always tell my British friends that they drive on the wrong side of the road; but, of course, to them, it's the right side. They tell me *I* drive on the wrong side. Right means two different things to us—opposite things. And if we carried it far enough, we'd create chaos in each other's cities."

"I think I understand your point, Senator. We've been talking about culture wars in America now for a long time. Different fundamental values honestly held by different factions with different presuppositions. But that tension is nothing new; it's part of the dialectic of American life."

Emily took a tissue from her purse, pretending to blow her nose, but actually wanting to dry her palms and give her something to do besides stare into Langer's piercing eyes.

"No," he said decisively. "It's different than that. If you have two cities, separated by this great gulf, you can no longer communicate, unless you have an interpreter who knows the rules of the other city." He seemed to stare past her at something on the wall over her right shoulder, and for a moment he was quiet, reflective.

She decided to wait him out. Maybe he's gone around the bend, she thought. Early Alzheimer's. Or, more likely, he's after something.

"Oh, forgive me," he exclaimed suddenly. "No southern hospitality here. I'm so sorry. May I offer you coffee or a soft drink?"

She seized at anything to break the conversation. "A Coke, if you have it. Thank you, Senator."

Langer hit a button and in seconds the door swung open. "Two Cokes, if you would, Joan. Thank you very much." And then continued as if there had been no interruption.

"Truth is the issue. You see that, don't you, Ms. Gineen?" He was staring at her again.

"I think I understand, sir," she nodded, still waiting him out.

"I believe in absolute truth," he said. "I believe that there is a point of ultimate reality, an absolute from which all truth as we know it flows. You don't, of course. I've read your articles."

"I believe in truth, Senator, but it is a truth we discover through debate and consensus. We find it in our collective wisdom."

"But truth is not subjective. It is not relative. It is truth. You see, I'm afraid this makes my point," he said. "We use the same word and mean something totally different.

"And this, Ms. Gineen, affects our entire view of life, and, of course, government. I believe, as most of our founders did, in a transcendent, binding absolute by which men and nations are judged. God, of course. I say 'of course' because I believe. Others call it natural law, as some of the founders did. Russell Kirk, in fact, said one cannot be a conservative without believing in natural law."

"I'm quite familiar with that, Senator. I've studied Kirk, and I read Leo Strauss when I was at Princeton. And, of course, I'm familiar with the founders' debates."

"But you don't agree with them either, do you?" Langer stared at her intently.

"No, sir, I do not. I believe our government was founded on the principles of a social contract, with ultimate sovereignty in the people. That's what consent of the governed means."

Langer continued to stare as he said, "So the people can do what they want. Each generation sets the terms of the contract anew and defines what truth is for their times?"

Emily nodded.

"But that's the rub. I can't accept that as a matter of conscience. Perhaps I should explain, Ms. Gineen, that I'm a Christian. I was saved as a very young man, taking Jesus as my Savior many, many years ago. Though I'm not as good a Christian as I should be perhaps, I take it all quite seriously. I believe Jesus when He says He is *the* truth. In Him is ultimate reality."

Gineen felt her cheeks flush. She shifted uncomfortably. She didn't enjoy talking about something so intimate as one's faith, and she hated the term "saved"—so smug and southern and Baptist, reminding her of her childhood in Alabama.

"Now not to pry—there's of course no religious test for public office—but I imagine you don't believe that the way I do."

"Well, I'm a Christian, Senator. I attend the Episcopal Church. Or, well, I used to. I haven't for some time . . . there are many reasons . . . but I believe faith is very important. It's also very personal."

"Of course. But I believe that if God is God, faith cannot be simply personal. God has spoken the universe into being. He has given a concrete, moral prescription for life. All law ultimately finds its roots in God's Word. All legitimate law, that is. That's where our natural law comes from."

Gineen took her tissue out again. *Oh no,* she thought. *And the White House tells me I need to work with this guy? I'm not gonna get out of here till he ties me down and converts me.*

"Of course I'm not trying to convert you." It was as if he had read her mind. "I simply want you to see how different our basic presuppositions are. And why, as a matter of conscience, I do not think that I will be able to vote for your confirmation, Ms. Gineen."

His blunt words came unexpectedly, and Emily felt her face flush again. What a terrible way to start. And the White House had told her Langer would take six or eight senators with him. This would be a terrible symbolic defeat for the incoming president, coming from his own party.

"I understand, sir," was the best she could get out.

"Of course I will explain that you are eminently qualified. It's simply a matter of conscience over deeply held beliefs. And it won't matter; you'll be confirmed anyway, of course. But at least I will have been true to my convictions. I'm sorry. I truly am sorry."

He's either a great actor or he really is sorry, Emily thought as she gazed into his eyes. "I wish, sir, I could persuade you otherwise. I approach these issues on their merits. I'm sure we'll be able to do that."

"Oh, of course we will try. We have to. But we'll really never understand each other. We'll never be able to communicate, because our words mean different things. And there are no interpreters—I mean, there's no one around you to explain what I mean, what I and maybe thirty or forty million Americans believe."

Langer let the words hang in the air. He took off his glasses and smiled benignly.

He can't be. He can't be, Emily told herself. Despite all of his pious philosophy, could he be angling to get her to appoint one of his people? Was this deal time—politics plain and simple? She detested this, but like it or not, she was in it.

She took a deep breath and stared at him, her blue eyes hard. "Would you happen to know any interpreter, Senator? Someone I might consider?"

"Oh heavens, there are many, of course, but I wouldn't be so presumptuous."

"No, please, Senator. If we are to work together, we must be able to deal the cards face up."

"I don't play cards, Ms. Gineen. Threw them away when I was saved, like the preacher told me to. Good thing, too. I'd have lost my shirt at poker. I'm just a transparent southern boy."

Emily had to catch herself to keep from rolling her eyes. Right. *This good ol' boy is a master manipulator. He could take your socks off without touching your shoes.*

"No, please, Senator. You must know some capable attorneys I might appoint to the Justice Department to, as you put it, be interpreters."

"Well, I'm not urging this, you understand, but the chief counsel on this committee—judiciary—is a very able man. His name is Paul Clarkson, and he's a brilliant attorney. He's smart, full of energy, committed... but I don't want to put you in a difficult position, Ms. Gineen."

"Not at all, sir. I know Clarkson. He's impressive. But he's rather young, isn't he?"

"He's thirty-eight but has a lot of wisdom for his years."

"Perhaps I could find a good position in the Office of Legal Counsel."

"Of course, of course. But I don't think he'd leave here for that. Who have you picked as associate attorney general?"

No poker player, huh. He's going for the number three position in the department.

"We have many candidates, sir. That's, of course, a critical position since the AAG runs the department."

"Paul has run this committee. I don't know how we'd do it without him...but I suppose, well, I wouldn't stand in his way, of course."

She stared at Langer, not caring if her anger showed. There it was—the deal, the horse trade—shamelessly laid on the table. And she determined, at that moment, that she would not sacrifice her honor. If she could not rise above this sort of thing, she'd simply go back to Harvard. Griswold had promised her her independence.

"I'm afraid he would not be mature enough for that position, Senator. But I will consider him for some post, I assure you."

"Well, of course, of course. You do whatever is right. But not mature enough? Hmmm. How old are you, Ms. Gineen? Ten years ago I wouldn't ask a woman that question, but things have changed a lot."

"I'm forty-two, Senator, and sitting in here with you has aged me well beyond that," she snapped.

"Well, that's right. We do a lot of maturing from thirty-eight to forty-two. But now I want you as attorney general to do what you think is right."

Gineen, furious, looked at her watch. She refused to sit here and be this wacko's prisoner any longer. "I appreciate your time, Senator. I must go. Will you have Clarkson call me?"

"Yes, indeed. Very important to have a strong associate, someone who understands Washington and, of course, this end of Pennsylvania Avenue. He'd be a good interpreter."

Langer escorted her to the door, and she willed herself to say good-bye calmly.

STILL FUMING, Emily called Bernie O'Keefe from the phone in her limousine and told him what had happened.

"This is Washington," he said. She could hear his chair squeaking as he leaned back. His feet were probably on the desk.

"I know where I am, Bernie," she said sharply. It infuriated her that he sounded so cavalier. "I'd like to see Griswold on this. He told me I would be independent, and I want him to back me up. I can't be held hostage to this kind of horse-trading."

"Look, Emily, you're the attorney general-designate. If you want to see Whitney Griswold, you can see him. I'll put you on the calendar for tomorrow morning. But I'll tell you exactly what he will do. He'll listen politely, tell you he wants to think about it, and then he'll call me and have me call you and tell you to hire Clarkson. So why don't we save all of us a lot of trouble."

Emily rolled her eyes and picked at a piece of lint on the leather car seat. How in the world had she ever gotten herself into this situation?

"Besides," O'Keefe continued, "it's a good move. You're the only southerner in the cabinet, and Clarkson will help you reach out to the Masterson people."

Emily leaned back and sighed. "That hypocrite Langer. All that rambling about truth, philosophy, and religion. He's one of those born-again types. All that stuff was just to get his boy a job."

"Or maybe, Emily, it was for power. He wants his man where he can be an influence. I can't blame him. This is politics. Get used to it. Look, small concession now and you'll be confirmed with a unanimous vote; stand on principle and the president's attorney general gets ten negative votes, the president gets slapped in the face, and the attorney general is crippled. Face it. You don't have much of a choice here."

Emily hit her palm against the armrest. "Right," she said sarcastically. "This stinks, Bernie. And stop smiling."

He laughed into her ear. "Yes, ma'am, Madam Attorney General, sir. Go home. Have a drink. Relax."

THE NEXT MORNING Bernie and Emily interviewed Paul Clarkson for two hours. The FBI completed their check on him within forty-eight hours, and by week's end the announcement had been made.

Two days before the inauguration, the Senate voted ninety-eight to nothing, with two absences, to confirm Emily Gineen as attorney general of the United States. Byron Langer gave an impassioned speech, assuring his colleagues that while there had been differences in the campaign, "This brilliant woman shows a profound understanding of the democratic process; we'll work together productively." Paul Clarkson's confirmation went without a hitch as well.

10

W HITNEY GRISWOLD'S cheeks smarted from the fresh
wind sweeping in from the northwest across the open
spaces of the Mall. A cold front had moved through only hours
before the Inauguration, clearing the skies and dropping the tem-
perature into the high thirties.

The president-elect, dressed in the traditional formal cutaway,
had just stepped through the door leading from the west front of
the Capitol building to the huge wooden platform constructed to
hold the VIPs. He stood for a moment soaking in the incredible
spectacle, shaking more from excitement than from the cold as the
military band launched into "Ruffles and Flourishes."

Immediately before him were the platform participants, all
turned toward him, smiling and applauding—the entire Congress,
the diplomatic corps, the members of his government to be.
Television cameras were everywhere; around the world, more
than a billion people were watching.

And beyond the stands was the sea of faces. Over one hundred
thousand. Like colored dots on a vast blue-gray background. The
applause came in waves. He could see hands moving seconds
before he was engulfed in the thunderous sound.

Beyond the Mall, in the distance, stood the Washington Monument, tall, erect, and proud. And beyond that the stately edifice of the Lincoln Memorial.

Step firmly, he reminded himself. *This is the picture the whole world will see.*

He had dreamed of this for twenty years but hadn't dared think about it since his big victory in New Hampshire. Against all odds, the pundits had said. *Well, we showed them.*

Remember, he told himself, *walk erect, not casual like Bush, no loping stroll like Clinton. People want a leader, firmly in charge, someone bigger than life.*

When Griswold was finally seated in the cupola at the front of the platform, the Episcopal bishop of Washington moved to the podium to give the invocation. As he did so, Griswold rehearsed his speech in his mind. The printed words of the address would flow across three sheets of nonreflecting, bulletproof glass surrounding the podium. If he paused, the words paused; if he speeded up, they speeded up. He could read and no one would be the wiser. But he had rehearsed his speech so many times that he had most of it committed to memory.

He scanned the crowd. They trusted him with their dreams for their children, their hopes for a better job or for decent medical care, or for just the freedom to walk around safely in their own communities. The American dream. Another president—the dream rekindled.

Overwhelmed by his own thoughts, Griswold almost missed the cue to take Anne by the hand and walk toward the chief justice. His knees felt wobbly, his heart was thumping, and a sudden sensation clutched the pit of his stomach. He raised his right hand, trying to stop it from shaking; then the roar of the crowd slowly faded. "I, John Whitney Griswold, do solemnly swear...."

Within moments he was the president of the United States.

Griswold's speech was an unusual blend of philosophies of government. On the one hand, he committed his administration to free market, supply-side economics. That meant lower taxes, free trade, all-out economic growth. "Opportunity" and "empowerment" were words he frequently invoked. But there was paternalism as well: He promised that government would fulfill its duty to preserve order and justice, that more police and sterner punishment would make the streets safe again, and that more medical and social programs would help the needy and the homeless.

But his strongest theme was social libertarianism. In fact, the line that drew the most sustained applause was his promise to "not only get the government out of your pockets but out of your bedroom as well."

"We will achieve the concord of which Cicero wrote," he thundered, "so that we can truly enjoy the rich life of a civil community. Decency and tolerance will once again be the distinguishing hallmarks of American life."

The crowd thundered back its approval.

Suddenly a surge of passion welled up within him; his face flushed. "But one thing we will not tolerate are those who would subvert our domestic tranquility. So help me God, we will do what we need to in order to protect the domestic order for the good and decent and caring people of our land."

His finger jabbed the air as he warned, "Let there be no mistake. Let those who would deny our most sacred birthright take notice: There is no price too high, no exertion too great, to safeguard our liberty. And I solemnly promise you I will do precisely that."

As he ended the speech and turned toward the door leading back to the Capitol, outstretched palms jutted toward him from the senators, congressmen and women, judges, and other dignitaries lining the steps. He basked in the glow of the sun and the thunderous roar from the crowd.

Capitol police and Secret Service agents elbowed one another to guide the first family to a brief reception in the rotunda. From there they were taken to their limousine which would lead the inaugural parade from the Capitol, down Pennsylvania Avenue, and on to the White House.

The Griswolds, for the first time, stepped into the long black Cadillac with its bulletproof glass and half-ton of armor plating. One front fender bore a flag with the Great Seal of the United

States, the other the Stars and Stripes. Four agents wearing sun-glasses and earphones climbed on the running boards, two on either side. A cordon of forty motorcycle police moved ahead, the rumble of their engines filling the air, and two station wagons full of agents and the president's doctor trailed close behind.

The parade route was lined with temporary bleachers, four hundred thousand board feet of lumber, all constructed for this one moment. But all Griswold could see were the faces, all colors and shapes, all smiling and waving flags and banners. Such genuine jubilation. *They trusted him.* He waved from side to side as did Anne. Robert and Elizabeth, however, sat stiffly in the jump-seats along with Major George Hughes, the marine aide, who was wearing dress blues with a gold epaulet draped from his shoulder.

The Secret Service had warned Griswold not to get out of the car. There had been more than the usual number of threats, and the police had spotted two suspicious-looking men in a car near Rockville, Maryland; they had found a high-powered rifle with telescopic sight in the trunk. The men were being detained in a suburban jail. One anti-abortion group was reported to be plan-ning to throw human blood on the president's limousine. Then there were all the usual crazies the agents kept files on, more than two thousand of them.

As the motorcade slowed the first time, Griswold noticed a group of school girls, probably from a parochial school because they were all wearing blue jackets, white shirts, and dark blue skirts. They reminded him of Elizabeth. They were standing just behind the barricades carrying "We Trust You" signs.

"Oh, Whitney," Anne sighed as he hit the door handle and jumped into the street. Major Hughes followed.

Instantly Robbie barked into his radio and four agents from the wagon in back surrounded the president, even as Griswold vainly attempted to wave them away. Taking long strides, he moved toward the girls and started grabbing hands. Television crews were running to catch up.

Just then Griswold looked up and saw two men, wearing black jackets and black watch caps, elbowing toward him through the crowd in front of the bleachers. When they were not more than twenty feet away, they unfurled a huge banner lettered in red: "Stop Killing Babies." The television cameras caught the scene of Griswold staring at the sign.

The crowd began to press in, and the police were having trouble holding the barricades. Troops in dress uniforms now closed the line. Finally, Griswold waved broadly to the cheering crowd and, just as the motorcade turned onto Fifteenth Street, walked briskly back to the limousine.

"For goodness sakes, Whitney, think of us if nothing else. You know the dangers," Anne said angrily, but the president just kept waving to the crowds as the limousine moved onto Pennsylvania Avenue, whose barricades had been removed for the occasion, and past the White House, where the driver turned through the northwest gates onto the grounds.

There, the first family was escorted behind the great reviewing stand, up steps covered with red carpet, and into a heated, bullet-proof glass-enclosed presidential box.

Robert's eyes lighted, "All right! Just like the owner's box at Shea Stadium."

Elizabeth also brightened at the spectacle. There were marching bands from every state, and floats with banners proclaiming Griswold's themes: "Bring Us Together," "We Trust Griswold," "The New Enlightenment," "Decency Again."

For the president, the most impressive display was the U.S. Marine Corps Marching Band led by the drill team of forty men marching in perfect precision without a command, spinning their rifles in the air, bayonets unsheathed and gleaming in the sun.

"Flawless, flawless! Bravo!" Griswold applauded. "Remember Tocqueville," he said to no one in particular, overwhelmed by the sentiment of the moment. This was the world's wealthiest and most powerful nation on parade, celebrating the oldest constitutional democracy on earth. "'America is great because America is good.' What's the rest of that quote?"

"'If America ever ceases to be good, she will no longer be great,'" said Robbie.

"Yes, that's it," the president said, rubbing his hands together after returning the salute of passing troops. "We will keep her good and great. That's why we're here."

FOLLOWING THE WHIRL of inaugural balls, the Griswolds, exhausted, arrived back at the White House for one last reception for close supporters held in the diplomatic receiving room in the basement. Then Major Hughes escorted the first family to the main floor where the head usher, Rex Leonard, two agents, and Juan Garcia, the navy steward assigned as the president's valet, were waiting.

After a day of bands and roaring crowds, the White House seemed eerily serene, and Robert and Elizabeth examined the portraits in the Great Hall as Leonard steered them to the family elevator at the west end of the hall.

"Welcome to our new home, kids," Griswold sighed. "We made it."

The agents explained that one of them would remain on duty on the main floor, one in the basement, and another was in the control room in the west wing. In addition, executive police were at their positions all around the grounds. The president thanked them, and the usher led the family into the elevator to the second floor.

The quiet now was almost unsettling. All alone in this huge place, thought Anne, you could almost imagine that all the stories about Lincoln's ghost were true. Elizabeth squeezed her mother's hand as Leonard led them to the right toward the west hall, where a beautiful living room separated the president's bedroom from the first lady's.

Most first families had kept the same, somewhat impersonal arrangement, and with good reason: the president often had to be awakened in the night. Some presidents, like Lyndon Johnson, roamed the corridors when, as was often the case, they couldn't sleep. Nixon had made a habit of sleeping from 11:00 P.M. to 2:00 A.M., then waking up to work for two hours in the Lincoln sitting room, then sleeping again from 4:00 until 7:00. Others, who had taken a more liberal view of marriage, had found the arrangement convenient for other reasons.

At the west end of the hall, the usher opened the door to the spacious room with its elegant Palladian windows, through which the flag, illuminated by a spotlight on the roof of the west wing, could be seen unfurled in the night breeze. Elizabeth let go of her mother's hand and, with a grin, dropped into the downy cushions of one of the bright yellow-and-cream brocade sofas. Robert walked around the room, then went over and peered out the window.

The Griswolds, who had stayed the night before in Blair House, had been given an earlier tour of their new home and thorough briefings by the Secret Service. All of their clothing and personal belongings had been delivered to the mansion precisely at noon that day, and the staff had already placed them neatly in closets and bureau drawers.

"Both the stairs and the elevator will take you to the children's bedrooms on the third floor. Would you like me to show you the way?" Rex Leonard asked.

"We're not children," Robert grumbled, just loud enough for his father to hear him and frown at him.

"No, Mr. Leonard, we've been through all the rooms," Griswold said. "We're fine. Juan, here," he said, nodding at his valet, "can help us, but you've been very helpful."

"Thank you, Mr. President. And remember, an agent will be at his station in the Great Hall downstairs all night. Any of the staff is, of course, available at your call."

"Yes, yes, much obliged, but we are just fine," Griswold assured him as the usher closed the door and left.

"Juan, the Dom Perignon, please—and Cokes for Robert and Elizabeth." The president grinned at his valet, who turned and headed for the kitchen just beyond the family dining room on the north side of the living room.

"I'm so tired, Whitney," said Anne. "I'm not sure I can stay up another minute."

"Just one glass, Anne! This is a night we'll always remember. A historic night for the nation—and for our family!"

Anne smiled and nodded, but Elizabeth was not impressed. "I don't like it here, Daddy," she broke in.

Garcia returned just then with a magnificent silver tray and a bucket full of ice with the neck of the champagne bottle just visible. Bowing slightly, he quietly retreated.

"You will, darling, you'll get used to it, and you'll make new friends." Griswold pulled off his tie and unbuttoned his collar.

"I like my old friends. Besides, it's creepy here."

Anne moved over and sat next to her daughter, putting her arm around her. "Everything will be fine, dear. You'll see."

Elizabeth ignored her mother. "Daddy, you promised if I didn't like it here I could go back to Hotchkiss. You promised."

They had made the decision to move Elizabeth to Washington, where she would attend the all-female National Cathedral School. Better for security, among other reasons. Robert, however, would stay at Groton. To Elizabeth, it didn't seem fair that she had to leave her old school.

"Elizabeth, you and I will talk about it tomorrow," said Anne while Griswold bent the wires back from the cork. "But you need to give the Cathedral School a chance."

"I can tell you why she wants to stay at Hotchkiss, Dad," Robert chimed in.

"Shut up, Robert." Elizabeth glared at her brother.

"She's got a boyfriend at school," Robert announced just as the cork flew out of the champagne and foam ran down over his father's dress pants and the handsome floral-patterned rug.

"Well, why haven't you told me about this, honey?" her father asked as he swung the foaming bottle back over the silver tray.

Elizabeth blushed, and her mother said, "We'll talk about it tomorrow, Whitney. Pour the champagne, please."

Griswold filled two crystal glasses to the rim and handed one to Anne. The children got their Cokes.

"To our beloved country." He raised his glass. "To keeping our trust. May we do everything we can—as a family—to make this a better and safer nation."

Anne took a sip. Griswold downed half the glass, then sat down and kicked off his black patent leather shoes.

"Well, well," he said. "A boyfriend. My little girl." He shook his head.

"She's not a little girl, Whitney," Anne said, slipping her arm around her silent daughter's shoulder. "She's a young lady."

"Well, we'll talk about that later, too. Great champagne, isn't it?" he said as he filled his glass a second time. He hit a buzzer beside the chair and Garcia appeared in the doorway.

"Juan, would you escort the children to their rooms and be sure they have everything they need?" He turned to the children, "It's very late. You get ready for bed, and your mother and I will be right up."

As Robert and Elizabeth followed Garcia out of the room, Anne walked over to her husband, leaned down, and kissed him lightly. "She'll be fine, dear. I'm going up to help her. We just need a little girl talk. You come in a few minutes."

"Good, Anne, thank you." Griswold was already reaching for the red folder the agent in charge had given him on security procedures.

ANNE HAD CHOSEN smaller rooms on the third floor for Robert and Elizabeth. They were adjacent to each other on the south side, across from the Washington Monument. There was plenty of space on the main floor, but she wanted them to have their own area, a more normal environment, away from all the guests and traffic. Besides, the third floor reminded her of their home in Greenwich, Connecticut. The ceilings weren't nearly so high as downstairs, and it had a homey feel.

Anne sat on the edge of Elizabeth's bed. "This button here, just press it, and Juan or Daddy will be here before you can blink an eye."

"Mom, this place is weird." Elizabeth's lip was quivering. The excitement of the day, the strangeness of the White House, away from all her friends and facing a new school . . . Anne knew her daughter was feeling overwhelmed and frightened, and she hugged her hard.

"I hear a noise outside the window," Elizabeth said.

"It's the wind, honey, just the wind."

"No, Mom, I hear something."

Anne stood up, walked to the window, drew the drapes to the

side, and looked out. "There's nothing out there," she said, "nothing except the most beautiful view in the whole world."

Anne reached up to unlatch the window and open it so Elizabeth could see that it was only the wind, forgetting that she had been told never to stand in the window at night, silhouetted against the light. There was no bulletproof glass on the third floor.

IN W-16, the Secret Service headquarters located in the basement directly under the Oval Office, Agent Callahan saw the red light flash before he heard the buzzer. He had been leaning back in his chair, sipping coffee, and watching a thirteen-inch television set on the back of his desk.

He jumped up, spilling coffee while yelling into his hand-held radio, "Alert, alert, red one, third floor residence, station six." A giant electronic map of the White House pinpointed the precise location of the alarm.

Oh, no, he thought. *The first night—just my luck. Only Matthews and Brown here with me.*

"Come in, Matthews. Where are you?" he snapped into the radio. "Move, man."

"I'm headed for the quarters, chief," came back the reply. "Brown's behind me."

Searchlights strategically placed around the White House grounds activated automatically. The executive police at the gate were alerted, and several drew their weapons. At the kennel across from the tennis court, two officers brought out two German shepherds. Executive police stepped out onto an Executive Office Building balcony, hand-held stinger surface-to-air missiles at the ready. They had practiced so many times it was almost a reflex reaction.

Griswold had heard the bell and bolted out of his chair. He needed an instant to orient himself, then realized the alarm was upstairs. He headed for the kitchen stairwell, bounded up the circular staircase three steps at a time, and turned into the corridor. But he was not as fast as Brown and Matthews, who were running directly toward him from the center stairwell, both with submachine guns at the ready.

The president froze as the two agents reached Elizabeth's door and swung it open so hard it smashed against the wall.

Elizabeth sat up in bed, screaming. Anne stood helplessly, a telephone receiver in hand.

"False alarm, chief," Brown spoke into his wrist radio. "All secure."

Griswold came in wide-eyed and breathless.

"I'm sorry, ma'am," Matthews said. "Did you open that window?"

Anne nodded.

"See that key there on the side?" he said and pointed. "That has to be deactivated first. It will turn green when you turn it to the right. You should have been briefed ma'am."

Robert was standing in the door, rolling his eyes upward and shaking his head. Elizabeth was sobbing.

"I'm sorry," Anne said. "We went over so many things in the briefing. I just forgot."

"You gentlemen are good. I'm impressed," said Griswold. "We're sorry for the alarm."

The agents returned to their stations, and Anne took Elizabeth down to her room for the night.

LATER, Whitney Griswold still could not sleep. He tossed for an hour, then got up, put on his camel-colored bathrobe and leather slippers, and walked down the hall to the Lincoln sitting room.

From this room, Abraham Lincoln had directed the Civil War. Griswold felt his cheeks flush and his stomach churn at the thought. Maybe he hadn't been kidding the family. Maybe ghosts did roam these corridors. He gingerly ran his fingers over the tufted yellow velvet chair in the corner before sitting down.

He stared for a long moment at the painting of Lincoln on the wall just inside the door. Then he checked his watch. 2:15. Doubtless there would be many nights like this. He'd been briefed by four of his predecessors, and all had warned him of the terrible pressures, the need for discipline and stamina.

"Only do those things that only the president can do," they had cautioned. "But even that is job enough for six strong people."

Though the problems seemed great at the time, he thought, being governor of a state with three million people was nothing by comparison.

The strange burning sensation in his stomach continued, and for a fleeting moment, Griswold found himself almost praying for wisdom. He'd never done anything like that before. He scribbled a little note on the pad next to his chair to ask the rector of St. John's to make that point—the need for prayer—in the service he would attend on Sunday. St. John's, directly across Lafayette Park from the White House, was known as the church of the presidents.

Still he felt that strange sensation. Might he, somehow, be the kind of leader who could heal the nation? Surely he was no Lincoln, but the nation needed healing. His own party was divided. The evangelicals who had supported Masterson had no use for him, and the feelings were mutual. The country was bitterly divided; abortion foes were increasingly militant. Homosexual groups were angry that the government hadn't done enough for AIDS, even with the new technologies coming down the pike. Minorities were increasingly restless, and the condition of the inner cities was horrible.

What was it Masterson had written to him, late on election night, after he had conceded? Griswold had a gift for remembering precise words; now parts of Masterson's fax came back to him. He had cast it aside at the time, laughing about it with Bernie. But now he remembered.

"You can with reason, love, and compassion begin to end the terrible divisions that are rending the very fabric of our common life," Masterson had written. "But it will take courage the nation has not known since Lincoln."

Griswold stared again at the great president's portrait. He remembered, too, that Masterson had promised to pray for him. He hoped he was doing so.

For several moments he sat quietly, contemplating all that lay ahead. The enormity of his own responsibility was overwhelming. But he remembered the old Yale professor's words: "to whom much is given, much is required." The time had come to fulfill his life's destiny. And that meant, now, in every decision he faced, every day, he had to do the right thing. People trusted him. He could not let them down. That meant pure politics was behind him now. He had to do his best to be a good president. Even a great one.

TWO MILES AWAY in a red brick federal townhouse in Georgetown, Bernie O'Keefe sat alone with his thoughts as well, sipping what he vowed would be his final Dewars on the rocks for the evening. He had had more than he wanted to count. Marilyn and the kids had gone to bed hours ago.

It had been a momentous day. His kids had loved it, but they were all returning to Boston that weekend—with Marilyn. She had insisted that the children finish their school year in Wellesley. They would decide later if they should all move to Washington.

His wife had inherited her Italian father's jet-black hair and her Irish mother's blue eyes. And from both she'd gotten a fiery temper and a stubbornness even more iron-willed than his.

Bernie had been making $700,000 a year practicing law and dabbling in politics. His $140,000 government salary would not support the mortgages on two homes, the pricey summer rental on Martha's Vineyard, and three kids in private school. And Marilyn wouldn't even think of public schools in D.C.

No doubt about it, politics had put more distance between them, Bernie thought, not that things had ever really been that good. He was always preoccupied—if not on the phone, then deep in thought. So Marilyn had made her own life, playing golf during the day, bridge at night, active in several charities. Even on this jubilant evening they had exchanged bitter words.

Bernie stirred his drink with his index finger. Good thing Marilyn was in bed; she hated that habit. She also thought he drank too much. Nothing new. Bernie took another sip.

Tomorrow we begin running the government, he thought. I still can't believe it. We've made it, and we're gonna make a difference. We're gonna bring things together, help the people, heal the nation.

For now, though, his drink was drained, and so was he. Bernie put his glass down, staggered out of the box-cluttered study, and made his way upstairs to the bedroom. Marilyn rolled over, looked at Bernie, then at the clock, shook her head, and went back to sleep.

11

T HE MARINE SENTRY at the door under the portico of the west wing entrance to the White House looked like he had just stepped out of a recruiting poster. He stood ramrod straight, his forearm snapped into a perfect forty-five degree angle so that his white glove just touched the tip of his polished black visor.

Emily Gineen noted that Anthony Frizzell, who had been the FBI director for five years, barely nodded in response to the sentry's salute. To be so preoccupied with the weighty matters of state that one hardly noticed others was one of the most visible marks of the Washington powerful; she had learned that already. Today, however, neither of them needed to feign the appearance of being weighed down by responsibilities. The president had summoned them to the Oval Office to discuss the Fargo killing.

The two were ushered immediately through the reception room, down the corridor running from the press room past the cabinet room, and into a small office where the two secretaries barely nodded, then returned to their word processors. A Secret Service agent motioned for them to wait just behind a door which, except for its bare, pencil-thin outline, looked like part of the wall; it was the side entrance used mostly by staff. There was a faint buzz, then a click, and the agent swung the door open.

For Emily, this citadel of power was as dazzling as it had been yesterday when she was sworn in. Though the day outside was gray and wintry, the room seemed flooded with light, illuminating the Great Seal of the United States embroidered in the large, deep-blue, oval rug that covered all but a narrow border of wood running around the room. To the right was a fireplace with birch logs crackling in the flames, and at the other end of the room, flanked by flags, Whitney Griswold sat at his desk.

The president, his half-circle reading glasses perched on the end of his nose, was studying a single sheet of paper. Harvey Robbins and Bernie O'Keefe sat quietly in two straight-backed Chippendale chairs on either side of the desk. The president bounded to his feet as they entered.

"Emily, come in. Good, good. And Director Frizzell. Thank you for coming." He shook their hands and pointed them to two empty chairs in front of the desk. Robbins and O'Keefe stood up, smiled, nodded, and sat down without saying a word.

"Getting settled in all right, Emily?" Griswold grinned.

"Yes, Mr. President. All twenty-four hours' worth. But everything is under control, sir." Emily feigned confidence. In truth, she had barely found her way around her new office.

"Good, good," the president nodded. Then his demeanor abruptly shifted as he leaned forward.

"Now, this is my first official meeting, except for yesterday's formalities, of course, and the CIA defense briefing—the spook community is all over a new president like a blanket." It was Griswold's way of impressing on the attorney general and FBI director the gravity of the Fargo killing.

"So let's get right to it. This is the first real crisis we have to face, and I want to hit it hard. Rotten way to start, but here it is." There was a stern intensity in Griswold's voice that surprised Emily. She nodded, as did Frizzell.

"I've, of course, read all your reports, Mr. Director, but I want it firsthand. I've got to make the decisions now." Emily's heart was pounding, and she was relieved that Griswold was staring at Frizzell, rather than at her.

"Let's begin with this letter." The president pulled from the sheaf of papers before him a copy of the open letter that had been sent to Levitz at the *Post*.

"What is this Holocaust Resistance? I want to know everything you know about these murderers—everything."

Frizzell hardly waited for the president to finish. "Well, sir, the bureau has been right on top of this since the shooting. There is no Holocaust Resistance as such. We're quite sure of that. It's got to be some person or persons who are part of the pro-life movement. This letter was to send you a message, sir, from the movement."

"Well, I've gotten their message. And they're going to get mine. My answer is act fast and stamp this thing out, or we'll have a new wave of violence like we had a few years ago."

"Yes sir," Frizzell said. "You've analyzed it precisely right, Mr. President. It's a warning shot. More to follow. But we'll beat them to the punch, I can assure you of that, sir."

Emily watched as the president nodded appreciatively. Frizzell, whose bureaucratic skills, particularly in promoting the FBI's image of invincibility were legendary, was in total control. She hadn't opened her mouth yet.

"All right then, Mr. Director, what leads do we have?" asked Griswold.

"We've got a hunt under way with a lot of good leads, sir. We'll get the killer. Rest assured of that. But I want something more. I want the whole conspiracy this time. We're spreading the net wide." Frizzell grinned.

"What do you mean 'this time'?" Griswold was leaning forward in his chair, one fist propped under his chin.

"Well, before, sir, like in the John Salvi or Paul Hill cases, we got just the gunman. But we suspected there were others involved. Grand juries were impaneled back then, but they botched it. We want them all this time . . . if we can get the prosecutors with us, that is." He glanced at Emily and smiled.

"Good, good," the president nodded.

"And we'll do it this time, sir, because we now have assets throughout the militant parts of the movement."

"Assets?"

Frizzell smiled, hesitated a moment, glancing at Robbins and O'Keefe.

"It's all right," the president assured him. "What do you mean?"

"An asset's an informer—an agent in their ranks. We've infiltrated most of the groups, including one here in Washington that is very interesting. They call themselves The Life Network and are supposedly nonviolent, merely wanting to expose the horrors of abortion, as they put it. But you never know. Then there's another group in Chicago. Actually there are eight or ten major ones across the country that we're certain of. Some are very, very dangerous, Mr. President, but we're inside."

Gineen watched Frizzell with admiration. According to his record, the FBI director had begun right out of Fordham as a street agent. A tough cookie who'd survived a big drug-bust shootout, he'd been decorated, promoted, and become special agent in charge in Memphis at age thirty-five. He'd made it onto the federal bench at thirty-nine and been named head of the bureau five years ago at age forty-two. Seemingly overnight he'd remade it in his own no-nonsense image. The street boys loved him, and no one in Justice ever crossed him. She could see why. He had taken over the meeting, knew more than the president, proved that the FBI was on the job, and made the situation sound so dangerous the president couldn't afford not to listen to him, all in three minutes. Yes, he was good, and this was Washington.

"Now, Director, is all this infiltration, this asset business, within the law? I want no wanton searches or other shortcuts in my presidency." Griswold tapped the desk with his index finger. The idea of stealing the other side's signals bothered him a little.

"Everything done in due process, sir. We have plenty of authority. These groups fall under the terrorist categories of the statute Congress passed after the World Trade Center bombing. With

groups like this we can do almost anything—all within the law."
He grinned. "So we just have agents doing their job, sir."

"If the agents were doing their job, Director, how come we
didn't know that these people were going to attack Fargo a week
before I came into this office?"

Frizzell didn't miss a beat. Most of the pro-life movement, he
explained, had remained nonviolent. "That's changing, though,"
he warned. "The problem is, these groups are loosely connected,
relatively independent cells spread around the country. Some simply run around carrying signs. Others, like this The Life Network
group in Washington, simply seem to be making information
public. And some of them are clearly trying to intimidate abortion
clinic workers. Even though we have the authority, our resources
are spread pretty thin. We just need more enforcement."

But the bureau was after them, he said. Like all zealot movements, there were very dangerous individuals spread throughout.
Frizzell used the word "terrorist" continuously.

While the FBI director was giving his detailed briefing,
Griswold leaned forward with his elbow on the desk and his chin
cupped in his left palm. His questions were sharp and quick: What
could be done to monitor the movement more effectively? Could
a conspiracy be proved? How would anti-racketeering statutes
apply? What was being done to search for the killer? Robbins and
O'Keefe were also listening intently, taking notes.

Griswold leaned back in his chair. "All right, then, we all
understand the facts. Let's get on with the job—fast. I realize these
people are testing me; the timing is deliberate, of course. But our
job is to get them before they strike again.

"What the nation has to know is that we're in charge. It
was, I think, 1918 or 1919 . . . check that Robbie . . . when
Calvin Coolidge, governor of Massachusetts, called out the
National Guard to break a police strike. Didn't say much,
Coolidge didn't, but he was quick and tough. Made him a
national figure and got him seated at this desk in short order.
Well, there's a lesson here. We need to act fast and tough . . . but
by the rules. Is that understood?"

There was a chorus of "Yes sirs."

"All right, Emily, you're in charge." Griswold's directive startled her. It was the first time he had addressed her since his initial greeting, but he was apparently well aware of the protocol. "I want marshals stationed at every clinic."

"We've got them spread around the country as best we're able, sir," she said. "We've got more marshals at abortion clinics than we do in the courtrooms."

"Get more if you have to, Emily. Whatever it takes. And I want the Freedom of Access to Clinic Entrances Act enforced. I mean tough. Get rough."

"Yes sir. The department has been using it in every instance over the past few years."

"Well, use it everywhere. You see, Emily, I want you to go after the whole movement here. These people claim that they're exercising peaceful protest, but by their violent language they are inciting violence. Wasn't it Oliver Wendell Holmes who talked about that?"

"Yes sir," Emily agreed. "There's a limit on free speech. You can't shout fire in a crowded movie theater."

"Yes, that's it. We're going after this whole movement. But I must tell you: We're to observe every statutory restraint and constitutional protection." Then he smiled. "But I don't have to tell you that. You're the professor of constitutional law."

Gineen nodded, but before she could reply, Griswold moved to Frizzell. "Director, put your best men and women on this. Spare nothing. We want to know what they're going to do before they do it."

"Yes sir, we will." Frizzell grinned.

"You call Robbie day or night if you need me. And from our end, Bernie here is my man. He knows me. He knows the law. You can deal with him as if you're dealing with me. Understood?"

Griswold didn't wait for the chorus but kept right on, the captain giving his oarsmen a pep talk. "And remember, firm action. Decisive. Quick. We nip this in the bud. Has to be done in days, not months. Understood?"

As there was another chorus of "Yes sirs," and Emily and Frizzell were going out the door, the president called out, "One more thing, Emily. We'll make a brief statement here, of course, in the press room. Any problem if we say we'll seek the death penalty for the criminal when apprehended?"

Emily stared at him for an instant while searching her mental casebook. Could it be prejudice? Could defense counsel use it? But before she finished her search, Frizzell assured the president that the bureau would have no objection.

Emily glared at him, then spoke firmly, "I'm the prosecutor, Mr. President, and I want a conviction. For the president of the United States to refer to the death penalty might be considered prejudicial—attempting to influence a jury. I'd recommend, sir, you just say we will prosecute to the fullest extent of the law."

"All right," the president nodded. "Got that, Robbie?"

AS FRIZZELL and Gineen left by the side door, Griswold turned to his aides. "Well, what do you think?"

Robbie, who had hardly opened his mouth during the meeting, broke into a grin. "Mr. President, this is more than we could have hoped for. Look at this latest poll I got just before the meeting began." He laid a single sheet of paper on the president's desk.

Griswold put his glasses on, sat back, and scanned the figures, pursing his lips and exhaling a whistling sound. "Well, well, Robbie. Good work. We've been doing something right, I gather." The poll was almost double the percentage by which he had been elected. "Sixty-seven percent," Griswold grinned.

"But look at the break-out of your personal qualities, sir," said Robbie. "Eighty percent list your decisiveness, 76 percent your integrity, 72 percent strength of character. You see, just what our focus group tells us. People are worried about crime and what they perceive as the breakup of our society. What they want more than anything else is a strong leader. They want order."

Griswold nodded. "But this killing will unsettle them. That can hurt us."

"No, I don't think so, sir, and if we work fast, I see it as an opportunity. You take charge. Crack down. These are the bad guys.

I say we go for them. Not just the murderer in this particular case, but the whole network, wherever we can find them," Robbie said. "Remember your history, Mr. President. Franklin Roosevelt. He became hugely popular by making the National Association of Manufacturers his public enemy number one."

Griswold nodded.

"And these are the fundamentalists, tops on everyone's bad-guy list—45 percent in Gallup's poll didn't want one living next door. It's a natural, sir."

Griswold nodded again.

"And I think you should put Frizzell right out front. He's so eager to please you, he'll be out in the streets with his Uzi blazing. I mean this character was born for this part. You think of a racket-busting cop, and you've got Frizzell, Eliot Ness reincarnated. Perfect. Besides, Bernie will like him. He's half Irish."

"That's all fine, Robbie, I understand the politics," said Griswold, "but remember, we must do the right thing. The campaign is over now."

"The right thing? Yes sir. These people are evil. They kill people. They must be stopped. And it happens to be the right politics." Robbie kept running his hand through his close-cropped hair, which he did on those rare occasions when he got really excited.

"Robbie's right, Mr. President." Bernie spoke slowly, subduing his natural impulsiveness to create the aura of the deliberate, thoughtful lawyer-philosopher. "You cannot separate politics from the art of governing. Your task, sir, is one of moral suasion. We're not interested in polls just to get re-elected," he paused with a wry grin, "but because they measure how well your persona and policies are moving this country."

"So what are you saying, Bernie? Be a lawyer now." Griswold was twirling his glasses by one stem.

"Go after them, Mr. President. Simple as that. I knew little about these groups before we came into this meeting. I thought this was one crazy knocking off one money-grubbing abortionist—neither one any good in my book. But this pro-life movement—what's left of it anyway—is dedicated to your defeat. They'll be nothing but trouble for four years. I've been worried how we're going to deal with them. But now, with incredible stupidity, they've handed you the sword with which you slay them," Bernie said, grinning widely.

"We're not just after a murderer here; we have a movement claiming credit. So you strike now, go for the movement, discredit it, break it up. The people are with you. They'll cheer you for it. Right now we can do anything—and we'll be rid of them—that will make life easier from here on out. Not to mention what it will do to show up the Mastersons and the rest of those renegades."

Bernie shook his head. "I can't believe their stupidity. If I didn't know that Robbie here was a man of exemplary integrity, I'd think maybe he wrote the letter himself."

The three men roared with laughter.

What had started out as an unpleasant intrusion into Griswold's first days in office didn't look so bad after all. Thoughts of what breaking the police strike had done for Coolidge and what campaigning against big business had done for Roosevelt danced in Griswold's mind. Yes, clearly this was an opportunity.

As Robbie left to brief Caroline Atwater and prepare a press statement, Griswold turned to Bernie.

"You call Gineen and emphasize how important swift, tough, decisive action is. We may need to do more here. Maybe wiretaps, more informers. She needs to understand that the job is not just to prosecute but to break a movement. These are subversives, really. Dangerous people."

Bernie was nodding.

"You know what to say. I obviously can't be quite so blunt, and of course you keep me out of it. But take care of it, Bernie."

His friend smiled and nodded. He knew exactly what Griswold wanted. Use whatever it takes, shove the other guy's face in the mud. This was the way Yankee Brahmins played the game. They used tough Irish boys to do their dirty work. Bernie had been faithfully doing this for J. Whitney Griswold for more than twenty years.

CAROLINE ATWATER called a special press briefing at 5:00 P.M. that day. The Griswold team already knew the tricks of the trade:

5:00 was perfect, just enough time for the networks to make their 6:30 or 7:00 feed but not quite enough for the commentators or critics to organize a rebuttal. This story would be covered, and it would get just the spin the White House wanted.

Atwater, standing before the blue screen with the rendering of the White House behind her, reviewed the day's events, referring to government intelligence reports indicating that the assailant in North Dakota had not been acting alone but as part of an organized conspiracy. She announced that more U.S. marshals would be dispatched to guard clinics and that all government agencies would cooperate with the Justice Department.

She concluded her prepared text: "The president has authorized me to say that he has ordered the attorney general to use every means at this government's disposal to bring the guilty to justice with the maximum penalty the law allows. But beyond that, this administration will not tolerate such terrorist acts. An action like this declares war on peace-loving Americans, and whenever that has happened in the past, Americans have responded. Let those who would challenge our freedoms know of our resolve: We will take whatever steps are necessary in defense of liberty."

"Who's declared war?"

"What conspiracy?"

The reporters stood waving their notebooks in the air, bombarding the press secretary with questions. But she smiled, folded up her briefing book, turned and walked off the platform without a word. Bernie had programmed her perfectly.

AT THE JUSTICE DEPARTMENT, Emily Gineen was handed a fax of Atwater's statement only moments before 5:00. She shook her head as she read. This didn't sound like the cool, carefully calculated Griswold she had met with only hours earlier. But then the call from O'Keefe hadn't made sense either. His instructions about "getting tough, breaking the movement" sounded more like overzealous aides than Whitney Griswold. The government clearly could overplay this.

Emily made a mental note to raise her cautions with the president the next time they spoke.

AT 5:20 P.M., Ben Thomas, Capitol Hill reporter for ABC, reached room 141 of the Russell Senate Office Building. It was worth a try to get a reaction from the ranking Judiciary Committee Republican.

Thomas was in luck. Langer was in and agreed. So the reporter's cameraman set up in the corridor with the door to the senator's office in the background, his nameplate perfectly framed in the lens.

Langer was used to the twenty-second rule and kept his remarks short and blunt. "Whoever did this despicable act must be brought to justice. But we should keep things in perspective. In the long and emotional struggle over abortion, there have been relatively few such incidents. So I would hope the government would not use this as an excuse to suppress legitimate dissent. In this city, there remain some who take the words of the Constitution quite seriously."

Perfect. One-third of a minute to the second.

Thomas sent his cameramen rushing to the Senate gallery where the tape would be fed instantaneously to New York. The editors would slide such sound bites in right up until the last minute, and it was a good take. New York always liked a little confrontation, and Langer was a pro. He was also a friend.

"All right, Byron, we're off camera now," Thomas said when they were alone. "What do you make of Atwater's statement? What's the White House angle here?"

Langer frowned, tightening his lips and folding his arms across his chest. "I don't know, Ben; I don't know. But it doesn't feel right. Doesn't feel right at all. We're heading for trouble, I think."

Langer looked up as if he had been caught in his own thoughts. Then he shook his head and said it again. "Big trouble."

12

I'M READY, if you'd like to take my order," Jennifer Barrett said to the young woman behind the deli counter. "I'll have the vegetable pita sandwich, hold the cheese, extra cucumber instead."

"As long as you're making one, you might as well make two of those," Alex Seaton added. "I'll have the same."

He took the bottle of seltzer Jennifer was holding and picked up two red apples from the straw basket on the counter. "Let me take care of this."

"No," Jennifer said. "Come on, let me pay. I invited you."

"You can take me next time." Alex grinned. *If there was a next time*, he thought.

They picked up their paper-wrapped sandwiches and headed to a table near the deli's picture window, which overlooked an ice-skating rink where wool-bundled children swooped and slid on the ice while their mothers hovered nearby, clumped in conversational knots. Jennifer unwrapped her sandwich and neatly smoothed out the white paper, folding it into a square. She paused, and Alex said a short blessing over their food.

"Thanks for buying lunch, Alex," she said when he finished. "I just thought I'd be bold and see if we could get together. I've moved around so much over the last few years, I've found that the best way to get to know people is to go ahead and take the initiative. If you wait for people to come to you, you end up waiting for a long time."

"I appreciate you giving me a call," Alex said. "Some people seem to think everyone should come to them; they're not willing to be the first to reach out. Do you feel like you're getting settled in Washington?"

Jennifer picked up a sprout that had fallen out of her sandwich. "I love it here," she said. "There's always so much going on. I haven't been able to find a full-time job yet, so I've been temping. I've worked at offices all over the city, and in some of the suburbs too. I really like it here in Reston, though—so many trees, and the bike paths are great.

"And some days I don't have work, so I just take the Metro downtown and walk around. The Smithsonian is tremendous, and I can't get over the fact that the museums are free. I lived in Philadelphia before this, and you have to pay to get in anywhere there. Even the zoo."

"Your federal tax dollars at work," said Alex. "Have you been to the Holocaust Museum?"

"I went right after I came," Jennifer said. "It was one of the most incredible experiences of my life. I think every adult in America should go there. It sears your conscience."

Across the room three young businessmen were looking for a table, balancing steak-and-cheese subs and Cokes on plastic trays heaped high with bags of potato chips. They made their way to the table next to Alex and Jennifer.

"Excuse me," said one as he bumped past Jennifer's chair. "You've got a nice view of the ice skaters." He smiled, and his eyes lingered just a little too long on her legs.

Jennifer's startling blue gaze was often so direct it was disconcerting, but now she broke eye contact with the young man almost immediately. "No problem," she said, then turned back to Alex.

"Have you been there?"

"Where?" he asked, momentarily distracted by the Neanderthal at the next table.

"The Holocaust Museum," she said, smiling and taking a bite of her sandwich.

"Oh, yes, I went there right after it opened," he said. "I've been back a number of times. When I look at the model of the crematorium at Auschwitz, sometimes I wonder if people in the future will one day look back at a model of an abortion facility, or one of these regeneration centers they're building now, and wonder how in the world it could have happened. Maybe they'll be as disgusted at the abortion holocaust as we are that the Nazis managed to murder six million Jews."

"Is that why you started the Network group?" she asked.

Alex took a long swallow of seltzer. "Daniel's the one who really started it," he said. "We've both been in the pro-life cause for a long time, but Daniel felt there needed to be a new organization with a more specific purpose than just being another protest group. He said we needed to expose the inner workings of the abortion industry: that if people see what's really going on, there's still enough of a core of common decency in our country that people would stand up against the regeneration centers. I kind of doubt it, though," he added. "And I wonder if it's really enough just to expose the evil."

Jennifer leaned forward slightly. "What about the shooting in Fargo?" she asked. "Do you support that kind of thing?"

"Of course not," Alex said quickly. He picked up his sandwich again. "What about you? Why did you get involved with us?"

She leaned back. "It's sort of a long story," she said.

"I grew up south of here, in Richmond. My father was an insurance executive, very successful. On the surface our family looked fine. We had a nice home, nice clothes, nice friends.

"But my dad was an alcoholic. He drank every night, but on the weekends he really went around the bend. And when he drank beyond a certain point, he was violent.

"My mother just took it. She was a classic enabler, if you're into those kind of tags. Didn't want to upset the applecart. My older sister compensated. She started looking for father figures everywhere. When she was a teenager, any older man would do. She was always getting involved with married men. And by the time she was twenty-five, she'd had three abortions.

"They were convenient, but they didn't help her at all. They just perpetuated the cycle she was on. No personal responsibility for her actions. More self-destructive behaviors. No self-respect. She just dwindled and dwindled as a person.

"The situation at home made me go the other way. When I was about sixteen, I decided that when women are weak, they get preyed upon one way or another. So I would be self-sufficient. I would be strong. I would take care of myself. By the time I left home for college, my dad knew better than to harass me, even verbally. Let alone physically.

"So I've always been in control, master of my own destiny, whatever. But about two years ago I realized I had over-compensated, that I did have needs I couldn't meet on my own. I worked with a woman who ended up inviting me to church, and I went with her. I decided I needed God. I take my faith very seriously. But now I'm not quite so self-sufficient."

Her smile gave Alex a strange feeling for a moment. He hadn't dated anyone since he and Sarah had broken up nearly a year ago, and he had forgotten that feeling.

"What are you waiting for?" Daniel had teased him. "You're a bachelor in your thirties. If you're planning to be a monk, then let me tell you something: You're in the wrong church."

At the time, Alex had told his brother, rather awkwardly, that maybe it was better for him to be free and unhindered, maybe he wasn't cut out to be in a relationship. Women took so much time, so much care and feeding.

Jennifer had finished her sandwich and was looking out the window at the skaters.

"Why don't we walk for a few minutes?" Alex said. "Do you have some time before you have to get back to your office? I've got the afternoon free. That's the great thing about being in construction: The winter months are lighter, business-wise, which gives me more time for the cause. Or, sometimes, for other things." He caught her eye, then immediately felt ridiculous.

But she smiled, looking at her watch. "I saw an espresso cart out there near the rink," she said. "Let's get some coffee and watch the skaters for a few minutes."

AS HE WATCHED the press conference clip on the evening news, Daniel Seaton thought about William Butler Yeats's poem again. The same four lines had been turning over in his mind ever since he'd heard about the shooting in Fargo:

The blood-dimmed tide is loosed, and everywhere
The ceremony of innocence is drowned;
The best lack all conviction, while the worst
Are full of passionate intensity. . . .

It was passionate intensity of the worst kind that had led to the murder in Fargo; now he could see it spilling over into official reactions here in Washington. We have to be so careful, he thought. Violence begets violence.

When Daniel and Alex had first discussed the idea of the The Life Network, they had talked at length about the narrow line they needed to walk. At the beginning they had brainstormed about whether there was any effective way to assault RU-486. Many pro-life groups had urged boycotts. The two of them had concurred but felt them to be of limited effectiveness.

Then had come the first clouds on the horizon regarding the regeneration centers. With the help of Lance and others, they had collected every article and clue they could find. Sympathetic doctors at Johns Hopkins, NIH, and other facilities had helped. Many medical professionals were shocked by the prospect of live-fetal-brain suctioning, and their group had gradually built a substantial network of friends in high and useful places.

After hearing the president's remarks, Daniel had gone into his office and deleted several key files from his computer. He had also pulled out his address book, a few manila file folders, and a list of phone numbers. Better to be prudent, he had thought. The time might well come when any concrete information and connections would need to be destroyed.

He didn't have time to memorize all the names and numbers tonight, though; Alex and the others would be here soon. So he sealed all the papers in a Ziploc bag and stowed the bag, for safe-keeping, in the bottom of his toddler son's diaper pail. When he showed Mary, she rolled her eyes but said nothing.

They would have to be extra careful as they made their next moves to fulfill their purpose. *Expose the deeds of darkness*, he thought. Right now the D and X procedure was going on behind closed operating-room doors, cloaked in secrecy by white-coated professionals with clean fingernails, eased by the complicity of many in the media. Dark deeds in a bright, sterile, enlightened environment. And those deeds were about to be multiplied many times over, destined to take place not just in research hospitals or laboratories but in well-funded, well-received processing centers across the country. The centers would somehow legitimize what would take place within them simply by the fact that they existed.

Still, they would have to be extremely careful. Daniel sighed. He knew he'd have to keep his eye on Alex.

AN HOUR LATER, Daniel and Alex, along with Mark Demmers, John Jenkins, and Lance Thompson, were on their way west out of the suburbs. The traffic was still heavy on Route 7, through the congestion of Tyson's Corner, past dozens of housing developments on the edges of Great Falls, Sterling, Ashburn, and through the town of Leesburg. On its outskirts, they had pulled off Route 15 and parked in the yard of a small complex known as Doggett's Garage.

Frank Doggett was a former navy pilot, now retired. He and his wife, Ida, owned this twenty-acre plot of land where Ida cultivated her garden and Frank had built up a small foreign-car repair business. He ran it more to keep himself out of trouble, his wife said, than for the income it brought in.

Frank and Ida had known Daniel and Alex's parents, and after their deaths, Frank had looked out for the two boys, ready to help if they had financial needs, ready to offer crusty advice whether they wanted it or not. Frank had also funneled a fair amount of money into the Network, underwriting various costs as they came up. He had even given Daniel a lovingly buffed, burnished, and cherished 1992 BMW 535i.

"I feel guilty keeping it," Frank had said. "It's just a toy. You use it for good." So Daniel had sold the car for $17,000 to a middle-aged attorney in Great Falls and put the money in a special fund earmarked for a special project he had in mind.

Now on this January evening, Frank welcomed Daniel and the other men at the front door of his comfortable home, almost as if he had been expecting them.

"Hello, gentlemen," he said, wiping his hands with a dinner napkin. "We've been listening to the news. That's some statement the president's press secretary put out. You guys need a place to talk, I bet. Just don't let me hear anything."

He led them over the frosty rutted mud past the back of his garage to a cinder-block outbuilding with a bathroom, a kitchenette, an old television set, and a few mismatched plaid sofas and folding chairs. When Frank's kids were teenagers, they had used it as a gathering place; now it stood empty most of the time.

Frank pulled two large metal space heaters out of the closet and flicked on a thermostat in the corner. "This'll warm up in a few minutes," he said. "But Ida will want you to have some coffee. I'll bring it over in a few minutes. Have you had dinner?"

"Yes, Frank, thanks," said Daniel. "But coffee would be great."

The older man grinned and lowered the miniblinds on the large front window, then pulled the door shut behind him.

"Cozy," said Mark Demmers. "I feel like I'm in a CIA safe house or something." The men took off their coats and pulled the space heaters closer to the couch and easy chairs.

"Do we have any idea who was behind the killing in Fargo?" John Jenkins asked.

"Absolutely not," Daniel said. He pulled out a faded orange Frisbee that had been lodged between the plaid sofa cushions.

"Whoever did it got angry and antsy and did the worst thing they could have done. You can't fight evil with evil. It doesn't work, it's stupid, and it's not Christian."

"I just can't believe that anyone would do this now," Mark Demmers said. "Shooting people does nothing but hurt us. Look at all the backlash after each killing over the past few years. Abortion doctors have become martyrs, and now, if you listen to the news, people in the pro-life movement are all terrorists."

"That's why our approach is right," Daniel said. "That's why we've got to keep going with our plans. No violence. Just exposing the abortion industry for what it is. More articles, more information in the right hands. People don't know what goes on in those places. If they see it—if we expose it—the public can't help but be revolted."

"Don't you think the time has passed for that approach?" Alex said. "Our hands are tied. I think we need to rethink some strategies."

"I've gathered that," Daniel said. "That's why I thought we should talk here tonight."

There was a noise at the door, and Mark got up to let Frank in. He was carrying a large teak tray balanced with a big thermos pitcher of coffee, five pottery mugs, and a napkin-wrapped basket.

"Hot cornbread," he said.

"Ida is amazing," said Daniel. "Tell her thanks."

He bent the Frisbee back and forth between his hands. "You know, when I was on the phone with Howard Fay in Chicago the other night, he alluded to something big coming down. I thought he was talking about the regeneration centers. But then he said something strange: 'Thank God for snow.' I let it go by, thought I must have missed something in the conversation."

Lance smiled and took a mug of coffee from Mark. "I don't think the snow in Fargo is a coincidence, do you?"

"I don't think anything is ever really a coincidence," said Daniel. "But we can't justify violence by the fact that the killer's tracks are being covered. Why? Do you think that's proof that God is on her side?"

Lance shrugged and smiled slightly.

"I'm telling you, guys, if this killing is traced to anyone we know, or the cousin's sister's aunt of anybody we know, then we're in for the type of times we've only read about in bad novels," said Daniel. "Judging from Griswold's press statement, he's going to use this to strike a blow for law and order. That means mostly order. The feds are gonna crack down in a big way. Now, more than ever, we have absolutely got to stick together."

"Well," Alex broke in. "That's fine. That's great. But all I know is that the first regeneration center is going to open in a few months. It's not enough to expose the evil, Daniel. You gotta explode it. And once that center's open they're gonna have so much security we won't get near it. We've got to go after it before it's opened."

Daniel rubbed his face in his hands.

"I'm not talking about people," said Alex. "Just take out the building. Blow it up. Disassemble the killing center. We can't just sit here."

Lance cleared his throat. "I know just the guy who can help us with that."

"Hold it," Daniel said, unusually abrupt. "Put the brakes on. I've got another plan here, a perfect opportunity for us, if everything goes right.

"I've been talking with some people in New York, and we think if everything breaks for us just right, we can pull something off that's pretty incredible. We've got a friend at NIH who says that they're moving forward with the training video there. You know about it, Alex. It's designed to train medical personnel who will work in the regeneration centers how to do the dilation and extraction procedure—shows the actual D and X. It's unbelievable, like a snuff film. From what I hear, they show the baby's head positioned in the birth canal, and then the doctor takes a pair of scissors and jabs its brains out. There's a voiceover, telling just how and where to do what in order to extract the brain tissue neatly and dispose of the corpse properly. It's absolutely unbelievable.

"Anyway, here's the deal. If a few things go right for us, we can get a copy of that video. And if about four thousand things go just right for us, we can get that video onto millions of television screens in America. We just have to knock off the evening news in order to do it."

By now, all of them were staring at Daniel, who was grinning with excitement. "I can't really tell you anything more about it at the moment," he said. "It's the New York group's baby. We'll just be helping in D.C. with a detail or two. We're calling it Gideon's Torch."

13

Friday, January 24

"WELL, I say they should line up all these people who say they're pro-life and haul 'em off to jail," an angry man yelled into the microphone from the front row. "All of 'em!"

"Thank you," said talk-show host Bill Donnell, spinning on his heel and running up the steps of the studio audience to poke the mike at a woman gesturing to him from the top row.

"He's right," she screeched. "They're all guilty by association. They've made it so every crazy out there thinks it's okay to take out a gun and blow somebody away. This has been going on for too long." She paused to take a breath, then added loudly, "These people should all be locked up."

The studio audience burst into applause, and Donnell cut to a commercial break.

"MR. PRESIDENT," you might want to look at Helen Jackson's editorial this morning," said Robbie. "She makes some good points here. It's the old argument—you know, just the act of protesting at a clinic or hospital incites people to violence. But she lays it out well: When these anti-abortionists call abortion 'murder,' they're leading people to believe that killing abortionists is justified.

"Let me see that," said Griswold. He skimmed the column quickly. Then he swung his chair around and stared out the thick windows overlooking the south lawn toward the Washington Monument in the distance.

"Maybe," he muttered, running his finger over his chin; he had shaved too hurriedly this morning. "Just maybe. We'll see what Bernie says."

DRINKING his third cup of coffee of the morning, Ira Levitz scanned Jackson's column. He shook his head angrily and scribbled a few notes on a pad for his own column. *Hannah Arendt*, he wrote, so he'd remember later to make the point that Arendt, the German Jew who'd escaped the Holocaust, had written that whenever a nation suppresses moral debates or attempts to silence those who assert positions based on deeply held moral convictions, the inevitable result is violence.

And what was it JFK had said? Ira tried to remember, tapping the pad with the end of his pen. Right. When peaceful revolution is suppressed, violent revolution is inevitable. Thomas Jefferson's point.

If Griswold listens to the Helen Jacksons, we're in big trouble, thought Levitz. If they clamp down too hard on the pro-lifers, stifle all dissent, they're just going to have more murders on their hands.

ANTHONY FRIZZELL studied the latest intelligence summaries on the most ominous of the anti-abortion groups. According to some fairly fuzzy information, Dr. Sloan's killer was rumored to be from the Chicago area, but the informant had no hard evidence. Frizzell's eyes sped from line to line.

"Nothing hard here, Toby." He turned to his special assistant, long-time agent Toby Hunter.

"No sir. Sorry. Our people have to be very careful. We're doing well, under the circumstances, to get this much."

"This much?" Frizzell echoed derisively, then swung around in his chair to stare out the window at Pennsylvania Avenue. "Well, beef up our office in Chicago."

"Yes sir. We can put forty extra street agents there."

"And, Toby, for now at least, don't put this in the daily report to the attorney general. Let's save it for a pleasant surprise later," Frizzell said with a slight smile.

Toby returned the smile. He knew his boss well. He would crack the case and then be there when the bust was made. Above all, he'd want to keep the politicians out. It was important not to share the spotlight. Not for his own advantage, of course. All for the bureau's good.

THE ATTORNEY GENERAL'S office is located on the fifth floor of the Justice Department, occupying the southwest corner of the massive old building. Many Washington powerbrokers measure the influence of their peers by the square footage and splendor of the office space they occupy; by that standard, the attorney general surely has power. The reception room is large and handsomely furnished, with ample leather sofas for visitors. The reception area, presided over by two secretaries, opens into the main office, which might pass for a great hall in a feudal manor house: long and high-ceilinged, with dark, burnished, mahogany paneling and portraits of former attorneys general lining the wall. A huge conference table occupies the center.

At the far end is a door leading into the attorney general's private suite, a more modest working office, and a generous private dining room.

Emily Gineen had been in this office only a few days, so she still found it somewhat overwhelming. The conscious and somewhat exaggerated splendor, the private stewards to attend every need, the young, bright-eyed interns from Harvard, Yale, and Stanford hovering, waiting to bring a brief or case at the snap of a finger.

As she had expected, the transition to her new role had not been particularly easy. Frederick was commuting back and forth to Harvard, their new home in Spring Valley was still crammed with unpacked boxes, and the children were not happy with their new schools. Just last evening, Kathy had sobbed as Emily tucked her into bed. She just didn't like Sidwell Friends, she told her mother, and she missed her friends at home. When were they going home?

Emily had stroked her daughter's curly hair and commiserated. "Just give it a little time," she said. "This is a great place to live. We're just having a bumpy time settling in. Are there any girls in your class you'd like to have over for dinner and a movie on the weekend?"

"No!" Kathy had sobbed.

At this point, her job was just as frustrating. Emily was used to an attorney's routine, examining cases, delegating research, pondering issues, consulting clients, and preparing arguments. She had never been in a position in which the amount of work to be done was absolutely limitless. It was triage: She delegated madly, judged in seconds what had to be done and what could be refused, and staggered home at the end of each day knowing she had just barely avoided total disaster for one more day.

The next morning she would emerge from her front door at 7:30 to find the limousine waiting, engine idling, in the driveway. Spread out on the back seat was *The Washington Post*, a White House news summary, and urgent faxes or memos that the Justice Control Unit had received during the night. By 8:00 she was at her desk, already fighting off the unrelenting series of demands: "The Civil Rights Division wants you to sign off on this proposed settlement,"... "the Criminal Division needs a budget fix,"... "Personnel has questions,"... "Senator so and so demands to talk with you personally,"... "This report needs your okay to go to the White House..."

By 7:00 in the evening Emily was reeling. Each day her briefcase grew larger with reading material, and after spending an hour or two with the children, she'd pore through papers until 2:00 A.M.

And on top of all this was the shooting of the abortionist in North Dakota. Griswold seemed obsessed with it. Bernie O'Keefe had called three times. The FBI had turned up only bits and scraps of information, though Frizzell had told her this morning that more problems could be in store for the future. But she was dubious about his agenda and skeptical about his motives. If his Oval Office performance was any indication, she knew this guy could operate.

Emily called O'Keefe about Fargo and the government's response. He didn't have any great insights for her. Then she'd sent an "eyes only" intelligence fax for the president, a single sheet that sounded very impressive but said next to nothing. She could imagine Griswold's reaction; he just wanted results. Period. Problem was, she had to walk a very fine line here, with pressure from the White House on one side but big trouble if she tried to cut any corners. Politicians like Byron Langer would love any excuse to nail the administration. He and others were already issuing high-sounding statements about not repressing the pro-life movement.

Maybe she should consult Paul Clarkson, she thought. She had met him only once, a perfunctory session at that. But he at least would understand Langer's camp. After all, wasn't he supposed to be "the interpreter"? Of course he was in Langer's pocket, but she'd take what she needed from what he said.

Emily picked up the phone line that automatically rang on her assistant's desk.

"Pamela, could you ask the associate attorney general to come in here—that is, if he isn't busy. Let me know if it's not convenient."

"GOOD MORNING, General," Paul smiled as he moved slowly from the doorway toward Emily's desk.

Paul Clarkson was almost impossible not to like—the kind of man every father prays will ask to marry his daughter, and he was the type who would ask, not announce. Unfailingly courteous but also smart and quick, he never seemed to press his intellectual advantage with others. His humility could be deceiving, however. With his curly auburn hair and a grin that accented two deep dimples, he was disarming.

It was impossible also not to feel sympathy for the man. Though only 5' 11" and 170 pounds, he had been a star linebacker on the Duke Blue Devils football team, making up for his lack of size with speed, agility, and a certain fearless abandon on the playing field. Then, in a big game against navy his junior year, he had met a bruising running back head-on. Paul had stopped him, but had been carried off the field on a stretcher. He had spent almost a month in the hospital, and doctors had to fuse his spine. Ever since he could walk only slowly, often painfully, with a cane or walker. He would never again bend his back or gain full use of his legs.

Turning his determination and energy into training, Paul used his mind the same way he had his body. In three years at Duke Law School, despite taking public issue with most of his professors whom he regarded as incorrigibly liberal, he never got less than an A. He graduated at the head of his class, winner of the moot court competition, editor of the *Law Review*, and Order of Coif, the legal honor society. He had his pick of the nation's best law firms but chose to clerk for a Fifth Circuit judge for two years then spent two years as a public defender in Atlanta. From there he moved to Washington, joined the Senate judiciary staff, and before he was thirty-three had become chief minority counsel.

"Sit down, Paul. And by the way, you needn't call me General or Professor or Mrs. Gineen, at least not when we work together in private. Just call me Emily."

"I'll try." Paul smiled and then nodded somewhat deferentially. "Thank you."

"I'm sorry that we've not really talked much thus far," Emily said. "I need to delegate more, I'm realizing. You're responsible for administration here, so I want to pass over a number of things in the administrative area to you."

"Certainly," he said eagerly. "I want to be as much help as I can to you." He paused, then added with a slight smile, "Emily."

"Right," she said. "Now, there are a few key areas I'd like to rely on you to handle." It was a modest list, but Paul nodded appreciatively as he took notes.

"Of course," she paused, staring intently at him, "you'll want to recuse yourself from anything involving the abortionist killing, I'm sure."

Clarkson looked startled. "Why?" he replied.

"Well," she said, feeling uncharacteristically awkward, "I thought that in light of your, uh, convictions and your close friendship with Senator Langer, I would not want to put you in an awkward position. I do not question your objectivity, of course."

Paul bristled. "No," he said firmly. "I took the same oath you did, and like you, I take it seriously. My job is to uphold the law, and I mean to do just that."

"I don't doubt that, Paul," she said, "but I understand that you are firmly committed to the pro-life cause, and our work right now very much involves anti-abortion issues."

Clarkson's face muscles tightened. "Well, you're right. My views are very much pro-life. That means I'm against the taking of innocent lives, but it also means I'm against the taking of an abortionist's life. What happened in Fargo is a heinous crime. I'll do my job."

Emily was relieved. Maybe Langer had done her a good turn after all. "I respect that, Paul. Some people—I don't mean any offense here—who are very conservative, religiously speaking, don't make the distinction you do. They can't separate their religious view from their private duties."

"Nor can I." His jaw was set. "If you mean those who say they are personally opposed but do it as part of their office, that's not me. That's hypocrisy. It's a cop-out. My faith affects all of my life. If you asked me to run an abortion clinic or order someone to have an abortion, I'd resign and be out of here in thirty seconds—"

"But that's exactly what I mean," Emily interjected. "I'm not interfering in your religious convictions. I just don't want to put you in an awkward position."

Paul seemed to relax just slightly. "I realize it sounds confusing. Let me just explain. I'm a Christian. No equivocation, no excuses. I know that makes some people in public office very nervous. But the fact is it shouldn't. Because it makes me a better public official.

I can do nothing contrary to my deepest convictions, but those convictions include not lying, not cheating, not bearing false witness—not altogether bad attributes for a person in the public trust.

"And if people understood, they'd realize that Christians believe government has been given the God-ordained job of preserving order and justice. So I view discharging that responsibility as my duty as a Christian as well as my duty as associate attorney general. So in the Fargo case, and in any others like it that may come along, I want those responsible prosecuted."

Emily sat back, tenting her fingertips beneath her chin, gazing at him intently. *He's really unusual,* she thought. *He's sincere about this. He's not just posturing to make himself look good.* She thought about Frizzell again.

"Well, just how would you go about prosecuting these unknown perpetrators in Fargo, Paul?" she asked.

As he gave her his lucid summary of the situation, Emily realized that he had already thought about the question and prepared his answer. His analysis was not only impressive but a challenge to conventional wisdom. The FBI, Paul argued, shouldn't have ultimate responsibility.

"They still play Eliot Ness games, want to rush in with guns blazing, get the bad guys, and haul them into court. That's the way the bureau thinks. They're cops, the best there are, but still cops. What we need here is a strategy," Paul argued, "to break the leaders, get to the higher-ups. This is a master political struggle." He ticked off various techniques for breaking conspiracies.

"Where did you get your criminal experience?" Emily asked.

"On the committee we worked with Justice strike forces in cracking down on drug cartels and organized crime. It's the same thing. But you can't rely on Frizzell...you, Emily, need to take charge."

For the next forty minutes Paul laid out options: wiretaps, reviews of Secret Service lists of known dangerous criminals or those who had made wild charges, obtaining search warrants after choosing the judge carefully.

"The right judge can be lenient on probable cause," Paul

explained. He also advocated "questioning" various leaders around the country, trying to get someone scared into testifying.

"Remember the killing of the three civil rights workers in 1964 down in Mississippi? Those three bodies were buried in a levee, and nobody would have found them to this day had not the bureau and Justice moved in, followed witnesses, knocked on doors in the middle of the night. They bullied it out of the Klan, and good thing they did. All within the law, but justice was done. Same kind of thing here."

Paul talked about the strategy almost clinically, like a lawyer advising a client, cautioning Emily on the limits of the law, the kinds of things Langer and others on the Hill would be sensitive to. Throughout, she took notes, smiling occasionally.

"Please understand," he said at one point, "I'm only offering alternatives, not making recommendations. I realize that the situation, as it develops, will dictate the course to follow." Emily agreed.

Before the meeting adjourned, Emily had unloaded other projects on Paul. He would handle the budget and personnel, call staff meetings, and perhaps deal with other parts of the Justice Department that weren't so sensitive.

"I'll want to get together again soon so we can assess progress on the Fargo case," Emily said as Paul got up to leave, rising from his chair with some difficulty. "And let me state once more, Paul, how impressed I am with your knowledge of the law. I'm looking forward to working with you."

After Clarkson left, Emily tucked her notes in her briefcase—just what she would need when O'Keefe called, as no doubt he would, around 10:00 this evening, probably with a thick tongue. She would give him quite an earful.

14

WHITNEY GRISWOLD walked briskly along the covered passageway from the Oval Office to the family quarters, looking forward to a quiet evening with his family, the first since his inauguration fourteen days ago. As he entered the living room, Elizabeth jumped off the sofa where she and her mother were watching the news together and ran to give him a hug.

"How was your day, dear?" Anne asked, rolling her eyes slightly as she bowed to convention. It seemed ludicrous to ask such a mundane question in the White House.

He rolled his eyes back, connecting with her playfully. "Oh, just the usual things, darling. Issues of national security, nuclear threats from Third World crazies with First World weapons, terrorists alive and well in the U.S....and how was your day?"

She smiled and nodded toward Elizabeth. "Your daughter had a big day."

Elizabeth smiled and straightened up proudly. "I made the basketball team!" she said loudly. "Coach Bell says he'll start me in the next game or maybe the one after that. Can you come? You've got to watch us!"

"Wonderful, Elizabeth!" he said, clapping his hands. "I'm so proud of you!"

"But will you come see me?"

"Well, we'll see," Griswold stalled as they all made their way together toward the dining room. He looked at Anne for support. It wasn't like the president of the United States could slip into the bleachers unnoticed. Just to set up the communications gear and do the security checks would cost about $100,000 and paralyze the school for a week.

They took their seats in the small family dining room just down the hall from the west end sitting room. Griswold sat at one end, Anne at the other, Elizabeth in the middle. The centerpiece was a large bouquet of fresh-cut flowers, and the table was set with the family china, not the official set used at state dinners. Anne had been clear about wanting a family feeling in this room.

"What a shame Robert can't be here," Griswold said. He smiled at Elizabeth, but the diversion didn't work.

"Daddy, you will come see me play, won't you?" She smiled at him. She had inherited both her mother's stubbornness and her father's appeal.

Anne took him off the hook. "We'll see, dear. I'll be there for sure, but you know Daddy has big responsibilities right now. But we'll work on it."

"Tell me about your schoolwork, dear." Griswold tried again to detour Elizabeth. "How about English? Do you like your teacher?"

"Okay, I guess, but Mrs. Martin is a drag." She was frowning, still thinking about the game, one more reason she didn't like what had happened to her life.

"How about history then? That was always a favorite for me. What are you studying?" he asked as the stewards were serving the first course, a chilled vegetable pâté.

"Oh, it's okay. We're studying the Civil War. You know, Daddy, two of the big battles were fought right near here. We talked about Manassas today. Can we go see it sometime?"

"Absolutely," Griswold quickly assured her. It would be easy for a president to visit a historical site.

"Daddy, my teacher said the Civil War was fought for moral reasons. To end slavery. But who would think slavery was moral? Why did people have to fight and kill over that?"

"At that time, there were people who believed that slavery was moral, just as there were others who saw it as horribly immoral," he said. "Today we can't imagine that anyone would condone slavery, but at that time, they did. The South believed that slavery was right; the North did not. And those two points of view led to a war. A terrible war."

Elizabeth listened. "But how do you tell which point of view is right?" she said slowly. "By which army wins?"

Griswold stared at his daughter, and the french bread stuck in his throat. He had to take a sip of water before he could continue. "Not necessarily," he said. "The moral point of view is the right point of view. What's right."

"How do you know what's right, Daddy?" his daughter pressed. Griswold looked at Anne. She was grinning slightly.

"You've been raised to know what is moral, Elizabeth," he said. "It's inside of you. You know when something is right, and you know what is wrong. Some people call it conscience—and families like ours understand that. We try to do right things, help others. That's why we're in this place."

Elizabeth nodded, but came up with one more zinger, just as the main course was served. "One of the kids in class asked if it's right to kill someone else for 'moral' reasons? I don't get it."

"Of course," the president muttered, cutting into his salmon.

"Whitney, did you hear the question?" Anne asked sternly.

Griswold looked up and smiled. "Sorry, sorry. I was thinking of something else. Ask me again, dear."

Elizabeth did.

"Decisions about war, where there is killing, are made by a majority in our society. When the majority votes to go to war and the government acts on it, then it becomes all right. I suppose you'd say that government decides that it's moral. It depends on the situation."

Just then Juan entered the dining room carrying a packet that had just arrived from Robbie.

"Thank you, Juan," Griswold said. "Just put it on my stand in the living room." It was, he was certain, more late dispatches from the National Security Council on the situation in Nigeria. The coup there was endangering the oil supply for several European nations, and American allies were concerned.

Glad for the interruption, he leaned back in his chair and turned to Anne. "And how was your day, dear?"

"We're getting organized, I think." Anne was, above all, organized. "Tea with the congressional leadership wives group. Sort of tedious, actually. And I've contacted the hospice national executive office. Their director is coming in next week. I think I'll give them a boost if you agree."

"That's a great idea, dear," Griswold said enthusiastically.

"And there's a new group called the Peacemakers. It sounds very interesting—helping people who are at the end of their lives leave peacefully and with dignity."

"Oh?" Griswold looked up. Assisted suicide was still not legal. The Supreme Court had decided that, but not whether the right to die was a protected liberty under the Fourteenth Amendment. So there were groups quietly helping suffering people find a dignified and compassionate solution. Despite the progress the country had made, it was still a controversial issue for many, particularly the Masterson crowd, the Religious Right.

"Look it over carefully, please," he said to Anne. "It's a noble enough work, I'm sure, but we don't want needless controversy."

Glancing at his daughter, he could tell she was still smarting because he had not promised to come to her basketball game.

"Listen," he said, reaching out a hand toward her. "How would you like to go to Camp David for the weekend? It's beautiful in winter. There's sledding, fires in the fireplace, cross-country skiing. We'll just get away, the three of us in the mountains. What do you say?"

"I guess it would be fun," she said, sounding less than enthused.

"Would you like to bring a friend along, someone from school perhaps?" Anne asked.

"Yeah," Elizabeth's face brightened. "Molly is my really good friend. She'd love it. Yeah."

Anne promised to call Molly's mother.

"I'll even leave here Friday noon," Griswold announced as he waved off the chocolate mousse dessert. He had weighed in at 210 this morning. No more sweets for a while.

"We can't. I've got basketball practice, Daddy."

Griswold nodded. "Okay, after school then." That was that. The president of the United States, whose every wish was someone's command, would, in this room at least, have to defer to the Cathedral School's basketball team.

AFTER DINNER, while Anne sat down in the living room with her folder of correspondence to be signed and Elizabeth stretched out on the rug with her schoolwork, Griswold headed for the Lincoln sitting room and his own "homework."

He settled into the comfortable chair in the corner and slid open the envelope. He skimmed the memos. Included just behind Nigeria was the attorney general's report on the Fargo shooting. Two hundred fifty words to say next to nothing. Killing for moral reasons indeed. These people were nothing but self-appointed executioners.

Moments later he was on the phone to Bernie O'Keefe, who was sitting in his study at home.

"You doing all right, Bernie?" Griswold asked. His friend sounded tired. No surprise.

"Fine. Fine. Just cleaning up a few loose ends, sitting here at the desk with a cup of coffee." Bernie grinned as he stirred his Dewars with his finger.

"Yeah, I hear the coffee's ice cubes tinkling," Griswold said dryly. "How are Marilyn and the kids?"

There was a pause. "They're back in Wellesley. Marilyn said they won't be down this weekend."

"I'm sorry. Anything I can do?" Griswold asked. "What about the box at the Kennedy Center, you know, the president's box?

Why don't you use it this weekend? Call Marilyn. She can't turn that one down."

"Thanks, Whit," Bernie said. "I really appreciate it. I'm not sure I can get Marilyn to come down if she doesn't want to, even for that. You know how she can be. But I'll give it a try." Bernie knew his friend knew just how stubborn Marilyn could be.

"Bernie, I've been thinking about this Fargo business," Griswold said after a slight pause. "It's been some time now, and I don't see that we know one thing today we didn't know the day of the shooting. Frizzell talks a good game, but that's it. I'd like you to call Emily and—"

"I'm one up on you tonight, for a change. I just hung up from talking with her. She's got some great ideas. We need to watch things, but if there are no breaks in the next few days, she's got a plan. A good one. She's sharp, and she's got style. I think you'll be pleased."

"Good. That's what we need, initiative. But now listen, Bernie, you keep on top of it. The only disturbing thing in Frizzell's report is the indication that there might be other things in the works. These are zealots, remember. People who will kill for moral reasons tend to be a little unbalanced. So we need to nip this thing in the bud.

"But remember Waco, the Koresh case, Bernie." Griswold stopped, letting the point sink in.

"Indeed I do," Bernie replied.

"Well, Janet Reno went bonkers, overreacted. We can't do that either. Of course we need to find them first."

"We'll find them. Gineen has some good strategies in mind. We'll watch things though, and I'll take care of it. You worry about Nigeria."

"Yes, Bernie, you take care of it."

Take care of it, Bernie thought after he'd hung up. He'd been taking care of it for years. Then he thought back to the first time, the time he doubted Griswold even remembered anymore...

IT BEGAN like countless other Wednesday nights in law school. It ended with the secret that cemented the bond between Whitney Griswold and Bernie O'Keefe for life.

At Yale, Whit and Bernie had fallen into a fairly disciplined routine.

Weekends were reserved for civilized dates with their girl-friends, both conveniently out of town. On Friday evenings, Whit usually went home. Anne would often meet him there, and they would go out to dinner parties, sailing if the weather allowed, and Sunday morning brunch with his family. He would get back to New Haven early on Sunday afternoon and study until early evening, when he'd meet Bernie for beer and pizza. Bernie usually stayed in New Haven on the weekend.

Both Whit and Bernie had come to assumptions about marriage to Anne and Marilyn, respectively, but wanted to wait until they finished law school. And until that happened, they weren't going to be totally fettered by relationships that would likely constrain them the rest of their lives.

Mondays, Tuesdays, and Thursdays were reserved for study, but Wednesdays were hump nights at their favorite local bar, with half-price drinks and free hors d'oeuvres.

So this particular Wednesday in April, near the end of their second year at Yale, found the two men working their way through their second Dewars and discussing the evening ahead. Two fellow students—female—had invited them over for a cookout later that night.

"I think it's okay to go," said Bernie. "It's not like it's a major commitment or anything. Just burgers on the grill and polite conversation with two law school colleagues who happen to be of the feminine gender. I don't think Anne or Marilyn would mind . . . even if they did ever find out, which they won't."

Whitney grinned. "Bull," he said. "If Anne finds out, she won't talk to me for a month."

"Do you really think that would be such a loss?" asked Bernie. He liked Anne as little as she liked him.

Whitney rolled his eyes and took another sip.

"Well, then," said Bernie, "let's make sure they don't find out. It's not a big deal." He drained his drink, signaled the bartender for another, and yelled down the bar to a friend five stools away.

"Hey, Tom! What you gonna do this summer?"

"Hogan and Hartson in D.C.," Tom shouted back. "It's a three-month internship. I'll check out the bars on Capitol Hill for you, Bernie. You want me to deliver any personal messages to Jimmy Carter?"

"Ask him what kind of dental floss he uses," responded Bernie. "Good luck!"

He turned back to Whitney. "He's smart," he said. "It's not a bad idea to do the D.C. thing. I've heard it takes awhile to get the feel of things there, and you're going to need that. Eventually."

Griswold laughed and swirled the ice cubes in his glass. "You're more ambitious than I am," he said. "Maybe we should just stay here, practice law, sail on the weekends, keep it simple. Maybe we should forget about politics. Too tiring." He smiled at a young woman two stools down.

"It is tiring," said Bernie. "That's why we've got to relax a little while we can. The package store is open till seven. Let's get a bottle to take with us to Jane's house."

Six hours later, the bottle was empty, and they were on their way home. Whitney was at the wheel as the April night rushed through the open windows of his Audi. Bernie was slouched in the passenger seat, clutching a beer in his right hand and singing the theme song from *Gilligan's Island* at the top of his lungs.

"...The weather started getting rough, the tiny ship was tossed. If not for the courage of the fearless crew, the *Minnow* would be lost..."

"The *Minnow* would be lost," echoed Whitney, squinting into the darkness ahead.

"You know, they just don't make television shows like they used to," reflected Bernie. "I mean, our generation grew up on great stuff... *The Dick Van Dyke Show*, *Bonanza*, *Mr. Ed*, *I Dream of Jeannie*... *My Mother, The Car*.

"Think of it! It's our common heritage, the ideas that made America great! A talking horse. A car that was somebody's mother. Four dudes living in the wilderness with a Chinese cook named Hop Sing. An astronaut who has a genie as a personal housekeeper...and her name just happens to be Jeannie!...What a great country!"

"You're raving," said Whitney. Usually Bernie drove them home, but tonight he had seemed unusually soused, so Whit was at the wheel of his own car.

The women had turned up with not only burgers on the grill but some sort of concoction they had called oyster shooters.

"Good for virility," they had teased. "Good for the brain, too. These really help you absorb the intricacies of the American system of jurisprudence."

"Why should we care about prudence?" Bernie had responded.

The shooters consisted of raw oysters shoved into the bottom of shot glasses, doused with a dash of cocktail sauce, then drowned in a combination of vodka and champagne and crowned with a pickled jalapeno pepper. The women were downing them with wild abandon.

Whitney couldn't stomach oysters very well, and the jalapeno didn't help any. He'd only had one and then stuck to Dewars. Bernie, who could eat anything, had raved over the combination of flavors and downed about six of them. So had Jane and Mindy. It had ended up being a far wilder evening than the mellow night on the patio they had expected.

But now the evening air felt so sweet and fresh, a promise of the springtime to come, and the two of them felt relaxed and confident. As Bernie continued singing off-key, Whit pushed the accelerator slightly and watched, detached, as the needle on the dashboard climbed.

The curve came too quickly. The car rushed into the turn, there was a sudden squeal of brakes as Griswold tried by reflex to adjust, and then everything spun out of control. There was the clipping thuds of the mailbox, the street sign, and then the telephone pole.

Bernie was out of his seat belt as soon as the car stopped. The shock and adrenaline somehow overcame the alcohol in his brain, and he assessed the situation quickly. The car was sideways in the street, wrapped against a telephone poll. Whit was slumped against the wheel, a little trickle of blood running down his temple.

Bernie clicked to attention. He opened the car door and deliberately crumpled the empty beer can in his hand, flinging it as far as he could into the trees. Then he ran around the car to the driver's side, forced the door open, punched open Whitney's seat belt, and dragged him from the car. The motion caused his friend to stir.

"What happened?" he said.

"Are you okay?" asked Bernie.

"I'm all right," said Whitney. "It's just that there's a telephone pole around my car."

"That's a small problem at this point," said Bernie. "Just keep quiet. Let me talk. I was driving. It's your car, but you were tired. Is your registration in the glove compartment?"

"Yes," said Whitney, who always kept everything in its place. "But are you okay?"

"I'm fine," said Bernie, licking his lips, rubbing his eyes, and bending down to look into the driver's side mirror. "I shouldn't have let you drive in the first place. I should have known you couldn't even handle the Dewars."

"A lot better than you could handle those oyster things," said Whitney. "Why are you doing this?"

"You're going to be a lawyer," said Bernie. "Think like one. You know the cops are going to come. You know we're both way over the top on the Breathalyzer. You know where we want to go in terms of your future. Somebody has to fix this mess, and I'm the only one here to save your butt on this one. Let's just say you'll owe me one."

Bernie raked his fingers through his hair, combing it back from his face. "I've got some Certs in the glove compartment," Whitney said, impressed that he had remembered this detail.

"Oh, those'll be a big help," said Bernie sarcastically. "Well, let's get 'em out."

He peeled a white mint and sucked on it. "We'll say I was driving, I had a few beers, and I'm so sorry. At the worst I'll go to jail for a night or two and lose my license for a while. Maybe the experience will help me when we get to criminal law. But we can't afford all that on your record. I'm sure your dad will take care of the car."

Bernie paused, looking at his tall friend now standing by the side of the smashed Audi. Whitney nodded toward the passenger seat, then rubbed his head with his shirttail.

"Okay," he said. "You know better than I do what to do." He paused. "And thanks."

Thus it had begun. That particular matter, as investigated by the New Haven police department, had resulted in a night in jail, a DUI citation, and a suspended driver's license for Bernard O'Keefe. It had also cemented the friendship—and commitment—of J. Whitney Griswold toward Bernie O'Keefe for a long, long, time.

15

Tuesday, February 18

THE RECESSED, round lights flashed along the edge of the subway platform, and a moment later the train thundered into the station. Late commuters hurried through the automatic doors, stuffing rumpled *Washington Posts* into fat briefcases, jangling car keys as they rushed toward the Metro parking lots and home. A group of students entered the train, settling into the padded orange seats and chatting casually.

As the lights flashed again and a bell sounded, warning of the train's departure, Alex Seaton darted between its doors. The train pulled out of the station, gathering speed.

Alex looked around, satisfied: No one had followed his last-minute jump onto the subway. The students and a few weary women who looked like maids or nannies, returning home to the city after a day in the suburbs, looked up for a moment without much interest.

Alex walked the aisle, steadying himself as the train rocked, and sat down with his back to the connecting door to the next car. He didn't put his briefcase on the floor, as most businessmen did, but placed the large, boxlike case gently on his knees then folded his hands over its flat surface, like a man contemplating evening prayers.

The train pitched and rolled to the next stops. Ballston. Clarendon. At the courthouse stop, Alex rose abruptly as the departure bell chimed, then jumped off the train, excusing himself as he passed through a group of attorneys clustered on the platform.

Eight minutes later, another D.C.-bound train arrived. Alex walked to the far end of the tracks, entered the first car behind the driver, and chose a seat adjacent to the section reserved for handicapped and elderly riders. The car's only other occupant, a middle-aged woman reading a paperback novel, looked up to register his arrival, then returned to her book.

Alex carefully opened his thick case and removed the A section of the *Washington Post*, turning to the story on page A-6. "Despite Construction Delays, Regeneration Center Moves Toward Completion." It was a small article, buried among the usual trash about Whitney Griswold's latest cabinet appointment and reports on the earthquake in California. Alex eyed it briefly, though he had already read it so many times he had nearly memorized it, then turned the page.

The train stopped in Rosslyn. "Last stop in Virginia," the driver announced. The lights flashed, then there was a muffled roar as the train passed under the Potomac River.

Alex stared into the darkness of the tunnel, feeling the irrational need to hold his breath. It was an odd sensation: the sense of being in a tube, tons of pressure outside, this fragile shell rushing along the canal in the darkness. Then a subtle change in the air, a breath, and they burst into the light again.

"Foggy Bottom—George Washington University," the PA system announced. "You are now in the District of Columbia. Doors open on the right."

Alex walked out onto the platform, carefully carrying his briefcase. He strolled to a pillar and looked at his watch, then eyed the platform again. A Metro security guard nodded in his direction as he glided up the escalator.

Alex walked to the elevator, entered, and waited inside for three minutes. He didn't want to be paranoid, but Lance had said that from here on out, they would need to assume they were being followed. He pushed the "ground-level" button. When he emerged on the surface, he walked quickly toward his destination.

Across the street, an ambulance sat in the curved emergency entrance of George Washington Hospital, siren off but its red lights still flashing. The hospital complex sprawled over several blocks adjacent to the mix of brick townhouses, nondescript dorms, and classroom buildings that made up the university.

Near the Metro stop, where its parking lot had once been, was the complex's newest addition: a long, three-story building, connected to the hospital by a second-floor glass walkway arching across Twenty-third Street. "Future Site of George Washington University Hospital's New Regeneration Center," read the sign affixed to the wooden wall next to the sidewalk. Development by Hughes and Crown." Dumpsters full of trashed construction materials rested on the bare ground in front of the main entrance.

This was the first time Alex had come downtown to see the building itself, but he knew about the forty well-appointed patient rooms, the four comfortable lounges, the snack area, the reception area, the doctors' conference rooms and offices, the counseling facilities, and the "staging areas," as the operating rooms where the procedure would actually be performed were called. He also knew what seven hundred pounds of high explosives, resting in the proper spot, could do to the center's concrete-and-steel reinforced construction.

He turned and walked several blocks down Twenty-third Street. Though there were people on the street, he knew instinctively he was not being followed. So he paused for only a moment when he reached Sam's Deli.

A bell strung on the back of the old-fashioned wood-and-glass door tinkled as he pushed it open. Sam's was a neighborhood hangout with eight booths, a counter, and a smattering of groceries and other essentials of college life: a self-serve coffee bar, plastic-wrapped packages of Nabs, Pop-Tarts, aspirin, deodorant, newspapers, magazines, and a big, glass-doored refrigerator full of cold beer.

The man behind the counter, known to the neighborhood as Sam though his name was Yasmir, nodded to Alex as he entered then went on wiping down the counter and watching the basketball game on the small TV mounted on a bracket near the ceiling.

Holding his briefcase with his left hand, Alex poured himself a cup of coffee with his right, fished seventy-five cents out of his pocket, and left it on the counter.

He moved toward the booth in the back, holding the Styrofoam cup carefully.

"Hey, how are you?" he said to the man in the booth, like any businessman meeting a friend after work. "Sorry I'm late."

Lance Thompson, sitting with his back to the door, looked up and grinned at Alex. "Hey, man," he said. "I'm fine. You owe me a cup of coffee, though. Make it decaf."

Alex sat down, placing his case between them on the table. "I'll get that for you in just a minute," he said, satisfied that no one was paying them any particular attention.

The basketball game was so loud it would drown out most of their conversation, and he had discovered that college students were so self-involved that their curiosity was rarely piqued by anything outside their own experience. The kids in the other booths and at the counter were intent on their books or their beers.

Nevertheless, Lance lowered his voice. "Do you have it?" he asked.

Alex nodded, his eyes indicating the briefcase between them. "Right here," he said. "I passed the center on the way in. The *Post* says it's due for completion by the beginning of September. It's too bad for them to go to all that trouble for nothing, isn't it?"

Lance nodded, then glanced at his watch. "I've got the van in that alley in the back," he said. "Let's go."

Alex gulped down the rest of his coffee, crunched the cup, and threw it in the plastic trashcan near their booth. He stood aside as

Lance headed toward the rest room in the back of the deli; from there he would go out the back door that led toward the alley.

Alex went out the front door. Sam was still wiping the same section of the counter, mesmerized by the Knicks and the Bulls, and didn't even register his departure.

A few moments later, Lance's nondescript white vehicle, the sort favored by electricians and carpenters, slowed near the curb, and Alex jumped into the front passenger seat. Lance headed back to the Metro stop, where he idled the van at the curb as if waiting for someone to emerge from the subway.

Alex stared out the darkened windows at the regeneration center. He noted the high fences, the checkpoint outbuilding between the narrow driveways awaiting security gates still to be installed. He balanced the briefcase on his lap as Lance pointed toward the checkpoint.

"I talked to a guy named Nick," he said. "He says that the plan is to hire an outside security company. Twenty-four-hour surveillance, sweeping guard patrol three times an hour, a canine unit on call. The whole building will be wired; the fence around the grounds will be electrified. It'll be like a prison camp, or maybe the White House. Nobody goes in or out except patients, staff, and doctors. They'll have armed security guards at the walkway between the center and the hospital. Once it's operational, there's no real way to get in...unless we get somebody on the inside working with us. I'm working on that."

Alex nodded. He knew that Lance's past had taught him that survival depended on uncovering every detail. He also knew that once those details were in hand, his friend would hesitate at nothing in order to execute their plan.

"Let's take a look at this," he said. "I used some of the treasury to get hold of these." He dialed the combination lock then snapped open the latches of his briefcase. Inside was a thick sheaf of blueprints.

"I looked for the load-bearing pillars in the parking garage," he said. "We can do it, once we have the supplies in order. I'm working on that. We can set them back a few million dollars and at least a year or so in time. And we'll give our friend Griswold another chance to read the writing on the wall."

Lance bent his head over the plans. "Our best hope is getting a plant inside," he said. "But if I can't make that happen, the other option is to use a woman. It's just that that gets a lot more complicated. And since Fargo, they're more suspicious of women posing as patients. If this was the Middle East, we'd just send in a suicide bomber."

"We're not the Middle East," said Alex. "Not quite yet."

Lance rolled the blueprints again, securing them with a rubber band. "I'll take these," he said. "And thanks for the briefcase. You'd better get out now. I'll call you later, once I've checked out a few things."

Alex climbed down from the van and watched it pull off into traffic. Then he stood on the sidewalk for a moment, gazing at the regeneration center.

He looked at the large color placard the architectural firm had put up, with its pretty pastel trees and vague figures strolling the walks of the center as if it were an English garden. The artist had drawn in extensive landscaping; large, curving flower beds filled with bright blooms lined the walkways to the main entrance.

Petunias, Alex thought with disgust. *Well, Auschwitz had flower beds, too. They always find a way to mask the truth.*

He looked again at the security gate then turned and walked back toward the Metro.

16

Thursday, February 20

O N S A T U R D A Y M O R N I N G, February 15, Emily Gineen and Anthony Frizzell had been summoned to the White House to meet with Bernie O'Keefe. For over an hour, the three huddled around a small conference table in O'Keefe's spacious, paneled office located directly above the Oval Office. There they reached the decision, which O'Keefe assured them he would clear with Griswold. Frizzell called the plan "Operation Steamroller." O'Keefe chose a more apt title: "Plan B."

Whatever it was called, it was simple enough. On February 20, agents would fan out to eight cities, all hotbeds of anti–abortion activity, and simultaneously at 4:00 P.M., EST (good for network coverage), would "visit" known leaders of the pro–life movement. No warrants needed; the agents were simply fact-finding. They would pound loudly on doors, flash badges, and make enough ruckus that as many neighbors and coworkers as possible would see them. They would "invite" the leaders to accompany them to the FBI offices. They'd also read them their rights, even though, unknown to them, their rights weren't in jeopardy. They weren't suspects; the agents would simply treat them that way.

It was the bully approach, and it had been used many times and to good effect in the civil rights days. With enough pressure, someone breaks. And at the very least, the pro-lifers would get the message that the government was not going to mess around with them anymore.

It was 7:45 on Thursday morning, February 20, however, that the first big break came. An urgent e-mail message from Chicago said that the Chicago office had a serious suspect and needed headquarters approval before acting. The agent in charge of the message center immediately called the situation room on the fifth floor and was given approval to route the message simultaneously to the assistant director for operations and to the director.

Seconds later, the screen in Toby Hunter's office started flashing, sign of an urgent transmission. Frizzell had just arrived at his desk and was lifting two thick leatherbound briefing books from his case.

"Chicago office, Chief," was all Hunter said. The Chicago office could mean only one thing.

"Get me Kane," Frizzell snapped, then grinned.

In seconds, special agent in charge Matthew J. Kane, a twenty-two-year veteran, highly regarded for his work busting the Cleveland mob, was on the line. He was one of Frizzell's favorites.

"Chief, we have a strong suspect. Very strong. A young Loyola College student, anti-abortion activist. Took this semester off. Fits the description, no one can account for her during the week of the shooting, and she has been talking quite a bit about saving lives of the unborn—"

"Any forensic evidence, ballistics, handwriting, any of the checks?" Frizzell cut in.

"No, but we've been following her for five days, and she certainly acts the part. She bought a large suitcase, and, get this, she has tickets—bought them three weeks ago—for a flight to Frankfurt, on to Warsaw, leaving tonight."

"Poland?"

"Yup. She's Polish-American. And she has a big man with her, also Polish. Maybe fiftyish. She calls him 'Dad'—but I think he's protecting her, or maybe there's some fooling around going on. Can't tell. Surveillance can't get a good view into the bedroom."

"You have to move fast if you're sure."

"I'm moving. Her flight leaves O'Hare tonight at 7:00, and after that, bye-bye. We'd be dealing with Polish authorities for months. You know what that means."

"Do you want to just question her, or do you have enough for an arrest?"

"Close call, Chief. If we just try to question her, she could tell us to buzz off. With a warrant, we can take her in and shake her up."

Frizzell was already repacking his briefcase. "See Judge Antonelli, no one else—only Antonelli—before court goes into session. We'll call him first, but he'll give us the papers we need. He always does."

Frizzell glanced at Hunter, who was on the extension phone. He nodded as he took notes.

"And don't move," Frizzell continued, "until I get there." He checked his watch. "We can have wheels up before 9:00...where is she now?"

"Home packing in a basement apartment, south side of Evanston," Kane replied.

"Okay, okay, let's see...Glenview, no, Meigs Field. Have an unmarked car there—no limo—at 9:45 your time. Don't talk to anybody."

Frizzell made a sweeping gesture with his arm toward Hunter, who immediately moved off the extension and called Administrative Services. The Justice Department Lear 35 with nothing but FAA markings would be fueled and ready to go at National.

"No press until we're sure, Matt," Frizzell warned. "You understand. But alert a friend or two. We want them at the scene right after the bust. You know how. Go to it."

"I've got you, Chief. See you at Meigs."

Minutes later, Frizzell and Hunter and one security agent were in the director's private elevator descending from the seventh floor to the garage where a black Chrysler was waiting. Even with morning rush hour traffic, they would make it to the FAA hanger at National Airport before 8:45. And before Frizzell even left headquarters, the copilot of FAA 79TD was already on board, doing his cockpit check, while the pilot was inside filing his flight plan.

SIPPING COFFEE at forty-one thousand feet, Frizzell and Hunter planned their day. They would drive immediately to the location, already staked out. Frizzell would stay in the car, within sight, and be signaled in when the suspect was securely in hand. Just a precaution in case anything went askew. The press was to be notified the moment they were certain they had the right person. She would be detained in the apartment until the press arrived, then escorted out, at which point Frizzell would make his appearance, preferably on the front steps.

"What have we missed here?" Frizzell asked as he handed the steward his cup for a refill.

Toby Hunter was a perfectionist with the kind of mind that seemed to have a built-in checklist. He was no strategist, but never missed a detail. Perfect aide.

"Just one thing, Chief. Should we notify the attorney general?"

"Good, Toby, of course notify. That's all, however. Nothing specific." He grinned. "Use the plane's fax and do it as we're landing. Anything else?"

"Nope, we're covered, Chief. Except for Murphy's Law. If something can go wrong, it will."

Frizzell tried not to show his irritation. That was Hunter's weakness. He was a fretter, too negative. But then the world must need negative people to keep the checks and balances going, Frizzell thought, because God certainly made a lot of them.

It was a dreary day in Chicago. The skyline did not break into sight until they reached six hundred feet on their glide path over Lake Michigan into Meigs. Everything looked gray, including the slushy remains of last week's snowstorm. Two cars were waiting beside the runway.

Frizzell, Hunter, and the security agent stepped down the plane's self-contained stairway. Frizzell nodded at Kane, shook hands quickly, and slid into the backseat of the second car, a dark gray Ford Crown Victoria. At 9:56 CST the two vehicles sped away.

DORRIE KISTIAKOWSKY was a twenty-two-year-old graduate nursing student at Loyola. She lived in a basement apartment in an older area of three-story brownstones, vintage 1920. Most of the lower windows in the building were barred, testimony to the decline of the once fashionable neighborhood.

Frizzell's car was parked half a block away but with a clear view of the suspect's house. Across the street, facing the other way, was Kane's car.

The plan was for Kane and two other agents to go to the front while two more agents staked out the back door of the building. Having studied the blueprints on file in the city's building department, the agents knew the suspect's apartment consisted of two rooms in the front and that there was an emergency door off the kitchen leading into the furnace room, and thence to a door opening to a back alley. No escape.

Kane half-saluted Frizzell, got out of the car, and walked alone down the street. When he was in front of the girl's brownstone, he nodded, then turned and opened a waist-high, wrought-iron gate. Two agents bounded from another parked car and followed. They walked down eight steps and turned to the right to the apartment's front door, partially obscured by the steps leading up to the main entrance. Kane stood in the center, the two street agents on either side. Kistiakowsky was classified as a dangerous suspect, so both men had weapons drawn.

The plan was to startle those inside, so Kane pounded his fist on the door several times. "Open up, FBI! Open up immediately!" he shouted, then pounded hard again.

INSIDE THE APARTMENT, Dorrie Kistiakowsky ran out of her bedroom toward her father, who was gasping and holding his chest.

"Be quiet!" she whispered, grabbing him by the arm. There had been two robberies and one rape in this very block over the past six months, in broad daylight. It could well be a trick.

The door was vibrating under the heavy pounding. Dorrie crept toward it, checked the dead-bolt, and activated the security alarm her father had insisted she install after the rape episode.

She pointed at the phone. "Dial 911!" she shouted. "Dad! Dial 911!"

Her father, who had been frozen for a moment, headed toward the phone, but then, clutching his chest, stumbled over a small footstool, knocking a lamp off its stand, and crashed to the floor.

Kane, hearing the noise, assumed the suspect was heading through the emergency exit.

"Hit it," he shouted, and the bigger of the two agents pulled out a crowbar, wedged it into the doorjamb by the dead bolt, and pulled violently. At the same time, the other agent hit the door with his left shoulder. The door shattered, and the men burst through. The girl was screaming hysterically; the older man was on the floor.

SEVEN BLOCKS away at the South Side substation a loud buzzer sounded at a computer control station. Officer Shick stared at the screen.

"Oh, man, another one! Down on Dodge Street. Probably another false alarm; we've had three in the past four days. But it's not a good area. Better check it out," he said, looking over at the only other officer in the station house.

Officer Bell, who had just completed his morning rounds, would have waited to finish his coffee, but this morning he had to be diligent. They had a visitor.

"And take Mr. McCartney here with you," said Shick. "He can see how taxpayer funds are used when these idiots don't know how to run their security systems."

Jim McCartney was a young *Tribune* reporter just assigned to the police beat, spending his very first day at this station in order to get indoctrinated. He grabbed his pad and followed the officer out the door.

MATT KANE approached the girl, his gun drawn and his badge flipped open. She was crying uncontrollably, leaning over the man's prostrate body and holding his wrist, obviously checking his pulse.

"Daddy!" she shouted.

Kane saw blood flowing from a gash on the man's forehead. He nodded at the phone, and one of the agents called 911. Just then two more agents burst through the rear door, and Kane waved them back.

"I'm sorry, ma'am," Kane said, "but I must ask you some questions. We'll call for medical help, and we'll take care of him."

"What are you talking about?" she shouted. "This is my father. You've killed him. He has a heart condition."

She ripped open the man's shirt, placed the heel of her hand over his heart, and began plunging her hand up and down, administering CPR. The agents hovered around her awkwardly; one got a damp towel from the kitchen and held it over the man's bleeding forehead.

Outside, the ambulance arrived, sirens blasting, at about the same time the police car did. A large group of neighbors was clustered around the front door. The paramedics rushed through them and loaded the unconscious man onto a gurney.

Officer Bell and the rookie reporter pushed their way through the crowd. McCartney pulled out a small thirty-five millimeter camera at about the same time Bell realized he was the only uniformed person in camera range. He accosted the men in suits; they flashed their FBI badges. Bell watched as they stopped the girl, who was trying to leave with the paramedics as they loaded her father into the ambulance.

"Wait a minute here!" Bell said to the agents. "What are you people doing?"

Kane, backpedaling madly, retreated to the kitchen and radioed Frizzell. "Get out!" he said simply.

The dark gray car, unnoticed, slid quietly down the street, and back toward Meigs Field.

SHOULD WE abort Plan B, sir?" Hunter asked during the flight back to Washington.

"Of course not, Toby. The AG herself ordered it. Why would you ask?"

"Well, we may not look too good this morning."

"No one will care. It only matters if we get the killer. Let's just pray Kane was right."

Toby noticed that the decision had now become Kane's.

"So why should we call off the AG's fireworks?"

"Murphy's Law, sir."

"Toby, stop that," Frizzell snapped and returned to the reports he had been scanning.

Even as they spoke, the wire services were carrying the story that the FBI had taken into custody a prime suspect in the Fargo abortionist doctor murder. Special Agent Matthew Kane acknowledged that some force had been used and that one innocent bystander, the suspect's father, was in intensive care from a myocardial infarction.

LATE THAT AFTERNOON, Emily, Paul, and Ted Foran, assistant AG for the criminal division, gathered in Emily's office as the field reports came in.

At precisely 4:00 P.M., EST, FBI and Justice teams had visited the homes and offices of anti-abortion activists in eight cities: Pensacola and Melbourne, Florida; Wichita, Kansas; Minneapolis, Minnesota; Tacoma, Washington; Portland, Oregon; Los Angeles, California; and Falls Church, Virginia.

The officials were meticulous, loud, and obvious. But courteous. These were simply fact-finding interviews. They apologized carelessly for neglecting to call and arrange the visits, though that was usual FBI procedure. They asked about pro-life opinions and activities, their questions blunt, their voices often weighted with suspicion. In several instances the agents left with a warning that they very well might return, and if the questioned parties were to take any trips, they should let the local FBI office know.

This countrywide barrage was intended as a shot across the bow, a chilling signal that the government was cracking down on pro-life leaders. It succeeded. It was also intended to reassure the press and public that the government was on the job. It did that—and much more.

Foran, an aggressive ex-Texas prosecutor, was jubilant at the incoming reports. Paul was more subdued, Emily cautious and anxious. The big story was Chicago, marred only by the heart attack of the suspect's father. But by late that afternoon, though he was still in intensive care, Dorrie Kistlakowsky's father was out of critical condition. The *Chicago Tribune*, however, the public information officer reported, was preparing a savage story that the bureau had disregarded the suspect's constitutional rights and botched the job completely.

The bureau was being less than helpful, Frizzell offering no information about the suspect. When Emily called him at 5:00 P.M., he informed her that the interrogation was still under way. He warned her that no information should be given to the press lest it be considered prejudicial at a later time.

Emily in turn called O'Keefe. He was with the president, she was told, but a few minutes later he called back from the Oval Office.

"Hold on," he said. Then Emily heard Griswold's familiar voice.

"Good show, Emily. We were elected to get tough on criminals, and we're doing just that."

"Yes sir."

"And don't let a little flak you'll take over that Chicago business throw you. The people trust the bureau. Let them handle it. They're the pros. This too will pass. How are your kids doing?"

"Fine," she sputtered with surprise. "Uh, thank you for asking, sir."

"Now look, you go home and spend an evening with them. We've got three years and eleven months, at least, in this place. We're going to make this government work. So stay strong for the long haul...and tell your kids their mom earned her pay today. Good show. Good show. That's what I like. Action."

Emily reported to her colleagues that the president was euphoric. "He likes action," she said dryly.

"I don't know," Paul shook his head. "We'll see."

He was more subdued than usual, Emily thought, and she wondered what he was thinking.

"Well, gentlemen," she said, "I have a presidential order to see my children, and I always obey the president. Paul, good job. Call me at home if there are any developments. Good job, Ted—and you tell your field people that for me as well."

She turned, scooped up papers into her case, and buzzed her secretary to order her car. For the previous two nights she hadn't seen the kids at all; they'd been asleep by the time she got home. Tonight would be different.

IT WAS 8:00 P.M. before Kane called on the secure line with the first real report. It confirmed the awful feeling Frizzell had had in his gut for hours.

"Not too promising, Chief. Our Miss Kistiakowsky says she was at a Christian conference when the Fargo incident took place, and so far it seems to check out. And she was getting ready to go to Poland all right, but she says it was to be part of a Catholic relief agency's work in some gypsy camps near the Slovakian border—"

"And that, I suppose, checks out as well," Frizzell sighed.

"So far it does. Of course, all this could be a cover. But I don't think we should hold her. We let her go over to the hospital to see her father, agents with her of course, and she got so angry she was nearly hysterical."

"What about getting the witnesses at Fargo to make ID?"

"They've seen her picture. They say she looks like the one. We're bringing them down in the morning. But it's real shaky. We can't book her, Chief; there's not enough. The magistrate would laugh us out."

"Has she got a lawyer?"

"Yeah, some buddy from the pro-life movement who doesn't know where the courthouse is, but I'm sure he could file a habeas writ."

"What's happening with the press?"

"All over us like flies in a pasture, but we've said nothing—not a word."

"Good. Say only that this is a major capital case, the usual stuff. Just buy some time."

"But she'll talk," Kane warned. "When we let her loose, she's gonna be all over the papers. She's that type. Probably sue us, too, if she gets a decent lawyer."

"Tell her we won't book her, but for her protection, until the witnesses come, we'll put her in a good hotel near the hospital, pay all the bills, cover the hospital expenses too. We've got to get some time here, Matt. Use your charm. Do what it takes."

"I'm sorry, Chief. We should have interviewed her first, but it looked like she was getting ready to take off—and who would figure the old man would have a heart attack?"

"Well, just keep the lid on, Matt, as long as you can." Frizzell hung up the receiver and sent Toby home. Then he called Clarkson since no one wanted to bother the attorney general at home with her kids and her husband, who had come back a day early from Harvard. Clarkson had passed the director's report on to O'Keefe, who had called Frizzell back immediately. Though it looked like the woman might not be the one, Bernie didn't think it cause for alarm. Certainly no need to bother the president. As for Robbie, he loved it. The government was acting. His tracking polls would show a blip-up the next morning, he was certain.

No one seemed concerned. The network coverage had been straight, the story about Mr. Kistiakowsky the only off-key note in a generally favorable report.

Frizzell sat there under the silent gaze of J. Edgar Hoover, whose portrait dominated the far wall of his office. He angrily threw his pen on the desk. So meticulous he was, prided himself on details. To botch this was unforgivable. Kane had misled him, of course.

He'll have to go, and fast, when the press hits, he thought.

He stared at the portrait. The old man seemed to be staring right back. What would he have done? That's a joke. He would have called the president and said, "We all screw up, don't we, sir?" And he'd have on his desk a file a foot thick on every indiscretion and dalliance his boss had ever committed since he was a teenager.

In those days the president knew full well what Hoover had. So the president would tell him he was a great American, and Hoover would pick up the phone, call three buddies in the press, and the whole thing would disappear.

But things weren't like that anymore. Too bad. Frizzell picked up his dictating machine, instructing his secretary to get a larger picture of Griswold on the wall behind his desk—and one of the new attorney general. Her predecessor's was still hanging. That kind of ineptness could be costly.

17

N O O N E, not even Frizzell, who knew the worst, expected
the firestorm that swept across the next morning's newspapers. The *Chicago Tribune* started it with a banner of the story,
and the *Post*, for its final edition, moved it above the fold. The wire
services were feeding new material hourly: stories from unnamed
hospital sources about the grave condition of Dorrie's father, then
from sources close to the investigation who admitted that the FBI
had arrested the wrong woman, then from other cities with
reports of bullying tactics by the bureau. By 11:00 A.M., the
ACLU's Washington office had issued a statement with a cautious
denunciation. When Congress opened at noon, a procession of
speakers took to the microphones and cameras, chastising the
administration for ineptitude at the very least.

By that time, Frizzell had worked out public statements so
positive that it made the agents look like death-defying heroes. If
the story worked, fine; if not, Kane would take the fall.

The bureau's public information office was working feverishly,
calling in chits. The agent in charge kept a lengthy list of all news
sources to whom they had leaked before, and these were the first

called. Even the most scrupulous reporters were reluctant to bite the hand that fed them.

At the White House, Robbie coached Press Secretary Atwater, who put a reasonably good spin on the story at her 12:00 briefing in the White House press room—and behind the scenes was frantically giving background briefings to friendly reporters. There was, she told them, evidence implicating Dorrie Kistiakowsky that couldn't be publicly discussed. No question, in time the case would be cracked.

Griswold called Robbins and O'Keefe to the Oval Office. Robbie, who, more than anyone else, had been goading the president to act, was unfazed by it all.

"Looks like a two-day story to me, sir," he told Griswold as Bernie sat slightly slumped in the chair, frowning, uncharacteristically quiet. The lawyer in him was always more tentative than the politician, and it was a tension he struggled with.

"But if the father dies..." Griswold said.

"A downer, but it wouldn't last...and he won't die." Robbie smiled. The polls had shown a tic up overnight.

"And we can fire an agent or two," Bernie chimed in. "The important thing is, we have the initiative. You were acting. It's what people expect. Leadership." Bernie was leading forward in his chair as if to add some momentum of his own to the campaign.

"Yes, yes, these things are going to happen, of course, gentlemen. We have to learn to take it in stride and not be thrown off. We'll keep the pressure on, Bernie. Don't let them use this as an excuse to back off. The sooner we shut down these terrorists, the better."

ONE PERSON not sharing in the self-induced euphoria was Paul Clarkson. He met with Emily for an hour, carefully reviewing all the information from the field. She was most worried about Mr. Kistiakowsky: first about his health and survival, and second about the possible civil rights violations. But on the whole, she said, the work in the eight cities had gone smoothly. The pro-life network was shaken, she was sure, and if they kept the pressure on them, someone would break. Somebody would talk.

Afterward, Paul walked the length of the south corridor to his own office to wait. He knew Langer would call. And he did.

"Paul, I sent you down to that swampland to keep the alligators tamed. What, for heaven's sake, is going on?"

"I understand, Senator. Chicago was a bad break. The FBI may have jumped the gun a bit."

"No, no. That's bad enough, but I understand. But these other eight cities, Paul. It looks to me—no, it smells to me like you people are trying to intimidate and break a movement. Can't you restrain those wild-eyed bureaucrats?"

"Senator, in fairness I have to tell you that this was my idea—"

"What! I sent you there to convert them, and they've converted you. Paul, Paul, you listen to me. These are our folks out around the country. Good, honest, God-fearing people who want to save babies from having their skulls crushed. That's all. One nut in Fargo doesn't taint the whole movement."

"There are elements in the pro-life network that are what could be called a terrorist operation, sir," said Paul. "I've seen the intelligence, and we have to bring them to justice. We need to do it before they discredit the good people."

"Paul, you and I need to talk. If you go after the killer, that's fine. Use the Eighty-second Airborne for all I care. But I'm warning you and your boss, you start trampling on civil rights or you use this as an excuse to stamp out legitimate dissent, and you'll have a real war on your hands right here at this end of Constitution Avenue where the people's representatives have the power.

"And listen, Paul, don't let your boss forget that all of her judges have to come past me—and all of her crime bills—and even her appropriations." Langer was steamed. Paul had worked for him long enough to know that the senator's cheeks would be flushed, his brow furrowed.

"And don't you forget," Langer's passion came through the phone lines, "that the right of civil dissent is at the very heart of a free society. Look at the civil rights movement: It wasn't so popular down home, but it was the essence of how a free society works. Or Vietnam. There's irony, for heaven's sake. I was prepared to die in the jungle—almost did—to protect the right of my peers at home to protest what I was doing. Sounds strange, I know. I hated them, but I'd die for their right."

"I respect you for that, Senator, and I agree with you." Paul could barely get any words in.

"But remember, the pro-life movement is the first one in the history of this republic to have its rights restricted—like what's coming down now." Langer paused for breath, and Paul spoke quickly.

"Senator, I share your convictions; you know that. But we have to enforce the law. It's different here than it was on the Hill."

"Never fails," Langer sighed, "send a politician to the executive branch and he becomes a statesman. The bureaucracy swallows even the best of them. You see here, Paul; you just get my message to the attorney general."

"Yes, sir, I'll do it today."

Paul hung up, chastened. He did live between two worlds. And in his heart he agreed with Langer. But as associate attorney general he had his duty to do. He picked up the phone to call Emily.

IRA LEVITZ sat in his cubicle at the *Post*, sipping coffee and scanning news accounts of the administration's campaign against the pro-life network. Turning in his chair, he knocked an empty Domino's pizza box on the floor. Crumbs and scraps of hardened cheese showered his lap.

It wasn't what he read that troubled him so much; he'd seen thousands of instances of bureaucratic overreaching and bungling. He and others in the press would rap their knuckles hard, and then the bureaucrats would draw their grubby hands back under their shells.

Maybe it was uncertainty about what to write. Usually he would mull over the ideas for a column for a day or two; then he'd sit down at the word processor and the words would pour out of him. But today, with only an hour to go, the words simply weren't there.

What was bothering Levitz was something he couldn't identify, a nagging sense that things were just not quite right. Over the years, he had learned to trust his feelings as much as his head. That's where the passion came from. And he didn't like his feelings today. He knew, deep down inside, that the country, without even realizing it, was crossing an invisible line.

Suddenly his fingers started moving on the keyboard.

> Only thirty days in office, and Whitney Griswold has arrived at the defining moment of his presidency. It started with a gunshot in Fargo and now hangs in the balance in a Chicago intensive care unit.
>
> At the risk of overstating, a common complaint about this profession, it may well be a defining moment for the nation. For in the Griswold administration's reaction to this wretched abortion clinic violence, we may discover that the defense of liberty costs us our liberty.

He stopped and rubbed his eyes. *That line's too cute,* he thought. *People simply won't see this. Don't want to. Crime is so bad in America that they'll welcome a police state. Anything for personal peace.*

The signs were everywhere, Levitz realized. Government SWAT teams, without regard for the Fourth Amendment protection against unreasonable search and seizures, were kicking down doors at night in public housing projects. Random roadblocks in Miami, Los Angeles, Detroit, and Atlanta. Threats to free speech. Curfews—nothing but martial law—in a thousand American communities.

He ran his hands through his hair and started again.

> When challenged by reports this week that the gestapo-style raids...

He went back, moved his cursor to the "gestapo-style" and struck out the words...

. . . on pro-life leaders might violate civil liberty, Griswold looked startled. "Why of course not," he said. "The first freedom is freedom from fear, and we are going to do what we must to guarantee that, for people in their homes, walking the streets, or exercising their constitutional rights in an abortion clinic."

Well, thank you, Mr. President. But perhaps you should study your history. Some seventy years ago another leader said almost exactly the same thing, and the people loved it. They welcomed fascism. It's an unfair comparison perhaps. Griswold is a decent man; Hitler was evil incarnate. But the fact remains: People will always choose order over liberty. And the most ghastly transgressions are often committed by decent, well-meaning people sitting in well-lighted offices, doing what they believe is right and noble.

Levitz sighed, drew back, saved the draft, and decided to come back to it in a few minutes. It was a wonderful, sunny day outside, brisk, clean air, maybe in the mid-forties. He'd walk to the park at the end of Connecticut Avenue, stop at his favorite cigar store on the way and indulge himself. And he'd clear his head.

Deep in his own thoughts, Levitz walked through the *Post* lobby, his trench coat swinging open. He hardly noticed the guard with the big grin until he heard, "Have a good day, Mr. Levitz." He grinned and waved back.

He made his way along L Street to Connecticut Avenue, passing the shining white edifice of the Mayflower Hotel, its bright flags snapping in the cool breeze. He thought how he must be careful not to let his own experiences distort his thinking. The passion for human freedom and human rights was, after all, in his genes. His mind moved back, as it had thousands of times before: He could see his grandfather, once a tall, stately gentleman—or so the pictures made him appear when he was professor of physics at Tübingen—being shoved from the train as it pulled into Auschwitz. He and Ira's grandmother were never heard from again. His own father had narrowly escaped.

America didn't have to worry about Hitler, or some madman plotting to exterminate Jews. But the moral vacuum of the '80s and '90s, had left people without any inner restraints.

And when there are no inner restraints, he thought, government has to increase force. But it's never enough. So it keeps
increasing. And eventually comes the Faustian bargain: You give up
your liberties, says the government, and I'll provide you security.
And the next thing you know, you end up killing Jews after all. Or
something like it.

Levitz stopped in Farragut Square where Connecticut Avenue
and K Street intersect, a beautiful patch of green in the middle of
the busiest part of the city. He looked around, taking a deep
breath. It was such a beautiful day.

He noticed a young couple sitting on a bench. The man
looked like a lawyer; so did the young woman. Both had short,
glossy hair and wore matching horn-rims that clicked as they
laughed and leaned together, talking quietly. Love blooming in the
park on this faux-spring day.

*What do they care about order and liberty and social contracts and the
Bill of Rights and writing deadlines?* thought Levitz illogically. He
felt an irrational impulse to walk over, grab them both hard, and
ask them if they realized that the social consensus in America was
unraveling and that they might someday, like his grandfather, be
on a train to a gulag or a camp. He had a perverse sense of humor,
so it took all his self-restraint not to do it. He could just see them
jumping up, screaming, running away, and then telling their
friends about the psycho who'd accosted them in the park.

And maybe they'd be right. Coat flying, slightly hunched
over, chuckling to himself, with cigar smoke billowing over his
head, Ira Levitz walked east on K Street, back to the *Post* to finish
his column.

18

Thursday, March 5
Arlington, Virginia

O N   T H E Virginia hills sloping down toward the Potomac
River, underneath the noisy path of jets thundering along
the river toward National Airport, lie the green slopes housing
Washington's quietest neighbors: the 235,000 graves of Arlington
National Cemetery.

The cemetery's formal entrance lies at the end of Memorial
Bridge, the gleaming white span over the Potomac River guarded
by huge statues of naked men with flaming swords and golden
horses. The cemetery itself rises up a steep hillside to the lawns of
the Custis-Lee Mansion, where the Stars and Stripes always fly
at half-mast. Not far away is the celebrated grave of John F.
Kennedy, its eternal flame still burning; and the grave of Robert
Kennedy, interred near his brother five years later; and the Tomb
of the Unknown, guarded night and day by the Honor Guard
Ceremonial Unit of Fort Myer's Third Infantry.

Despite its tourmobiles and visitors' center, Arlington main-
tains its quiet dignity as the final resting place of presidents, gener-
als, admirals, astronauts, and thousands upon thousands of ordinary
men and women who gave their lives in the service of their country. The nation's history is marked and measured in its headstones:

The Civil War. The Spanish-American War. World War I. World War II. The Korean Conflict. Vietnam. And then there are the less celebrated skirmishes that claimed much smaller numbers, but still demanded the ultimate sacrifice: Beirut. Granada. Kuwait. Somalia. The simple, rounded white-granite stones stretch out in uniform, heartbreaking rows, dotting silent hillsides and guarding grassy meadows.

On this particular morning, a slow procession wound its way up one of the cemetery's quiet drives to a green canopy draped above a freshly dug, perfect rectangle of red Virginia clay. Beside it were three precise rows of folding chairs. At a discreet distance, atop a small rise, an army band waited, along with four soldiers at attention, bearing flags.

The cortege topped a hill near the gravesite. An army officer walked slowly, leading a large, glossy chestnut horse who strode the familiar road, occasionally snorting and shaking his head from side to side. Its saddle was empty; a gleaming pair of high black boots were turned backward in the stirrups.

All was quiet save the measured clop of the riderless horse's hooves on the pavement—and the echo of four more horses behind, pulling an open, large-wheeled cart bearing the flag-draped coffin: Colonel Carl Lee Miller was coming home to Arlington for his final rest. Behind the caisson walked his widow, children, and grandchildren.

On a hillside nearby, two men stood erect near a copse of trees and a grouping of graves. Their arms angled in salute as the caisson rolled by. Then, as they watched the funeral procession move to the gravesite, the two resumed their conversation.

"Thanks for meeting with me, man," said Lance Thompson. "This was the best place I could think of where we could talk in private. But I forgot they would be having funerals. It sure brings back the memories."

His colleague was a tall black man with close-shaven salt-and-pepper hair. He wore round wire-rimmed spectacles, had a large, rather flat nose, and when he grinned, a gap between his teeth offset his otherwise rather forbidding appearance.

James Jones had served with Lance in the army's Special Forces in the Gulf War. Though the two had not been in the same unit, the unique challenges of the deserts of Iraq and Kuwait had drawn them together in a way they hadn't anticipated: They had been part of a tiny, top-secret, multioperational force chosen to infiltrate Baghdad and neutralize Saddam Hussein.

The two men had dropped into the dark skies above Baghdad in camouflage chutes, made their way to the Iraqi leader's hidden compound, slit the throats of the guards at the entrance, used a minute amount of plastic explosive to blow their way into Hussein's bunker, and there had found the Iraqi leader engaged in an interview with an American journalist.

Before they could recover from the shock, an entire squad of armed-to-the-teeth Revolutionary Guards had sprung into action. The two infiltrators had thrown smoke bombs, sprayed the room generously with their Uzis, and barely escaped in the resulting firefight. But as they were running toward the door, James had returned to break the news camera, still rolling, and destroy the film. Lance had then torn back through the wall of troops and dragged his friend out of the bunker.

From there they had fled by foot through the streets, hiding in garbage dumps until dawn, when they had connected with their helicopter unit and been spirited out of Iraq.

The bizarre scene had been buried. The western journalist's memoirs, helped along by a large and anonymous financial contribution, had not mentioned the incident; neither had any reports to the joint chiefs and the president. But ever since, Jones had said he and Lance were blood brothers for life.

After the war, Jones had retired from the military and started a small security company. Aided by loans extended to minority-owned businesses, he had built his company, even in the security-saturated Washington area, into a scrappy, good-bargain agency whose employees combined military-style precision with an unusual ability to blend into the background. Many diplomats and government attachés used their services, and, increasingly, so did private companies looking for top security at a good package price.

For all these reasons, it had seemed only natural that his company would bid for a new contract on a soon-to-be-completed building in D.C.'s Foggy Bottom area. The owners seemed unusually skittish, and several other security groups had already been screened out of the action for one reason or another. Now, essentially, it was down to his company and one other. But James Jones was determined to get this contract. He had special, personal reasons for wanting to be in charge of security for the regeneration center.

"I think it's all just about in place," he told Lance. "We bid as low as we could without making it suspicious. And we've thrown in a goodie they seem to like: additional checks and sweeps based on information we obtain ourselves from subcontracts with private investigators and networking with police units. You can tell they've gotten more jittery since the Fargo thing. They liked the idea of additional intelligence and information gathering on possible threats to security."

"I guess there's nothing more we can do, then," said Lance. "It sounds like you guys have everything in place. We just gotta hope they sign you."

"Right," said Jones. "And I think they will. Hey, you remember my boy Justin? He's graduating from college in May—"

"No way," said Lance. "He was a high school football player last time I saw him."

"Well, he finished out as right tackle this year at Maryland," said Jones. "He's a big boy. But he's coming into the business with me after he graduates, and he's starting from the ground up. That means if we get this contract, he'll be working the night shift at the center this summer—"

"That's perfect," said Lance. "You are too smooth, my man." He looked at the funeral canopy in the distance. "I don't know quite when we're going to be ready to move. But I know we gotta do it. All the talk these people do isn't accomplishing anything. People are dying. Little people. I just need a little more time to work on the white brothers—they're a little slow, if you know what I mean."

Jones laughed. It was a longstanding joke between them.

"It's because they've never been in war," he said. "Sometimes people wait until the situation hits 'em right over the head before they understand where they are. And usually by the time they understand where they are, it's too late."

"Right," said Lance. "And this *is* war. It has been for some time, but now it's too far gone to ever go back. That's why things are heating up. We can't talk on the phone anymore unless we're both at pay phones. There can't be any traceable connection between us…so don't call me. It's too chancy. If I need you, I'll put an ad in the personals section of the *Fairfax Journal*: 'Gay black man seeks same for discreet, explosive good times.' Check every day. If you see that ad, meet me here at noon."

Jones sighed. "'Gay black man seeks same'?" he said. "It was easier in Iraq, dealing with terrorists…but I'm with you, brother."

They looked around for a moment, then hugged vigorously, clapping each other on the back. For good measure, in case anyone was watching, they each looked down, touched the headstone nearest them, crossed themselves, then headed in opposite directions down two different cemetery paths.

Suddenly the hills echoed with the final tribute to Colonel Carl Lee Miller: the three sharp explosions of the salute—seven guns fired perfectly in unison—then a trembling moment of silence; then the clear, throbbing notes of "Taps" filling the quiet air of the cemetery.

Lance Thompson's eyes filled with tears, as always, and he turned, hand over his heart, then saluted a farewell to the fellow soldier he had never known.

19

Saturday, March 21

EMILY GINEEN guarded her weekends. With Frederick home from Harvard and the kids home from school, weekends were family times at their large brick Georgian-style Rockwood Parkway home in the Spring Valley section of northwest Washington. On Saturday evening they usually cooked up a huge batch of chili or pizza and watched videos or played board games.

But on this Saturday morning she made an exception. Director Frizzell had sounded so insistent on the phone the night before: issues of grave national concern, he said, that were better not put in writing. So Emily had invited Paul to join the two of them at her home, 9:00 A.M., for one hour only.

Paul was first to arrive, wheeling into the circular driveway in his old red Volvo. Emily watched from the window as he swung his legs out first, grasping the door handle firmly, and then thrust himself upright; at almost the same instant, he clutched the two canes just behind the seat. It required perfect balance, but she imagined he'd had lots of practice.

A few moments later, at exactly 9:00, a black Chrysler arrived. The security agent in the passenger seat bounded out to open the rear door for Director Frizzell. He strode up the front walk in his suit and tie.

Emily shrugged to herself and opened the door. She was wearing jeans, a turtleneck, and a gray sweatshirt with a black Labrador stenciled on the front; Paul had on khakis and an Irish knit pullover. She escorted her two visitors to her cherry-paneled library, a spacious room at the far end of the first floor.

"Help yourselves, gentlemen," she said, pointing to the pot of coffee and stoneware mugs on the coffee table. She then sat in one corner of her brown-leather sofa, the kind one finds in musty Boston law firms. Frizzell took the leather wingback chair that looked new and didn't match the sofa; Paul chose the upright, lacquered, Hitchcock chair with the Harvard seal on the backrest.

"I felt it extremely important," Frizzell began, "to share the latest intelligence with you, much of which lends itself to some interpretation. This room is secure I assume?"

Emily nodded. Security checked it at random times but at least every month.

"Good. First let me show you this." He picked up a large folder. "We've had psychological profiles prepared on the more notable anti-abortion leaders. A lot of the observations here are, of course, quite predictable, but what I found interesting was a pattern that emerges. Interesting and, I must say, disturbing."

Emily resisted the urge to fidget as Frizzell explained the bureau's facility for psychological analysis. "So reliable that the CIA even asked for help."

Why are bureaucrats so obsessed with proving their own importance? Emily wondered as she sipped her coffee. Insecurity perhaps, or to justify budgets? After all, the bigger the budget, the more important the job is perceived to be.

"And what did you find?" she asked, glancing at her watch.

Frizzell cleared his throat. All of these leaders, to no one's great surprise, seemed to be single-minded, zealous in their cause, and, in some cases, exhibited behavior bordering on obsessive/compulsive, he said. They were generally without fear for themselves and evidenced definite psychopathic tendencies. The report was filled with technical jargon, but Frizzell frequently interjected a layman's interpretation.

"In short," he laid the report on the coffee table, "very dangerous people, prone to violence, with Messianic complexes. The CIA tells us that these profiles are not unlike Muslim terrorists who want to die for Allah. It's their ticket to paradise."

"The CIA has read these? It's against the law for them to spy on American citizens."

"Oh, they're not involved, other than to give us technical advice, sort of an informal understanding," Frizzell shrugged.

"But clearly here," he continued, "we have certain signs of imbalance. For example, we understand that some of these people actually claim to hear voices they believe are divine messages."

Paul frowned slightly. He wondered what Frizzell would say if he told him that God had spoken to him at times. Not audibly, but in distinct inner convictions. Like the time he had sensed God's clear leading about spending two years in Atlanta as a public defender. He decided to say nothing.

"Nothing surprising, Director." Emily smiled, nodding, her eyebrows up, as if to ask what else.

"The urgency, you see, is that I think they're about to strike again. These types of people could do just about anything. They hate the president, and I fear they might go to any lengths to embarrass or discredit him to make their point."

Emily nodded again.

"The most critical information is contained in one informant's report. One group seems to have a plan. They've even named it."

"Plan B?" Emily interjected. "Operation Steamroller?" She couldn't help herself.

Frizzell looked at her coldly. "An operation they're calling 'Gideon's Torch.' We don't know anything specific. They're very security conscious. Some of the conversations, though, have alluded to 'lighting the darkness and exposing evil deeds.' Our analysts say this could be violence, perhaps even spectacular violence to make a point...I mean, lighting the darkness could refer to some violent explosion."

Frizzell then explained the grave possibilities. Four and a half pounds of highly enriched uranium, capable of being used in a nuclear weapon, had recently been stolen in St. Petersburg, Russia. Intelligence reported that organized crime groups there had the components to construct nuclear weapons and were offering them for sale. Just a year earlier, a nuclear weapon produced in North Korea had been intercepted on its way to Iran. The CIA, he pointed out, was diligent, as were the other intelligence organizations. But this kind of thing could always slip through. And there were plenty of less exotic ways to concoct huge lethal explosives. Messianic zealots talking about "torching" something could not be ignored.

"Which group is it that's developed the plan?" Emily asked.

"That's another part of our concern," said Frizzell. "It's the one right here in Washington. The one called The Life Network."

"Why all the torch stuff?" she asked.

"We've looked into that. You can tell a lot about these types by the imagery they choose. Our analysts presume the metaphor comes from the Old Testament, where there's an account about an ancient battle between the Israelis and the Midianites. The Israeli commander was a man named Gideon. His army was overwhelmingly outnumbered, but he won the battle. Used torches as weapons."

Paul started to say something, then thought better of it. Frizzell had his facts skewed, but perhaps now was not the time to correct the FBI director, nor the time to seem overly familiar with the biblical text in question.

"So what do you propose?" Emily asked Frizzell.

A laundry list, he said. Authority to put bureau agents or marshals in selected major hospitals across the country, in addition to those already posted at clinics; authority for "deeper" surveillance and wiretaps; and a "supplemental budget allocation of perhaps fifty million dollars to pay the bills." And the president needed to be apprised of the profiles, Frizzell added.

It was 9:45. Emily thanked the director and assured him she would read the profiles and weigh all he had said carefully over the weekend.

"Please do not underestimate the gravity of this situation," he said. "My experience over the years tells me that this is a matter not to be taken lightly."

Frizzell left first, and Emily motioned for Paul to remain. She was learning to trust his judgment.

"Well," she said when they were alone, "what do you think?"

"I dunno. He's very shrewd. And remember, he was badly stung by the Chicago fiasco. I think he's covering his butt. Then again, he may be genuinely concerned. Still, I can't help but wonder if he isn't seeing this as a chance to puff his budget—and his own importance."

"But he's got informers. He wouldn't dare misrepresent the intelligence," Emily pressed.

"But he might also not understand everything quite right. 'Gideon's Torch' for example. It comes from the book of Judges, chapter 7. It's a great story: Gideon's men, three hundred of them, blew their trumpets and shined their torches in the night—and their enemies fled. The torches weren't weapons. That's pretty mild stuff by Old Testament standards."

Emily smiled. "I knew your Bible knowledge would come in handy one of these days. Anyway, I don't think we'll rush into the Oval Office with this one yet. But we will consider wiretaps and surveillance."

Paul looked surprised. Emily didn't notice this, but she did think he was showing a little more pain than usual as she walked him to the front door.

20

DANIEL SEATON woke groggily, feeling as if someone was calling his name. Even as he swam to the surface of consciousness, the fragments of the dream still clung to him, like seaweed from the depths.

He sat up in bed, looking over at Mary, who was on her side, one knee raised up to her chest as if she was running in her sleep. He looked at the clock. Nearly four o'clock.

The dream was slipping away even as his mind cleared. It had been a mixture of Old Testament and modern times, the type of dream he'd often had during his seminary days. Moses on the Metro. Noah at the National Zoo. His brain had no problem pairing biblical characters and twentieth-century Washington, D.C. Sometimes, in fact, the former seemed more real than the latter.

And this dream in particular had seemed so real, even though it didn't make sense. In it, he and Mary and Alex and Lance and the others had been marching in a line around the White House. He could still see the pointed tips of the wrought-iron fence separating the sidewalk from the green lawn. They had been carrying pro-life protest signs in one hand, torches in the other.

Then the president and the first lady had come out to the fence, and the president had reached through, his hand extended toward Daniel's.

"You're right," he had said. "I've changed my mind." And Daniel was nodding.

Suddenly the Secret Service were all around the president, so Daniel backed up slightly. There was an enormous terra-cotta pot positioned on the sidewalk, full of red geraniums; Daniel backed into it and knocked it over. There was a huge crash. And then he woke up.

He wasn't into literal dream analysis, but this dream made sense.

The FBI invasion of their home a month earlier had shaken him. Four men, pounding loudly and flashing badges, had charged in without warning and begun reading them their rights, even though he had assured them there was no need for that. He and Mary would answer truthfully anything they were asked.

At first he had been surprised when the agents had asked about the Network by name. But he had answered deliberately, without restraint, telling them that the The Life Network was an informal, voluntary group of like-minded and seriously committed Christians sworn to nonviolence.

No, he said, they knew nothing of the open letter to President Griswold or of anyone involved in the abortionist killing in North Dakota. He often preached vigorously against anything of this sort, he said.

He and Mary had been exhausted by the time the agents left their home after warning them, in so many words, not to leave town.

The other elements were equally recognizable. He had been so focused on Gideon's Torch for so long the dream had mixed the biblical account with the desires of his heart.

WHEN DANIEL was a child, one of his favorite Bible heroes was Gideon, a man who had used cunning, not violence, to outwit and defeat the enemies of Israel in a thrilling story of psychological warfare.

In 1150 B.C., the armies of the Midianites had amassed in the great valley adjacent to Mount Moreh, south of the Sea of Galilee and just north of the borders of modern-day Israel's West Bank. The Midianites had allied themselves with the Amalekites and other eastern, nomadic armies and settled into a seven-year occupation of the nation of Israel, devastating their crops, possessions, and storehouses.

Now 135,000 troops were camped in the valley, their tents billowing in an occasional breeze, which also carried the odors of roasted goat, human sewage, and strange Oriental anointing oils to the nostrils of the men of Israel, peering down upon them from the heights of Mount Gilead. The Jewish soldiers could hear the rough shouts of drunken soldiers, the barking of dogs, even the chatter of the women and children accompanying the camp.

The Israelite commander, Gideon, was young but not untested. His reputation and his devotion to the strange God of Israel were well known to the Midianite leaders. They had heard tales of this Jehovah's delivering power against Israel's enemies. They believed the stories enough to be unnerved by them, but not quite enough to quit the fertile land.

Gideon's command had initially consisted of thirty-two thousand troops—hardly a reasonable hope against the vast eastern army. And yet God had told him to reduce his fighting force, so it would be absolutely clear that their victory over the Midianites was the work of God, not men.

Thus, Gideon had informed his soldiers that whoever was afraid was free to leave. Twenty-two thousand Israelites, hearts pounding in their chests from the sight of the vast opposing force, clutched their cloaks and gratefully returned to their tents.

But the ten thousand remaining were still too many. God told Gideon to winnow down his fighting unit even further, and soon there were but three hundred men left.

As the darkness deepened, each man was given a ram's horn trumpet, a clay pitcher, and a torch. The pitchers were inverted over the torches to protect them from the wind and to hide the light from the Midianites until Gideon's men were all in place.

But just before the battle was joined, Gideon and an assistant named Purah had crept from rock to rock until they reached an outcropping where the last patrol of the Midianite advance guard kept watch around a crackling campfire. Here they heard one soldier tell another of his strange dream of a loaf of barley bread rolling into the camp and upending the general's tent. His comrade, raising his eyebrows and thinking of the strange stories from the past about the Jewish God, had no question about the interpretation: It was the army of Gideon, the Israelite commander, he said. Their God was going to cause the Israelites to prevail.

Grinning with tense exultation, Gideon and Purah crept back to the waiting Israeli troops. And even as they did so, the strange dream and its chilling interpretation were repeated from watch to watch, carried via couriers throughout the camp, building into a common premonition of disaster that fed on the dark edges of the Midianites' pagan fears.

Before midnight that evening, the three hundred Israelites, now divided into three companies, crept silently into position above the valley where the Midianites slept. By now the sentries had all heard the strange dream and jumped at every crackle in the dry desert grass.

Suddenly the night exploded. On signal Gideon's troops all blew their trumpets, broke open their clay pitchers, and raised their torches in the darkness. The abrupt convulsion of light and noise terrified the jittery sentries, who leaped to their feet, drew their swords, screamed, and slew one another in the chaos. Meanwhile, the soldiers in their tents, groggy with sleep and fermented drink, stampeded in panic. Those who weren't cut down by their own troops fled, shrieking and stumbling, into the hills.

Daniel loved the strange story of Gideon's battle. He loved the parallels between the ancient victory and their modern mission—the victory of light over darkness, of truth over fear. It was fitting that they had named their project Gideon's Torch.

PAUL CLARKSON arrived at his office a few minutes after 7:00 Monday morning. He liked to use the limited-access highway in from Virginia that was closed to vehicles with fewer than two occupants after 7:00 A.M.; he also liked to get a headstart on the paperwork while things were quiet.

As he glanced through the agency summary for the day, his eyes stopped on a criminal division report recommending that a proposed prosecution be dropped.

Eight Act-Up protestors had smashed vials of contaminated blood on the door of the Senate Appropriations Committee to protest inadequate funding for the regeneration centers. The Capitol police had arrested them, and the protestors were then released on their own recognizance.

The event had been widely covered on the networks and in the press. The U.S. attorney first announced he would prosecute for criminal trespass and assault with a deadly weapon (the blood tested HIV-positive), but on review, the department was now contending that they could not make the charges stick; even if they could, it wouldn't be good policy. A prudential call, the assistant AG argued.

Clarkson remembered an earlier case that had outraged him when he was on the committee. Over a hundred Act-Up activists had hurled condoms and desecrated the sacramental elements at St. Patrick's Cathedral in New York. Judge JoAnn Ferdinand sentenced four of them to seventy hours of community service. She was the same judge who had sentenced pro-life rescuers charged under the same disorderly conduct statutes to fifteen-day prison terms.

Act-Up had used such tactics for years. In 1989, protestors invaded the headquarters of the Burroughs-Wellcome pharmaceutical firm, protesting the price charged for the AIDS drug AZT; some even chained themselves to desks in the offices. Later, other demonstrators disrupted the New York Stock Exchange for trading Burroughs-Wellcome stock. The response: With much fanfare, Burroughs-Wellcome gave a million-dollar donation to the AIDS cause.

Clarkson finished the report and stared at it a moment. He thought about the Saturday morning meeting and Frizzell's information and comments.

Gideon's Torch, he thought. *Exposing the darkness. No doubt there is darkness.* He added the report to a small pile on the right side of his desk.

21

"MR. SMITH, I think I'm gonna get what you want," Alfonzo Rojas said into the pay phone. "I got a call from NIH early this morning. They've got a big videotape duplication order for me. From the gynecology unit. I'm gonna pick it up at three o'clock this afternoon."

The long-distance wires from Bethesda to New York crackled for a moment, and Alfonzo watched the cars roar past on Wisconsin Avenue as he strained to hear.

"That's great," said "Mr. Smith," whose real name was Bill Waters. "I'll catch the next shuttle and meet you at 3:30 at the pickup point."

"Right," said Rojas.

After he hung up the phone, he crossed Wisconsin Avenue, retrieved his old, rust-colored Honda Civic from its parking meter, and headed back to his office.

IN A RESIDENTIAL section of Bethesda, Maryland, not far from the busy downtown grid of restaurants and shops, sprawl the 260 acres of the National Institutes of Health. The disjointed campus includes high-rise apartments housing doctors and their families; the Children's House, where children with cancer play on the green grass; a low, white building with what appears to be a crumpled UFO on its roof, housing the national medical library…and on it goes.

Federally funded, the hospital complex welcomes patients from all over the world, patients whose conditions have defied conventional treatment, patients who are willing to engage in experimental therapies. Sterile testing laboratories adjoin chaotic offices resembling a cross between a clinical research facility and the back room of a fraternity house.

Ringing faxes and phones compete with the visual displays of computer monitors; beside these, piles of open books and pamphlets are half-hidden by scribbled notes and half-eaten sandwiches and bottles of Evian water. Nearby are the patient wings where critically ill men, women, and children receive test protocols developed by the enthusiastic, blue-jeaned young researchers who live in the labs.

One of the most secure buildings on campus houses the animal research laboratories. Staff and doctors entering the building must wear proper identification. Vendors and civilians are not allowed in at all, for on the top two floors live a colony of meticulously maintained, exotically diseased mice, dogs, rabbits, and research monkeys costing $20,000 apiece, all locked carefully away from the rabid denizens of the People for the Ethical Treatment of Animals, who have vehemently vowed to free their fellow mammals.

Security for the human mammals at Building 10, an ugly glass-and-brick high-rise, is not so stringent. Marked by a grotesque black-metal sculpture at its entrance, Building 10 houses inpatients, outpatients, hordes of researchers, and, in its patient wings, any number of critically ill individuals. It is a hubbub of activity at nearly any hour, day or night. So no one took any particular notice of Alfonzo Rojas as he stepped onto the central elevator and pressed the button for level B-2.

The car descended into the bowels of NIH, and Rojas stepped off into an underground labyrinth of wide, dark corridors with stained, spotted floors. Occasional double doors opened into grimy, subterranean boiler rooms; as always, he half-expected to see shackled, slave labor manning the boilers in the darkness.

He eventually emerged into the medical arts and photography branch. Here the doorways were painted shocking pink and other bright colors to create an illusion of cheerfulness.

Whistling slightly, Rojas tapped on one of the pink doors. A receptionist let him into the television production offices, a well-lit area, with plants, a few padded chairs, and cream-colored dividers separating a claustrophobic warren of cubicles crammed with videotaping equipment. Here a media staff produced training videos, from script to finished product, for the various institutes of the NIH, as well as medical facilities throughout the country.

The videos, generally about twenty minutes in length, gave overview information on anything from the proper care of laboratory animals, to procedures for new surgical techniques, to the correct procedure for filling out the laborious paperwork needed to apply for an NIH grant. The media office also provided stock video clips for news affiliates' use when they ran NIH-related stories: photography of cancer cells, backgrounders on various laboratories, and quotes from NIH officials. The production offices also had monitoring devices for taping network and local newscasts so any mentions of NIH could be culled for the files.

"How're you doin' this afternoon, Cindy?" Rojas said warmly to the receptionist. "I'm here to pick up a master video to be copied for distribution. Some kind of training video. Beth called earlier this morning."

The receptionist smiled. "Yeah, this is a big order," she said. "They're in a big hurry for it, too. I'll get Beth for you."

She picked up the phone and buzzed an extension. "Beth," she said. "The gentleman from TapeMasters is here."

Almost immediately Beth emerged from the cubicles in the back and extended her hand. "Hi, Alfonzo! How're those babies of yours? Got any new pictures?"

Rojas gave her a huge smile and reached for his wallet. He pulled out a plastic sheaf featuring a small, dark-haired boy and a tiny girl with huge brown eyes and gold pierced earrings.

"They're doing beautiful," he said. "Things are a little tight for us on the money end, if you know what I mean. But we wouldn't trade our twins for anything."

"I know what you mean," said Beth. "But I don't know how your wife does it. We've just got one, and she keeps us going all the time."

She put a videotape on the counter of the receptionist's cubicle as Rojas pulled a clipboard out of his soft-sided briefcase.

"This is a big order, right?" he said as he began filling in the work order.

"Right," said Beth. "I usually make these training video copies here myself, but I can't handle this many very easily. They want fifty dupes, and I need them in three days."

"Okay," he said. "Here's the work order. Just sign here. We'll get these back to you by Thursday."

Beth handed him the video, a one-inch Beta cassette in a dark blue-and-gray jacket with the NIH seal on the spine. Rojas glanced at the long, official title quickly—fetal tissue something or other. This was it.

He gave Beth a copy of the work order, initialed it, and stuck the video and the clipboard into his briefcase.

"Thanks," he said, smiling. "We'll get right on this. I'll call you when it's done. You all have a great day."

"You, too," the two women echoed as the door swung shut behind him. "Thanks a lot."

ROJAS ASCENDED the elevator, exited past the ugly black sculpture, and got into his Honda. At the corner of Center Drive and Cedar Lane, a few blocks down, he turned right. A big, unmarked van was idling there. He parked at the curb and walked up to the passenger door. There was a stocky young black man at the wheel and a slender white man on the passenger side. In the back, Rojas could see snaked cables, sophisticated-looking video equipment, and a small pile of video cassettes.

"Did you get it?" asked the white guy, the one Rojas knew as Mr. Smith.

"No problem," said Rojas. "It's the one you want."

He handed his briefcase to the man, who extracted the video and looked at the spine, smiling. "Great!" he said simply. He reached into his rear pocket, pulled out a thick sheaf of twenty-dollar bills, and tucked them into the side flap of the briefcase.

"Alfonzo," he said. "Here's a thousand dollars. Why don't you go get yourself a cup of coffee and come back in forty-five minutes?"

Rojas's eyes widened at the bulge in his briefcase flap, and he thought of the twins. This was the best thing that had happened to him in a long time. He took the briefcase and looked at his watch.

"Thanks," he said. "I'll be back at about 4:15."

"Great," said the man. "I'll have the rest of your payment and the master for you when you come back. Enjoy your coffee—make it an espresso."

As Rojas headed back to his Honda, Bill Waters smiled again, looking at the video in disbelief. Getting it had been almost too easy; but what it would eventually unleash would be hard indeed.

22

SPRING IS something you not only see but feel in Washington. And for Whitney Griswold it felt very good. His tax overhaul had won editorial plaudits and was enormously popular in the opinion polls. People seemed to like his leadership style—his no-nonsense approach to issues. Crime continued to dominate public concern, but he and his attorney general had positioned themselves well, having sent a tough new sentencing bill to Congress and recommended federal jurisdiction for more capital offenses.

The polls showed him riding almost as high as he had been right after his inauguration. Robbie's grin as he entered the Oval Office each day assured the president that things were on track.

The only sour note remained the unsolved Fargo killing, and in that regard Griswold was discovering the sobering truth about the presidency: The chief executive sits in the most powerful office in the world, atop a bureaucracy employing more than 3 million civilian employees, 1.75 million military personnel, millions of offices, resources, budgets, and brain power...but it is not unlike sitting atop a huge, cold-blooded dinosaur, massive, obstinate, and sluggish. The president can kick, cajole, scream, pound on its armor-coated skin, but though it may occasionally stick up its head and stare back at him blankly, it moves at its own deliberate pace, one enormous plodding foot at a time.

Though Frizzell dutifully provided a daily intelligence report on the progress in the case, it contained less information than Griswold could pick up on any television broadcast.

"FBI and Justice are doing their best," Emily Gineen assured him. "They just haven't gotten the break they need yet."

Each morning, during his session with his senior advisors, the same ritual was repeated. Irked by the media drumbeat—the leaks and sensationalized stories and editorials demanding action—Griswold would lean forward, tap his desk, and order Bernie to order the FBI to step up its work. Bernie would agree and call Frizzell, who in turn would notify his field offices of "intense interest at the highest levels." And then the bureaucracy did what it would have done anyway.

On the foreign policy front, things seemed to be going smoothly. Then, in early April, new Arab-Israeli tensions erupted, thrusting Griswold into long sessions in the Cabinet Room with his national security team. General George Maloney, a square-jawed, battle-decorated hero, was proving to be one of the best of Griswold's appointees. He was tough, taciturn, but fluent in six languages and with a versatile mind that could wrestle with three major problems at once without missing a beat. Griswold liked his take-charge, can-do attitude.

This time, the problem was on the Israeli side. Right-wing factions had wrested concessions from the ruling party, and there was serious talk about renouncing the pact with the PLO and cracking down on infractions of the Gaza Strip agreements.

Some groups in Israel, Griswold thought, always wanted war. They were no better than the Islamic zealots or, for that matter, the zealots here at home.

"This must have been a great job when Calvin Coolidge had it," Griswold grinned to Robbie after a particularly long day. Still, his morale was good.

Buoyed by the polls and the fresh beauty of the cherry blossoms,

Griswold decided to keep a month-old promise to his family: a long Easter weekend at Camp David. Robert was home on spring break, Elizabeth had Good Friday off, and basketball was finally over, to his enormous relief.

Aware that things were not going well in Bernie's family life, Griswold invited him and his family to join them for the weekend at Camp David. To Bernie's surprise, Marilyn agreed, and his kids were excited. Griswold had even sweetened the offer by proposing to send a special air mission King Air to Hanscom Field in Bedford, Massachusetts, to pick them up. Not really within the rules, but he wanted to help patch things up for his old buddy.

Late on Friday morning, *Marine One*, the big, specially fitted CH56 helicopter, painted olive green with the telltale white engine housing, swooped in over the Mall, approached the White House across the south lawn just above the treetops, and then reined back, its nose jutting upward, and hovered clumsily to the ground.

While the awkward bird sat on the landing pad, motor whirring and blade spinning, members of the White House press corps were ushered to the usual observation position in front of the rose garden on the walkway between the mansion and the west wing. Unless the president chose to come over and talk to them, not a very common event, they had only one reason to stand there: to observe and write about the crash if the president's helicopter went down.

The Griswolds walked briskly out of the south diplomatic entrance on the first floor, escorted by Juan, two Secret Service agents, and General Maloney, who was carrying a large briefcase. Captain Slattery, naval aide to the president, also carrying bags, and the president's doctor were close behind. Griswold held Anne's hand with his left and waved to the reporters with his right, flashing an even broader grin than usual.

The family filed across the red carpet rolled out from the chopper's steps, and Griswold returned the marine sergeant's stiff salute—something he still felt awkward about, never having served in the military—and then turned and waved once more for the cameras, ducked his head quickly, and went through the door, which swung shut seconds later. With its twin turbos whining, the machine, vibrating hard, rose, banked to the right, and swooped back over the south lawn, leaving the reporters to return to the press room empty-handed once again.

Marine One followed the Potomac River west and north across Chain Bridge, the Beltway, then Great Falls. In less than thirty minutes, a thousand feet in the air and fifty miles from the capital, they approached the foothills. Soon the heavily wooded Catoctin mountaintop came into view.

As the chopper descended, armed marines in fatigues waited at the edge of the landing area. A navy commander wearing a field jacket with the presidential seal saluted smartly when the front door was let down and the president and his family descended. The Griswolds got into golf carts driven by Secret Service agents and headed down a winding road.

"This place is creepy," Elizabeth said. Men with guns were everywhere, behind trees and along the roads and paths of the mountaintop retreat.

Other Secret Service agents scrambled ahead. At the first bend in the road, an agent lifted his radio. "Amos to control. Searchlight and party on road to Aspen." "Searchlight" was the president's code name.

"Control to Amos: Stay on the air."

"Searchlight now in Aspen. All secure."

"Roger, Amos. All secure. Out."

Two agents took their positions in Elm, a small building camouflaged in the foliage with an eight-foot wide darkened window from which all approaches were visible. From these quarters, packed with electronics, including closed circuit TV, they could watch both the front and rear of Aspen, the big presidential cabin, a rambling cottage with a huge stone fireplace, a rustic great room, cozy down sofas, and a picture window overlooking the pool and woods. The agents in Elm could also monitor the main gates, the helicopter pad, and every path within the fenced compound.

Griswold called to be sure Bernie had arrived and was being well cared for in Sycamore, one of the nicer cottages scattered through the woods. Built in the '70s when Richard Nixon had brought many world leaders there, the newer lodges were rustic on the outside, luxurious inside.

"Listen, Bernie," said the president. "You and Marilyn just take some time together. This isn't a working weekend. Just have some fun."

"Thanks," Bernie responded. "We've needed something like this for quite a while."

"We'll leave you alone tonight—but we'll have dinner together tomorrow night, okay? Just like old times."

"Like old times," Bernie echoed. "Thanks, Whit."

THE FIRST AFTERNOON, the first family enjoyed a walk in the woods, a game of horseshoes, and an informal dinner. Anne had given them a reprieve from their usual low-fat diet and granted the children's wish: a cookout. Big, fat hamburgers on the grill, "the way Daddy used to cook them," were Elizabeth's words.

The president would cook? The stewards scurried to locate a charcoal grill and lighter fluid, while the Secret Service hurriedly secreted fire extinguishers in the woods just to the side of Aspen.

"Like old times," Griswold grinned, pulling Elizabeth to his side as he lined eight half-pounders on the grill over the fiery coals. All at once, he felt a bubbly sensation in his stomach. He realized what a great moment this was. He was enjoying being president and he was enjoying even more, at this moment, being a father. He looked into his daughter's face, radiant in the glow from the embers. So innocent and pure. And Robert—what a great kid, doing well in school. And Anne was a wonderful woman. He was fortunate to have her. Life was good, Whitney Griswold thought as he sipped his glass of chilled Sauvignon Blanc.

"Daddy, why is today called Good Friday?" Elizabeth broke her father's reverie.

"Well, honey, it marks the day long ago that Jesus Christ was crucified."

"But what's good about that?"

Where does she come up with these questions? Griswold wondered. He'd never really thought about that himself.

"Well, it has religious significance. But I don't know why it's called that," he answered slowly, hoping his daughter would change the subject but knowing she wouldn't.

"We went to the cathedral this week to listen to a lecture. The man said it was good because Jesus paid for our sins. But why did he have to die?"

Griswold shoved his spatula under the hamburgers where the fire was hottest. "It's a religious symbol. It's like He had to suffer in our place."

"Why?"

"It's part of the story. The people didn't like what Jesus taught: that we should love one another. And that's the important thing. Our family are Christians, so we do the good things Jesus taught, like loving one another. Do you understand that?"

"No, Daddy. The man said we are sinners, all of us. And that Jesus died for us, in our place."

"Who was this man?"

"His name was Mr. Greene. Michael Greene, I think. And he said that crime and all the bad things—and wars and everything—happen because of our own human nature. Is that so, Daddy?"

"Michael Greene . . . from where?" Griswold asked, trying to place the name.

"England," Elizabeth said. "From some place where the Archbishop of Cadbury lives."

"Wait," said Griswold as the information clicked into place. "You mean the Archbishop of Canterbury, dear. Michael Greene is at Lambeth Palace there. Well-regarded, I'm sure, but if he was being so negative about human nature, he must be terribly out of date. Old-fashioned, like the Middle Ages. People are good, dear. We know that today."

"Mr. Greene said we are born in sin. I don't get it."

Griswold frowned. "Of course not. What a terrible thing to say."

Why would they teach such things? he wondered, nodding at Anne and making a mental note to have her check with Elizabeth's teacher.

"But why *do* bad things happen then, Daddy? Why do people kill each other and all the crime and everything?"

"That's what we're doing something about in the White House, dear. Your mother and I, and you and Robert, are very fortunate. We have a good family, good parents, good training, good homes. But many people just never have a chance. They're poor, or their parents didn't help them. Or they never got a good education. It's really not their fault. Then there are some people who are bad, and we have to arrest them and put them in prison and try to teach them to do good things with their lives. We're working very hard on that right now."

Elizabeth nodded.

"You see, with the right policies in our government, we can end a lot of bad things. We can cure a lot of the conditions that cause people to do wrong things in the first place."

"What about war, Daddy?"

"Well now, honey, that's a very good question and happens to be exactly what I'm spending most of my time on these days. And if we could just learn to trust other people—I mean look them in the eye and tell them the truth—I believe we wouldn't have any wars." Griswold was gesturing with the spatula now as he talked. "Like what I'm doing right now in the Middle East. I look straight into those Arab and Israeli leaders' eyes—"

"Whitney!"

Robert, bored, had drifted over to the fish pond, so Anne saw it first—the flames shooting up and the shriveled hamburgers looking like hockey pucks. In the trees, an agent rechecked the location of the hidden extinguishers.

"Oh, oh, sorry. I'd better turn these." Griswold struggled to turn the charred burgers, but they stuck to the grill and broke apart.

Anne cleared her throat. "Juan," she called. "Could you bring out some more hamburgers, please? We seem to have worked our way through the first batch already."

Then she smiled, and Elizabeth laughed as she watched her father fling the burgers into the woods and then scrape down the grill with the metal spatula.

"Do you think squirrels like burned hamburgers?" he asked.

"They're vegetarians, Dad," Robert volunteered.

"Thanks for that insight, son."

Elizabeth started up again. "So what does Easter mean, then, Daddy?"

"Well, dear, it means we should all be like Jesus. Good people, kind and patient." He gritted his teeth slightly. "Very patient."

Just then Juan arrived with a hastily assembled platter of plump pink burgers.

"Okay, now," said the president, "let's try this again." He slid the spatula under the first burger; it wobbled, and he promptly dropped it into the black dust next to the grill.

Elizabeth laughed again, and Griswold pretended to smile.

SATURDAY was a great day for the president. With his Camp David windbreaker zipped to the top, he took a long, early morning walk alone in the woods. (As alone, that is, as any president ever can be; two agents with radios flanked him, tramping through the woods, and a third followed on the path a respectable distance behind.) He whipped Bernie soundly in three rounds of tennis during the morning, took the kids all around Camp David on one of the electric carts, and bowled with Robert before dinner, all without an interruption. (General Maloney was in the main office, just down the road from Aspen, ready to alert the president should anything of importance occur.)

That night the Griswolds and O'Keefes dined together around the large oak table at Aspen. The kids were off at Laurel in the staff mess, eating hot dogs, french fries, and enormous amounts of ketchup, settling in for an evening of first-run films in the private theater. Anne was back in control of the adult menu: sautéed Dover sole and steamed vegetables.

Anne couldn't remember the last time the four of them had sat down like this and had a leisurely dinner. The wine flowed, along with Bernie's Dewars, and the combination of the relaxed schedule, the alcohol, and the crisp air reminded her of days long gone, back when they were in school and their dreams were young. She and Marilyn leaned their elbows on the table and started reminiscing.

"Remember Barb Brookstone?" Anne said, using a pair of silver shears to cut a cluster of grapes. "Try these, they're perfect." Marilyn took the grapes and then passed the fruit tray to Bernie without looking at him. The men were preoccupied in some hot discussion about the Middle East.

"How could I forget her?" Marilyn said. "Remember when she got her skirt stuck in the top of her pantyhose and no one told her until the party was almost over?"

Anne laughed. "Well, I'd lost track of her over the years, but she sent me a wedding invitation. Funny how when you're in the White House everyone comes out of the woodwork. She's getting married—third time—to this Viennese count or something whose bloodlines go back to the last czar of Russia. So she'll be related to the English royal family and the new Russian aristocracy...great career move, right?"

Marilyn smiled. She vaguely remembered Barb as the sort of woman who always had to have a man at her side. She had traded them in often, and she always traded up. Once Barb had said something to Marilyn at a party, something about Bernie, appraising him with her cool blue eyes. He wasn't great-looking, but he had great potential, Barb had said. "He's going somewhere."

At the time Marilyn had loved Bernie for his laugh, his heart, his wit, his energy, his Bernie-ness. She'd never thought much about where he was going; she just knew she wanted to be with him. She'd shot back a barb at Barb. Something about feeling reassured about the caliber of the O'Keefe gene pool, and that she'd stick with him for the sake of future generations.

But now those future generations were eating hot dogs, Bernie was two sheets to the wind, as usual, and he and Whit were laughing as if they were fraternity boys.

Maybe I could compete with just the alcohol, Marilyn thought. *Or just the White House. But I sure can't compete with them both. I haven't had Bernie's full, sober attention in a long time.*

Just then the president leaned across the table. "Listen," he said. "I've got a great idea! This has been tremendous, just the four of us together again. Why don't we go horseback riding tomorrow morning? The kitchen will pack us a picnic breakfast. Champagne, orange juice, croissants, fruit...it'll be great!"

Bernie grinned and nodded. Anne smiled, too; the weekend had really relaxed Whitney already.

But Marilyn frowned, a well-worn vertical crease coming between her eyebrows. "I'm sorry, but I'll have to respectfully decline, I'm afraid."

Bernie flushed. No one turned down the president.

Whitney looked surprised, then smiled winsomely at Marilyn. "But why?" he said. "The weather report says it's going to be a perfect day, Marilyn. The trails are safe. The horses are great."

Marilyn smiled. He really did sound sincere. "I really appreciate the invitation. It sounds wonderful. But tomorrow is Easter, and the children and I will be going to Mass. We always do."

Bernie sputtered. "But Marilyn—"

She turned toward him, her eyes steady. "Won't you be coming with us, Bernie?"

MUCH LATER that night, Whitney Griswold shook his head as he thought about the dinner. "And I thought tensions were tough in the Middle East," he said, as he leaned down to take off his slippers. "Tough times for Bernie."

"Well, I'm not so sure about that," Anne said, raising her eyebrows. She was sitting in bed reading a copy of the new definitive biography of Eleanor Roosevelt. "I'd say tough times for Marilyn."

23

Thursday, April 16
New York City

B ILL WATERS looked up from the editing machine. It had
been a simple job. So far. Getting his hands on the NIH training video had proved easier than expected. Extracting its visceral
contents, recording an additional message, and splicing the two
together had also gone smoothly. The new tape timed out at four
and a half minutes.

Though Gideon's Torch was an ambitious plan, it was also reasonably feasible, providing everything broke just right. Though it
sounded preposterous, bumping ABC News's satellite uplink and
interrupting their programming wouldn't really be too difficult,
given the resources they had in place. What would be difficult
would be getting their own message up and keeping it going for
four and a half minutes—an eternity in the world of television.

But their people were at their posts. The tape was ready. All
they needed now was a disaster of some sort within a hundred
miles of Washington on a Saturday or Sunday so that *ABC World
News Tonight*, which was broadcast from D.C. on the weekends,
would send out a certain satellite news-gathering—or SNG—truck
manned by a certain operator for an on-site report.

The truck in question—a white van with a satellite dish on top, with uplink capacity to any transponders the networks used and a phone that could reach anywhere in the world—was privately owned, as were many contracted for news reports. It had been designed to provide news-gathering capacity at crisis spots, but with much more ease than the huge network vans with their towering radio mast transmitters, huge white dishes, and megatonnage. The networks tended to contract the smaller trucks for short-notice projects in confined spaces, such as Amtrak train wrecks on the Boston-to-Washington line, row-house fires in Philadelphia or Washington, and inner-city drug busts.

Fortunately for Gideon's Torch—absolutely providential, thought Bill—the operator of an SNG truck based in D.C. had proven himself a friend to their pro-life ideals. Only at the lower levels of the operation had they paid people for services rendered. Like Alfonzo Rojas at TapeMasters. A good guy, focused on the concerns of his own life, worried about providing for his family, he didn't mind taking some money for what in his mind was an insignificant action—getting one extra copy of some dull medical training video. But at the higher end of the operation, you couldn't depend on hired guns; you had to have people in place who were committed not because of dollars but because of ideology.

Hired guns can be rehired by a higher bidder, thought Bill, and their opposition would always have more money than they did. But the people now in place at ABC in New York and Washington believed in the cause. So much so that they were devoting considerable creative effort, at considerable risk, to get their message on the air. One of them was a promising young man Bill had met at a church-sponsored building-renovation project in Harlem. His name was Reginald Warner.

Washington, D.C.

Everything about Reginald Warner was huge. He carried about 275 pounds on his 6' 3" frame and walked with the characteristic pigeon-toed gait of a linebacker, his giant thighs rubbing against each other like enormous twin hams. His head was shaved on the sides, with his curly black hair two and a half inches long on top, tightly coiled yet erect, a buzz cut with an attitude. His dark, clear eyes were spiked with lashes so thick and curly they looked like tight spirals on his lids. His big white teeth split his good-natured face whenever he smiled, which was often.

Reginald would have been even more imposing were he not just seventeen years old, finishing his junior year of high school. When he was older he might seem more like a bulldog, but for now he was an enormous, big-footed puppy—friendly, sweet, and bumping into whatever was remotely near his path.

Reginald had been raised in Harlem in a home that defied the statistics: his no-nonsense mother exacted obedience from him and his five brothers and sisters in everything from the length and care of their fingernails to the status of their homework. And the Warners were the only family for blocks around with a father in the home. Reginald's dad worked for the New York transit system, and the scheduled comings and goings of buses and subway trains gave a grid, a backdrop of consistency, to the home.

Their spiritual structure came from the family's second home. Almost all day Sunday, and on Wednesday evenings and Friday nights, the entire Warner family was lined up, overflowing their worn pew at the Faith, Hope, and Love Missionary Baptist Church on the corner of Grady Avenue and Stokes Street.

The Warners had cultivated a fruitful life in Harlem's barren blocks by avoiding shades of gray about the temptations of modern society. Consequently, Reginald thought about life in terms of absolute right and wrong. He wasn't narrow; it was just that rules and structures had provided a bastion of protection for his family in a neighborhood where too many young people confused liberty with license. He had seen many friends pay the consequences of that confusion.

Given his mindset, it was not surprising that Reginald had developed an affinity for short-subject black-and-white documentaries. His teachers marveled at their young student's proficiency with a video camera. Despite his natural clumsiness, he had a deft ability to juxtapose visual images to communicate truths that were more than the sum of their parts. He had a way of capturing the realities and the unfulfilled potentials of urban life in the crosscutting of a few living portraits, a few simple words on a script.

Assisted by a grant that supplied news-making resources to the inner city, his teachers had encouraged Reginald in his documentaries, and eventually a three-part series had made its way to a local news affiliate, then to the network. This had resulted in Reginald winning a six-month internship at ABC News in New York and Washington, D.C. Only too glad to give wings to their precocious student, his teachers and principal had granted a special dispensation, and Reginald was now spending the last term of the school year learning the ropes of network news.

He was having an especially good time with the network staff in Washington, where ABC's weekend news broadcast originated. It was the first time he had traveled beyond New York, and he loved being in the capital city. He marveled at Washington's clean streets, its marble monuments, its manageable crisscross of important streets. And though its delis weren't up to New York standards, there were still plenty of places that made a mean steak-and-cheese sub. Reginald ate them two and three at a time.

24

"I DREAMED ABOUT my baby last night," Amy O'Neil said to Mary Seaton. It was a Saturday afternoon, and the two women were sitting on a park bench at the playground just a few blocks from Mary's home.

"Right after my abortion I used to dream about her all the time. It doesn't happen that often anymore, but I guess things lately have dredged up a lot of memories...

"I dreamed that the baby was tiny, about as big as a sparrow. I carried her in my pocket. I'd check on her every once in a while to make sure she was okay, but then it was like I was at a football game, and there were all these people in the stands, and then the stands started to cave in, and people were running against each other, pushing and shoving, and I was running, trying to get outside the stadium through this long, dark tunnel.

"In the tunnel I was terrified, but I couldn't run fast enough. My legs were like lead. But I got to a quiet place, and then I realized that I had forgotten to keep my hand on my pocket, and I looked, and my baby was gone.

"I panicked and started screaming, and no one would help me, and I was trying to run back into the stadium against this huge wall of people, and I couldn't get in and I couldn't find my baby. It was horrible."

Amy's blue eyes filled with tears, and Mary put her arm around her shoulder. "That sounds awful," she said, "but it was just a dream. God is taking care of your baby. She's safe with Him. You'll see her later."

It was at times like this that Mary realized how vulnerable Amy was. In some ways she seemed self-assured, at peace, despite all she had been through. In other ways, she seemed much younger than her years, prone to emotional mood swings that made her just a bit volatile.

Amy dabbed at her eyes, ineffectively, with the sleeve of her cotton sweater. "I know," she said. "It's just that sometimes late at night, or in nightmares, it seems so overwhelming. She was so little, so vulnerable, so helpless. And now everything is all upside down: This abortionist in Fargo gets shot, and the newspapers and the television and the police and everyone are acting like it's the crime of the century. I mean, it's awful. But what about the babies?

"I don't understand why they're cracking down so much on the pro-life movement. Don't they see who's at stake here—the babies who can't defend themselves?"

Mary rolled her eyes, shook her head, and focused on the playground. They had brought the children here to run off steam; she figured that maybe an hour of swinging, leaping, and sliding might begin to wear down the edge of their seemingly boundless energy. At home they had been bouncing off the walls, driving Daniel, herself, and anyone else who happened to visit their home slightly crazy.

"Abigail!" she shouted at her four-year-old daughter. "Give your brother a turn on the swing. You push him for a while. He doesn't know how to pump his legs yet."

Abigail looked up, waved, and leapt off the still-moving swing. "Sure, Mommy!" she shouted.

Wonder what she's plotting, Mary wondered. That's a little too cooperative.

She turned back toward Amy. "We just have to keep moving forward, carefully," she said. "The way the government is cracking down means we have to conduct ourselves as prudently as possible. It doesn't change our agenda, though."

Amy bent down to retie her tennis shoe. "Well, what is our agenda at this point?" she asked. "I feel like we're kind of in a holding pattern."

"Sometimes being in a holding pattern is the smartest thing you can do," said Mary. "We don't want to act rashly."

"But what are we going to do?" asked Amy. "Thousands of babies are being killed every day we wait. And the regeneration centers will be up and running soon. Aren't we going to do something? I heard Alex say something to Daniel about Gideon's Torch...is that the code name for something?"

Mary looked at Amy sharply, a bit surprised by all her questions. She had noticed, though, that Amy would sometimes swing just a bit between depression on one hand and excess energy on the other. Nothing major, but maybe she was a bit manic.

"I don't know," said Mary rather unconvincingly. "If we all knew everything there was to know these days, none of us would get anything else done. I have a family to raise; you have a job to do. We have to fulfill those responsibilities first. Our roles within the Network group are going to ebb and flow, depending on how we can best be useful for different tasks. We're not in charge of this thing; we're the foot soldiers. John Jenkins was on the Hill all week, gave out some articles to congressmen. That sort of thing is going on all the time. We just perform our duties when we get the orders from the commanding officers."

She said it all rather lightly, wincing to herself; her analogy sounded so sexist. Women doing what men assigned them to do. But it was true; they weren't in charge. Daniel and Alex and others were orchestrating the big plans. Especially the one that would be coming down next.

She watched Abigail pushing Mark on the swing, her small mouth set in a straight line.

"I think you know a lot more than you're telling me," Amy

said, a bit petulantly. "You're not just a foot soldier; you're married to the general. You've got to know what's going on! What about pillow talk and all that?"

Mary laughed, trying to steer away from the issue. "You wait until you've been married twelve years and have three children," she teased. "By the time our heads hit the pillow at night we are out, snoring like banshees."

Amy smiled, evidently deciding to pull herself into a better mood. "Remind me not to get old and gray and have three children, then," she said. "When I'm married, I'm going for *amour*. Surprises. Negligees. Keep the romance alive."

Mary sighed. "Great. You can be the Total Woman for your generation."

"Who's the Total Woman?" asked Amy.

"Never mind," said Mary. "She was before your time."

In the distance, Abigail swung her little brother too high and too far, and Mark sailed out of the swing into a weeping heap on the mulched playground surface. Mary could tell it was an angry cry rather than a pained or panicked one.

"I'll be right there," she shouted. "Abigail, you tell your brother that you're sorry!"

She turned back toward Amy. "Listen," she said. "If any operations come up, you'll know what you need to know when you need to know it. Until then, we'll all just stay at our posts and keep our mouths shut." She smiled to take the sting out of her statement, then ran toward Mark before Amy had a chance to respond.

25

A T ANY GIVEN moment, dozens of domestic, unmanned communications spacecraft gently orbit the earth like a ring of miniature moons 22,500 miles above the equator. Tin cans with wings, they serve as sophisticated shortstops, receiving the signals thrown to them on transponders that amplify and transmit the messages, then throwing them back to earth within a fraction of a second.

It's an impersonal process for the stuff of daily life: telephone conversations, bank transactions, financial and business information, and, of course, television programming—all broken down into digitalized bits of information, crammed together to save space in a process called multiplexing, and beamed into space.

Those signals take the form of electric and magnetic fields vibrating at right angles to each other at the same frequency, traveling at the speed of light. And anyone with the right tools—a transmitter and dish antennae—can create a satellite uplink, sending a message to the orbiting parking lot in space. One need only identify an empty transponder of the hundreds available, call one's recipient and have him turn his receiver dish to the right coordinates, and beam up the information. The transaction would take only seconds, and the satellite's owner would never know. And even if the unauthorized use was noticed, it would be difficult to locate the perpetrator: an uplink beam is extremely narrow, and a search plane with radio-monitoring equipment might take weeks to find it. By then the bootleggers would be long gone.

So using empty transponders for information uplinking is not particularly difficult. But sabotaging television programming is: in order to get a message out to a broad audience, one has to ensure that people are watching. That means bumping and replacing scheduled television programming.

THE METAL BIRD floating in the cold reaches of space, mechanically processing the signals from earth, was not subject to human passions, which was fortunate, for such passions abounded at the Washington headquarters of ABC News on DeSales Street, just around the corner from the heart of Connecticut Avenue and the Mayflower Hotel. According to the red digital numbers on the clock dominating the control room wall, it was 6:28:44 P.M., with the network news broadcast due to air at 6:30 P.M., EST. The air in underground Studio B and its adjacent control room sparked with electricity, primed to ignite at any moment.

In the studio, ABC weekend anchor Amanda Dawson sat in the swivel chair behind the large gray anchor desk on the set. Leaning against the walls were the backdrops for the sets for such programs as *Nightline*, as well as the wall-size photo of the Capitol dome used for remotes from Washington for New York's *Good Morning America*. But for this broadcast, the familiar newsroom backdrop was set up.

Dawson sipped coffee from a white Styrofoam cup, leaving huge red lipstick marks on its rim; through long practice, she managed not to smear her teeth in the process. She was already wired for sound, a microphone clipped to her lapel. A coil of clear thin cable snaked up her back and connected to an earpiece that linked her by audio to Hal Humsler, the executive producer in the control room. Before her lay the news script, timed to the second by a small army of writers, producers, and technicians.

A few feet away, out of camera range, the TelePrompTer scrolled down through the first report. On it, sentences were broken into three- and four-word fragments, the typewritten periods and other punctuation augmented by big, black-marker, hand-written additions to emphasize the potently stilted style that was the trademark of the anchor's delivery.

The lights on the set, automatically set by computer, were remarkably low, thanks to the sensitive Fuji boom cameras the network used. The lowered lights kept the heat down in the studio and also lowered the tension level on the set to some degree. Or so the technicians thought.

MEANWHILE, though the control room was almost dark—so the directors, producers, and assistants could better see the lighted computer displays and the forty-nine video monitors lining the walls—the tension level was anything but low.

The control room felt like something between the austere expertise of the space program's Mission Control and the escalating desperation of a party of people trapped together in a large freight elevator. It was built on two levels: a higher room, perhaps fifteen by twenty feet, separated from the lower level by sliding glass windows.

In the lower room, technicians orchestrated everything from sound, to dissolves between video images, to the graphic titles appearing on the screen. They could also, by means of the digitized D-2 machines and quick human sweat, call up standard video footage such as shots of the floor of the House of Representatives, should the producer call for such last-second augmentations to the newscast.

Down a step and out the door, past the red "on the air" light, was the entrance to the studio. And a few steps down the narrow hall from that was the submarinelike confines of Master Control, the brains of the whole operation, manned by two grizzled network veterans named Dutch and Mike. Mike ran audio; Dutch ran video.

Orange cables hung like intestines from the belly of the control panels stretching from floor to ceiling on both sides of the narrow rectangle. The two men, evidently immune to claustrophobia, sat side by side at a small desklike area extending from the middle of the long wall of panels. From there they monitored everything beaming up from the satellite dish at the top of the building on the uplink, determining frequencies, wattage, and other technical considerations.

During periods of bad weather or thick cloud cover, they blasted their signal up to the satellite at eighty-three watts, though normally they illuminated the bird at about seventy-five watts—what the techies called "full saturation." The satellite would take a hundred-watt hit, but such a strong signal normally wasn't necessary. From D.C.'s heading position—a near-semicircle from about twenty degrees above the terrain to twenty degrees in the opposite direction—there were fifty-four satellites in range, with between twenty-four and thirty-six transponders on each.

Dutch knew he could easily knock his competition off the air. All he would have to do would be uplink to the same coordinates, same transponder, as NBC or CBS. But the result would simply be competing signals—double illumination—and a lot of snow on viewers' screens. A gentlemen's agreement between the networks, not to mention a 1986 federal statute, kept that from happening. Dutch had no particular desire to mess with the other networks nor go to jail—particularly so near retirement.

ON THE forty-nine screens of the control room were transmissions of those rival networks, NBC, CBS, and CNN; the scrolling script of the TelePrompTer; various camera angles; the net return—the actual downlink of the news coming from New York to Washington via a fiber-optic line; video footage of the correspondents' taped reports; and, at this particular moment, closeup shots of Amanda Dawson's nostrils.

On a standard evening, the only live element of the news was the anchor's script-reading, usually about 230 seconds of the whole, or less than four minutes of air time. Commercial messages took more than six minutes of the broadcast. That left about seventeen minutes for the correspondents' reports, which were taped—usually perilously close to broadcast time—unless news was breaking even as the news was airing. In that case, a correspondent would wait at his or her site and do live interaction with the anchor, usually in the form of short questions and answers.

Though these live interchanges amounted to just seconds, they often caused problems and added to the tension level of the control room. Tonight, because writers were still gathering intelligence regarding Senate reaction to the president's proposed crime bill, the broadcast would have a short live tag at the end from Capitol Hill correspondent Rob Bickhert.

Typically the news was broadcast live for those on Eastern Standard and Central Standard Time, then the tape replayed later for Mountain and Pacific—unless there was breaking news, in which case the anchor remained on site to redo the broadcast·for the West. When that happened—like tonight, because of the crime bill—everyone had to stick around, and the network was contractually bound to provide dinner for the entire crew. For Reginald Warner, sitting in his usual spot on a stool in the back row of the control room, these were his favorite nights.

"A M A N D A ," said the executive producer into the microphone built into the control panel at his station.

Hal Humsler was a tall, thin, intense man in his late forties, his hairline receding and his sharp, hooked nose protruding. He habitually bobbed his head when he was angry, which was fairly often, particularly when he neglected to take his medication. Because of his beak, his bobs, his long, thin legs, and his rather widely spaced pale-blue eyes, some of the less respectful crew members called him the Blue Heron." But never to his face.

Hal had produced the weekend news for several years, and though deep down he enjoyed the work and the people, his habitual intensity usually got the best of him. *ABC World News* had held its number one spot for some years now, but the weekend post made Hal feel like he was on second string. Ratings couldn't help but decline on the weekends; that was a fact of life. Their advertising time sold for only $40,000 for a thirty-second spot, compared with as much as $75,000 for a comparable weekday slot. And he couldn't help but notice that their advertisers catered to the older segment of the population, the La–Z–Boy folks who stayed home on the weekends and watched the news, then settled in for the Saturday night lineup.

Just look at tonight's sponsor, he thought. The company that had paid more to get the billboard slot and their logo on screen near the top of the program, as well as the first commercial, was Attends. *Great*, thought Hal. *Diapers for adults.*

He scanned the program sheet in his hand. Typical. Here were Attends, Listerine, Centrum Silver, Dr. Scholl's, Efferdent, and Metamucil. It read like the pharmacy shelves at the home for seniors where his mother lived. *What I wouldn't give for a good condom ad on the weekend*, he thought.

But the commercials weren't as bad as the fact that real news just seemed to wait for the Monday-to-Friday shift before it happened. Earthquakes, hostage situations, assassinations—none of the good stuff ever happened on Hal's watch. Even those now-classic mesmerizing hours of live television, the celebrated O. J. Simpson white Bronco police chase on the freeways of L.A., had happened on a Friday. Hal kept waiting for a Saturday or Sunday disaster of some sort...anything to spike his ratings.

He bobbed his head and drummed his fingers on the desk where he sat, just in back of the glass window at the control desk. Before him was a complicated panel of switches and buttons, a video monitor, and a bank of sophisticated controls. His senior producer sat to his right, the timer/researcher to his left on a stool before a computer monitor crammed with files, a production manager and an operations manager to her left, and in the corner, a frazzled technician in front of a vertical video monitor and controls.

Behind them was a flat table manned by two technicians and a small flock of assistants who served as runners to the studio and the operations deck. Behind them were two interns: the kid from New York and a young girl from Florida.

As Hal spoke into his microphone, which fed into the clear coil snaking into the anchor's ear, Amanda Dawson continued to sip coffee, then rubbed her tongue over her gums and used a long red fingernail to floss between her two front teeth.

"Amanda!" he said again. Louder.

Oblivious, she laughed, apparently at something a lighting technician had said, and closed her eyes while a makeup person dabbed powder on her face.

"People!" said Hal to the crew in the control room in a measured, clenched tone, "Amanda cannot hear me. I cannot hear Amanda. We need to hear each other. We are going on the air in two minutes. DO SOMETHING!"

The sweating technician in the corner, with multiple cords coming out of his ears, began punching buttons on a side monitor.

"Amanda!" said Hal again. "Wave if you can hear me!"

Amanda looked up and waved, her lips moving. No sound came out.

Humsler took a deep breath and exhaled slowly, a relaxation technique his therapist had recommended. He turned to the frantic man in the corner, who was flipping buttons madly.

"We are halfway there," Hal said calmly, even as he snapped a pencil in two between the clenched fingers of his right hand. "It's nice that Amanda can hear me. But perhaps I need to point out that I also need to be able to hear Amanda, so I can direct this broadcast. Maybe I would not be so concerned if this did not happen rather often, LIKE EVERY SINGLE WEEKEND!"

His scream was cut short by Amanda's voice coming through his earpiece.

"All right," he said, as everyone exhaled together. "That's much better. Thank you. Why don't we do the news now?"

The technician in the corner popped a Rolaids in his mouth and kept hitting buttons.

"Thirty seconds," said someone in the lower control room.

Amanda took a last swig of coffee, put the cup behind her, straightened her blouse, and pulled on the sleeves of her jacket.

The control room population watched the clock. Then came the countdown...six, five, four, three, two, one...

"From ABC," the announcer intoned as the dramatic trademark music throbbed, "this is World News Saturday...here's Amanda Dawson."

"Good evening," she said, nodding crisply toward the camera. "With America's crime rate up 16 percent over a year ago, the president's long-awaited crime bill is at the forefront of focus in our nation's capital tonight.

"Though the president's plan has received the endorsement of many, conservatives and liberals alike, it must still overcome tough opposition on Capitol Hill.

"As ABC's Rob Bickhert reports, Senator Byron Langer is leading a movement of those who believe the president's plan may lead to infringements of individual liberty. Some have even suggested that the plan is motivated by retribution against a very few and endangers classic American civil rights for the many."

"Twenty-nine seconds," said the assistant in the control room.

As the monitors switched to Bickhert's report from Capitol Hill, taped only fifteen minutes before air time, Dawson reached behind her for more coffee.

Hal spoke into his mouthpiece. "Amanda, your hair is sticking up a little on the right side." She reached up and patted the right side of her head. "No," he said. "Sorry. I meant your left side. My right; your left." She smoothed the other side as the makeup person rushed to assist. "Great," said Hal.

Bickhert's report ran for two minutes. Amanda wet her teeth as the studio cameras rolled, at 2:39, into the broadcast for the second story, an augmentation to the first.

"The president's desire to get tough on crime echoes his campaign promises to restore order to American society. But President Griswold's actual plan is a far cry from the niceties espoused by Candidate Griswold last fall. David Bawman reports."

"Eighteen seconds," said the control room as Bawman's taped piece, a commentary on the disparity between the then-candidate's remarks and the now-president's actions, began to roll.

As it did, talk in the control room turned to the consuming issue of sandwiches. An operations person in the corner hung up from booking additional satellite time for the extra West Coast broadcast and punched the automatic-dial button for Arnie's Deli.

"Sandwiches for fifty," she said. "Just like last time...chicken salad, tuna salad, ham, turkey, roast beef, on mixed breads. Then do about a dozen vegetable and cheese combos on pita...and six steak-and-cheese subs."

Reginald Warner grinned in the semi-darkness of the back row.

"Amanda," said Hal into his microphone. "We're running about four seconds over now. Just speed up the thing about the vice president slightly."

Amanda nodded just as Bawman's taped report ended and they went live again. A square stock photo of the vice president floated in the air just above her left shoulder. If she were to lean too far toward it, it would block her face.

"Vice President Stuart Potter is recovering from surgery at Bethesda Naval Hospital," she said briskly. "Potter tore his Achilles tendon yesterday morning while playing basketball at the House of Representatives gym. He underwent more than an hour of surgery...and is expected to be released from the hospital tomorrow."

"She picked it up perfectly," said the assistant in the control room. "We're right at five minutes for bumper one."

"Coming up," said Amanda, "the fired head of the American Civil Liberties Union meets the press...a southern town rebuilds itself a year after a tornado reduced its dreams to rubble... and later in this broadcast a high school athlete shoots for the Olympics...from her wheelchair."

The announcer's smooth voice took over as the ABC music came up. "World News Saturday," he said, "brought to you by Attends."

There was a general groan in the control room. "Attends again?" said an assistant director.

Meanwhile, Hal and the senior producer were conferring on the phone with a writer. "We're going to a live feed from Bickhert at the end of the broadcast. Amanda will need to ask him a question. Something like, 'What's happening now on the Hill, Rob, with this unusual Saturday session?' Then Bickhert needs to respond with something tentative, like, 'Well, Amanda, Senator Langer is caucusing, even as we speak, with aides and colleagues in the Senate. Their plan of action is not yet determined. But one thing is certain: Langer and like-minded legislators are not going to let the president off easily on this one.'

"Something like that, okay? Tentative, but still teasing the fact that there's going to be a war on this issue. Just write it up; we'll have a runner there in a minute."

Hal looked at the clock. The Listerine commercial was just finishing. They were due up again at 6:40. The only other live element in the broadcast was the sports report: Jack Tyler live from New York before he introed the tape on the high school basketball player...not a big thing.

Tyler was usually reliable, though the chemistry between him and Amanda was absolutely nil, so Hal kept the interplay between the two pretty minimal. All Amanda had to say was, "Now to New York...here's Jack Tyler...good evening, Jack." No joshing back and forth.

And then the live thing at the end, maybe fifty-five seconds of wrap-up between Amanda and Rob Bickhert. Shouldn't be a problem. He wasn't going to run any accompanying video, just Bickhert standing up live at the Capitol. And Bickhert was a pro.

Hal's stomach was settling down. He breathed in and out a few times. It looked like it was going to be okay. For tonight.

26

Wednesday, April 22

EMILY MET Paul Clarkson at her private elevator in the Justice Department building.

"Hate to ask you to go with me, Paul, but these guys on the Hill...well, I need my interpreter. I think Langer was right."

"I'm happy to do it," Paul said. "Crime bill, huh?"

The elevator descended into the underground parking area, and they walked to the waiting Lincoln town car. As Paul swung himself into the car, laying his canes on the floor, Emily pulled papers from her case.

"Rayburn Building," she told the driver, who already had explicit typed instructions. The car accelerated up the ramp onto Tenth Street into blinding sheets of spring rain.

"This statement, Paul, I should have given it to you sooner, but I've been pressed. Here, check it. I don't want to sound high-handed to the Democrats. Congressman Peyton can be a bear."

"Sure can. Let me see it." Paul took Emily's statement and immediately underlined two sentences at the beginning. Then his eyes skimmed down the pages of the document. "Here, on page four, I'd leave this out altogether."

Paul suggested several more changes, and Emily nodded appreciatively. Then the limousine stopped on Constitution Avenue, at least a block from the jammed intersection of Constitution, Pennsylvania, and Third Street at the base of Capitol Hill. One by one, cars were timidly navigating through the huge wading pools that had collected at the corner.

"Frizzell's done it to us again." Emily shook her head and arched her eyebrows in a look of resignation.

"Not another Chicago," Paul frowned.

"No, no. But get this: He goes to the White House last night for the dinner for President Landos...then at one this morning, who calls me, wakes me out of the beginnings of a very sound sleep?" Emily didn't wait for an answer. "The president...'Uh, hope I didn't wake you, Emily.'" She lowered her voice several octaves in a rather remarkable imitation of Whitney Griswold. "'Didn't disturb you, I hope,' he says. 'Oh, no, Mr. President,' I said, rubbing my eyes and slapping my cheeks."

Paul chuckled and nodded sympathetically.

"He's in the Lincoln sitting room, he tells me, and just thinking about the terrorists. Frizzell just happened to mention in passing at the state dinner that something big was about to pop. Could be very serious. 'What are we doing?' he asks. Must be prepared—and all that. Hopes we'll do whatever it takes: more agents, task force, surveillance."

"That Frizzell is a piece of work," Paul said, stroking his chin. "He's going to get his budget one way or another."

"You don't take advantage of a social event like that. The man is power mad, if you ask me." Emily sighed.

"The old Plato quote is right," said Paul. "'Only those who don't seek power are fit to hold it.'"

"Problem is, if we applied that criterion, Washington would be a ghost town," Emily replied. The limousine inched forward, its front wheels entering surging water up to the hubcaps. The rain was pelting hard on the roof.

"But the fact remains, Paul, we've got to do more. The president is right, we can't afford any more political heat on this. People are screaming out there."

"We've got over twelve hundred men and women assigned right now," Paul said. "It's overreaction."

"The president wants it."

"He's the boss," Paul said, but shook his head.

"And he asked if we are doing enough with wiretaps and surveillance—wants us to use the conspiracy laws to widen the net. I mean to head off any new incidents. Just legitimate security."

"Frizzell really got to him good." Paul stared straight ahead as the rain began pounding even harder, driven by a rising wind.

"Robbie and the others are pushing on the president too. They say he can't get hurt, can't get tough enough to suit the public."

Paul smiled.

"Okay, what is it? Your old comrades that you're worried about?"

"No, Emily, my job is to enforce the law. My personal views aren't at issue here," he said. "You know that. But when public passions dictate like this, we're headed for trouble. 'Get tough, hang them, just leave me and mine alone.' That's what people want."

"Well, that's our job, isn't it? To secure our citizens' right to live peaceful lives?"

"Yes, sure. But you can't do it with naked force. You need the willingness of people to be governed. That's what self-government is all about. The founders called it republican virtue, the idea of duty and responsibility."

"Save that for the philosophy class, Paul. Right now we've got a real-life problem."

"No, Emily. *This* is the real-life problem. People want to do their own thing. They see liberty as the right to do what they want, but it isn't. Liberty is the right to do what you *ought* to do. So now we have chaos because we have no moral consensus—which, I might add, has always been supplied by our religious beliefs." He paused, then added, "It was Aquinas who once said that 'without a moral consensus, there can be no law.'"

"Very trenchant."

"Yeah—and very true. In a free society that honors virtue, you have 270 million policemen; in a society that mocks virtue, you can't hire enough policemen."

"Maybe," she shook her head. "But we have the rule of law in this country that protects us. For heaven's sake, Paul, you need to sit in on one of my classes at Harvard."

"What's the rule of law? Is it what these people on the Hill say it is...?"

Emily feigned a cough and groaned.

"...Or does it rest on truth—truth that is true because it is true, not because someone votes it in?"

Emily looked out the window.

"You've got to see where this is leading us, Emily. Griswold never will. There are only two restraints on human behavior. One in here," he pointed to his heart, "the inner restraint of conscience. Moral. And the other out there," he pointed to the street, "the outer restraint of force. Police. The less you have of the inner, the more you need of the outer. Take away people's Bibles and you will replace them with bayonets."

Emily's eyes met Paul's. She saw his passion and intensity and realized that he had really thought these issues through; she, for all her legal training, had never thought a lot about them.

"And remember that Levitz column? He was right. When the restraints of conscience break down, when there is chaos, people welcome force. They'll do what every society in history has done. They'll trade in their liberties—oh, just a little at first, then everything."

Emily shook her head, mostly amused. "That's not about to happen here, Paul. You know that."

"Yes it is, Emily. We could put on wiretaps, call out the troops to guard clinics and neighborhoods—the president would love that idea—we could arrest suspects, intercept mail—all to enforce the law—and they'd line those streets." He pointed out toward Independence Avenue as the limousine slowly climbed the House side of Capitol Hill.

"They'll line those streets waving their flags, cheering...then we can put on our armbands and take them to the camps."

"Paul, you're being melodramatic," she laughed.

"Emily, I am associate attorney general, I'm loyal, I'll do my job. But I want you to think about where things can lead us."

"Think? How much time do I have to think in this job?" Emily said dryly as the limousine pulled into the wet circular drive on South Capitol Street.

"Emily." Paul put his hand on her arm, which startled her momentarily. "The issue here is truth. If truth retreats, tyranny advances. A democracy cannot survive if the law has no other authority than force."

Emily stared at him a moment then again sought to dismiss the strange conversation. The driver held an umbrella over the open door. Then she grinned, relenting. "Well, Paul, let's go give these honorable representatives some lessons in truth."

Flashbulbs popped as Emily was escorted through the main door. Paul followed slowly, getting very wet.

27

R EGINALD WARNER stood at a phone booth on Connecticut Avenue, just outside the Metro stop. During the week
the area was clogged with commuters, but late on Sunday afternoon there weren't many people around.

He dialed the number he'd been given. Area code 212...New
York. He wondered how his parents were. He missed his family.
They would appreciate what he was doing; it was like he was a spy
for the underground railroad or something...

Bill Waters answered on the third ring. "Yes?"

"The truck has been activated," Reginald said. "There's been a
disturbance at Lorton prison. It's a hostage situation. They've
called for the SNG truck. It should be there in forty-five minutes.
They'll be doing a live feed on the news tonight."

"Right," said Bill. "Thanks, Reginald."

Waters hung up and looked at the briefcase on the desk before
him. Inside it was the tape...or, actually, just a copy. The original
he'd made had been taken to D.C. three weeks ago and was now
on its way to Lorton prison in a white satellite truck.

He smiled. God *had* provided a way to get His message out.

5:09 P.M.

Agent Thomas Pilch at the FBI command center picked up the special phone line set aside for incoming information from assets in the field.

This is Orange 2," said the woman's voice. "I expect to be able to confirm soon. It is New York. Something big is coming down. More later."

6:12 P.M.

Finally, thought Hal Humsler as he sat at his control room post, his feet drumming the carpet under the desk. The air around him was electric with activity, but Hal felt less than his usual stress. He hadn't even taken his medication today, but he had an unusual sense of well-being. Finally, a break from the humdrum Mickey Mouse exchanges with New York! Finally, a Washington-based crisis—on the weekend!

If there is a God, thank You! he thought. A voice in his head was saying that it probably wasn't really much, just a prison riot at Lorton; maybe it would just be arbitrated down to nothing in a few hours. *But at least they have hostages*, he thought. None injured yet, but there was potential for tension and drama. Finally! Some breaking news!

6:20 P.M.

At the small house behind Doggett's Garage, in spite of the warm spring evening, the windows were closed and the blinds tightly drawn. Inside, Daniel Seaton and his friends had gathered. Some sat on the old plaid sofas, sipping coffee; some paced the room. A television set, sitting on an old brown TV cart on wheels, was on, its volume low.

"I can't believe they're really gonna pull this off," said Alex, the tension evident in his voice.

Daniel, too, was wound tight. He sat on the sofa, tapping his fingers on the water-ringed surface of the wooden coffee table. He felt a mixture of things, his stomach in a knot and his mouth dry. It reminded him of a long-ago debut in a college theater production...or his feeling just before he stepped out in front of the church the day he and Mary were married. He thought of the scramble in his brain just before his oral comprehensives in seminary. And he remembered how he had felt on that long-ago day when he had heard that Ronald Reagan had just been shot outside the Washington Hilton.

It was an odd pastiche of memories, but they all shared the stomach-churning sense of significance that he felt inside.

As he looked around the room, he could tell the others were feeling something similar. Lance stood in the corner, occasionally peering out the window blinds, calm but at full military alert. Alex paced, stopping periodically to stretch his legs, the way he did before a big race. John Jenkins sat quietly on the sofa, cracking his knuckles. Mark Demmers guzzled coffee from a thermos.

The television droned on. The local ABC affiliate was winding down its Washington-area newscast before the national news came on at 6:30. The sportscaster finished his golf coverage. Next was the entertainment critic's review of a new action film starring an aging Arnold Schwarzenegger teamed with a child actor from Singapore. Then they were teasing reports on the Lorton situation: update to come on *ABC World News Sunday*, next.

6:25 P.M.

Up in the family quarters at 1600 Pennsylvania Avenue, Anne Griswold was relaxing with her daughter. It had been an unusually quiet Sunday, and the beautiful spring afternoon had coaxed her from her usual preoccupation with schedule and protocol. An hour ago she and Elizabeth had walked the White House grounds, looking for purple violets in the lush emerald grass.

Though Secret Service agents had trailed behind and she knew there was a video camera in every tree, she had felt a sense of freedom. Perhaps it was the scent of wisteria blossoms in the air, an elusive link to springtimes past, before life had gotten so complicated.

Elizabeth had had three friends over for Sunday lunch; she was fitting in more and more with her classmates at the Cathedral

School. And, she confided to her mother, her friend Molly—one of the girls who had come for lunch—had told her that her brother thought Elizabeth was beautiful. Half the girls in her class had crushes on Molly's brother. Anne had smiled, vaguely remembering that feeling from a hundred years ago when she was eleven going on sixteen.

And now, best of all, they had the evening off. No official events, and tomorrow seemed far away. So she and Elizabeth were sitting on the tufted yellow sofa before the mammoth entertainment center in the White House family quarters. They would dine later, hopefully with Whitney. He was in a meeting, something about the Middle East. But for now Anne sipped a glass of Chardonnay, Elizabeth a Coke; they shared a bowl of popcorn while they watched the evening news together.

6:30 P.M.

Hal Humsler tapped his pencil on the panel before him as he watched the control room clock tick down the seconds.

Amanda was wired, in more ways than one, her revised script before her and the TelePrompTer poised with her opening lines.

"Six, five, four, three, two, one," chanted the assistant. It was 6:30:00.

ANNE GRISWOLD brought the sound up on the remote control. The familiar theme music sounded. "From ABC," said the announcer, "this is World News Sunday...here's Amanda Dawson."

Elizabeth pointed at the anchor. She dreamed sometimes about going into broadcasting. "I like her suit, don't you, Mom? It's such a pretty color."

Anne nodded, smiling, and popped a cluster of popcorn into her mouth.

"Good evening," said Amanda Dawson, looking more serious than usual. "An inmate uprising rages this evening at the District of Columbia's Lorton prison complex, located in the Virginia suburbs. A group of prisoners has taken control of part of the institution.

"The inmates are holding an unknown number of guards hostage and are armed with weapons that were evidently smuggled into the facility. They have not yet issued any demands. For more on this tense situation, we turn to ABC's Jim Warren."

"TOO LONG," said the assistant in the control room. "We're already running over, right out of the gate."

It was 6:30:34. In Master Control, Dutch punched a button and switched the uplink feed loop to the SNG satellite truck remote at the prison.

Standing fifteen feet from the white truck at Lorton, correspondent Jim Warren took his customary breath before the camera's red light went on and he would begin his report on the hostage situation.

Inside the truck, at precisely the same moment, the operator flipped a switch and popped the altered NIH videotape into the uplink drive. The standard encryptions the network used as a protection against such sabotage posed no problem: a week before, Reginald Warner had gotten hold of a digitized decoder card. Effusive with questions about just how the signals were scrambled and unscrambled, he had engaged in a conversation so innocent and enthusiastic that the operations person who had explained it all to him had felt gratified that she could help such a nice young intern learn the ropes.

Outside the truck, oblivious, Jim Warren continued his report as the cameraman filmed.

BACK AT THE television studio, no one had noticed when Reginald Warner left his customary observation spot on the back row at precisely 6:30:30 and wandered into Master Control. Part of his internship involved lots of question-asking, and Dutch and Mike usually welcomed his visits. Tonight things were hot because of the live feed at the top of the broadcast, but that didn't affect Dutch and Mike as much as it did the producers and directors. Especially the Blue Heron, who, according to reports from the control room, was flying high.

So Dutch and Mike smiled when the gregarious young intern came into their submarine carrying a tray balanced with steaming 16-ounce cups of coffee, then frowned a little as he negotiated his huge bulk in the narrow confines of Master Control, then shouted in horror as Reggie tangled himself up in some of the cables, twisted, and crashed on top of them, knocking them both to the floor.

The scalding coffee flew up in the air, suspended in space for a horrifying moment, then splashed over the central part of the control panel, as well as on Dutch, Mike, and Reggie himself. They all yelled in pain; what they were feeling would turn out to be first-degree burns, according to the emergency room medics who would see them later. Some of the coffee even splashed up on Dutch's glasses; with his eyes squeezed shut in panic, it would take a few moments for him to realize that they weren't burned. Meanwhile, the three were a shouting, tangled mass of arms and legs. It took a full minute for Reggie to untangle himself and get his 275 pounds off the other two.

Reggie's maneuver didn't divert Master Control for the full four and a half minutes. But it was a start.

ANNE GRISWOLD stared at the television screen. There was a moment of snow and static, and she wondered if the transmission had somehow been affected by the situation at Lorton. Things must certainly be in upheaval there.

Then a picture came into focus. But it wasn't the ABC correspondent, and it wasn't the anchor desk in the studio. It was something entirely different. It looked like an operating room scene.

Then Anne slowly realized what she was looking at. A patient was lying on a gurney, draped in white sheets. It was a woman. Her legs were straddled wide, feet resting in stirrups, as if she was going to deliver a baby. The camera was pointed directly into her cervix, which was fully dilated.

Anne froze, her wine glass halfway to her lips.

There was a pause, and then the sound—the voice of an off-camera narrator—caught up with the picture.

"...Candidates for this elective procedure are placed on the operating table in a sterile, yet pleasantly nonclinical setting. Nurses stand by to reassure the patient.

"The surgical assistant places an ultrasound probe on the patient's abdomen and scans the fetus, locating the lower extremities.

"Once these are found, the surgeon introduces a large grasping forceps through the vaginal and cervical canals into the corpus of the uterus.

"Based on the image on the sonogram screen, the surgeon is able to open the instrument's jaws to firmly grasp a lower extremity. The surgeon then provides firm traction to the instrument and pulls the extremity into the vagina...

"At this point, the right-handed surgeon slides the fingers of the left hand along the back of the fetus and 'hooks' the shoulders of the fetus with the index and ring fingers (palm down). Next the surgeon slides the tip of the middle finger along the spine toward the skull while applying traction to the shoulders and lower extremities.

"While maintaining this tension, the surgeon takes a pair of blunt curved Metzenbaum scissors in the right hand. The surgeon carefully advances the tip, curved down, along the spine and under his or her middle finger until he or she feels it contact the base of the skull under the tip of the middle finger.

"The surgeon then forces the scissors into the base of the skull. Having safely entered the skull, the surgeon spreads the scissors to enlarge the opening.

"The surgeon removes the scissors and introduces a suction catheter into this hole and evacuates the skull contents. With the catheter still in place, the surgeon applies traction to the fetus, removing it completely from the patient."

The film had been edited to mesh clips from the actual procedure with the narrator's description. Anne saw the fetus's tiny body positioned in the birth canal, its thin leg grasped firmly by the surgeon's forceps like an animal caught in a trap.

She remembered how it had felt as Elizabeth and Robert had

slipped out of her, how even then their little bodies had had tone and resistance. She had touched Elizabeth's tiny fingers just after she was born; she had gently pushed her little arm, and her daughter had pushed back. Anne had been so proud. Even a few seconds after birth, her daughter was a fighter.

This fetus appeared to be a fighter as well. She seemed to resist a little as the gloved hands of the doctor positioned her, hanging out from the birth canal. The doctor held the scissors, then jabbed them through the base of the soft skull. The fetus jerked, then hung still. The tube sucked out the brain. Then the tiny limp body slid from its mother, broken and bloody in the jaws of the doctor's forceps.

Next to her, Elizabeth broke out in a huge sob, her hands over her eyes.

Anne jumped. She had forgotten her daughter was right there. She put down her wine glass, pulled Elizabeth toward her, put her daughter's head in her lap, and turned her away from the television screen. She rubbed Elizabeth's head gently but continued to watch, mesmerized.

THE CONTROL ROOM was in a state of suspension. Dutch and Mike hadn't shut down the sabotaged uplink; Hal wasn't sure where they were or what was going on in Master Control down the hall. New York was on the phone, the producer there screaming that something was wrong with their switching system and they couldn't bump the broadcast off the air.

"Get it off, get if off, GET IT OFF!" New York shouted into Hal's ear.

Maybe that was when he snapped.

He was still feeling great, with that crisp-edged clarity that often came on the manic side of his mood swings, enhanced by the fact that he hadn't taken his lithium. He felt a delectable sense of power: New York was begging him to do something. He also had an idea beginning to form on the fringes of his brain.

As the video progressed, the control room was eerily silent. People's mouths were open, everyone frozen in position, looking back and forth from the video to Hal. Only the senior producer was shouting at him, echoing New York: "Get it off, get it off, get it off!"

In that second, it all came together for Hal. The first commercial break wasn't due until almost five minutes into the broadcast, and this thing, whatever it was, might well be the best thing that had happened to weekend ratings in years. He looked at the switchboard. All the phone lines were lit up.

He looked over to the upper row of video monitors: NBC and CBS and CNN were still blathering on with their regular scheduled programming. Whoever was doing this, whatever it was, the saboteurs had chosen ABC. On the weekend. On his watch. It was the chance of a lifetime!

He flipped the microphone switch so everyone in the control room, the studio, and down the hall in Master Control—whatever in the world was going on there—could hear him.

"LEAVE IT ON!" he shouted, his eyes bugging out of his head. "I don't know what it is, but leave it on. At least until the first commercial break! Trust me, people. If anyone goes down on this one, it'll be me."

ANNE GRISWOLD continued to watch in disbelief as the grisly video dissolved to a new scene.

A man faced the camera, his face in total shadow. As he began to speak, it was clear that his voice had been electronically altered.

"What you have just witnessed is not footage recovered from the files of Nazi Germany," he said.

"This *actual video* is currently in use in medical schools across America, equipping doctors to suck the brains from live, unborn babies in ever-expanding numbers. *This* is what the coming regeneration centers are all about.

"Americans are being told that the regeneration centers are the great new hope for cures for cancer and AIDS. That is a lie. The regeneration centers are nothing but killing centers.

"Mothers who once aborted their children at ten or twelve weeks are now being encouraged—and even paid—to wait until the third trimester of their pregnancy, when the unborn baby, if born, could live outside the womb.

"Instead, these babies are tortured to death in the most gruesome manner possible, as you have just seen.

"These deeds of darkness must be exposed to the light. Americans must not allow their so-called freedom of choice to open the door to the greatest holocaust in human history.

"We must reject the regeneration centers and turn back this bloody tide before it is too late. Surely Americans can look within themselves to a core of common decency and stop this grisly killing!"

The television screen went snowy again, and the next thing Anne saw was a bewildered Jim Warren, limply holding the microphone in his hand. He was still standing there as the scene flipped back to the studio in Washington. Amanda Dawson was pale and strained, a strand of hair hanging over her forehead as she prepared to deal with the utterly unscripted challenge before her.

"Ladies and gentlemen," she began, but Anne Griswold had heard enough. She hit the mute button on the remote and, still holding Elizabeth, picked up the phone on the end table.

"Nancy," she said when her assistant answered, "get me the president." Her voice shook with anger and shock. "I don't care what meeting he's in. Just get him for me. Now."

28

A CCORDING TO old World War II movies, the White House situation room is a hubbub of activity, with fleets and armies arrayed on huge charts, and screens with troop movements descending from the ceiling. But the National Security Command Center, known as the situation room, is, in fact, an ordinary cluster of offices in the west wing basement, entered through a small door just across from the White House senior staff dining room.

Normally, the White House was quiet on Sunday. Tonight, however, it was abuzz with senior staff in meetings and the press room on dull alert. The president, General Maloney, and the secretaries of defense and state were gathered in the situation room, along with assorted aides and note takers, though the latter were superfluous since everything in the room was automatically taped.

The president had just taken the secretary of defense's recommendation to order a task force consisting of the *JFK*, escorted by six frigates and one cruiser, along with two LPHs, amphibious ships loaded with a regiment of marines, to steam toward the Israeli coast. The move might enflame hotheads on both sides, but

Griswold felt the risk was worth it. Today's bombing violence could make it necessary to evacuate American citizens in the Middle East in a hurry.

"All right," Griswold said, the decision made, "what's next on the list?"

The secretary of state was starting to suggest a personal call to the Israeli prime minister when Captain Slattery walked into the room, moved quietly around behind the president's chair, and passed him a single sheet of paper folded over. Griswold shook his head, then Slattery leaned over and whispered in his ear.

"Excuse me, please," Griswold said to the group, but looked annoyed as he took a portable phone Slattery handed him. He cupped his hand over the mouthpiece as the others around the table engaged in obvious conversation to give him some privacy.

Anne sounded nearly hysterical. He had never heard her like this.

"Now calm down, Anne. I can't help what's on the evening news. I've just sent an attack force to the coast of Lebanon."

"Well, tell them to turn around and come back here to ABC!" Anne shrieked. "Don't you hear me? It was a live abortion!"

"I'll get someone to call the network, dear."

"No! No! You don't understand! Elizabeth is so traumatized she can't even talk."

"What do you mean?" he asked. "Elizabeth saw this?"

Suddenly the president's face flushed with anger as he held his hand over the receiver and told Slattery, "Get O'Keefe on the phone right now."

BERNIE O'KEEFE stood in his mahogany-paneled office wearing only a starched white shirt and blue-and-white-striped boxer shorts, fumbling with the suspender buttons of his tuxedo trousers. He was supposed to host the president's box at the Kennedy Center that night, a black-tie symphony benefit for AIDS research. He was already running late for the dinner before the concert, an event featuring a blue-ribbon bevy of Hollywood stars and producers.

The loud persistent buzzer on the president's direct line went off just as the final thread holding the button holding the suspenders to the trousers popped. With a string of expletives he hurled the trousers onto the tufted corner sofa and headed for the phone.

"Yes sir."

Griswold was on a fast boil. A live abortion on the evening news...his daughter traumatized...get troops moving...take over the studio.

"Let me get this straight, sir." Bernie was seated now at his small conference table, scribbling across a yellow pad with his maroon Mont Blanc pen.

Caroline Atwater, who had seen the broadcast in the press room, had run up the main west wing stairway and down the long corridor to Bernie's reception room, arriving only moments after he picked up the president's call. Bernie's secretary, Barbara Shannon, a plump, gray-haired woman who had taken care of her boss through every conceivable crisis for more than a decade, tried to fend her off.

"Please, Ms. Atwater, don't go in," she said, jumping up from her desk. "Mr. O'Keefe is on with the president...see the red light is on...and besides—"

"That's exactly who I want, the president." Caroline threw her head back. "I'm sorry, move aside."

She swung the door open, and there was Bernie O'Keefe sitting at a small conference table, his shirt draped open exposing a hairy chest and rumpled layers of flesh, his white legs punctuated by boxer shorts and dark socks.

Caroline shrieked. Bernie held his hand up, pointed at the door, and shouted, "Shut that!"

"No, no, sir, I wasn't saying 'shut that' to you, Mr. President. It was to Caroline...Yes, sir, I understand, yes, sir." Bernie was nodding, waving off both Caroline, who was somewhere between shock and revulsion, and Barbara, who had tried to get to the door before Caroline.

Bernie hung up, darted to the sofa, and threw his pants to

Barbara. "Can you get that button back on for me?" he asked in a lather. "National emergency!"

"What? The button?" asked Barbara.

"No!" Bernie shouted at Caroline. "Terrorists on television!" He grabbed his jacket and draped it around his middle.

Barbara took the pants and went off looking for the sewing kit she kept in her desk for such emergencies.

"Come in, Caroline; maybe you can tell me what's going on," said Bernie. "The president didn't see it, but he's out of control. Have you called the network?"

"I can't get through," she said. "Their phone lines are jammed, and their correspondents downstairs are as much in the dark as we are."

"That's hard to believe," said Bernie drily. "Sit down while I call the attorney general. Would you like a drink?"

The press secretary glanced over her shoulder. "Desperately," she said. "What do you have?"

Bernie pointed at the credenza. "And make me one too—a double on the rocks."

Emily Gineen hadn't seen the broadcast, so Bernie recounted as much as he knew. It sounded even less believable than when the president had told him about it, so he took refuge in talking tough.

"Look, Emily, the president of the United States is in orbit. The first lady is in shock. What is this, some kind of banana republic where rebels take over the country by seizing radio and TV stations? We give you $10 billion a year, armies of FBI agents, and somebody can hijack a television network and you don't even know it? Maybe I should call the Defense Department and get the army out."

He bulldozed ahead, ignoring her questions, mostly because he had no answers himself.

"Now, I suggest you get back to the department and get your butt in gear. Call me as soon as you do, if that's not too much to ask. The president would like to know what's going on. He'd also like to get a SWAT team to the ABC studios on DeSales Street."

Bernie felt better after he'd vented for a moment.

"Get on it, Emily! I don't mean to sound harsh, but this is absolutely unbelievable. Thank you. Yes. Yes."

Bernie dropped the receiver hard in the cradle, muttered some more expletives, and took a large gulp from the glass Caroline had set on his desk.

"Welcome to Nicaragua," he sighed.

At that very moment Sharon Holmland, Caroline's special assistant, fresh out of Columbia University Journalism School, arrived breathless in the outer office with urgent news.

Barbara, pants and needle in hand, shrugged and opened the office door for her. Sharon froze at the sight of a half-naked Bernie O'Keefe, jacket wrapped around his ample waist, sipping scotch, and her boss sitting across from him, drink in her hand as well.

"ABC has just announced that it appears that someone hijacked their satellite transmission," Sharon spoke to her boss, trying not to look at the president's counsel.

"Wonderful!" Bernie exclaimed. "We'll call out the air force, not the army." Then he turned to Caroline. "You schedule a press briefing right away. We've got to get a presidential statement and avert a panic here."

ACTUAL EVENTS did little to avert a panic. Two vans filled with an FBI anti-terrorist team roared to the network's studio, where ambulances were already on the curb. The agents, wearing black jackets and carrying H&K MP5s and sawed-off shotguns, stormed the building, which was already in utter chaos.

Griswold left the situation room and the fast-breaking developments in the Middle East to return to the family quarters in the mansion. He was sitting with one arm around Anne, the other gently stroking Elizabeth's hair, when Bernie arrived. The two men adjourned to the Lincoln sitting room and talked to the attorney general, now in her office. The president also called Frizzell, who gave him the most thorough report he'd received so far while resisting the temptation to say "I told you so."

"Bernie," Griswold said somberly, "this is close to anarchy. An assault upon the established order that no responsible government can tolerate. We must toughen up my statement."

Robbie, who had appeared out of the woodwork, had already drafted something stronger.

Caroline Atwater announced to the White House press corps that there would be a special 8:30 briefing so she could read a statement from the president. The networks would carry it live—"providing," Griswold muttered to Bernie, "they can keep control of their own satellites!"

The phone lines were jammed. Statements cascaded from Capitol Hill with senators and representatives calling for congressional hearings, demands for Griswold to act, scathing denunciations of anti-abortion terrorists and the "religious bigots who spawned them," and one hapless Pennsylvania congressman who demanded the air force "shoot down" the offending satellite.

Platoons of young marines in battle dress, M-16s in their laps, sat in the Marine barracks at Eighth and I Southeast awaiting a command. At Fayetteville, North Carolina, the eightieth battalion of the Eighty-second Airborne were put on standby. Somewhere in the jumbled first moments of the crisis, O'Keefe had called the deputy secretary of defense, asking that units be put on alert. No one had bothered to call them off when it was discovered that there hadn't been an attack by terrorists after all.

"LADIES AND GENTLEMEN, please." Caroline Atwater stood before the blue screen with the drawing of the White House behind it. The red lights indicated the networks were on live, but in the back of the room the buzz continued.

"Please," she intoned pleadingly. "Before I read the president's statement, let me simply explain what we know at this point."

She then referred to an ABC press release from corporate headquarters in New York, explaining that the evening news, like all programming, was transmitted to a preassigned target frequency received by a satellite leased to the network; the signal was in turn transmitted back to receiving units on the ground across the country which in turn transmitted them either by transmitters or by cable to individual receivers. No one had yet determined how, but it appeared that someone had displaced the regular uplink and replaced it with the abortion video.

Atwater then explained the actions Griswold had ordered for Justice, the FBI, and other investigative arms of the government.

"The president is committed," she put emphasis on every word, "to exposing and bringing to justice those responsible for this act of piracy."

"'I deplore this act of terrorism,'" she read, "'which offends the sensibilities of every law-abiding, decent citizen in this land. It is an outrageous invasion of our privacy to bring such an offensive, grotesque scene into our living rooms.

"'I know what it means: My own daughter was deeply wounded emotionally. This is a direct attack on the authority and legitimacy of the American government, no less seditious than a physical assault upon our elected leaders or institutions.

"'It is, in short, insurrection, which will not be tolerated. This government will act swiftly and decisively, of that the American people can rest assured.'"

When the press secretary finished reading Griswold's statement, the room erupted, several dozen journalists shouting at her at once.

Caroline sputtered for a moment; then Bernie O'Keefe walked over from the doorway, took her gently by the arm, and led her off the platform and back to her office. The networks were then forced to cut away to their own studios, where their anchors gave their interpretations of this profoundly unsettling assault on the collective national psyche.

29

BERNIE O'KEEFE passionately hated his buzzer alarm, but it was the only thing that really roused him. He either slept right through the clock radio's music or news reports, or else he hit the snooze bar and went back to sleep. But the horrible shrill ring of the old windup alarm always got him. Now he knocked over two magazines and an empty glass to get to it: 6:30 A.M. after a long, surreal night.

He rubbed his eyes and raised himself on one elbow. What he could see—and it was all still blurred—looked terrible, reminiscent of his room at Yale where there was always total disorder, clothes strewn everywhere, a big towel draped over the dresser top. And his head throbbed horribly.

Not that he had the usual excuse. He'd been in the Lincoln sitting room all evening with the president, who'd offered nothing stronger than decaf. So he'd had only a couple in the office and one big one before going to bed.

His legs felt heavy as he steered them toward the bathroom.

The forties are cruel, he thought, staring into the mirror. Sagging jowls, puffy sacs under each eye, the right one slightly bloodshot. He still thought of himself as the kid at the top of the class, son of a construction worker who had made it to the White House, always the youngest in any group of peers and surely the smartest. He didn't look it today.

Bernie splashed cold water on his face and ran his hands through his auburn hair. He needed a haircut. When Marilyn was here she nagged about such things, but now his hair, like everything else, was out of control. Actually, though, he liked it longer; it reminded him of his courtroom days.

Now, that was fun, he thought. There was nothing like standing there matching wits with your opposing counsel, like two gladiators going into combat, and only one could survive. He'd almost always won, and even when he didn't, he was in charge. It was his show. He missed it.

TWENTY MINUTES later Bernie was shaved, showered, dressed, and in the kitchen washing down his aspirin and handful of vitamins with a large glass of orange juice. The coffee was brewing, the beans freshly ground and the water slowly dripping through. The stronger the better.

He stared out of the kitchen window at the bricked-in courtyard at the rear of the house. The sun was still low, the yard still cast in long, deep shadows. When they had looked at the house, Bernie had imagined a little oriental garden and patio furniture, maybe with a trellis full of vines along the wall of the carriage house behind.

But all he saw today were two patches of green, with unruly grass sprouting out in corners of the yard. The bricked pathways were uninviting, covered with green moss. And the kitchen, as he looked around, seemed no more inviting. Empty bottles—dead soldiers, Bernie called them—filled a brown grocery bag in the corner, an empty peanut butter jar and mounds of crumbs on the countertop, and a sink piled with dirty dishes. Good thing the maid came tomorrow.

All at once he missed Marilyn and the kids and the big open lawns of their Wellesley home. He and Marilyn had had their share of difficulties, both of them with explosive tempers, but the house was always neat and full of cheerful noises with kids running in and out. Often at night, in years past anyway, he and Marilyn would linger over the kitchen table and talk about the kids and school and his cases. Bernie would have his Dewars and maybe a hunk of cheese and some grapes, Marilyn a glass of white wine.

That was all before the politics, which Marilyn detested. Also, though she never said it in so many words, Bernie knew she resented Griswold. She thought he used people, especially her husband. Bernie knew she was right.

She still said she'd be moving down when the kids were out of school in June, but Bernie knew about that too. She wouldn't. And he really couldn't blame her. There was nothing for her here.

Life moves on, doesn't it? You can't go back; it never works. He sighed and poured his coffee, black and steaming. He took great gulps, rolling the hot liquid down his throat. He loved the sensation of that first strong cup in the morning, almost as much as he loved that first tinkling glass of Dewars in the evening.

Bernie cleared a space on the cluttered kitchen table and spread out the *Washington Post.* The headlines screamed: "Anti-abortionists Hijack Network." He gulped more coffee. His head throbbed. "Public Outraged" was the smaller headline over a background piece by the *Post's* national political editor.

"Pro-choice Leaders Demand Griswold Act," was the second lead. O'Keefe read fast: The heads of six national organizations, including Act-Up, NOW, and Planned Parenthood, were demanding greatly expanded federal efforts. "Muslim terrorists have been deported," argued Jade Worthy of NOW. "Why shouldn't these equally dangerous individuals be locked away for good where they can do no harm?"

The newspaper confirmed what Bernie already knew: his agenda for the next few weeks. He would be chasing a bunch of wackos, putting out statements, putting out fires, calming the president, writing legal opinions, studying polls—and all for what? Had these people really thought they would change anyone's mind?

He flipped quickly to the back of the A section to see if

Levitz's column would be in today's edition. Yes, there it was. He must have written it late last night in order to get it in.

He's Washington's conscience, thought Bernie. *Though that's a contradiction in terms.*

Last night anti-abortion extremists set back their own cause by an act of terrorism. Now they have not just committed murder, as in Fargo, nor merely attacked the rule of law, but assaulted the very means by which what the founders called domestic tranquility is sustained in our nation.

Strange paragraph construction, thought Bernie. Levitz must have written quickly.

Like it or not, television is the one instrument that provides national cohesion. In earlier days, Americans met in town halls for political discourse; today our town hall is in everyone's living room. Television has become the lifeline of the late 20th century community. It is the tie that binds us together.

"Scary thought," Bernie muttered.

Free societies cannot survive without free civil discourse. Only with the open exchange of ideas can we form shared values and assumptions about life—what philosophers call the moral consensus.

The extremists who stole last night's broadcast stole free discourse as well, attempting, one supposes, to achieve ends they believe good by evil means. They would do well to heed Solomon's words: "He who pursues evil will bring about his own death."

"To pursue evil is to bring about one's own death." Bernie repeated the words to himself, then heard his driver rapping on the front door. His limo had arrived.

JUST A FEW MILES to the west in Spring Valley, Emily Gineen crisscrossed her spacious kitchen, grabbing milk from the refrigerator, hauling boxes of cereal from cupboards, boiling eggs on the stove, and anxiously staring at the coffeepot. Each time she passed the table, she would stop for a spoonful of strawberry yogurt, her own breakfast staple.

Before she had time to finish the kids' breakfast or hers, her limo pulled in the drive. She kissed each of the children as she headed to the front door.

"Mom!" said Kathy, pulling her back for a moment and giving her a strong hug. "Have a great day. Hang in there!" Emily hugged her back fiercely. *So sweet*, she thought. Both of them knew she was under the gun. She picked up the *Post* and poured herself a big mug of coffee to go. Rosemary would see that the kids ate their breakfast and got off to school.

As she passed the dining room window, Emily was struck by the incredible beauty: explosions of pink and vivid red and white from the banks of azaleas. It was a glorious day. She was glad she could soak that in; somehow she knew she would need it later in the day to offset all the ugliness awaiting her.

There were, after all, no precedents to draw upon; no attorney general before her had had to face an issue quite like this because no terrorist group had ever hijacked a television network.

In the back of her limousine, Emily spread open the newspaper. She scanned the front page and stopped on the background piece headlined "Public Outraged." The *Post's* national political editor had an uncanny sense for what people were thinking.

> No event in recent memory has created such instant indignation. Americans take in stride the garbage strikes, poor postal service, power outages, tornadoes, yes, even wars, but the message today is clear: don't fool with our television.
>
> That was what pollsters discovered in an evening survey of 320 homes. It will no doubt disappoint the hijackers to learn that far less outrage was directed at what was shown on the film than at those who interfered with the broadcast. According to recent surveys, television is the prime source of news for 70 percent of Americans. . . .

Emily chuckled at the irony. Paul really had a point the other day when he said that Americans just wanted to be left alone to live their contented lives, and they expected government to provide that privacy. No great passion over great issues, no raging national debate over policies or the nation's future. Just let me get my six-pack and watch the tube, get my kids into a halfway decent school, and be able to walk around the block without getting mugged.

Maybe that's all we should shoot for, Emily thought for a moment.

Then she turned to Ira Levitz. Most of the column scolded the terrorists who had hijacked the network. But near the end, the pundit called for moderation in the government's response. The closing paragraph, in fact, sounded like Paul Clarkson himself might have written it.

> As president, Whitney Griswold must also be a moral leader. For only he can break this ugly downward spiral of repression and violence.
>
> To be sure, Mr. President, enforce the law. But at the same time rebuild our nation's sense of decency and civility. Our moral values are in tatters.
>
> When people feel they cannot speak, their frustration spills over into violence. The president must choose: He can seek to restore free and open moral discourse in which those with minority views are not driven to the margins—or he can continue the current crackdown and watch as the violence continues.
>
> The president would do well to heed the words from the prophet of old: "Come, let us reason together."

Nice phrase, Emily thought. But columnists make it all sound so easy. They don't have to make it happen. They just sit at their word processors and pontificate. Still, a good point.

THREE LEVELS beneath the White House is the old World War II bomb shelter, a subterranean labyrinth of gray hallways punctuated by rooms with triple-thick steel doors, used for miscellaneous secure and secretive purposes, including the dental chair used for filling presidential cavities.

Whitney Griswold had chosen one of the larger rooms to

house his elaborate physical fitness equipment, primarily an antique rowing machine equipped with an ergometer. The year he graduated from Brown, the university was replacing its ancient, one-ton, cast-iron machines with sleek, lighter, and cheaper ones. Griswold, sentimentally attached to the monstrous old machine and the heroic memories it evoked, had bought one.

After his election, the navy had lugged the thing to the White House basement, and at 6:30 every morning, Griswold would strap his feet in, adjust himself on the seat, and grip an oar handle.

The oar, on the starboard side because it was the same position he had rowed, was cut off halfway and connected to a large, mechanical pivot, which in turn, drove a cast-iron flywheel two feet in diameter and weighing eight hundred pounds. There was a crude brake to create resistance, consisting of a strap wound around the wheel and attached to several two-pound weights called stones—a reference, oarsmen always said, to the age in which the machine was invented.

The object was to set the flywheel counter to zero and then row as hard as possible for six minutes. One's score was measured by the number of rotations clocked in the wheel. It took incredible fortitude to overcome the intense physical pain, but Griswold had learned, as champions do, how to best the system.

With exactly the right cadence and an extra push, the brake strap would begin to bounce at its resonant frequency, thus releasing some of the load. The only problem was that the noise from the weights clanging as they swung wildly was ear-splitting, so much so that the more senior Secret Service agents always managed to avoid the early morning detail, laying it off on junior agents.

But for Griswold, it was pure exhilaration. Sweat streaming down his face and soaking his shirt, breathing hard but perfectly synchronized with his legs and arms, the man and the machine became one. He could almost feel the shell gliding through the rippling waters of the Narragansett River. Pain would give way to euphoria as he reached his full stroke—and then there was a deliriously joyful sound of iron and steel colliding as the stones flew through the air.

The old machine was important to Griswold. It reminded him of his own golden days, affirmed his belief that some things in life had permanence, stability, connection to the past. And the challenge was fresh every day.

"Crew is a sport of the mind," he frequently told his young agents, who stood silently cursing their ringing ears. It was a challenge to the will to ignore pain and persevere to the finish line. Bernie, the old football player, used to kid Griswold that crew, the sport of the select few, was the only one in which the participants moved backwards, since they always sat facing the rear of the boat.

The doctors had told the president that he should taper off because eventually the strain would be too great and he couldn't stop all at once. But Griswold was not only disciplined, he was compulsive.

After his exercise, he would take alternating hot and cold showers, wrap himself in a terry-cloth robe, and use his private elevator to go to the second floor quarters. There Juan had his suits and shirts and shoes arranged so that Griswold could dress quickly and be in the hall in time to kiss Elizabeth good-bye as she was escorted to school. By 7:15, not a moment later, Griswold was at his place at the end of the table in the family dining room for his breakfast of orange juice, yogurt, and coffee.

Other than weekends at Camp David and his two trips out of Washington, this was the first morning of the nearly four months into his presidency that Griswold had missed the routine.

Elizabeth who, complaining of horrible dreams, had come in to sleep with her mother during the night, then awoke early, still visibly disturbed over the television broadcast. Anne had summoned him early, and instead of his morning routine, he sat with Elizabeth in the small breakfast room while she ate.

He tried to get her talking about school and soccer, but Elizabeth's thoughts were elsewhere.

"Daddy, was that film real?" she asked. "I mean real people, not actors?"

"I think so, dear. I haven't seen it. But remember, this is a medical film. It is meant for doctors to help them do their work better. It has to be very realistic."

"It was totally gross. Blood and everything."

"Any operation would be very sickening to watch, dear. But that's what doctors and nurses must do to save lives and make people well. But you should just put it out of your mind."

"Daddy, do babies feel it when they're killed?"

Griswold felt his heart pound and that heavy sensation come into his stomach that he always felt after a fight with Anne or when some very bad thing happened. "No, no, dear, and they really aren't babies. They are not born. They aren't persons. So you needn't even think of that."

"It looked like a baby."

"I know, dear, but the age of consciousness comes much later. Like you—what's the earliest you can remember anything?"

"Hmmm." Elizabeth thought for a moment. "I think when I fell and cut my forehead and you took me to the hospital. I remember lying on the table."

"Of course. And you were three, almost four at the time. So these babies...er...I mean fetuses, they are not babies. They don't know or feel anything."

"But Daddy, this baby wiggled around. It jerked. The doctor stuck a pair of scissors in its head." Elizabeth shook her head, put her spoon down, and pushed her cereal away. "It was horrible."

She looked up. "Since you haven't seen it, why don't you watch it, Dad?"

"Well, I've got a very busy schedule. A meeting at 9:00 this morning with all of my advisors to discuss the film, in fact."

"Promise me you'll watch it so you can tell me what you think."

Griswold hesitated, but knew he couldn't avoid it. "Yes, dear, I promise."

"Cross your heart."

Griswold made a cross over his heart, and though it wasn't easy, forced a big grin. "All right, Elizabeth, get your books. And remember, guard that goal in the soccer game today."

"Yes, Daddy." Elizabeth started toward the hall, then turned.

"And you remember, you watch that film. You promised."

More tired than if he had rowed six minutes, the president went to the breakfast table where Juan had arranged in a neat pile beside his place the *Washington Post*, the *Wall Street Journal* and two folders, a red-leather binder marked "Intelligence Summary—For the President's Eyes Only," which contained overnight dispatches compiled by General Maloney, and a black binder containing the president's news summary. The red folder, as always, was on top, the first thing the president read.

This morning he fished down, picked out the *Post*, scanned the front page, and then turned to Ira Levitz.

30

J. WHITNEY GRISWOLD considered tardiness the moral equivalent of slothfulness, one of the seven deadly sins. It was 9:04. Robbie, Emily, and Frizzell were seated in front of the president's desk. Griswold was reaching for the phone when Bernie O'Keefe, slightly out of breath, came through the side door.

The president's half smile and voice evidenced his irritation. "I'm happy, Counselor, that you could grace us with your presence."

"Sorry, Mr. President, a very important call, getting the latest intelligence."

In truth, Bernie had been talking with Marilyn, who had called him at his desk about their eldest son's failing grades, and she was mad at him, too, when he had to cut the conversation short to get to the president's office. This had been a double loser.

"You know, obviously, why I have called this meeting," Griswold began somberly. "We must in the next hour assess what has happened, review our options, and I will also expect your recommendations. We must be decisive.

"I should warn you that the National Security Council is meeting now, so we may be interrupted by an emergency—like the outbreak of war in Israel—which some of us might perhaps find a welcome diversion from the rather bizarre matter at hand."

The group chuckled.

"Emily, you get us started here. What are the grounds for criminal action? I don't remember reading any cases in law school about theft of a network's air time." Griswold leaned back, resting his elbow on the chair arm and propping his fist under his chin.

"No, Mr. President, it is somewhat novel. But my people have found the pertinent statute." She looked at her notes. "It is 18 USC 1367, the Electronic Communications Privacy Act passed in 1986. Twenty-five-thousand-dollar fine and a ten-year sentence."

Griswold leaned forward and made a note as his lawyer's mind kicked in. "Any precedents?"

"Yes sir," Emily grinned. "You'll love this one. In 1987 a technician at the Christian Broadcasting Network was apparently sitting in the control room with nothing to do. *Lassie* or *The Waltons* or some other rerun was going out of CBN. So he started scanning satellite transmissions and came across a hard-core pornographic movie being beamed in on the Playboy channel. He sat down at a scripting machine and made a few biblical graphics; you know, terse little messages like 'Repent, the kingdom of God is at hand.' Then he beamed them up from CBN's transmitter and superimposed the words over the Playboy broadcast..."

Bernie let out a huge laugh. "Can you imagine? In all those homes and bars, people watching a couple go at it on the screen and then all of the sudden there's writing on the wall screaming, REPENT! Aaauuuggghhh! Probably had people on their knees or rubbing their eyes all over America!" Bernie slammed his hand on the chair arm, almost doubling over.

Even Griswold couldn't contain his laughter. Then he asked, "What did they do to him?"

"Jury convicted, $1,000 fine, and 150 hours community service." Emily looked again at her notes.

"Not enough." Griswold shook his head. "No deterrent there. Do you suppose that's what happened in this case?"

"We can only speculate," Emily replied. "But the FCC tells us that a hijack like this is relatively simple to do. There are three hundred earth stations that can transmit and no way to tell where the signal comes from. In this case, it was probably from a mobile satellite van. You can even rent them for a few grand."

"Clever," Griswold said thoughtfully. "But too easy, too dangerous."

He stared at Emily. "If we don't come down hard and fast, every nut in America will be doing the same thing. We've got to prosecute to the hilt."

"Yes, sir," Emily nodded.

Then he turned to Frizzell. "And you, Director, you find those who did this."

Frizzell could hardly wait to answer. Information from assets had pretty well pinpointed those responsible, he told the president. Arrests could be made quickly, probably within twenty-four hours.

"Good! Go to it!" Griswold leaned forward. "Okay, Robbie, my speech to the nation will be tonight. I'd like to wait until tomorrow, after the arrests, but the country needs to hear from me quickly. I'll say that we know the perpetrators—"

"No, sir, mustn't tip them off," Frizzell interjected.

"And be sure to always say 'alleged perpetrators,'" Emily added.

"Yes, yes, of course. Be careful of the language. You watch that, Bernie."

"Right. We'll just say that 'the FBI is diligently pursuing the investigation and we expect swift action. Justice will be done.' Are we agreed?"

Everyone nodded.

"So much for that," Griswold said. "But we must now examine some broader questions. Robbie has given me a very disturbing report." He held up a sheet of paper. "You explain, Robbie."

Harvey Robbins's power had increased dramatically in the first four months of the Griswold presidency. Viewed initially as a cold-blooded campaign technician and administrator, he had slowly but surely gained influence over policy. Whoever controls the president's schedule, Robbins had discovered, controlled the issues agenda.

But Robbins was also winning sometimes grudging admiration for his computerlike mind and shrewd political insights, which included mastery of poll data and demographic research. A polling service headed by J. D. Sindberg reached six hundred homes between 6:00 P.M and midnight every night so that issues and attitudes could be tracked day to day. The service was located in Sioux Falls, South Dakota, but Robbie had a direct line installed in his office so that he could often listen in as interviewers were questioning respondents. He'd learned that he could sense the intensity of issues simply from the tone of voice of the people being polled.

"The events last evening," Robbins began, "precipitated a dramatic change in public opinion. For example, the percentage responding in the affirmative to the question, 'Is America on the right track?' dropped from 57 percent to 44 percent; the percentage giving approval to the president, from 59 percent to 51 percent. That is the greatest single movement in one night that J. D. remembers since the market crash in '87. And the voices are angry, impatient."

"For heaven's sake, one interruption in the network news for five minutes wouldn't do that," O'Keefe, never a great fan of the pollsters, scoffed.

"It sure has, Bernie. Maybe in some ways it was a minor incident, but it had a big symbolic effect. It's like the last straw—proof that life is really out of control, that this is an ugly society, that people can't feel secure even watching television in their own living rooms."

Robbie adjusted his chair, turning to face the others as well as the president. He squinted, creating deep furrows in his brow, then gestured toward them with his pen. "This presidency is at a grave crisis point. All our backup data shows the public wants someone to take charge. Last night's broadcast and the Fargo shooting are being seen, quite correctly, as a direct assault on the authority of this office. The American people will watch very closely, and what they decide now may stick with us for the rest of this term."

"What are you saying, Robbie?" Emily asked. "We'll move

immediately. Director Frizzell here says we can have arrests in twenty-four hours; the president will be on TV tonight."

"Not enough." Robbie stood and paced to the left side of the president's desk, adjusting his rep silk tie and looking very stern. The sun, reflecting in from the french doors leading to the rose garden behind him, silhouetted his short blond hair.

Bernie knew Robbins well enough to know his agenda: He was testing his new-found authority, and he was also plowing the dirty political soil so the president could be the statesman. Bernie'd seen the one-two routine before.

"Not enough," Robbie repeated. "We have to break this movement. Finish it off. The people want this president to take charge. They want order."

Just what Paul was talking about in the car, Emily thought to herself. *We must keep all this in perspective.*

"All right, Bernie, Emily, you tell me what steps we can take under existing statutes to bring this violence to a halt." Griswold pointed to each one. Robbie had set him up perfectly.

Bernie liked feeling like a lawyer again. He traced the statutes in case law, beginning with *NOW v. Scheidler,* in which the Supreme Court had held that anti-abortion protestors, even if they had no economic motive, could be considered "racketeers" under RICO, the tough laws enacted to break organized crime. The anti-abortion movement as a whole could be considered a conspiracy, and anyone could be drawn in if they had any connection to a "racketeer influenced corrupt organization," as the New Covenant Church in Pompano, Florida, discovered when its church building was confiscated because it had allowed Operation Rescue workers to meet there before rescues. And under FACE, the Freedom of Access to Clinic Entrances Act, any interference with abortion facilities was a federal offense.

"Tie those in with federal civil rights statutes," Emily interjected, "or the new anti-terrorist laws. You, Mr. President, just have to make a finding as to who *is* a terrorist. Then we can do anything we want. We can spread the net to anyone who has ever been involved in an abortion protest. We can go as far as you want legally. As a law professor, I question whether these statutes go too far. As attorney general, I have to say they are the law, and I'll enforce them."

"Good. We'll start to crack down on the known activists first. Agreed?" The president looked around. O'Keefe seemed troubled, but Frizzell was enthusiastic.

"Absolutely, sir." Emily nodded. Robbie grinned.

"I'll announce this evening," the president said to them, "that I am directing the attorney general to treat as conspirators all those who have aided, abetted, or assisted *in any way* those whose conduct violates the law, that grand juries will be impaneled in each major city, and that we will prosecute to the fullest extent of the law. We must be very clear in our intentions. Do you agree?"

"Yes sir," said Emily. "I understand your point. We'll draft the language carefully."

"All right, but be clear."

Bernie sat silently. *Just because a law can be enforced,* he was thinking, *doesn't mean it's prudent to do so.* As a litigator, he had always counseled clients to be sure they knew what they were getting into before they rushed into the courtroom. Once in, he would say, it's hard to get out; and it can be bloody. His advice was always to try to settle first.

"Mr. President, remember that letter Martin Masterson faxed you on election night?" Bernie asked.

"Of course I do."

"Well, do you suppose we could invite him in, along with Senator Langer and a few others? See if we couldn't get the responsible elements on our side. *Reason together.* Maybe build a little consensus before we get too far down this road. It's just a thought."

Robbie didn't give the president a chance to answer. "No one has heard two peeps from Masterson since the election. Langer... well, I wouldn't trust him if he came in here on his hands and knees carrying an olive branch between his teeth.

"Come on now, Bernie." Robbie's eyes were darting. "These

are the 'responsible elements'—is that what you call them? They've called us 'baby killers' and worse. Their speeches are what caused the crazies to go off the edge. No, it's too late for that."

"I like to be a peacemaker, Bernie, but Robbie's right," said Griswold. "It would be a sign of weakness. I've shown restraint. My door has been open. But now the train is out of the station, and they've missed it."

The president turned to Frizzell. "Director Frizzell, I've read how the FBI destroyed the Klan in the '60s. Glorious chapter in your bureau's history. Wiretaps, infiltration, some heavy-handed stuff—but it brought an end to that evil. It's unbelievable, but less than half a century ago we were lynching African Americans in this country." Griswold shook his head.

"I want you to go after these people in the same way," he said. "It may sound extreme, but these people are extreme. Wiretaps, infiltration, whatever it takes—but you go after the leaders. Hard!" He startled Emily by smashing a fist in his open palm.

Frizzell sounded gleeful. "Yes, sir, we will."

Bernie remembered what Levitz had said in the paper that morning: *The extremists . . . attempting . . . to achieve ends they believe good by evil means . . . would do well to heed Solomon's words: "He who pursues evil will bring about his own death." . . . The president can seek to restore free and open moral discourse . . . or he can continue the current crackdown and watch as the violence continues.*

"Now, Robbie has another recommendation we need to consider," the president continued, turning to his chief of staff. "Go ahead, Robbie."

Oh, boy, Bernie thought. *Old Robbie set this one up. He's been lobbying for weeks.*

For years, Robbins said, the mayor of the District of Columbia had urgently requested authority to call out the National Guard to help patrol some of the gang-ridden combat zones in the capital. The White House had always said no. But the truth was that crime was out of control in D. C.: eight hundred homicides a year, 60 percent of the African-American males between nineteen and thirty-one in jail or on parole, and the statistics were getting worse by the day.

People had debated why it was getting worse. Some said it was part of a general moral breakdown; this administration believed it was the lack of educational and economic opportunities and that its empowerment programs in time would bring change. But for now there was a crisis. The police couldn't handle it. Just two thousand Guardsmen could bring an immediate sense of order.

"But what's that got to do with this TV business or the abortion controversy?" Emily asked, looking perplexed.

"The breakdown of order. All part of the same general problem. It's time to act, and if we do it all at once," Robbie replied, "the public will be overjoyed."

"I may include a declaration of national emergency in my statement tonight," said Griswold. "Robbie has come up with a statute that I think covers us on national emergency powers, one that was passed in 1976. What would you think of that, Emily?"

"I want to reflect on it, Mr. President, study the law." She frowned. "It's an extraordinary measure to take, and, of course, that statute—I happen to be familiar with it—closely regulates what you can do. For one thing, Congress can overrule you."

"Well, there are plenty of good precedents." Griswold had obviously thought about this. "Nixon activated the reserves to move the mail during the 1971 postal strike—and there was even emergency detention of anti-war protestors. Bush brought in the army during the L.A. riots. No, I think the constitutional power under Article II is clearly there—even without a statute."

"I'll need to look carefully, sir. It's a major step."

"But let's look what it would do," Griswold said. "It would send an important signal and give us all some added authority. And we should give the guardsmen police powers. Let them make arrests," he continued. "It may be our best chance to finally break the back of street violence—at least here in D.C. where we are responsible."

"We have to do something. I'll certainly agree with that, sir," Emily said. "The statistics are horrible. It's a vicious cycle, really. There's no law and order in the big cities, so criminals know they can do whatever they want. And I'll admit, doing this would send a signal that we mean business."

"Even if Congress raises a howl—and they will—think what we're saying: The president has this situation in hand." Griswold set his jaw, ready for battle.

"Let Congress scream." Robbie rubbed his hands together. "Who do you suppose the public will back in that fight? Ha! Joe Sixpack wants safe streets—and he doesn't want some crazies invading his television set. No, we need to draw the line."

What is it about this room? Bernie wondered, looking around at the flags behind the president, the exquisite rose garden through the french doors, the rug with the Great Seal of the United States in the center. *People come in here with good, clear, level heads and within a few months they become raving powermongers.* He should, he realized, raise all the warning flags, but so far no one had talked of breaking the law, and the political analysis was unassailable. Bernie decided he'd talk later with Griswold.

"Let's remember that those who have preceded me in this chair have had to take extraordinary measures in times of great national crisis," said Griswold, standing to indicate the meeting was over. He scooped up two folders, one red and one gray.

"Roosevelt faced the problem, of course, of the Japanese Americans—citizens put in detention camps without trials. What he did sounds repugnant now, but at the time it was the only thing he could do. Lincoln suspended habeas corpus. It was a measure of their greatness that they acted to avert what imperiled the republic," Griswold said. "What we're facing is no less a challenge than what those men faced. We have to act accordingly. Are we agreed?"

"Yes sir." Frizzell was first, then Emily, who said, "I agree with your analysis, sir. I'm satisfied. We have no choice."

Griswold looked at Bernie. "And you?"

"Yes, I think so, sir. I want to work on the language of your speech very carefully, however—and look at the statutes."

"Good, good." Griswold picked up his folders and headed for the situation room.

THE PRESIDENT spent the next two hours closeted with his National Security advisors. Meanwhile, Bernie informed Caroline Atwater of the president's plan, and she called each of the network's liaison executives, requesting that five minutes be cleared at 8:00 P.M., EST, for a major presidential announcement. Bernie then contacted the president's top speech writer, Jack Carmichael, who assigned two of his assistants to begin drafting the president's statement.

Emily returned to the Justice Department, where she asked the Office of Legal Council for draft language for an executive order declaring a state of emergency. Impossible to do adequate research by 5:00 P.M., she was told, to which she replied, do it anyway; it's for the president. Then she summoned Paul to her office.

By 3:00, they had looked over the first drafts and returned them for rework. Then an idea flashed across Emily's mind. She leaned back in her chair and looked at Paul. "What would you think if the FBI were to break the Fargo case today? I mean, make the busts and let Griswold announce it tonight?"

"Terrific, Emily. Of course, the president and his palace guard would be euphoric. But the bureau's not ready—unless you know something I don't. I mean, they've got some good leads to that one woman—the one in Chicago—but according to Frizzell's latest report it's not a sure thing."

"Let's see." Emily grinned as she reached for her phone. In a matter of seconds Frizzell was on the line.

"Director, I've been thinking ... this report you gave us last week about the Fargo suspect in Chicago ... we just might be able to do something for the well-being of this nation."

Emily swung her chair around and explained what an arrest

might mean, how Griswold could announce it, with the FBI moving in even as the president spoke.

"Sounds good, General." Frizzell would like nothing better than to be part of Griswold's address to the nation. "But there are just a few problems. We haven't nailed this one down yet."

"Like what?" Emily said as Paul quickly slipped the bureau's latest summary under her nose. "Says here your lab got some positive tests, physical description fits to a T, travel records establish that Ms. Pignato was in the area at the time, and we've got an informant's report that she boasted about having done a 'big job.' What more do you need?"

"We have no motive and no connection to the movement." Frizzell did not sound his exuberant self.

"There must be something. People like this don't come in from Mars." Emily was surprised at her own enthusiasm. It was a real role reversal. Here she was, the thoughtful and deliberate attorney general pushing the trigger-happy FBI director.

"We've looked, believe me. Not even a scrap of literature lying around. No testimony, nothing, nada."

"Remember John Salvi? I mean he had no ties to the movement, but they found some pro-life stuff in his apartment."

"We've looked. Nothing."

"You've searched thoroughly?"

"Yes, ma'am."

"With a warrant I suppose? No, forget I asked."

"We have our ways."

"Well, perhaps your agents could *find* some literature when they visit the suspect again?"

There was a pause.

"If I understand you, the answer is yes," said Frizzell, "but there are great risks you may want to consider."

"I was a prosecutor, you may recall, Mr. Director," Emily responded coldly.

"Yes ma'am. There are some other things that trouble us however. She's only twenty-five but has a rap sheet as long as your arm. Spent two years at Dwight in the Illinois system. Numbers stuff. Lots of family ties."

"Good, good. The record helps...casts suspicion."

"No, not really," he said. "Because in this case it just doesn't fit the anti–abortion zealot profile."

"Neither did Salvi. He was nuts, but he did it."

"You're the attorney general. If you tell me to do it, I will. But we have her under surveillance. Eventually she'll slip and lead us to others. Then we will have a conspiracy. If we move now, we may never know. It could compromise the case."

Emily shook her head and bit her lip. Griswold needed a break; she could just see him announcing it on television with just a touch of a smile. But compromise the case? She knew better. What in the world had gotten into her?

"In addition, General, I think we're going to bust the New York gang in the morning. That's great timing. The president says tonight we're going to get them, and in the morning, we do."

"That's good, Director. You just sit tight. I want to think about this, and I'll call you."

"We'll need time to set it up."

"I know, I know." She hung up.

Looking down, Emily could feel Paul's stare. He was smart enough to figure out from her end of the conversation what was going on. She was angry at herself; she had never suggested anything remotely like planting evidence before, and now Frizzell had one on her. She had gotten carried away.

"So, it's not such a good idea?" Paul broke the silence and smiled, giving her a reprieve.

"Well," she said, feeling uncharacteristically awkward, "we won't complicate the president's task tonight. It'll be hard enough as it is. And we'll continue investigating to find the connection. We know there has to be a conspiracy. Break the case prematurely and we could lose it."

"Right," said Paul. "Let's just get through tonight. We'll talk later."

"Let's get to work then," Emily agreed, visibly relieved.

ANTHONY FRIZZELL leaned back in his big chair and placed a call at 7:20.

"Bernie," he said. "Tell the president that we'll make the bust in the morning. Everything's going fine. And tell him to stick it to 'em in his speech tonight."

He paused, relishing the moment. On the issues that mattered, he knew a lot more than Bernie O'Keefe.

"Bernie," he continued. "Griswold may take some heat for what's coming down, especially from some of our favorite friends on the Hill. The whole Langer crowd. If you run into any trouble, feel free to give me a call."

He heard a quick, deep, impatient sigh from Bernie.

"Well, I know you need to go," said Frizzell. "But just remember, I've got some information on tap that may be of help to you in the near future."

Frizzell hung up, leaned back with his hands behind his head, and smiled at the picture of J. Edgar Hoover.

AT 7:45, the president was escorted into the small dining room adjacent to the Oval Office, where a cosmetician wielded pancake makeup and powders. As she swabbed away at his face, he joked, "It's like getting a corpse ready for showing, isn't it?" It was an old line, but she laughed.

At 7:55, Griswold took his seat behind the desk with a thin sheaf of papers before him. The Oval Office looked like a Hollywood set. Two cameras on large rollers were positioned in front of the desk, with lights beaming down from both sides. Behind the cameras were reflector lights illuminating the ceiling and bathing the room in a chill white light, which caused the walls to sparkle. Thick black cables snaked across the rug and into junction boxes in the hall. There was a backup system for everything and a generator on standby in the basement.

Behind the president were the two traditional stands of flags and a table between them with a bust of Lincoln prominently on one side. On the other side was a picture of the Griswold family in a burled walnut frame and a picture of Griswold at the helm of his sailboat. Robbie had wanted that photo moved, on the grounds that only one-quarter of 1 percent of the American people sailed; but Griswold was adamant. There was also a framed letter he had received during the campaign from an eight-year-old dying of cancer. "Heal our nation," proclaimed the crayoned letters.

At 8:01, the red light flashed on camera number one, directly in front of the president's desk, and the senior technician nodded and pointed at Griswold, who cleared his throat and began.

"My fellow Americans. This is the first time since I took the oath as your president nearly four months ago that I have believed it important to address you directly from this office. Events of the last twenty-four hours have moved me to do so.

"For just as evil forces have threatened our national security at various times during our history, so now have unwholesome forces, hostile to free democratic society, threatened our domestic security. We have always risen to these challenges, and we will do so now."

He reminded viewers of Fargo and explained that these same forces, "bent on subverting the democratic process," had now hijacked a network broadcast. He told of the effect it had had on his own daughter. Then he assured the watching millions that he had directed the attorney general and the director of the FBI to "swiftly bring to justice those responsible."

In the back of the Oval Office Robbie was watching on the monitor. "Perfect, perfect," he kept muttering. Griswold had mastered the timing, the pauses, the modulation of his voice. Robbie could already see the polls rising.

As he had been coached, Griswold exuded self-assurance, firmness but no hint of alarm. The nonverbal message was clear: The situation was under control because Griswold was in control.

"The anti-abortion movement may have started with deeply held personal goals. But no longer. They have become dangerous terrorists, and their random acts of violence are undermining respect for the law, so much so that other reckless forces in our culture are being unleashed, threatening the very security of our neighborhoods and homes.

"The first freedom," Griswold said, nodding directly into the lens, "is freedom from fear. This administration, I assure you, will do what must be done to guarantee that freedom for every American.

"And to that end I am signing an executive order tonight." He reached for the black folder to his right, opened it, then took his thick, black pen from his inside jacket pocket and scrawled his signature on the open page.

He looked up again, speaking softly, reassuringly.

"This order declares a state of national emergency.

"It's necessary to augment the police force of the District of Columbia which is, after all, the seat of government. Accordingly, two thousand National Guard troops will be called to active duty in the morning. This is secondarily necessary to reenforce the authority of law enforcement officials who may have to make very quick decisions in emergency circumstances. This is not new: Similar authority has been invested in America's peace-keepers by my predecessors when the national interest was similarly threatened.

"You elected me president, and I swore on my oath to uphold the Constitution and faithfully discharge the laws of this great country. Let no one be mistaken. This is precisely what I will do.

"Together we will meet this challenge and do our duty with the same courage and resolve previous generations of Americans have demonstrated.

"God bless you, and God bless this great land of liberty."

Robbie and other staff members standing in the doorway burst into applause the moment the red light went off. Griswold stood, grinned, and gave a thumbs-up sign.

IN HIS North Arlington home, Senator Byron Langer slumped back in his chair.

"I knew it. I felt it coming," he said, staring at the screen as the network anchor appeared, standing under the lights on the White House lawn, ready to debrief the nation.

"Mark this day, Lily," he said to his wife. "One day this will be remembered as a very dark moment in the history of our republic."

31

Monday evening, May 11

"THANKS SO MUCH, Dawn," Mary Seaton called up the stairs to the baby-sitter. "We really appreciate your help. They can each have *one*—I repeat, one—story. Then into bed. No negotiating. Daniel and I will just be gone for an hour or so."

Mary paused. Daniel was at the front door, his hand on the knob, impatient to go. Upstairs she could hear muffed chaos; the children must be bouncing on the beds—or off the walls—while they got ready for bed. But Dawn could handle it. She was only fifteen, the daughter of a neighbor, but she was great with kids. Mary decided she wouldn't worry; she and Daniel should escape while they could.

They eased out the front door and down the front walk. She and Daniel needed to talk, but things had gotten to the point where they felt they could not speak freely in their own home. Mary remembered a friend telling her years before about living in Iran as undercover missionaries. She and her husband had had to whisper in their home, had been followed when they went out to the market, and an Iranian member of their little Christian community had actually been killed by government agents. It had sounded surreal, but Mary now understood, at least somewhat, how her friend must have felt.

Daniel grabbed her hand and pulled her down the sidewalk, walking quickly, as he always did when he was upset. They both looked behind them, all around them. No one seemed to be following; in fact, the neighborhood was unusually quiet.

After they had walked in silence for a block or two, Daniel sighed, then spoke softly.

"This thing is really getting to me," he said. "I absolutely cannot believe the response during these past twenty-four hours. It's like a bad dream. I have not seen one thing in the media about the video itself. Everyone is just screeching about network sabotage and if your TV can be violated, then the nation is going down the tubes. Never mind that babies' skulls are being crushed and their brains sucked out. No, just don't mess with our TV!"

Mary's stomach turned over sickeningly. "It's still so early," she whispered. "This is just the first wave of reaction. People will come to their senses."

"That's what I thought!" he hissed back at her. "I thought the video would be the bucket of cold water that would shock people out of their stupor. But all they seem to care about is to find and prosecute the terrorists who dared to mess with their regularly scheduled programming. It's ludicrous!"

"I think that'll still happen," said Mary. "People *have* been shocked. But they're in denial. That's why they're all overreacting. They're shifting the focus to the TV issue because they aren't willing to face the regeneration-center issue. Maybe it'll just take a while for people to face facts."

"That's a nice psychological analysis," Daniel said. "But I'm afraid. What if Gideon's Torch ends up backfiring? It seems to me that all it's accomplished so far is that we now live in a police state. I mean, we've got the National Guard patrolling D.C. like this is Haiti or some Third World dictatorship. There's probably a tank formation rolling down Route 7 toward Falls Church even as we speak..."

Daniel sighed and clutched Mary's hand tighter. "I believed the video was the clearest way possible to expose the regeneration centers. We showed them what will happen; people actually saw the procedure, right in their living rooms. I thought no one could watch it and turn away. Evidently I was wrong."

A FEW MILES away, Alex Seaton and Jennifer Barrett were also walking in the darkness, strolling the C&O bikepath in Reston. Usually they ran this route, their conversation carried on in short, breathy bursts, but tonight they didn't want to risk being overheard by other joggers on the trail.

While Daniel was mourning people's lack of response to the video, Alex was angry. He was furious that Americans could look at a baby's death on television—a murder committed coldbloodedly by those sworn to save lives—and not rise up in indignation against the perpetrators of that death. He was furious that President Griswold—hypocritical co-conspirator that he was—was self-righteously loosing troops on the streets. Griswold was the criminal.

Alex was also mad at himself. He was furious that he had allowed himself to be cajoled into even believing that something so benign as putting a video on television could work. He was angry, too, that his strategies had been ignored. Lance was right. This was war, and you don't win wars by hoping the bad guys change their minds. You win by taking out enemy targets. One by one.

In spite of his inner turmoil, Alex was silent. Jennifer walked beside him, also quiet. He appreciated that about her; she didn't need to be constantly chatting in order to feel secure. Their relationship had moved along rather well, he thought. She didn't require some of the mysterious attentions, gratuitous phone calls, and constant affirmations that had mystified him in earlier relationships with women. She obviously enjoyed his company, but she didn't pressure him. As a result, he was moving faster with this relationship than he ordinarily would. They had spent a lot of time together lately. They ran together nearly every day, had gone to a few movies, and had spent several very nice quiet Sunday afternoons in one another's company.

He took her hand in the darkness. Her fingers were cool and dry.

"What's on your mind?" she asked.

"I just can't believe everything that has happened in the last twenty-four hours," he said.

"I don't think anyone could have imagined how much of a stir the video would cause," she said.

"Not the right kind of stir," Alex said. "It's all turned into a huge mess. The pro-lifers are the villains in people's minds. Not the butchers who carve up defenseless babies. I don't get it."

"No one gets it," she said. "How's your brother doing?"

"He's devastated," said Alex. "I mean, it's not like he had anything to do with it," he added awkwardly. "But he can't believe people's reaction. I guess he's sort of naive about human nature."

"What about the people in New York?" she asked. "I mean, they're the ones who did it, right?"

"We don't know who did it," Alex said quickly. "We don't want to know."

"Alex, you can be a little more open with me, you know," she said. "There's more information floating around than you seem to realize. I heard Mary and Amy talking after church yesterday, and one of them mentioned something about a big project in New York. You need to be really careful with security; the feds are going to be on your tail from now on, and the less anyone knows, the better. Especially the people on the fringes—like Amy. She's too young and too volatile. She could easily let something slip."

Alex felt a twist in his gut. Amy had been acting sort of strange lately, he thought, especially in the past week or so. He'd thought that maybe she was jealous because he had been spending time with Jennifer. She'd seemed a little evasive, a little abrupt, a little cool. "Hell hath no fury like a woman scorned," suddenly popped into his mind. But Amy hadn't been scorned; he hadn't really made any overtures toward her before Jennifer appeared on the scene. But maybe she somehow felt slighted. She was one of those mysterious emotional women he didn't understand.

32

Tuesday, May 12

A NTHONY FRIZZELL stood, hands clutched behind his back, staring from his office window at the mass of cars crawling slowly in both directions along Pennsylvania Avenue. He had spent the night in his office so he could stay in touch with the field, getting only four hours sleep on the daybed in the side room, but he felt exhilarated. He was made for battle, and he knew it. Probably would have been a great general if he had lived in a different era.

He checked his watch: 7:20 A.M.

"It's amazing, Toby," he said without turning his head. "Every year the traffic starts earlier and earlier. All these people hurrying to get to their desks and make all the machinery work. Worker ants." He gestured grandly toward the Capitol to the left, then toward the White House to the right.

"Most of them don't have a clue," he concluded, swinging around toward his assistant. "Are you sure everything's in place?" Frizzell stood with arms folded, leaning on the back of his overstuffed, black-leather chair.

"Yes, Chief. I've gone through the checklist with Martin himself.

Every item is covered. Solid. They should be calling in here in, let's see..." Toby Hunter looked at his watch, compared it with the digital clock on the wall. "In eight minutes, thirty seconds."

"Everything covered?" Frizzell said again.

"Yes sir. No more Chicagos."

"Let's go then, Toby."

The two men strode down the hall to the command center. The duty officer and the assistant director for operations both stood as they entered.

"Thought we'd come down here where we can watch," said Frizzell. "All set for 7:30 gentlemen?"

"Yes sir. Enjoy the show, sir," the assistant director said, flipping on a huge TV screen that took up most of one wall. It was connected by closed circuit to cameras in the back of a mobile control van parked near the corner of Broadway and Roosevelt Avenue, not far from LaGuardia Airport.

The camera panned the busy intersection; cars heading west jammed the roads. Then the camera swung back to a side road off Roosevelt, to a tavern just to the right, then down the street to a long string of townhouses, 1920s vintage, most of them in need of paint and repair. The camera zoomed to the front door of number 1246. Through the speakers overhead in the command room came live transmissions. Frizzell could hear a voice counting down the seconds, "Ten, nine, eight... three, two, one, go."

The back doors of a parked van marked "Perucci's Bakery" burst open, and twelve men, some carrying H&K MP5 subguns, others riot shotguns, and one leading the way waving a .45 pistol in the air. They were wearing Kevlar helmets and black, heavily padded sweatsuits with FBI in huge white letters on their backs.

Twelve more poured from another van, then two groups from parked cars. Within seconds, FBI sharpshooters with high-powered rifles had taken up positions behind parked cars and in two doorways across the street. Roaring past the cameras, with lights flashing, came a herd of New York City police squad cars and one wagon.

It all happened so fast that only trained eyes like Frizzell's could follow the action. The alleys were covered, men with rifles peered down from rooftops, a helicopter swept into view. Two agents knocked on the door, then swung themselves back against the wood columns of the front porch. The agents waited to the count of five, then used a battering ram on the door. It collapsed into the room, shattering the glass panels, and, with bulletproof shields in front of them, they burst through the doorway.

A few minutes later, four men and three women, all handcuffed, were being led down the front steps. Then, one by one, they were herded into the back of the police van.

Frizzell grinned and gave a thumbs-up. It was a textbook operation, surgically clean and quick, over in seven minutes, start to finish.

While the vans and their escorts sped off away from the camera, the New York police pushed back curious bystanders and began blocking off the area with sawhorses and yellow tape while FBI crews moved in to examine every nook and cranny of the building.

"Get me Martin," Frizzell ordered. "I want a confirm on this before I call the AG or the president." He strode out of the room, headed for his office. Toby trotted ahead to put through the call.

By 8:15, seven suspects had been taken into the Jackson Heights headquarters; two others, including a priest, had been picked up on the lower east side of Manhattan; and three had been arrested in Yonkers. It was the New York cell of the The Life Network, at least all known members. In Washington, D. C., Reginald Warner and the satellite news-gathering operator had also been detained.

Emily Gineen had just arrived at her office when Frizzell called.

"Congratulations, Director," she said. "That's faster than I thought possible. Good work."

Emily picked up her direct White House line. "Get me the president, please."

All in all, this might turn out to be a pretty good day, she thought.

Probably not, her gut responded.

BY 9:30 A.M., Senator Byron Langer had spread out on his desk four statute books, a well-worn little volume containing the Constitution, and a long memorandum from the Library of Congress detailing every invocation of extraordinary powers by any president since Washington had called the troops out for the Whiskey Rebellion in 1794—when farmers in western Pennsylvania, Virginia, and Carolina fought off the feds collecting their excise tax on whiskey. There were, to Langer's surprise, hundreds of such precedents; there were fifteen national emergency declarations in the relatively tranquil years of 1979 to 1993 alone.

He reread Article II of the Constitution, under which many presidents, including Lincoln, Roosevelt, and Nixon, had declared national emergencies: the so-called implied powers of the presidency. *Dangerous if abused*, he thought. It was a small miracle indeed that through all these years this delicate balance of government powers had been maintained when there was so much latent power in the executive. *The system is so fragile; it depends entirely upon men and women of good will to protect it.*

Then he reread the act Congress had passed in 1976 attempting to regulate the statutory declarations of national emergency that have been authorized under 470 separate provisions. Congress had attempted to rein in the power of the executive branch by determining that presidential declarations could be overturned by a joint resolution of the Congress.

If Griswold decided to act under Article 2, Congress had no specific authority to overrule him, and he might well get away with it. Even mild-mannered George Bush had called out marines and soldiers to put down the L.A. riots in 1992—forty-five hundred of them with orders to shoot if fired upon. The crisis was so grave that very few people had ever questioned him.

Langer leaned back in his chair. Presidents had acted unilaterally before. So why did Griswold's actions bother him so much?

The man had no consistent convictions, that was the problem. And he wasn't a conservative. Oh, sure, Griswold talked like a conservative on economic issues; he was pro-business and free market and railed against big government. But he was also a social libertarian, bending with the breezes on social issues and political judgments. In Langer's mind no one could subscribe to social liberalism and at the same time be a true economic conservative. Somebody had to pay the bills, after all, for the libertine lifestyle such liberalism unleashed. You eliminate all social conventions, people go on welfare or get AIDS, and the government ends up paying the bill. So inevitably one philosophy destroys the other.

And the social liberal ended up, no matter what he said, supporting big government. This was what happened to men like Griswold. No matter what they said, whether they were right or left, they were utopians. Ideologues, in fact. These kind always figured you could create incentives, social engineering really, and thereby create the so-called good society.

But it was nonsense. No matter how good the policies, government can never create the good society. That comes only from people *being* good. *By a change of heart*, Langer thought. Public virtue depends on private virtue, the moral life, the very thing Griswold so disdained.

No, Griswold was a utopian ideologue, like so many who called themselves conservatives these days. But Langer considered ideology and utopianism the real enemies of true conservatism. He believed in the established order of things, of wisdom handed from generation to generation. He was especially fond of T. S. Eliot's description of the "society of permanent things." He believed in a tradition of republican virtue based on respect for covenants of the past; he believed that citizens were moved to their own civic responsibility not because of some political decree but because of gratitude for the liberty their forefathers made possible.

In Langer's view, one took hold of such enduring truths and guarded them with everything one had. And that's why, he realized, Griswold frightened him so much. The man was a good politician, keen, quick, and articulate, able and well-meaning. But he had no tie to things enduring, no belief system bred in the bone. Of course he had descended from umpteen generations of New Englanders. But roots did not go deep in New England's rocky soil. As Langer saw it, Yankee aristocrats believed they were born to govern and therefore had the instincts to do so. Their reliance was in themselves, not in enduring truths.

Griswold was decent but not deep. And surely not of Langer's school of conservatism.

Langer stared at the pile of papers on his desk. The laws, the precedents, the Constitution—they were one thing. But in today's environment, how could written statutes stand against an opportunist who fanned public passions and preyed on people's fears?

Byron Langer sighed and closed his eyes. He had a foreboding sense of doom, like watching from a distance as two locomotives hurtled toward a railway junction.

He shook his head, then leaned forward and hit his intercom button. "Get me the attorney general, please."

EMILY WAS WORKING in her inner office. Spread out before her were the same four statute books Langer had on his desk, along with a memorandum of precedents the Office of Legal Council had hurriedly assembled. Around the desk were her four most trusted assistants, including Paul Clarkson. She was expecting Langer's call, and had, in fact, told her secretary to put it through immediately.

Emily had slept only four hours, but she did her best to sound bright, chipper, and confident.

"Madam Attorney General, I have a question," Langer began, "which I ask in a most constructive spirit. My deepest desire, I assure you, is to avoid a constitutional crisis."

"It's my deepest desire as well, Senator."

"Well then, tell me please, what are the specific extraordinary measures the president and you contemplate under this executive order?" he asked calmly.

"We will allow the National Guard to make arrests. There are many precedents for it, Senator, as in Los Angeles with George Bush or during the '60s anti-war and civil rights riots."

"Yes, I understand, though I have difficulty seeing that this crisis begins to approach those."

"We have reasons, Senator."

"Oh, yes, of course. You'll tell me it's your intelligence reports, I suppose. That's usually the case. What else?"

"We will put marshals or deputized guardsmen on duty at earth station transmitters. We can't have a repeat of the other night."

"Oh, my," Langer gasped. "Like Nicaragua, where the military guard the communications. Apart from the symbolism, don't you think that has some ominous First Amendment implications?"

"No, Senator. It's a mere precaution."

"And what about search and seizures?"

"We are looking at all the authorities at this moment. We may, as President Clinton did, take some extraordinary measures in this regard. I hope you realize, Senator, that this is a very dangerous national conspiracy we're up against. Very dangerous."

"No, Madame Attorney General, this is a very dangerous response. It is an unwarranted usurpation of power that cannot help but pose a grave constitutional threat, and I will oppose it with all the strength at my command."

"I'm sorry you feel that way, Senator." Emily was not surprised, but she paused a moment, wondering whether to attempt to persuade him. She decided it was pointless. "We, of course, respect your right to dissent."

"May I ask under what authority the president has made this decision?" Langer spoke slowly, deliberately.

"Well, we have thus far concluded it is within his implied powers under Article II of the Constitution."

"There are 470 statutes giving him emergency authorities. Why not one of them?"

"Well, sir, we considered the 1976 act but decided it wasn't necessary—"

Langer cut her off sharply. "Under the 1976 act, of course, Congress can overrule the president. That probably never entered your deliberation. But let me assure you, this will not stop us. The

Congress will not have its authority disregarded. Before we head down that road, I beg you to reconsider."

"We'll consider your views, certainly, Senator, but we've studied this issue very carefully."

"Mrs. Gineen, I have come to respect you, but I must say that I believe you are reading from a different Constitution than the one on my desk. In any event, we will soon see. I must as a courtesy tell you that at noon today I will file a joint resolution to override the president's order. He has his implied authority under Article II; the Congress has its explicit authority under Article I—and we will not shirk our responsibilities."

Emily hung up and looked at her associates. "Well, he's against us. No surprise there, of course. But he says he'll file a resolution to block the president's order." She looked quizzically at Paul, whose expression was grim.

"We're playing this one on his home field, Emily, and he seldom loses at home," Paul said somberly. "This will be bloody."

Emily called Bernie O'Keefe, and within thirty minutes six White House congressional liaison assistants were leaving West Executive Avenue, their limousines headed for Capitol Hill.

AS SOON AS the senator finished his call to the attorney general, he summoned his speech writer, legislative assistant, and personal secretary. Still a judge by temperament, Langer dictated the outlines of the case while his aides scribbled notes furiously.

First he framed the issues: Could a president be stopped from asserting extraordinary powers under Article II? There were 470 specific situations giving the president emergency powers; didn't that mean Congress intended to define such emergencies? In which case, Congress could block him. Finally, what would happen in the event of a constitutional confrontation?

Then he began to recite just a few of the precedents, going back to Washington. There were hundreds to study; he told his legislative assistant to put absolutely everyone to work on this one.

At that point, Langer drew himself up straight in his chair. This would be, he said, a principled defense of the Constitution. No politics, no petty vindictive feelings.

"Take the high ground here, Josh," he exhorted his speech writer. "The very viability of our government is at stake here. This goes to the very heart of our republic."

With his staff at work, Langer set out for the minority leader's hideaway office in the Capitol; from there he went to the majority leader's expansive office just off the ornate Senate reception room. With the latter sympathetic and the former passionately pledging support, he then strode through the corridors, confronting colleagues and visiting offices in the three Senate office buildings. Since senators seldom drop in on one another, he created quite a stir and also managed to see many of his colleagues. Few wanted to turn him down face to face, especially when the issue he championed had to do with the protection of senatorial prerogatives.

By noon, Langer had lined up an impressive list of twenty-six cosponsors for his resolution, an unusual alliance of liberal Democrats, civil libertarians who relished the thought of embarrassing a Republican president, and evangelical Christian conservatives who distrusted Griswold and saw his power grab as a not-so-subtle attempt to break what remained of the pro-life movement.

Langer checked with his office and was told that legislative counsel had drafted the resolution and research was nearly completed. The senator then phoned the majority leader and was granted permission to introduce the resolution and speak for thirty minutes at noon the next day. By then he might have close to a Senate majority on his side.

Langer's strategy was announced to the Senate press gallery, and the news arrived in newsrooms around the country minutes later, about the same time it hit at 1600 Pennsylvania Avenue.

DESPITE THE domestic crisis, Whitney Griswold had maintained his scheduled activities for the day. This included a National

Security Council meeting, a carry-over from the day before, to deal with the fast-developing events in the Middle East. The 10:00 A.M. meeting included the secretary of state, the secretary of defense, the director of the CIA, and top NSC staffers.

CIA director James Quarles's briefing included voluminous information about the inner workings of the Israeli government, provided by CIA assets—Israeli officials sympathetic to Americans, if not by ideology then by augmentation of their numbered Zurich bank accounts.

As Quarles spoke, Griswold doodled on his scratch pad, centered on the black-leather desk pad with "The President" engraved in blue. Months earlier he had realized that Quarles, a career intelligence officer, gave more information than anyone needed simply to prove how proficient his agency was. Besides, Griswold's mind was not on the maneuverings in the Knesset, but on his daughter. Elizabeth had had another bad night's sleep.

Griswold had learned from early childhood to maintain a cool and dignified composure under all circumstances, but inside his anger raged. He'd like to get his hands on those terrorists who had traumatized his little girl. Or at least get them behind bars. Good work on Frizzell's part, hauling in the New York gang this morning. He scribbled a note to call Frizzell and congratulate him. Coax him on. Do more. Get the rest of the bunch. Suddenly anger gave way to a burst of enthusiasm: He, Whitney Griswold, would have a role in cleaning up this kind of pernicious influence in American life.

The meeting ended at 11:30. Griswold started for the south door, which led directly through the secretaries' spaces and into the Oval Office. Then he paused and, impulsively, walked to the right into the hallway, startling both the Secret Service agents at the main Oval Office entrance and two low-level staffers passing by, one of whom backed up against the wall, flushed and flustered. Griswold shook hands with both. Then he turned right and walked straight down the corridor to the door at the end and into his press secretary's office.

Caroline Atwater was on the phone; she quickly hung up and

stood behind her desk. Griswold thought she looked particularly attractive this morning, with the light streaming in the windows giving a lustrous sheen to her soft glossy hair. Such a wholesome look.

He walked to the front windows and looked across the north lawn. "Good view," he chuckled. "You can watch the sharks swim by, can't you?"

Caroline laughed. There was a pathway right past her windows where the members of the press could walk from the press room to the front lawn. Just off the path outside her windows was the place where television correspondents often stood for network reports from the White House.

"Are we getting beaten up?" Griswold asked.

"Too early for editorials. The ACLU issued a rather tepid disapproval. Most others seem supportive, although there is some restlessness on the Hill. But not bad so far, sir," Caroline replied.

"Good, good." Griswold turned and looked her in the eye. "But it doesn't matter. We'll do what we have to do—do what is right—and not let these armchair journalists intimidate us. You stand out there, Caroline, and face them down," he commanded, pointing at the press room. With that, he gave her a thumbs-up sign, a pat on the shoulder, and marched out.

It was time, Griswold reasoned, to buck up the troops. The leader has to be firm, strong, self-assured. Others sense it if he isn't.

This was the first time the president had walked randomly through the corridors, opening doors to the wide-eyed gaze of secretaries. Griswold gave each the thumbs-up sign, a word of encouragement, and then moved on, two agents now trailing behind him. He ended up at the southwest corner suite of his chief of staff.

Robbie, also on the phone, stood, but kept the conversation going. Griswold took a seat at the conference table and watched his assistant. Robbie never skipped a beat in his conversation, showed no emotion, let alone signs of stress.

"Well, what does your stargazer tell us, Robbie?" the president asked when he'd hung up.

"Wonderful, Mr. President. Almost brought you a note in the NSC meeting. Your approval is up ten points—biggest one-day jump yet—and it more than makes up for yesterday morning's drop. The speech was a home run, sir, nothing but glowing comments. All positive. Calls and faxes are coming in by the thousands, overwhelmingly supportive."

"Good, good," Griswold grinned, visibly relieved. He rubbed his face with his large, bony hands.

"Only concern Sindberg picked up—and not really a negative— was a little uncertainty, people worried about what will happen next. It's understandable. This thing is volatile. But they sure hate the anti-abortionists. We've picked a good enemy."

"We won't let up, Robbie, until they're all in jail. The country will be better off without that movement. They're terrorists."

Robbie answered his intercom. "Yes, bring it right in." He turned to Griswold. "A statement by Langer. Better get a grip on your seat, Mr. President."

After his secretary had brought in the statement and left, Robbie read it aloud: the announcement of the resolution to be filed the next day, one quarter of the Senate already in favor, the speech planned. It was all there, and it ended with a bite, "The Congress of the United States will not be intimidated. The Constitution will be defended."

"Sounds like he's at the Alamo, but he won't get thirty votes," Robbie scoffed.

"The Democrats might see this as a chance to embarrass me." Griswold frowned thoughtfully.

"They're not going to get on the side of the religious right—not even for partisan politics."

"I don't know. I don't know." Griswold started to get up. "Call Bernie. He told me he knew about some things that might come in handy with Langer sometime. Don't tell me about it though . . . just see what you and Bernie can do."

"I understand." Robbie grinned.

Griswold held his head high and marched into the corridor. Then came the self-assured grin and the thumbs-up sign again as he passed more startled staffers and one visitor who was so unsettled he couldn't respond when the president said hello.

Griswold headed past the Roosevelt room and into the Oval Office, but not before greeting the Secret Service agent guarding the door with a punch on the arm and a "Good job, good job."

AFTER THE CALL from Robbie, Bernie O'Keefe called Frizzell. "Yesterday you told me if I ever needed a little information on Senator Langer to let you know."

"It doesn't involve the bureau, you understand," Frizzell said. "We're not into that. That went out with Hoover."

"Okay, but what is it?"

"Call William Johnson, assistant secretary of defense, personnel and readiness. Tell him you understand he has a sensitive file that you would like to see. The Langer file. He'll know. He may insist that you make it a presidential directive."

"Thanks, Tony."

"No, no thanks to me. We never talked. Wipe your recorder clean. I'll do the same here."

"Understood."

"Oh, and by the way, if you can't get the file, call me. I just might know where a copy is."

"You're a good man, Mr. Director. A good man." O'Keefe could almost see Frizzell's smile.

THE MARKET took Griswold's speech well, opening twenty-eight points up. By 10:30, it was up fifty-two points. The big traders already loved Griswold's tax package; now it appeared he might get domestic unrest under control. Wall Street liked nothing better than churning markets and quiet streets.

At 1:00 P.M. when Langer's statement became public, the market reacted to uncertainty by beginning erratic movements. Within thirty minutes, the gains were almost erased. Minutes before closing, it plunged thirty points—an eighty-point swing in four hours.

By 6:00 P.M., two 2,000 D.C. National Guard troops arrived at the D.C. armory in full gear. There, routine drug screening eliminated 175; another 190 had legitimate reasons to be excused. By 7:00 P.M., nearly 1,600 were mustered in, but it was a disorderly lot, looking less like an army than a crowd laughing, shoving, and pushing, waiting to get into a football game.

The battalion commander, Colonel Pierce, and the D.C. police captain, briefed the officers and non-coms then broke the battalion into squad size units assigned to police details across the District.

The first unit arrived at 9:30 P.M. in two Humvees to take up their position at the corner of Sixteenth and R Streets, a turf ruled by drug dealers and prostitutes. The D.C. police normally only drove through the area, usually looking straight ahead, allowing the dealers to duck into the shadows, though most didn't even bother to do that.

The guardsmen didn't know the rules. They parked both Humvees on R Street and began to unload. One young guardsman, a Corporal Jefferson, heard some commotion in a doorway on R Street and started toward it, his M-16 at the ready.

Jefferson had never had riot training, so he hadn't been warned that one can see out of darkened doorways but not into them. Six loud shots cracked through the darkness. Several rounds embedded themselves in Jefferson's Kevlar jacket, but one went clean through his Adam's apple, and he crumpled to the ground, blood gushing from the severed main artery. He was dead within a minute.

The other guardsmen, twelve in all, scattered behind street posts, cars, and fences. All at once, a volley of fire erupted, lighting even the darkened recesses of the streets.

There was no return fire, the drug dealers having fled through the rear, but by the time the squad leader, Sergeant Chambers, had restored order, two prostitutes were dead, two bystanders wounded by ricocheting bullets, and one guardsman had been shot through the arm by friendly fire.

Across town, two armored personnel carriers loaded with two squads of men pulled into an RFK Stadium parking lot. The back doors burst open and troops jumped out and immediately dispersed to patrol the Anacostia riverbanks. The shadows under the East Capitol Street Bridge usually sheltered an assortment of homeless folk and cokeheads. This night, as four scared young guardsmen moved along the bank, peering into the darkness under the bridge, a fusillade of rocks suddenly showered down on them, launched from a group of teenagers atop the bridge.

Most bounced along the bank, but some hit the troops, and one landed on a guardsman's helmet, making a nerve-shattering noise. In pure reflex, the guardsmen fired blindly at the bridge. One thirteen-year-old was killed outright; another, only ten, was gravely wounded and taken to D.C. General Hospital.

Six other shootings were reported that night, three involving the Guard. In an Anacostia bar, three individuals were stabbed, two fatally.

"SOME NIGHT!" D.C.'s mayor looked grimly at the report the next morning. "We call out the Guard, and instead of our usual quota of two dead, we have seven killed, one gravely wounded, and three others hospitalized, not to mention about $300,000 in reported property damage. And that's only because the lawyers haven't gotten into it yet."

"It'll get better," his aide said stiffly.

"Sure it will," the mayor said dryly, shaking his head. "No problem. Next we'll just bring in the Eighty-second Airborne and clean out the Guard."

33

WILLIAM JOHNSON was a tall, bookish man with unkempt brown hair. Squinting through thick glasses and
wearing rumpled tweeds, he looked more like a college professor
than a high-ranking government official. In fact, he had graduated
at the top of his class when earning a doctorate at Stanford
University Business School and had been a human resources whiz
for Apple Computer. Apart from his involvement as a community
activist in Marin County and head of the Audubon Society for
northern California, Johnson had had no experience in politics
before coming to Washington. Thus, Bernie O'Keefe's call sent
him scurrying to his agency's general counsel's office, where he
was advised to accede to White House directions regarding a matter as sensitive as a personnel file only if issued with the president's
authorization. There were standard procedures for such things.

At 9:00 A.M., as instructed, carrying a small, black-leather bag
under his arm, Johnson entered the northwest portico, was saluted
by the marine sentry and shown to the main reception area. The
smiling secretary quickly checked his ID and showed him to a blue
damask sofa. Out of nowhere a red-jacketed steward appeared with

a silver coffee service. The china cup had a narrow silver rim and, on the side etched in silver, the seal of the president.

Moments later, two cabinet members breezed by into the corridor to the chief of staff's office.

The Israeli ambassador soon arrived, and General Maloney came into the reception area to escort him back to his office.

Johnson watched through the window as a camera crew set up just in front of the portico and two senators were escorted to the cameras.

Upstairs in his corner office, well aware of what was transpiring a floor below, Bernie O'Keefe rifled through morning reports, occasionally checking his watch. *We'll warm him up for ten minutes,* Bernie mused, smiling slightly.

But then the report of the Guard's first night in D.C. wiped away the smile. Bernie had had doubts, expressed them to Griswold in fact, but no one was thinking in terms of restraint these days. "Show action. Get hold of things," Robbie had said, and the president had followed his lead.

O'Keefe called Barbara Shannon in and instructed her to go downstairs and get Johnson.

"Don't bring him up in the elevator," Bernie said to his secretary. Rather, she should walk him by the cabinet room, where the doors were always open, stop in front of the closed doors to the Oval Office and whisper that the president was in, then pass the Roosevelt room, where some of the senior staff might still be lingering from the 8:00 meeting. She should then walk him upstairs, pointing out General Maloney's office in the northwest corner on the way. It was a circuitous route, but Johnson would not know the difference; and by the time he got to Bernie his eyes should be popping.

The president's counsel was on the phone when his secretary showed Johnson in; he waved his visitor to the straight-back leather chair in front of his desk and kept talking, taking notes, and then said, "Yes, sir, I'll do it, sir."

There was only one person from whom O'Keefe would be taking orders, Johnson realized. He tried to glance unobtrusively around the room; the walls were covered with photos of O'Keefe and the president, some dressed informally. William Johnson was, indirectly at least, in the presence of the president.

"Dr. Johnson. Your reputation precedes you, sir." Bernie bounced out of his chair and thrust his hand across the desk as soon as he hung up the phone. Johnson rose awkwardly, smiled, and nodded.

"Coffee, Coke, anything?" Bernie looked up over his gold-rimmed reading glasses as he moved some papers off his desk, clearing the pad in front of him and taking out his Mont Blanc pen. Johnson, clutching the briefcase in his lap, declined.

"We are both very busy, so we'll waste no time here, Mr. Secretary," Bernie began, removing his glasses and setting them on the desk. Assistant secretaries liked being called "Mr. Secretary."

"The matter of which we spoke on the phone has been discussed, I should assure you, at the highest levels. It is also, I should add, a matter of utmost security and sensitivity. I'm sure we can trust you to respect that?"

Suddenly, unexpectedly, Johnson felt defensive. "Why, of course, sensitive indeed."

"So I would suggest, Mr. Secretary, that we not request that file which is in your briefcase. It is there, I assume?"

Johnson nodded.

"Not officially, that is. It needn't be logged in or anything of the sort." O'Keefe spoke so reassuringly that Johnson could feel his tightened muscles relax.

"As counsel to the president, at this point I should merely like to glance through the file. I cannot decide unless I see it whether it warrants a formal request. Should we decide to make such a request, it would have, I assure you, full authorization. I understand the protocol, of course."

O'Keefe seemed to have anticipated Johnson's well-rehearsed objections, and he certainly sounded eminently reasonable, more so than Johnson had expected. And he could hardly deny the president's counsel a look at any government document.

"Of course, sir. If you just want to skim through it. You are acting, of course, as counsel."

"Of course."

Johnson opened the case and pulled out a legal-size, yellowed folder with a large metal bar clip across the top. He handed it gingerly to O'Keefe, who smiled reassuringly and leaned back in his chair, perched his reading glasses on the end of his nose, and started to thumb through the pages, almost as if indifferent to the contents.

"Must be tedious work wading through all this bureaucratese. They must have a course over there that teaches bureaucrats how to say one page's worth of information in six," O'Keefe laughed.

Johnson chuckled and relaxed another notch.

Suddenly the door opened, and Barbara was standing in the doorway. "Mr. O'Keefe," she said in a matter-of-fact tone, "the president is on line two. Israeli matter." Then she walked over and tapped Johnson gently on the arm. "National security, if you don't mind," she whispered.

Johnson did, but he followed her meekly. He heard O'Keefe pick up the phone and say, "Yes, sir, Mr. President," before the door closed.

Barbara showed Johnson to a large armchair, offered him a copy of the president's news summary, and gave him more coffee in another of those china cups with the silver seal.

Inside his office, Bernie laid the receiver on the desk, turned to the fax machine on the table behind him, removed the clip from the folder, inserted the papers he needed in the machine, and punched the green button marked "copy." In just over three minutes, he slid the copies into his desk drawer. Then he carefully reassembled the folder and laid it on his desk under a large blue folder marked "For the President," which he laid open. In less than five minutes, he buzzed Barbara to show Johnson back in.

"I'm so sorry, Mr. Secretary," Bernie said. "Simply one of the hazards of this office."

"I understand, of course. I have the same problem with the secretary of defense," Johnson lied. The secretary hadn't called him in four months.

"Now let's see." Bernie lifted the folder marked "For the

President" and slowly closed it, laying it almost under Johnson's nose. "Where was that file? . . . oh yes, right here." He leaned back and began thumbing through it as casually as before. "Can't be too careful, can we?" he asked, looking over his glasses.

"No," Johnson said. Then, "In what way do you mean that?" Now he was curious.

"Well, it appears here that there is some evidence of, shall we say, instability. We must know these things because, of course, we share information with Congress that is, well, actually above top-secret classification."

Johnson immediately agreed. "Indeed we must be careful."

"Thank you, Mr. Secretary," O'Keefe said, closing the folder, handing it across the desk, and standing all in one quick motion. Johnson instinctively stood also.

"It will not be necessary to take this any further, Mr. Johnson; nor do we need to trouble the president with this. He has so much on his mind these days, and as I look through this, I see no need for us to have this folder," Bernie said.

O'Keefe had established what in the White House is called "deniability": The matter could not be traced to the president.

Johnson seemed almost disappointed, as if his visit had somehow been diminished in importance. But he left clutching the pair of gold-plated presidential cuff links that Bernie had given him rather effusively. The White House bought them for $2.49 a set.

As the door shut behind Johnson, O'Keefe picked up the phone. "See if the president can take this call, please," he directed the operator. Seconds later, Griswold was on the line.

"I've got it. Dynamite."

"Good. Bernie, you take care of it."

34

Wednesday, May 13

PAUL CLARKSON was in conference with Emily when the call came from O'Keefe. They were both surprised by the demand that Paul come to the White House immediately. O'Keefe would normally have called for the attorney general. Furthermore, he sounded insistent, almost angry. "Drop everything; be here in ten minutes," he had said.

Emily dispatched Paul in her limousine, and shortly after 10:00 the black Lincoln was waved through the southwest gates.

There was no delay in the reception room this time; Paul was immediately taken to the elevator and escorted down the long corridor as fast as his canes would allow. Barbara showed him into O'Keefe's office, where Bernie was eagerly awaiting him, the papers on his desk now neatly arranged, with only one file sitting in the center.

"We have exactly two hours, Paul," Bernie said, unsmiling, "so let me get right to the point. This administration naturally respects the right of any senator or representative to dissent from its policies. But your friend, Senator Langer, is going beyond the bounds. He is threatening to undermine the government's sworn duty to maintain domestic order. That is government's first task, as I know you agree."

"I understand, Mr. O'Keefe, but you don't know Senator Langer. This isn't politics. He's a man of real conscience and conviction. I spoke with him last night and—"

"Conscience? Conviction? I don't think you know him as well as you think, my friend. And please, call me Bernie."

"Oh, no. I'd stake my life on that. I know him as well as any man can. I worked for him closely for five years, remember."

"All of us, I suppose, have secret hiding places, inner recesses that we never open to others, maybe not even to ourselves, Paul. Your friend, the good senator, was quite a war hero, wasn't he? I'll bet he sat around regaling you with great war stories."

"What are you getting at?" Paul said angrily. "Don't beat around the bush with me."

"All right. Fair enough. Let's see here," Bernie said, opening the file in front of him and picking up the top sheet. "First Lieutenant Byron Langer 0622873, commissioned ROTC, June 6, 1966. OCS, Fort Benning. Qualified for Airborne, good officer." Bernie looked up and saw Paul glaring at him, deep furrows on his brow.

"After jump school, assigned to Eighty-second Airborne, then qualified for Ranger School, from which he graduated. Hot stuff, a regular Rambo, top of his class.

"Arrived in Da Nang in July 1967, just when things were getting very hairy over there. Eager young man—he volunteered for behind-the-lines stuff. Military advisory group in Laos, working with Montagnard fighters. They were mean little devils in the highlands who would cut out the enemy's heart and eat it, literally—"

"Could we get to the point here?" Whatever O'Keefe had, he was relishing the moment, Paul thought. This man was cruel.

"Well, our good friend here is choppered in to a Montagnard camp just in time for an attack by the North Vietnam regulars. They shoot the place up pretty good—so good that Langer's platoon is decimated. He's petrified, loses his men, and goes bonkers. He runs away. The platoon sergeant saves the day, rescues the men and Langer. The sergeant gets the Silver Star, and Langer gets an army hospital at Clark Field in the Philippines for two months—'battle fatigue,' or, in layman's terms, a nervous breakdown."

"I don't believe it." Paul was angry. Langer had told him stories about Vietnam for years.

"Right here in black and white. Got his commanding officer's statement in front of me."

"What about his medal? I've seen it. It's in a case on the bookshelf in his office."

"Oh, that's the best part. Lieutenant Langer goes back to Vietnam, to a supply depot near Saigon. No more boom-booms for him. He works his butt off and comes up with a system to get supplies of cold beer to Khe Sanh and other hot spots during the Tet offensive. The doggies in the field are so happy, General Westmoreland gives him the Legion of Merit...for, it turns out, getting beer to the troops." Bernie leaned back in his chair and laughed loudly. "Isn't that rich?"

Paul stared at him, furious. "So you want to blackmail Langer and get him off your back. That's the little plan here, right?"

"Whoa!" Bernie leaned forward in his chair and raised his hand, palm out like a traffic cop. "Not so fast, my friend. We would never do something like that. We just thought...rather, I just thought...you might simply explain to your old boss the wisdom of the president's action here—"

"Bull." Paul knocked over one of the canes that had been leaning against the arm of his chair. "You want to shut him up. Well, I'm not gonna play ball with you."

"That's fine. I just thought you might like to spare your esteemed senator some embarrassment. Just an act of Christian charity, you know. He doesn't exactly occupy the high moral ground here. And it seems to me a good lawyer could certainly be able to explain why it's in everyone's best interest that he get behind the president."

Paul leaned over and recovered the cane, lifting himself slowly from the chair. Bernie thought he was leaving, but instead he walked to the narrow window that looked over the parapets of the west wing roofline toward the mansion. He stared out for a few minutes. Bernie waited. Finally he turned.

"I'll talk to him, because I care about him. He's my friend. That's the only reason. I want him to have a chance to spare himself if he chooses to. He's entitled to that," Clarkson said. "But I can't tell you how badly I feel for you. Sitting in this beautiful office, day after day, doing the president's dirty work for him. It stinks in here, but you're so full of yourself, you can't even smell your own odor." He paused, then added, "How do you sleep at night?"

Bernie sat still, startled, for a moment. No one had talked to him this way since sixth grade in parochial school. Then he shook his head, dismissing the thought. Clarkson's little lecture was a small price to pay for what they were about to gain. The fate of the nation—or at least the fate of Whitney Griswold's presidency—hung in the balance, and there was one hour and forty minutes to keep it from tipping over the edge.

"We'll talk about things like that some other time," he said, trying to sound gracious. This guy was so black and white. "Why don't you call the senator from here? You may not see it now, but it's for the good of the country. Stop him from filing his resolution. The nation can't afford that kind of constitutional crisis." He stood and extended his hand.

"Right. I understand," Paul said, ignoring Bernie's outstretched hand. "I'll call from your secretary's desk, if you don't mind." He gathered his canes and made his way to the door, then turned to look at Bernie. "Listen, if you ever need to talk about something more than garbage like this, give me a call. It must get pretty rancid up here sometimes." He opened the door and left.

Bernie, still standing behind the desk, watched as the door closed. The guy's got spunk, he thought. He's better than the pompous 'war hero' he's trying to defend. Langer had it coming. Pretending to be something he's not. Clarkson may say it stinks here, but at least we shoot straight about who we are.

Right, his conscience echoed, ever so slightly. *And you, the great constitutional lawyer, are gleefully bending the Bill of Rights for J. Whitney Griswold?*

Bernie stood for a moment, shrugged, and picked up the phone. There was work to be done.

AT 11:15 that morning, several guardsmen and a D.C. police officer stumbled onto a drug deal near the intersection of Columbia Road and Eighteenth NW, an area surrounded by hot Latin restaurants and lively sidewalk cafes. The policeman was unscathed, but both guardsmen were hit, one seriously. Again a bystander caught a ricocheting bullet. Colonel Pierce issued a bulletin to all units to withhold fire unless fired upon. In each of the incidents the night before and this morning, the troops had shot first.

By 11:30, as news flashed over the wires, the market was down another sixty points.

PAUL CLARKSON could not remember ever feeling more uncomfortable. It was like he had eaten a huge meal and it simply wouldn't digest. A huge lump, just sitting in his gut. He fought back touches of nausea.

Langer's secretary escorted him into the senator's office to wait. The senator was still in a meeting at the Capitol, she said, lining up more supporters for his resolution. Paul glanced around the room at the familiar books and pictures. He had great memories of this office, when he and the senator had teamed up to fight for the causes they so passionately shared.

Paul walked to the bookshelf. It was there, all right, in the glass case: a small bronze medallion hanging from a pin by a red silk ribbon. The Legion of Merit. For the first time Paul realized there was no printed citation under it. Beside it was another medal with purple silk, the Purple Heart. Not far away were pictures of Lieutenant, later Captain, Byron Langer, with his men, a happy-looking band of warriors in their combat gear.

"Well, Paul, I'm glad you came today." Langer smiled broadly as he walked through the door. He took off his coat and came over to Paul, placing both hands on his shoulders, a near embrace. Paul knew he had at least fifty-one votes in his pocket. He'd seen him this way only a few times before.

"I'm afraid I'm going to have to challenge your president, Paul. Teach him a lesson, in fact. But it is very important for the country," Langer effused. He was in high form. "The Constitution judges us, we don't judge it."

"He's not my president, sir," Paul said so bitterly that Langer stopped abruptly.

"What's going on?" he asked.

"It's you, sir," Paul said, then paused, not knowing how to begin. "Sir, I respect you more than any man I've known other than my father. And my feelings are unaffected by what I must tell you. We're up against people without principle or conscience. Hollow men. They'll do anything right now to stop you—"

"Of course. Don't you think I know that? I've been in this swamp a long time—"

"This is something else, sir. Believe me, whatever they call it, I call it blackmail. They want you to back off this resolution—and if you don't do it right now, they're going to smear your military record."

"Smear what? What are you saying, Paul? Come out with it." The senator's eyes darted to the string of photos on the wall.

"The White House has a file, Senator. I cannot vouch for its authenticity, of course, but they say you didn't get your medal in combat—"

"Bull," said Langer abruptly. "What else did they say?" His heart was racing; he could feel the flush in his cheeks and the heavy weight in his stomach.

"That you broke down in combat, sir. Battle fatigue. Not that anyone would blame you..."

Langer's heart was thumping so hard he wondered if Paul could hear it. He rolled his eyes back and looked up. *Thump, thump, thump...*

T H U M P, *thump, thump.* The noise of the chopper was deafening, blades rotating loudly against the steady whine of the Huey's turbines. Lieutenant Langer could feel his heart thump as well, straining against the huge nylon harness fastening him into his bucket seat. The machine seemed to be brushing the tops of dense green foliage. In the open doorway, a sergeant with linked bandoliers of 7.62 mm shells over his shoulder straddled an M-60 machine gun, one of his boots actually hanging out the door. The gun was trained at a forty-five degree angle, ready to spew its lethal load at the first sign of life on the ground.

Langer glanced at his platoon sergeant, Jim Howard, an old Vietnam hand on his second tour, sitting next to him. He could show no anxiety; Howard would pick it up in a heartbeat.

Thump, thump, thump. The Huey was vibrating so hard you wondered why the rivets didn't fly off in all directions. It bore its battle scars proudly, metal patches all over the fuselage.

Suddenly the machine lurched upward. It wasn't easy to see ahead, hard to move with a steel helmet rubbing on the padded collar of his flak jacket and a fifty-pound pack on his lap, with canteens and ammo belts dangling from it. But Langer could lean forward far enough to see a small mountain not five hundred feet ahead. The Huey strained and pulled, nose pointed down, as it scaled the side, thrusting ahead as it reached the top.

They were in Laos, he figured, probably fifty miles west of Con Thien and the DMZ, and they were heading north. This was not only illegal—the politicians in Washington created absurd artificial boundaries for this war that sure didn't bind the North Vietnamese regulars—but exceedingly dangerous, way behind enemy lines. That's why the major at the controls was hugging the tops of the banyan trees.

Suddenly the jungle was behind them and they were over open, rocky terrain; even at this higher altitude, they were an inviting target. *Oh God, protect us,* Langer breathed. He glanced around at the ten men, most of them silent; some, he was certain, were praying as well.

For twenty minutes the Huey roared up over the hilltops and glided down the slopes; then the thumping intensified, and the machine shook and quivered. The gunner stiffened. The crew chief, a master sergeant doubling as copilot, turned around in the cockpit and screamed some command which no one could hear, but they had done it so often, everyone knew instantly what to do. As the skids hit, Langer and his men released their harnesses, grabbed their packs and weapons, and nearly dove through the open hatch, hitting the dirt and falling forward. By doing this, the chopper, never more vulnerable to enemy fire than at that moment when it was immobile, could lift off without waiting for the troops to get away from the spinning blades. It was a discipline troops learned fast; stand up and you could be decapitated.

The bird lifted, and Langer signaled his sergeant to send hand signals to the two other squads, one to the left and the other to the right, that had been similarly disgorged by two other Hueys.

Langer and his platoon were reinforcing a Green Beret company, advisors to a small Montagnard army in the Laotian hills. Each night Montagnard patrols, along with their U.S. advisors, ranged the eastern slopes of the mountains setting ambushes for North Vietnamese troops coming down the Ho Chi Minh Trail. Of late, however, this company had been taking some heavy casualties, and Langer's troops were there to give the veterans a break.

The choppers had come into the compound at dusk when visibility was reduced for the enemy snipers and mortar men. At the north and south ends were two forty-foot-high observation towers, assembled with rough hewn jungle wood. The entire perimeter, perhaps six-hundred feet square, was protected by electrified fences and rolls of razor wire. Outside, the area was studded with land mines; inside, bunkers were strategically placed so that machine-gun and automatic-weapon fire could saturate every direction, defending against an attack.

The base gave a great sense of security. Each night the enemy, scattered throughout the area, would lob in mortar shells, but the troops almost became used to them. Seven months earlier a North Vietnamese regiment had assaulted the base, but the Montagnards repelled them, then pursued them down the slopes, killing every single attacker. They had sliced the heads off the dead and wounded and carried them back on sticks.

By 11:00 that night, Langer had dropped off into a deep sleep in his bunker when the sirens blared. He had already been briefed that the siren was only to signal a massive assault. As he grabbed his helmet and came up out of the bunker, the first waves of North Vietnamese troops were assaulting the east fence.

Langer was completely disoriented; he started running, he thought, toward his platoon area. Two mortar rounds landed just behind him, hurling him forward into the soft dirt. He came up with a mouthful, shaking his head and recovering his helmet. Everything seemed to be in slow motion and sounded far away; only later would he discover that his right eardrum had been blown out.

Everything was ablaze. The defenders fired flares that arched high over the camp; shells exploded all around. As he recovered his balance, Langer ran toward his platoon stationed on the northeast corner. He stumbled over the bodies of two soldiers. One was groaning, his entrails protruding from a huge gash in his gut.

"Medic, medic!" Langer screamed, but his shouts were lost in the explosions of mortar shells on either side. As he turned away, reeling, a shell hit the two soldiers. Too late for the medic.

Dazed and shaking violently, Langer reached his position. A radioman was kneeling next to his commanding officer, calling for help. Langer heard the steady rat-tat-tat of automatic weapons and saw dozens of men in khaki suits running straight at him. His position had been overrun. Langer pulled out his .45 and emptied the magazine. Two bodies fell to the ground. Another GI came up out of his hole, blasting his M-16 on automatic, cutting down the others.

Langer was crouched down, reloading, when the mortar shell hit to his right. The soldier next to him caught the full blast. His arm flew past Langer's head and pieces of flesh splattered against his face; he looked down and saw blood all over his tattered uniform. The last thing he saw was more men in khaki coming at him...

He woke up in a hospital bed at Clark Air Force Base. Padded leather straps held his wrists and ankles. Two doctors, one with a used syringe in his hand, were standing over him. For nearly two months, it turned out, he had been in some twilight zone. Except for superficial wounds and a punctured eardrum, he was unhurt—physically.

They told him what had happened. The base had held out, somehow. Half the Americans had been butchered. They had found him in the fetal position under some rubble. There were only sixteen survivors from his platoon; they had been rallied by the platoon sergeant. He had been treated both with electroshock and heavy doses of antidepressants.

THUMP, thump, thump... "Senator, are you all right?" Paul was standing over him holding his chin cupped in his hand. He sounded far away. "Are you all right, sir?"

He shook himself, loosened his tie, and ran both hands through his hair. He had to get control. "I'm sorry, Paul. I'm okay. Some sort of flashback or something."

Langer took a deep breath. "I guess I always knew it would come to this at some point," he said without looking at Paul. "I can't believe it, though. I was negligent to leave myself so vulnerable, stupid to allow it to happen in the first place."

"Senator, you don't have to explain," Paul said. "I can't imagine what you went through in Vietnam. None of us know what we'll do till we're put to the test. No one could hold that against you."

"But that's not it," said Langer. "I let this myth kind of grow on its own. When I came home, I just wanted to forget it all. I never talked about Vietnam.

"But then when I ran for office the first time, somebody put 'decorated Vietnam vet' on the campaign literature. That was true enough, so I didn't object; I didn't even think much about it at the time. I should have. But then on the stump, well, you know, the story got a little better and better. Not so much by me as by all those well-meaning, wonderful people who want you to succeed so desperately so they can get a job or a favor. Pretty soon you begin to believe it all yourself."

"Senator, you don't have to explain," Paul repeated.

"No, Paul, it's a relief to talk about it. Even Lily doesn't know it all," he said. "So these kind and decent gentlemen in the White House want to make it all public?"

"They didn't say it in so many words, but that's the threat."

"Well, I have to do what I have to do. I couldn't live with myself if I didn't. Those gentlemen in the White House are going to bring down this country. They have no respect for the Constitution. I have to do it."

"Yes, sir, you do." Paul was being disloyal to his present position, and he knew it. But he was in such anguish for Langer, he could not resist. Besides, he wondered if Langer wasn't right.

"Anyway," he added, "people are much more forgiving than you think."

"Maybe," said Langer. "But you know who'll chew me up will be my own constituency—the Christian Alliance. I've noticed they're not very forgiving when one of their own falls."

Paul winced. He had noticed that too. "You're human, sir. Some Christians are so smug and self-righteous, they put everyone off, and they're usually hypocrites anyway. If a person who is known as a Christian falls, and admits it, then people can identify with him. The people who matter will stick with you."

"Sounds good, but can't you see the press, too? They hate us 'right-wing Ayatollahs.' They'll crucify me. And the worst thing is—I deserve it. I broke the first rule: Never hand your enemy the sword with which to kill you. Stupid. Stupid." He shook his head then got up and walked to the window.

"Senator, just face right into it. Tell exactly what happened. The people will understand."

Langer continued to shake his head as he gazed over the green park in front of Union Station. A limousine pulled up at the Russell Building's First and D Street entrance, letting out an obscure sub-cabinet official Langer knew vaguely. The man walked as if he was the president himself. *Washington*, thought Langer.

"They'll call me a hypocrite, Paul—number one hypocrite. I've been the hawk on military issues, and now it comes out that in battle I cut and run. I can't face it."

"Hypocrisy, Senator, is the tribute vice pays to virtue. Hypocrisy is better than men like Griswold and O'Keefe who don't know there's any difference."

"Good philosophy. Try it on the editorial board of the *Post*." Langer walked back to his chair. Then he turned back.

"Thank you, Paul. Whatever happens, you've been a good and decent friend. You go back and tell them you really twisted the screws on me. Protect yourself. I need thirty minutes alone to think it over. What time is it?"

"It's 11:30, sir." Paul answered, disturbed. Langer was staring straight ahead at the wall, not even bothering to look at his watch, the wall clock, or the chronometer sitting on his desk.

"You sure you're all right, sir?"

"Yes, yes, thank you." Langer managed a faint smile. "You go on now."

After Clarkson left, Langer buzzed his secretary. "No interruptions, please, for the next few minutes." Then he sat, continuing to stare at the wall.

O'KEEFE WAS with the president in the small dining room off the Oval Office when the dispatch came in at 12:30. Juan passed the paper to Griswold who scanned it, jumped up, threw his napkin down, came around the table, and grabbed Bernie's hand, pumping it hard.

"Listen to this, Bernie! 'Senator Byron Langer, who until noon today had vowed to block President Griswold's declaration of emergency, has had a sudden change of heart. Briefed in the last hour by administration aides, Langer says he has been made aware of sensitive information convincing him of the gravity of the national crisis. He has concluded that President Griswold's actions are justified.'

"And listen to this, Bernie: 'Leading senators expressed consternation at the dramatic turn of events. Majority Leader Keenan announced that consideration of the resolution will be delayed. According to informed Senate sources, Langer's decision throws into doubt the Senate's ability to veto the president.'

"Have we got a team? Good work, Bernie. And call that AAG over at Justice. We ought to promote him. Make a note of that, Bernie. The next slot is his, or maybe he wants the bench."

O'Keefe pushed his plate aside as Griswold smashed his fist into his palm. "Good job. Leadership, that's what it is."

Robbie joined them seconds later, grinning broadly. "This is the way things are going to work around here," he enthused.

"The trains are running on time," Griswold said, slamming Robbie on the back.

35

IRA LEVITZ dined at Dick Morton's at least three times a week. He usually hit the Washington landmark about noon, where one of Dick's minions, or often Dick himself, would lead Levitz to his favorite table, already stocked with half dills and matzo crackers. Here, he would hold forth with assorted Washington insiders.

Today, however, his meal was interrupted when Dick brought the phone to him at 12:45. Levitz's guest, Chief Judge Satterfield of the D.C. Court of Appeals, an authority on constitutional law, made a rather obvious effort to look away while Levitz gripped the receiver to his ear.

"What?" he exclaimed. "You're not serious. That's incredible. Incredible!" The judge glanced at him, noting the columnist's neck turning an odd shade of purple.

Levitz threw his napkin on the table, where it landed in his plate of chicken livers and coleslaw. "Impossible," he yelled. Those at surrounding tables were now listening. "Impossible!"

He clicked off the phone and lowered his voice. "Do you know what Langer has done?" he said to the judge. "Withdrawn his resolution. He's backing Griswold!"

Satterfield looked startled. "Why?"

300

"Who knows! I'm heading for the Hill. You'd better finish your soup and get back to your courthouse fast. The way things are going, the army may have gotten there ahead of you."

In minutes, Levitz was downstairs, raincoat under his arm, three steps off the curb on Connecticut Avenue, hailing a cab. He brushed right ahead of two middle-aged women to grab the first taxi that stopped.

"Russell Office Building," he barked.

LEVITZ BOUNDED up the steps of the Russell Building at the First and D Street entrance, then turned right to the first office.

"Ira Levitz to see the senator," he growled.

"How are you, Mr. Levitz?" Langer's receptionist stood immediately. "Let me take your coat. I'll see if he's in."

"He's in. Otherwise you would have said he was out," he snapped, hanging on to his raincoat.

"Yes sir," she answered patiently, then made her way through the large mahogany door into the next office.

Levitz lit up a long, dark cigar, ignoring the smoke-free environment of the Senate, then pulled his small notepad out of his raincoat pocket and started scribbling.

Less than a minute later, a bright-eyed aide in his early twenties came through the door, asking if he could help. The senator simply wasn't available, he said, much as he was sure Senator Langer would have wanted to see Mr. Levitz.

"Young man, you go right back through that door and tell the senator I am here to see him and him only. Tell him I know why he changed his position, and I'm waiting." It was a tactic that had worked before, as it did now.

Two minutes later, the same young man returned. "Follow me, please, sir."

THE FIRST THING that struck Levitz was how ghostly Langer appeared. His skin had a grayish tone. His eyes looked reddened like he had an allergy. His hair was limp, as was his handshake. But he was as courtly as ever.

"Please sit down, Mr. Levitz," said Langer. He stepped around behind his desk and sat in his high-backed leather chair, then pulled an ashtray from his drawer and pushed it toward Levitz.

Levitz dropped into the nearest chair, folded his raincoat across his lap, and propped his notepad on top.

"I know why you're here, Mr. Levitz, and all I can say is that I have come to understand the urgency of our domestic crisis in ways that I had not before. I felt my decision was the only one I could make as a responsible public official." Langer spoke slowly.

"Just what information do you have today at"—Levitz glanced at the wall clock—"1:30 that you didn't have at 9:00 this morning when your office confirmed your speech plans? What in the world changed your mind, Senator?"

Langer's mind was moving slowly. Was Levitz bluffing to dig for information, or did he already know what had happened?

He decided to chance it. "I'm not at liberty to explain in great detail, but I can say that I know a great deal more about this conspiracy than I did before. I'm also aware of intelligence about the general breakdown of order in our cities that is of grave concern, Mr. Levitz."

"That's an old dodge, Senator," Levitz said bluntly. "What did they offer you? The Supreme Court? Air force planes at your disposal? A few million in pork?"

"Nothing," Langer said with conviction.

"Well, whatever it is, I want to tell you, man to man, you are betraying your trust, Senator, and I will say so in my column tomorrow—unless you can persuade me otherwise," Levitz said angrily. "Frankly, I'm shocked. How could you do this? You must see where those people in the White House are taking us!"

"It's the only responsible decision," said Langer dismissively.

"Bull," shouted Levitz. "It's a sellout. I don't know for what or why, but it is absolutely unconscionable. For years you've shown courage and a respect for the Constitution, for the law, for truth—and now you're no better than they are. What in the world happened to you?"

Levitz waited for Langer to speak, but the senator just sat there, staring vacantly at him.

"In fact, Senator, you're lower than they are. They're unprincipled, self-centered pragmatists who do whatever it takes to get what they want. They're amoral! We've known that for a long time. But you know right from wrong..." Ira trailed off, then picked up again. "And if we lose our liberties—God forbid—it will be because people who knew better did nothing. Don't you care?"

Levitz waited again, certain that Langer would reply this time and he'd at least get a quote or two...something, anything.

"I'm sorry you can't see my position, Mr. Levitz. I'm truly sorry." Langer's words were perfunctory, and his eyes seemed to stare past Levitz. His flesh looked almost transparent. Levitz wondered if he was ill.

Angry and confused, Levitz jumped up, flapped past the secretary, and flew down the corridor to see the majority leader. Somewhere he'd find someone with some honor and conviction.

AT 2:00 P.M., the White House announced that National Guard units would be activated in Miami, Baltimore, New York, Los Angeles, Detroit, Atlanta, Houston, and Dallas.

Because of the "success in the District," Caroline Atwater told the press corps, this additional action was deemed advisable and fulfilled this administration's pledge "to make the nation's streets safe again for every American."

She reminded the press that for the past three years Guard units had been detailed to the Miami police to help curb the epidemic of tourist killings. This action, therefore, should be viewed in context as "administrative escalation," a nice phrase Atwater herself had invented.

The press secretary had no comment on Senator Langer's announcement, except to say the president had phoned the senator to express gratitude for his putting the public's interest first.

EMILY GINEEN had scheduled lunch from 12:00 to 1:30 with the House Judiciary Committee. The subject was the crime bill, and she couldn't cut it short.

Paul had not returned to the Justice Department after his visit with Langer but had sent the limousine back for Emily to use. He had then walked to his old office in the Capitol. It hadn't been reassigned yet, and he went in and sat at his old, scarred mahogany desk for a long time. He wasn't sure why; he just knew he needed to. After a while he took a cab to the Justice Department.

AT A FEW MINUTES after 2:00, Emily made her way to Paul's office. She hadn't been there before, and she immediately noticed the photo of his family on the desk. "What a beautiful family, Paul. Beautiful!" She leaned against the desk corner. "What did Bernie want?" she asked cheerily.

Like a doctor describing a particularly painful operation, Paul clinically repeated exactly what had transpired: the meeting with O'Keefe and the confrontation with Langer. He left out only the references in the report to Langer "cutting and running" and being "found in the fetal position." All the while he talked, he avoided eye contact, staring out the window. Emily watched him intently, concentrating on the whole ugly story.

When he finished, there was a long silence. Then Emily pushed herself away from the desk and walked toward Paul's bookshelves, staring at the neat rows of volumes in the case, then at a framed quote penned in flowing calligraphy hanging on the wall... "Civil authority is a calling, not only holy and lawful before God, but also the most sacred and by far the most honorable of all callings in the whole life of mortal men."

Emily cast her eyes down to see the quote's source. John Calvin...who obviously wasn't well acquainted with the dirty tricks of civil service in Washington, D.C., she thought bitterly.

"I can't stand this," Emily said, whirling back to face Paul. "I hate politics. Griswold told me this office would be removed from politics, that we'd be able to work above all of this stuff—and now here we are, in garbage up to our necks.

"I mean, I've never agreed with Langer, and I never particularly trusted him; I felt like he was always manipulating things to get his way. But I knew he was a decent human being. I knew he had convictions. That he cared about something besides himself."

Emily slumped in the chair opposite Paul's desk and looked at her fingernails as if she had never seen them before. She didn't say anything for a while. Neither did Paul.

Finally, she looked up. "Paul," she said, "you are associate attorney general. You did your job. There is a higher interest here. The very heart of government is to maintain order and justice. This hurt, but it's a personal matter. Don't let it affect you so much that you feel like you didn't do the right thing. There's more at stake here than one man. It's the government."

Paul nodded, not knowing what else to do.

"As for me, well, I guess I've got to get used to this. It was so easy at Harvard; I could just look at cases and facts and opinions, all so stable and uncluttered. But that wasn't reality, I guess."

"Reality?" Paul echoed. He looked at Emily and raised his hands, palms up.

AT 2:45, a rumor swept Wall Street, already unsettled by the announcement of further Guard call-ups: The administration was readying a plan to limit the independence of the Federal Reserve Board—something that had been kicked around for years. It was one of those Washington secrets everyone knew: Griswold felt the Fed was being too tough on interest rates. The market closed fifteen minutes later, down 270 points.

Robbie walked into the Oval Office shortly after 3:00 with the alarming news. Griswold, who two hours earlier had sailed the heights of elation, now felt the crushing weight of his position. Except for dealing with his wife and daughter, he wasn't accustomed to such mood swings.

"Alan tells me that Nixon faced a crisis like this in '71," Robbie said clinically to his boss. "Bottom fell out, a 10 percent drop in one day, all over the reaction to Vietnam. Nixon called every big money man on Wall Street, a hundred of them, to dinner in the state dining room. Wowed them. Next day the market soared one hundred points and then some."

Griswold stared for a moment, then tapped his fingers on the desk. "Hmmm," he said. "Good thinking. You call Lucy in the social office. I'll call my wife. She'll get the menu and all that. Good, good. When do we do it?"

"Tomorrow night," Robbie replied.

Griswold arched his eyebrows. "Impossible."

"Lucy says she can pull it off."

"You've already talked to her?"

"Of course, sir. I knew you'd agree. I have the invitation list being put together right now. We'll get on the phones, and by 6:00 tonight we'll have a hundred leaders invited. No spouses. Working dinner."

"Robbie, you're amazing," said the president. "All right, let's go. I suppose you've called my wife too."

"No, sir, I leave the hard jobs for you."

Griswold laughed. He felt better already.

AT 4:00, Senator Byron Langer's office issued a two-sentence announcement: The Senator, suffering from exhaustion, had been admitted to Walter Reed Army Hospital. His condition was stable, although he was undergoing cardiac examination.

The president called Mrs. Langer to express his concern and wish the senator a speedy recovery.

AT 7:15, Bernie O'Keefe, leather attaché case in hand, exited the west wing through the basement door onto West Executive Avenue, where his limousine, a black Chrysler, was waiting. The driver, Scott Hubbard, an army sergeant, hustled around to open the door.

"Home, sir?" he asked.

"No," Bernie said. "Kelly's tonight."

Hubbard always suggested "home," hoping he'd influence the answer. Going home meant he'd be through for the night. But Kelly's, a Georgetown bar and eatery, meant he'd have to either wait or return for O'Keefe later, usually much later. Recently, however, Kelly's was the regular destination.

Kelly's was a Georgetown landmark, a cozy Irish pub and Washington watering hole since the Kennedy administration. On weekends the bar featured live Irish music and attracted throngs of singles; on weeknights Kelly's drew professionals in post-work recovery from all over the city.

Bernie pushed through the crowd, waving to a few regulars, and stood at the end of the long curved bar, waiting for a stool. He was in luck. A couple who obviously had been at the bar for some time were just coming to the climax of a long-simmering argument. The young woman leaped up and flung a couple of dollars on the bar.

"If *that's* the extent you're willing to commit, then forget it!" she shouted. "I'm outta here!"

The young man, abashed, picked up his car keys from the bar and threw a few dollars down as well. "You're being totally irrational!" he hissed. But she was already plunging into the crowd.

"So sue me!" she shouted.

He leaped off the stool and followed her.

Bernie raised his eyebrows at Henry, the bartender who had been at Kelly's for twenty years. "Makes me feel at home—like the old days with Marilyn," he joked.

Henry picked up the crumpled bills and wiped down the bar where the couple had been. "They'll be in here later this week," he said. "They love to fight."

Reminds me of Marilyn, Bernie said again, this time to himself.

"What do you want tonight, Bernie?" Henry asked. "Anything to eat, or just some Dewars?"

Wonderful, Bernie thought. He doubted that the bartender even knew his last name; to Henry, he would always be just Bernie. The fact that he was counsel to the president of the United States didn't mean a whit. *They say that only in church is the ground level, everyone equal at the foot of the cross*, Bernie thought. But he'd seen those religious people operate, with their head tables and their power cliques. Where the ground was really level was in a good bar.

"Thanks, Henry," Bernie said. "Yeah, I'd like a menu."

The bartender handed him a menu, left for a moment, and came back with a double Dewars on the rocks. Bernie sipped, then loosened his tie. The laundry had put too much starch in his shirt, and it had irritated his neck.

"Good job today, Bernie. That old coot on the Hill saw the light, huh? 'Bout time. Imagine trying to block the troops. Give us more, I say."

"You like the Guard on the street, Henry?"

"Sure do. Guy left here the other night with his girlfriend, got up onto P Street where they'd left their car, and two jerks with a gun waited till they got into the Mercedes, then held them up and took the car. The guy resisted. They shot him twice in the head. If I could get away with it, I'd have an M-16 right behind the bar here and blow 'em away myself, like I did in 'Nam."

"That's right, you were in Vietnam," Bernie said. "I forgot." He passed his glass back for a refill.

"On the DMZ, Third Marines. We took a pounding and then came home to the real enemy."

Henry poured another generous drink and handed it back. "Let me tell you, Bernie, and you tell your boss. I talk to people all day long, and folks out here like what he's doin'. Keep it up."

Bernie thought about Robbie and his obsession with Sindberg and his polls. He could see why Robbie listened in to the live calls; there was something energizing about hearing what real people thought, instead of just staffers and bureaucrats and politicos.

"I'll tell him, Henry."

"I mean it. You knock heads out here, put these animals away, clean up these streets. Lock 'em up. Fry 'em. We've had it. You do that and we're with you."

"Thanks, Henry." Bernie had heard the man's political views before, but he was surprised at the intensity in Henry's expression tonight.

The bartender left to wait on some customers at the other end of the bar, and Bernie stared into the mellow golden fluid in his glass. The pain was lessening.

Henry came back a few minutes later and refilled Bernie's glass. "What do you want to eat?" he asked. "You gotta eat when you're putting away this stuff like that." He had seen a lot of people drink a lot of alcohol over the years, but few of them could hold it like Bernie.

"I'm not really hungry," said Bernie.

"You gotta eat," said Henry again. "Just have some soup and a burger or salad or something. The onion soup is good tonight."

"Right, Mom," said Bernie. "You order something for me."

Henry left again and returned with a steaming crock of soup and some french bread.

"You seem a little quiet tonight, Bernie," he said as he laid the meal out on the bar. "Tired?"

"Henry, have you ever killed a boar?" Bernie asked abruptly.

"A bore? Yeah, we get 'em here all the time. I wouldn't kill 'em just for that, though."

"No, I mean the animal—the wild pig."

"No, don't know that I've ever even seen one, aside from my wife's mother, of course. Have you ever hunted boar?"

"Yeah," said Bernie, looking into his drink. "A real little one. Last animal I ever shot."

"That's a shame. I go to a farm in West Virginia after wild turkeys. I love it. What's wrong with hunting?"

"Oh, it's fine. Just not for me. Forget it." Bernie took a big gulp of scotch, and Henry left for another customer.

But the moment was still stuck in Bernie's thoughts. It had started as a wonderful weekend, right after he and Marilyn were married and before the kids. A client belonged to a private hunting preserve in New Hampshire, thousands of acres stocked with elk, deer, and wild boar.

The first morning, Bernie and his client, a big game hunter, were stalking an elk. They moved up the tree line silently and came to a clearing with a view to a distant field. Bernie's client spotted him first, the boar trotting across the field. "Too far away," he said. "Can't be sure how big he is, and you couldn't hit him anyway."

But Bernie eagerly leaned against a tree, got the animal in the crosshairs of his scope, lifted the high-powered .30 caliber just slightly to compensate for trajectory, and squeezed ever so gently. *Poom*, the rifle butt recoiled into his shoulder.

"Bull's-eye!" his companion shouted as the boar rolled over.

The two men walked briskly toward the fallen animal, which proved to be well over three hundred yards away. When they approached the animal, they could see he was lying helpless but in great agony, flailing his left front paw in the air. As they closed in, they could also see he was very young, maybe only fifty pounds. Though arguably the ugliest creature on the face of the earth, the boar's face had a pathetic expression, as if he were asking for help.

Bernie's companion drew his .38 pistol and shot the animal through the head. Then he gutted it, except for the liver, tied its feet together, and dragged it back to the camp.

Bernie had never hunted again.

"Another one, Bernie?" Henry asked. His glass was empty.

"Yeah, sure, one more," said Bernie, shaking his head. "And Henry...never kill a boar."

36

Wednesday evening, May 13

R OBBIE LOOKED at his watch. Only 8:30. Which meant the phones had been going at Sindberg's headquarters in Sioux Falls for only two and a half hours. Yet already the pattern was clear, and it was startling. So much so that J. D. Sindberg himself had called. People were rallying behind the president in astonishing numbers. They didn't care what he did as long as he cracked down on extremists and terrorists and criminals. Get rid of 'em.

Robbie jumped up from his desk in his McLean home, rubbed his hands together, and paced around the room. He couldn't contain his exuberance. He picked up the phone and asked the operator for the president.

"I'm sorry, sir," she replied. "He's on the tennis court with Mrs. Griswold."

Robbie then asked to be patched in to the army's signal corps network. "Get me the military aide with Searchlight," he ordered.

Seconds later, the aide on duty, Commander Hall, was on the line. "Have Searchlight call me at home," Robbie instructed him. "In between sets, of course. There's no crisis."

Minutes later Griswold called, struggling for breath. "What's up, Robbie?"

"You are, sir. Sindberg thinks you could be up five to eight more points in approval ratings tonight. He says the respondents all sound the same: Knock heads. They're with you, sir."

"Excellent!" The president was still gasping. "And oh, Robbie . . . thank you."

IRA LEVITZ had never felt worse. For one thing, his column was due at 9:00 P.M., precisely thirty minutes from now. It was an inflexible deadline; any later, and he'd be bumped from his regular space, replaced by a gushy background piece written by David Johnson about how Griswold had reached his momentous decision. That kind of soft journalism revolted Levitz.

For another thing, he was hungry. He'd had nothing for dinner but Heath bars and an old piece of pizza he'd found in the microwave. And he was angry—at Langer, Griswold, and the whole crazy world of Washington and its currency of pride and power and puffery. And his legs hurt. Cramps from sitting too long.

All of this added up to an apparently terminal case of writer's block. So he did what he often did when this happened: don't wait for grand inspirations; just write. Get it on paper. Then you can fix it.

Levitz took several deep breaths and stared at the screen, hating it, hating Washington, hating the *Post* because they wouldn't let him smoke in the building. Then his fingers began to move on the keyboard.

> Once again J. Whitney Griswold has proven himself the consummate politician. Someone evidently opened the Oval Office windows, and the president has wet his finger to the wind and knows which way it's blowing. If the people want action, crackdowns on criminals, then J. Whitney Griswold is ready to give them what they want in the circus called Washington.

"Yes, the president has asked not for whom the polls toll; he knows they poll for him," Levitz wrote wickedly. "So too apparently do a group of suddenly weak-kneed, compliant senators. But President Griswold and company should learn from history, lest they be doomed to repeat it."

Doomed. Did he really believe that? Yes, and then some. Once you give up liberty, the process begins to feed on itself. And there is never enough. Much is never satisfied with less than more. The obsession with order, with power, with control, always leads to the same end. The despots of every century end up on the ash heap of history.

Providing the Guard learns to shoot straight, some measure of order may be restored to our nation's troubled streets. Though it will be at an awful price. A people who cannot govern their own behavior are incapable of self-government. Troops in the streets are but a signal of the death of the American experiment.

But Griswold's second objective may be even more frightening. For the government to believe that it can suppress by brute force a movement driven by the deepest convictions of conscience is to ignore the most dramatic testimony of the twentieth century.

The words were flowing now. But was he being too supportive of those maniacs who had hijacked the network news? Two days ago he'd denounced them. Was he reversing himself? Would readers be confused?

No, he thought. His position had been consistent. It was Griswold who'd flipped, virtually declaring martial law.

He started writing again.

What has sustained American democracy has been the most fragile, yet the most enduring of all its qualities—its moral consensus. The values held in common that inform our consciences, restrain our behavior, and encourage virtue. These come at the very deepest level from the religious impulse, the conviction of a higher power which calls us to live righteously and compassionately. The impulse to be good and do good. It is the weakening of this impulse and the resulting collapse of private virtue that has led to the loss of civic virtue.

But tanks in the streets will not restore it. Force leads only to further tyranny. Or, perhaps, to an equally frightening prospect: revolution.

The essence of a free society is that different points of view can contend openly and freely in the democratic process. People have to believe that the system works, that they can make a difference. But when those doors are closed, when different points of view are declared out of bounds, frustration mounts. People move from the mainstream to the fringes. Violence erupts. And then, from somewhere in the heartland of this great nation, will arise a modern Oliver Cromwell.

Levitz's leg cramps increased along with his sense of frustration. Did it matter? Who really cared? Would anyone even get the reference to Cromwell and the overthrow of the British monarchy?

"Call off the troops, Mr. President," Levitz concluded. "Before it's too late."

He looked at his watch. Five minutes to nine.

He read through the column quickly. It was bumpy but passionate. Had some life to it. He keyed in a few changes, ran his spell check, and copied the file to the managing editor's terminal. Within fifteen minutes it would be read, checked for libel, and in type, just as the giant presses began rolling. The earliest edition would be off the press at precisely 10:30.

Levitz pushed back in his chair and rubbed his thighs. A White House messenger would be at the L Street entrance of the *Post* to pick up a copy at 10:35. It was the same every night. Griswold's aides would be poring through the paper within two hours.

"I hope he looks to the lessons of history," Levitz said to himself as he got up and stretched. "Well, at least I hope it scorches his butt."

He reached for his raincoat. Time to go home.

37

"MRS. BROWNSON, please cancel my appointments tomor-row afternoon. I'll be dining with the president," the managing partner of Goldman Sachs had ordered on Wednesday afternoon, his effort to sound casual betrayed by the slightly ele-vated level of his voice. He was not alone. The White House invitations had come by phone, and in New York, Chicago, and elsewhere across the nation, America's financial movers and shak-ers got ready to move. Personal and company pilots were alerted to get their Gulf Streams ready and flight plans filed; in more fru-gal circles, first-class reservations were hastily confirmed.

Meanwhile, Harvey Robbins called out the marines. The marine lieutenants, that is; those stationed in the honor units whose job it was to make Washington properly Washingtonian. In dress blue, gold braid, and white gloves, they were individually dispatched in White House cars to meet each arriving guest at National Airport.

Everything went flawlessly until 4:00 P.M., when Lucy Cabot, the White House social secretary and long-time friend of the Griswolds, discovered something suspicious. She knew New York City well and was surprised to see that the address of Herbert

Greenberg, managing partner of the investment banking firm of Baer and Morgan, was listed as Seventh Avenue and West Thirty-fifth, the heart of New York City's garment district.

Angry with herself for not noting it sooner, Lucy called Robbie, who immediately called the secretary of the treasury, Josh Wainwright, who had recommended Greenberg. Minutes later the information came back to Lucy: Wainwright's secretary had mistaken the Herbert Greenberg of Greenberg Garments, a cut-and-stitch sweatshop, for the Herbert Greenberg of the prestigious Wall Street firm.

"We'd better get word to Greenberg immediately that he's not invited," Lucy advised flatly.

But Robbie, aware that the press would seize the story as a potentially embarrassing tidbit, vetoed that. A hasty strategy conference convened in his office and a plan was designed. Two White House assistants would stay with Greenberg at all times, keeping him away from the other guests as much as possible and also keeping him at great distances from the president—and light-years away from the White House press corps who would be let in once during dinner for a photo opportunity. Beyond that, Robbie suggested prayer.

THE HIGH-CEILINGED state dining room on the west end of the main floor of the White House is dominated by an extraordinary brass chandelier hanging in the center and the portrait of a pensive Abraham Lincoln sitting with his chin supported by his right hand. The portrait hangs over the fireplace whose original mantel design called for a lion's head; Theodore Roosevelt changed that, appropriately, to an American bison. The deep gold in the draperies is accented by the gold brocade chairs and gold tones in the muted patterned carpet.

Normally for a state dinner the room was set with twelve round tables seating ten each. But Robbie wanted a working boardroom feel for this group, so straight tables had been arranged in a giant square, with the center empty and twenty-five chairs on each side.

The president's place was with his back to the fireplace. Two seats away to his right would be the attorney general and two seats to his left, Secretary of Treasury Wainwright. Wall Street loved Wainwright, a zealous supply-sider and tax-cutter. Then around the tables, scattered among the Wall Street guests, would be other cabinet officers and White House aides.

Herbert Greenberg, sandwiched between the two aides, would sit in the corner closest to the president, where he would be most obscured from Griswold's view. As it turned out, his short body was barely visible anyway, his round face peeping over the wine glasses, his shoes barely touching the floor.

The guests arrived at 6:30 and were ushered upstairs, where they were greeted by members of the cabinet. After everyone was seated in the dining room, the head usher appeared at the door and announced grandly, "The president of the United States," and Whitney Griswold strode into the room, smiling and shaking hands left and right as a marine band contingent played "Hail to the Chief."

Dinner was a feast of regional American dishes topped off by a selection of Hawaiian sorbets. Over demitasses of coffee the president spoke informally with the guests seated near him. Several were old friends from Brown and Yale, a number had been Greenwich, Connecticut, constituents, and others frequented the same clubs Griswold had belonged to in New York City.

Then the president began the evening's program with a glowing introduction of Emily Gineen, who, he said, would describe the character of the crime crisis and terrorist threats that had prompted the White House's current course of action.

Emily, wearing a simple black linen dress and pearls, stood, her back to the draped southwest window, and spoke easily for several minutes, profiling the situation: Violent crime was up 700 percent since the 1960s, and police were so overtaxed that law enforcement had effectively broken down in the inner cities. She then traced every major historical instance of the invocation of emergency powers since Abraham Lincoln.

"This administration," she concluded, "with scrupulous adherence to our fundamental constitutional liberties, will restore order to our streets. It is government's first obligation, one that demands courage and boldness, but we will not shrink from the task." She smiled as she looked around the room, connecting directly with her audience, then sat down as the bankers, investors, and money gurus applauded her warmly.

Wainwright followed with a less-inspiring speech, but he pushed all the right tax and growth buttons so important to this crowd.

Then it was Griswold's turn. He began as relaxed as Emily had been, but with a firm, direct, even blunt tone.

He first reassured the crowd that the rumors about limiting the Fed's independence were totally unfounded. The group applauded heartily. Griswold then turned to domestic matters. "Our crime bill puts real teeth in our laws, giving police and prosecutors the weapons they have long been denied," he said, and was again interrupted by a burst of applause. Robbie, watching, smiled and checked his watch.

Then Griswold spoke of the missing ingredients in American life, the qualities he had learned on "the playing fields of Groton and Brown," the things many in the room believed they had acquired in similar settings: decency, tolerance, civility.

"These religious bigots—who are, in fact, quite unchristian by my definition—will not be allowed to pollute our social environment," he said. "Free religious expression, always. Violence and obstruction of the rights of other law-abiding citizens, never."

On that line, delivered powerfully as Griswold jabbed his index finger in the air, the powerbrokers of Wall Street rose to their feet in enthusiastic applause.

Emboldened by the response, Griswold ignored his typed 3 x 5 cards and leaned toward the group. "Let me say something that I trust will not be misunderstood. I probably could not say this in a more public setting for fear of being called racist, which, as you all know, I most certainly am not..."

Emily tried not to look as startled as she felt.

"...but the truth is," continued Griswold, "the crime crisis in

America is quite localized. If one were to remove the African-American crime rate from the overall statistics, our national crime rate would be lower than the Belgians', lower than most of Europe, and below average for industrialized nations."

Around the room of mostly white faces there were raised eyebrows, quiet gasps, then nods of understanding. Emily was horrified. The figures were true, but the crime rate had to do with the breakdown of the family, which was epidemic in the inner cities—which happened to be predominantly black. For Griswold to use the stats the way he was doing was exploitative, fueling prejudices of the worst kind.

But it worked. Though a few faces were still frowning, most of the crowd had locked in with Griswold. He had merely articulated what they had thought all along. Robbie was grinning.

Griswold went on to explain that the National Guard was, therefore, the only feasible solution. Many of the soldiers, after all, were minorities, so racial tensions would be minimized. The troops also could be targeted exactly where the problem was: the inner cities. This was further grounds for their support for the president's inner-city empowerment legislation.

"Once we cure the root problem—that is, jobs, education, better housing—then we will no longer need the Guard," he concluded.

Once again the applause rang out from the bulls and bears of Wall Street; they had just experienced Whitney Griswold at his most adroit, skillfully manipulating the crowd. But Bernie O'Keefe, watching them, thought they reminded him more of sheep, baaing on command of the shepherd. *It worked, but it's a cheap shot at the blacks. Robbie must've cooked that one up.* He shifted uncomfortably in his seat.

Robbie, too, was uncomfortable, but for a wholly different reason. His eyes were trained on Herbert Greenberg, who had enjoyed his meal with great relish, had sipped appreciatively on the wine selection, and now was nodding gravely and moving his lips as if he wanted to speak.

Robbie, who had watched him carefully throughout the evening, willed the little round man to silence. *You may not open your mouth . . . you may not open your mouth,* he repeated silently. The press had just been let in, the evening had gone perfectly, and this man must not be allowed to say or do anything to call attention to his presence.

But then it happened. Robbie had the sensation he was in a dream, everything in slow motion; he couldn't move fast enough to stop the horrible thing from happening.

Herbert Greenberg raised his hand, signaling a question.

The aide to his left, eyes wild, wrestled his arm down, hissing in Greenberg's ear. Startled, the short, stocky man stood up. The aide on the other side attempted to pull Greenberg down by the back of his jacket but succeeded only in rolling him backward on his heels, off balance. Greenberg clutched the tablecloth desperately, and plates, silverware, and wine glasses rolled and tipped to the floor.

Robbie knew at once he had made a crucial tactical error by not alerting Griswold. He had hoped that Greenberg would not be noticed so there would be no need to concern the president, who had a tendency to fret over such things, and who, incidentally, would blame Robbie for not being more careful.

Griswold started toward Greenberg just in time to collide with the secretary of treasury, who had thrust his chair backward to avoid the splatter of wine from the tumbling glasses. Robbie winced when the president got to Greenberg first and helped steady him as the waiters converged on the scene.

"I'm so sorry," Griswold said with instinctive graciousness. "You have a question, sir?"

"Yes, sir, I do," Greenberg said, still wiping the melange of pineapple, mango, and papaya sorbets from the front of his jacket and pants. "First, thank you for inviting me and having me met at the airport."

The president nodded.

"I haven't been in Washington since the wife and me drove through here twenty-two years ago on our way to Miami Beach. On my fiftieth birthday, in fact. Now we own a condo on the beach and we fly. You can do it cheaper than driving, you know."

By now Griswold's eyes were wide, his mouth frozen open in a half smile. Robbie knew what he was thinking—and it wasn't good.

"My partner and me," Greenberg continued, "we started our business forty-two years ago. Just the two of us, it used to be. Back then you could go uptown on the subway for a nickel and it's a $1.25 today, which you should do something about." He looked sternly at the president.

"But we've worked hard, twelve to fifteen hours a day, and because of that we now employ forty people. About half Spanish and half black—on two shifts. That's forty off the welfare rolls that you don't have to worry about."

Robbie could feel the knots in his stomach. Bernie caught his eye and sliced his finger across his throat. Some of the guests were looking at each other with arched eyebrows, shaking their heads. Griswold stood motionless, arms folded, a dreadful, sickly smile on his face. And Greenberg kept going, telling the president his whole business history, while the television cameras kept grinding, the flashbulbs popping.

Robbie gestured for Caroline to get the press out. Envisioning herself herding some horrible stampede, the press secretary knew that was impossible. Now the other guests were clapping for Greenberg, a few calling for him to sit down.

But the applause snapped Griswold out of his trance.

"Now, now, gentlemen and ladies," he said, raising both hands, palms outward. "We've just heard a very sincere account of how from humble beginnings one man built a good, successful business. We thank you, sir, for creating those jobs by your ingenuity, enterprise, and hard work. This is the American dream, which we are pledged and determined to keep alive."

Greenberg was still standing, trying to ask his question, which was about minority job quotas, but the crowd drowned him out with sustained applause for the president. The two aides, gently this time, got Greenberg back into his chair. Robbie, breathing heavily, took his napkin and wiped his brow as Griswold asked if anyone else had a question.

"Mr. President," a middle-aged man whom Robbie knew to

be the head of one of the largest mutual funds in America, rose to his feet. "Michael Novak has written, sir, that the American system is like a three-legged stool; one leg is the free economic system, the second is our free political system, and the third, our moral base. And clearly, Mr. President, there is an ethical collapse in this country. What can you do to strengthen the moral leg?"

Griswold could answer policy questions all day with one hand tied behind his back. But no one had asked him a question quite like this in a very long time. He hesitated just a moment, searching to recall Novak's thesis, but showed no emotion.

Then he grinned. "Good question, good question. I see it as government's first task to punish wrongdoers and reward right behavior. That establishes the moral norms. Beyond that, we must create a climate of economic and political freedom, the first two legs of the stool, which will in turn encourage the full creativity of the American people. If we provide the freedom, we will allow the basic goodness and decency of Americans to flourish. That's precisely why we are pursuing our present policies: to achieve order and preserve freedom so decent people—and Americans are that—can live decently. That's the moral answer."

The man who asked the question did not applaud, but the rest of the room did. The sound signaled the end of the evening, and the Marine Corps band began to play. The press people were ushered out, and Griswold started around the table pumping hands.

Robbie's knees were still a bit weak, but he knew all was well. Everyone was smiling.

THE NEXT MORNING, the market opened 140 points up and kept rising. Sindberg himself called Robbie to tell him that the president was now at the highest point of his presidency: 67 percent approval. In his euphoria Griswold apparently had forgotten about Greenberg. Robbie, not a religious man, thanked God.

"Just one thing, Robbie," Griswold said, twirling his reading glasses by their stems and leaning back in his chair, propping one leg on his bottom desk drawer. "That Novak question. I've been thinking about it. I've got to be a little better prepared on stuff like that. Government can create virtue by the right policies; I've always believed that, and I still do. But I don't think I convinced that fellow—who was he anyway?"

"President of Federated Investors. Very devout Catholic."

"I see. Of course. Probably a religious right-winger. Still, we ought to be ready. Have you read Novak?"

Robbie shook his head. Conservative Catholics weren't on his reading list.

"Well, I haven't lately. It's pretty right-wing stuff, I remember." Griswold kept twirling his glasses and half smiled. Robbie knew he had not read him either.

"Have Carmichael's boys do a little analysis for me. Put someone on this, Robbie. Read his stuff and give me a summary."

"Yes sir."

"That's it for now, I guess." Griswold sat upright, a signal he wanted time alone. Robbie gathered his papers.

"And, uh, Robbie, good job last night."

"Thank you, Mr. President. But you made it, sir. You were brilliant."

"Yes, yes... and, uh, Robbie," he said, just as his assistant reached the side door. "Give my warm regards to our friend Herbert Greenberg."

Robbie blanched, nodded, and went out the door. Griswold reached for the direct line to the private quarters in the mansion. Anne answered.

"A terrific morning," Griswold said, then proceeded to tell her about the polls, the feedback from the dinner.

She listened without response until he finished, then said, "That's wonderful, Whitney."

"So I've got an idea. It's a beautiful day. My schedule isn't too bad. Why don't we pick Elizabeth up after school and drive out to Middleburg. No big fuss, just two cars. We can have dinner at the Red Fox Inn. They won't advertise I'm coming."

"But, Whitney, you know wherever we go, it creates a fuss."

"No, we can do this."

"And I'm in the middle of packing. Everything is spread out on the bed. Maria's helping me. I'll be at it all day."

On Saturday Anne would be flying to Martha's Vineyard to supervise the opening of their twenty-two-room summer home on Starbuck Point, an exclusive enclave on a neck of land at the entrance to Edgartown Harbor. As soon as school was out in June, the family would spend as much time there as they could squeeze out of the schedule. The Secret Service and military had already taken over the basement, built a guard post, installed electronic devices and communications gear, and Anne wanted to get it all back in order. She hated mess.

"But, dear, that can wait. This is a great day for us and the country. We should celebrate, like the old days." Griswold was almost pleading.

"Oh, Whitney, of course. How insensitive of me. Whatever you'd like."

Anne put the phone down and stared out the bedroom window at the Washington monument in the distance. It was a gorgeous day, her husband was in a wonderful mood, she was looking forward to Martha's Vineyard, and yet she had this awful feeling. She remembered when she was a small girl, putting the furniture back in her dollhouse one day. Everything was in place perfectly; she was kneeling, reaching into the bedroom with a tiny rocking chair, and then she lost her balance and knocked the house over, scattering all the furniture.

Should she say anything to Whitney? Certainly not. He'd probably dismiss it anyway. But it was real; it wouldn't go away. She thought of Elizabeth, then realized she was tearing her cuticle, something she hadn't done for years.

Maybe a ride in the country would be good for them.

38

Friday, May 15

BERNIE O'KEEFE couldn't remember a morning when he
had felt more miserable, at least not since the awful time five
years ago, a time he had almost totally blocked out of his memory.

He opened the top drawer of his dresser and fumbled through
piles of handkerchiefs, a traveling iron, a box of buttons, three
packs of hemorrhoidal suppositories, and miscellaneous luggage
tags. In the corner, behind some old used airline tickets, he found
the small round vial filled with pills, five milligrams each of
Xanax. The label had a red warning sticker: "Avoid alcoholic bev-
erages while taking this medication." Bernie shook his head
slightly—he never drank in the morning—and threw two pills in
his mouth, swallowing them without water.

Dr. Nikkels had told him to take one at the first sign that stress
was getting the better of him. Maybe he'd waited too long. The
black veil had descended. For four hours in the night he had
clutched his pillow and tossed fitfully, his heart racing, his
thoughts dark and clouded, in the grip of that awful feeling of
helplessness he remembered from before. Around dawn, he had
fallen into an hour of sleep; then the horrible alarm had rung.

His temples throbbed, his head felt like it was an eighty-pound ball of iron.

And the awful thing was that he was alone. Marilyn had held him in her arms the time before, stroked his head while he had sobbed in the night. Now she was in Wellesley, and the way things were going, she probably wouldn't be particularly sympathetic if he called her. He couldn't talk to any of his colleagues at the White House, or even the White House doctor. He knew the rule there: Walk the corridors with your back to the wall. Somebody was always waiting to sink the knife in and take your place in the inner circle. He could think of a number of people who would be overjoyed at the thought of Bernie O'Keefe having a nervous breakdown.

Bernie tried to absorb himself in the intelligence summary awaiting him on the back seat of his limousine, but he couldn't concentrate. He could focus his eyes, and he saw the words, but he couldn't process the thoughts. It made him angry, and he was already raging inside.

At the dinner last night he had put his finger on what had been troubling him for weeks. Robbie was now totally controlling Whitney Griswold, manipulating him with his polls and his little divisive bits of information, exploiting the man's darker side. It was infuriating, and as Bernie's limo worked its way through the morning traffic, he got angrier and angrier.

When his car arrived at the west wing at 7:45, Bernie leaped out and headed straight for Robbie's office. It was time to set a few things straight. He walked by Robbie's secretary with hardly a glance and through the big mahogany door. Robbie was at the conference table, his back to his desk, his two young assistants seated on either side, scribbling instructions into their notebooks.

"Bernie, come in, come in." Robbie could be irritatingly cheerful in the morning. He waved Bernie to a chair at the table.

"Got more good news from Sindberg. The boss is staying right up there in the polls. Look at this, Bernie." He slid a paper across the table.

By now the Xanax had made its way into Bernie's central

nervous system, numbing it slightly. He took a look at the paper: The approval was holding near 70 percent.

"Impressive, all right, impressive." He handed it back to Robbie. "Could we have a minute?" he asked.

Robbie motioned to his assistants, who were both wearing almost identical gray suits and red silk ties. Bernie called them the beaver patrol: young and eager, obsequious around Robbie, brusque with most everyone else. They got up after Robbie nodded and quietly slipped out.

"Jeez, you look rough this morning, Bernie. You all right?"

"I'm fine," said Bernie quickly. "Just a short night's sleep. But there's something I need to say to you...I don't want you to forget, Robbie, that Whitney Griswold and I go back together a long way—twenty-five years. I know this man, his good side and his bad side, and I know when someone is manipulating—"

"Wait a minute. What are you talking about? Look at these polls. We're playing this thing like a violin—"

"Live by the polls, and you die by the polls. This is the president of the United States, Robbie. He's not a marionette. You can't just put him on stage, pull his strings, and make him dance."

"Bernie, are you sure you're okay? This is the way every White House is run. The president's out front. That's his job. He's the public face; he's scripted according to the game plan that's already set. You can't run the modern presidency any other way. Not with the media in your face. Look what happened to Clinton when he tried to wing it."

"Yeah, I know. But Whitney Griswold is a good man, Robbie. Let him be president. I trust his instincts."

"What's eating you?"

"Last night at the dinner. That crack he made about the black crime rate. Emily didn't give him that; I know, because I've talked to her. I didn't give it to him, it wasn't in the briefing material, and it's not Whitney Griswold. It was a cheap shot, Robbie. Those fat boys from New York loved it, but it was a cheap shot. The cause of crime doesn't have to do with race, and you know it."

"Maybe he read it somewhere. Maybe he isn't scripted all the time."

"You planted that one, Robbie. Don't manipulate him."

"Right. And who are you to moralize? Politics is a rough game. Just ask Byron Langer."

Bernie's cheeks flushed. "That's different," he snapped. "That hypocrite had it coming. He lied about his war record, he blackmailed us into hiring his man, and don't forget that he was just about to launch a major torpedo right at us."

"Listen, Bernie," Robbie's eyes narrowed as he glared, "my job is to keep this man in this chair for the country's good. What do you want? The bigots cramming their narrow-minded values down our throats—or the Democrats who will bankrupt us? Whitney Griswold is this country's hope."

Bernie got up. It was almost time for the 8:00 staff meeting. "I believe that," he nodded. "Let's just remember that it's Whitney Griswold who is president. We aren't running a puppet show here."

Bernie stopped in the men's room before the meeting. As he splashed water on his face, he was disgusted to see that his hands were shaking.

Later that morning, he found Dr. Nikkels's card in his desk drawer and placed the call. He couldn't face what he'd gone through before: the deep black holes, the long counseling sessions, the Prozac. The doctors had called it clinical depression. It had been so bad, there were times he'd wished he was dead. He couldn't go through all that again. He'd have to see if Nikkels could just send down some pills.

While he waited for Nikkels's nurse to get the doctor, he rubbed his temples. He felt exhausted.

39

Friday, May 15

Paul clarkson arrived at the attorney general's office a few minutes before 4:00 and found the other assistant AGs already gathering around the big table in the conference room. Director Frizzell was setting up a chart board, and Lieutenant General Childers, assistant chief of staff for the army reserve and the Guard, was also on hand.

Paul was making his way to his chair just as Emily entered from her private office at the other end of the room. She slid quickly into her place at the head of the table.

For the next twenty minutes Frizzell briefed the assembled executive team on the progress of the bureau's investigation of the anti-abortion groups. All those who had been involved in the Gideon's Torch operation had been apprehended, he assured them, including a young broadcast intern and the man from TapeMasters who had "loaned" them the original tape to copy. The suspects were being held, awaiting preliminary hearings and arraignment. None had been able to meet the $500,000 bail set by a government-friendly judge.

Furthermore, five churches in the New York area at which the

Gideon's Torch people had held meetings were being charged under RICO statutes as part of the conspiracy. The civil division was moving aggressively to confiscate assets. Several businesses that allegedly had supported the members were being vigorously investigated and would likely be charged as well.

Undercover assets were still in place, and more anti-abortion leaders were being "visited"—Frizzell smiled when he used the word—and interrogated extensively.

"Our only problem at this point," he explained, "is in knowing who could be tied in by overt acts, but we're casting the conspiracy net wide. Extensive phone taps. Physical surveillance. Particularly where we can't infiltrate. If anything is coming down the pike, we'll know about it."

He warned them, however, that more terrorist acts were possible, even likely, and security at the White House was being significantly augmented. But violent acts were possible anywhere.

"These are dangerous people," he reminded the group.

Agents in each field office would soon begin visiting anyone visibly involved in the pro-life movement. It was a huge task and would take months.

"Won't that, at the very least, border on harassment?" asked the assistant attorney general for civil rights.

Frizzell grinned. "Sure. We're dealing with terrorists."

Any clinics that had ever been targets of protest at any time were being given round-the-clock protection by U.S. marshals and FBI personnel. Even the regeneration centers, still under construction, would receive federal protective security in the weeks ahead, just as soon as more personnel became available. "Our resources," Frizzell said, looking pointedly at Clarkson, "are being taxed to the limit. I have submitted a supplementary budget request to the associate attorney general's office."

As for progress in the Fargo case, Frizzell concluded, the bureau had a very strong suspect but had to be careful not to act precipitously; she was being kept under active surveillance, and it was hoped would lead them to others involved in the conspiracy.

General Childers, a tall man with rugged features, a one-time

West Point all-American fullback and a decorated veteran, followed. He lacked the adroitness of Frizzell and occasionally stumbled as he read from his briefing papers. The report was also anything but inspiring: thirty-two shooting incidents involving guardsmen; a number of the victims were innocent bystanders. Arrests were up in each city where the Guard was working, but also, surprisingly, were homicides—sharply up in D.C. and L.A. There were no questions for Childers.

As the briefing concluded and the staff assembled their papers to leave, Emily signaled Paul to her office. "Let's talk a few minutes," she said, leading him toward the doorway.

"Of course," he said. "But I do have a little time problem."

"Oh? Well, I guess it could wait until tomorrow."

"If it could wait, that would be great. I really need to go. I'm sorry, but I promised Paul Jr. I'd be at his Little League game tonight, and it starts early, at six o'clock."

The bottom was falling out in the country, terrorists were on the rampage, and the associate attorney general was heading to a Little League game? Emily raised her eyebrows.

Paul smiled. "A long time ago, I promised June that whatever happened in my work, I would not neglect my family. I promised my son I would come to his game tonight, and if I break that promise, he'll never forget it—"

Emily stopped him. "I really do understand. That's great. It helps to cut through the garbage and distinguish between the important and the urgent. I should get home too. Where's the game?"

"In Great Falls, near where I live."

"Good, I'll drive you out. We can talk in the car. I'd like to see your son."

"It's way out of your way, Emily," he said.

"Well, that'll give us a chance to talk. No problem."

AS THE BLACK Lincoln wound along the George Washington Parkway in bursts of speed and abrupt stops—traffic was at its worst before six—Emily seemed unusually reflective.

"It's beautiful," she said, looking at the spring growth, the wildflowers, and lush green embankments. To the right they could see the Potomac, its waters higher than usual.

"Paul, what do you think?" She turned toward him. "Is all this we're doing going to work?"

Paul smiled and shrugged his shoulders slightly. "Maybe, for a while at least, if we can get the Guard not to shoot everything that moves—and if there are enough of them."

"But only for a while?"

"Yup. Levitz's last column was right on."

"What would it take to really stop crime, Paul? What do you think would really work for the long run?" she asked.

"Put kids in Sunday school."

"Oh," Emily shook her head, annoyed, "you religious people are all alike with your simplistic, cute answers. Langer did that with me too. Be serious."

"I am being serious," Paul said. "There was a study done in England by a professor at the University of Reading. He found that when Sunday school attendance was at its peak, crime was lowest. When Sunday school attendance declined, crime went up, in direct proportion. A group of scholars studied the data and came up with the answer: Put kids back in Sunday school."

"Look, that all sounds very nice, but we were elected to lock 'em up. The criminals, I mean. You don't want the government to get into the Bible school business, do you?"

"No, I sure don't," Paul said. "Government can only do so much. I mean, we can help in little ways by the standards we set in the laws we pass. But government can't create virtue, Emily. That has to come from within the people themselves. Individual lives changed. That's what God alone can do."

Emily stared at Paul for a moment, then shook her head. "So we're just keeping our finger in the dike, trying to hold it all back, right?" she asked tiredly. "Trying to keep the troops from killing innocent citizens. Trying to keep Frizzell's storm troopers from taking over the Capitol. Right?"

"Just about," he sighed.

"Got any constructive ideas, Paul? Any good news?"

"I can tell you where the really good news is, Emily."

"You going to get your Bible out?"

"Sure," he chuckled. "You ready?"

"No, not today."

A FEW MINUTES before six, they pulled up behind a chain-link fence. Beyond it, groups of parents were standing or sitting on the wooden bleachers, chatting, watching their kids warm up around the softball diamond.

As Paul got out of the car, a boy spotted them. "Hey, Dad!" he shouted with a grin, tossing the ball to a teammate and running around the fence.

"You remember Attorney General Gineen, son," said Paul. The boy took off his hat and shook Emily's hand.

Emily had seen him the day Paul took his oath of office, but now looked him over more carefully. With his close-cropped, curly hair and beautiful smile, Paul Jr. was a copy of his father.

"Thanks for the ride, Emily," Paul said. "I'll see you on Monday."

She watched them for a moment as they walked away. Paul walked slowly, leaning on one cane, his other arm around his son's shoulders. Paul Jr. was carrying his father's briefcase.

It's incredible, she thought. Most of the politicos she had come to know in Washington never got home from the office before midnight and prided themselves on their "commitment." *I know one thing*, she thought. *Paul Clarkson does have his priorities straight.*

Emily got back in the limousine. "Home, please," she said to the driver.

KELLY'S WAS JAMMED, as it was every Friday night. Bernie couldn't get a stool at the bar; he had to stand behind somebody else.

"Hey, Bernie, how's it going?" Henry grinned, waved, and headed for the Dewars.

"Great," Bernie yelled. *No problem*, he thought. He'd popped his last two Xanax hours ago, before lunch. Dr. Nikkels had prescribed some sleeping pills and recommended Valium. Nothing stronger, he said, until he could examine Bernie.

In any event, he was feeling better, and the first sips of scotch were soothing. Bernie always liked the feeling when the 86 proof hit his stomach. On an empty stomach it took only seconds for the alcohol to penetrate the walls of the intestinal lining and enter the bloodstream. He could feel the warm glow before his second sip. It was comforting; life was really bearable after all.

He'd fly to Boston tomorrow night, see the kids, and then Nikkels had agreed to see him at his home on Sunday. With a plane from Andrews, he'd be gone less than twenty-four hours.

Within a few minutes he had edged his way into an open spot next to a young man with a ponytail and an earring in his right ear. Henry was wiping down the counter.

"Good day, Henry?" Bernie asked.

"Yeah, no complaints."

"Big weekend?"

"You bet. We're taking the boat to Lake Anna tomorrow. Can't beat it." Henry smiled. "The kids love to go down there."

"What kind of boat?" Bernie asked.

"Century 21. Nothing fancy. Fast, though. Kids like to water-ski. Me, I just float around with a few cool ones."

"Is it worth it?" Bernie asked suddenly.

"Is what worth it?"

"Life. You work your tail off in this place, full of smoke and noise, listening to everyone's gripes—you hear more than most shrinks do. You work all week so you can zip around on a lake on Saturday. Is it worth it?"

"I never thought about it, Bernie. It's what I do. I mean, I might like a bigger boat. And my wife wants a bigger house. I don't know why. We've got four bedrooms and three kids. But I wouldn't trade with most of the people who come in here every night," he said. "No, I guess I've got it okay. Why do you ask?"

O'Keefe drained his glass and put it on the counter. "Just wondering," he said. "I'm doing a poll." He shoved the glass toward Henry. "Get me one more, would you?"

Henry knew he never meant only one more.

40

IT WAS STILL quiet in Rehoboth Beach in mid-May. The big crowds didn't start coming until Memorial Day weekend, when the summer season kicked off with a bang. Then all the boardwalk shops opened, beach umbrellas sprouted like colorful mushrooms in the sand, coconut suntan lotion wafted in the breeze, and the waves were dotted with bobbing heads, while children built sand castles and adults lay nearby, baking and basking in the latest Tom Clancy or John Grisham novel.

Incorporated in 1891 as an alcohol-free Methodist retreat town, by the 1990s Rehoboth's well was no longer dry, most of the Methodists were gone, and three distinct populations worshiped at the shrine of sun and sand. Each had its own particular amusements and hangouts.

First were the families, who staggered onto the beaches in landing parties carrying more equipment than the troops at D-Day. They set up elaborate camps stocked with coolers, umbrellas, chairs, sipper cups, playpens, strollers, sunblock, plastic shovels, buckets...and when they tired of the ocean, they made their way across the sand and up the wooden stairs to the boardwalk's dubious delights: miniature golf, Wack-a-Mole, cotton candy, fudge, and funnel cakes.

Rehoboth was also a magnet for D.C.-area single professionals. They traveled lighter than the families yet still made the two-and-a-half-hour trek from the city each weekend with solemn ritual. To avoid the bottlenecks on the Chesapeake Bay Bridge, they would linger downtown after work on Friday evenings, waiting for the traffic to die down. Many gathered in groups at the rooftop bar of the Washington Hotel, whose breezy clusters of comfortable sofas and low tables overlooked the Treasury Department and the White House. It was one of the best views in Washington.

By nine or ten at night, they would head east for the beach, stopping sometimes at the landmark Red, Hot, and Blue restaurant on Route 50 just before the Bay Bridge. The Memphis barbecue was a Washington ritual: pulled pig sandwiches to go.

FINALLY, in recent years Rehoboth also had built up a substantial homosexual community. They kept mostly to themselves, sunning on what the locals had called Poodle Beach until a city ordinance prohibited the nickname as a hate crime.

The locals were still allowed to note that the gays had the lock on the best restaurants in Rehoboth. If you wanted a really good meal, the best places to go were the Blue Moon or Syndey's or LaLa Land.

But the undisputed king of Rehoboth cuisine drew from all three of the town's populations: the legendary Grotto's Pizza, with multiple locations in Rehoboth and its next-door neighbors, Dewey and Bethany Beaches. A trip to Rehoboth was not complete without the experience of sitting on one of the ancient white benches on the boardwalk with noisy seagulls circling above and a huge, hot, triangle of Grotto's extra-cheese pizza in your hand, oozing oil down your chin with each bite.

DANIEL AND Alex Seaton had come to Rehoboth Beach every summer of their lives. After their parents had died in the plane crash, the boys had held on to the family's summer home on Columbia Avenue, a pine-lined residential neighborhood near the heart of town. Number 31 was modest yet comfortable, a snug bungalow with a generous screened porch.

Whenever Daniel and Alex were there, childhood memories merged with recollections from the years since, especially all their late-night discussions on the porch with friends. Such conversations usually came after an evening spent laughing and pounding the red-seasoned shells of blue crabs with wooden mallets, then plucking out the tender meat.

Most of the memories were from an earlier, more innocent time. Before J. Whitney Griswold. Before Gideon's Torch. Before violence and ugly confrontations. Before things had gotten so complicated.

This evening found the two brothers, along with Lance Thompson and John Jenkins, sitting on the beach in the light of the setting sun, a Grotto's pepperoni pizza between them, the grease seeping through the cardboard box and into the big old bedspread spread out beneath them.

Recent events and the arrest of their friends in New York had made Washington feel too alien. The walls seemed to be closing in. So Alex had suggested that the four of them, the inner circle of the D.C. cell, take an overnight and go up to Rehoboth.

"Staring at the ocean is always therapeutic," he'd said. "And I can't think straight with federal troops on the streets of D.C. I feel like I'm in a movie."

Even as they ate the pizza, however, he found himself looking around to see if they had been followed. The public beach off Columbia Avenue was about a quarter mile from the end of the boardwalk; he could see the big street lights just beginning to come on, spiking the wooden walkway at intervals.

As they faced the ocean, behind them were several hundred yards of sand, dunes, and to the northwest, the quiet, exclusive neighborhoods of Henlopen Acres. If anyone wanted to overhear their conversation, they would have to march across open sand and plop down on the blanket with them.

DANIEL TOOK another bite of pizza and stared at the sea. The sun was setting, and the pink glow from the clouds reflected slightly on the foamy curl of the cresting waves. It was his favorite time of day.

He thought of how many summers he had sat on this sand and stared at the ocean. Sometimes he had prayed and struggled with decisions here. Like whether or not to go to seminary. And he had come here and gazed at the sea, in a grinning daze, before he had asked Mary to marry him.

He and Mary had come here when Dan Jr. was a baby; he had slept under an umbrella in his mesh playpen while they stretched out on the sand, relaxed, and dreamed about the future. The fall after their parents had been killed, he and Alex and the rest of the family had come here for Thanksgiving; it had seemed appropriate to gather together in a place that had brought them so much joy.

Constant yet changing, the ocean was Daniel's touchstone, the place that tied him to his past and freed him for his future.

But he had never been at the beach in such turmoil. Even as they ate this ordinary pizza, looking like any average group of guys relaxing and talking, he noticed that Lance was not facing the ocean, but toward the west, like a sentry. And driving Route 50 east, headed to the beach, well under the speed limit, Daniel had noticed that he himself had flinched each time he saw a police car. *Why do I feel like a fugitive?* he wondered.

Lance startled him; the usually silent sentry spoke. "I think the time has come to do something," he said simply.

"We have done something," Daniel responded.

"It didn't work."

"We don't know that," Daniel said tentatively. He was talking like Mary, though without much conviction. "Changing people's minds takes time."

Alex wadded up his paper plate and napkin and thrust them into their trash bag. "We're out of time," he said. "The video didn't do anything but make people mad. At us. The government has cracked down like we're Colombian drug dealers, except they treat the drug dealers better.

"Look, Daniel, let's just lay it all out. We've done everything we could over the past two years. We've protested peacefully. We've sent mailings to people who influence public opinion. We've called legislators. We've protested some more. Written articles.

"And we've gone the extra mile to accomplish something unprecedented in the history of broadcasting: We actually showed a third of the nation what will happen in the regeneration centers. We've taken every conceivable route within the system—and then some—to expose the evil. Gideon's Torch: We lit up the darkness, right?"

Alex turned toward John Jenkins, who was watching Daniel. "John, you're a businessman. Would you continue a project that had failed on every single count? No. You'd learn from the failure, cut your losses, and take another strategy."

Daniel thought of Bill Waters. They had gone to school together. He had seen his friend's familiar face, briefly, on the network news. Two federal agents were leading Bill, manacled. There had been a million reporters, all shouting questions. It was chaos, and yet Bill had had his head up, looking directly into the television cameras, his expression neither defiant nor cowed. Then one of the agents had put his hand on the crown of Bill's head and pushed him down into the unmarked car...he wondered when he'd see Bill again.

Lance spoke again with his characteristic brevity. "Alex is right."

Daniel sighed and started digging a hole in the sand with his fingers. "I've always argued against Christians working outside the system. No one ever thought this would be easy. But we have to exhaust every avenue of reasonable nonviolent action."

"They're exhausted, man," Lance said. He was beginning to sound like the chorus in a Greek tragedy.

"I'm exhausted, too," said Daniel. "Maybe Gideon's Torch hasn't worked. I don't want to sound holier-than-thou, but I've never been too concerned about what works; I've tried to think in terms of what's right."

"But it's gotten a lot more complicated," Alex responded. "We haven't gone outside the system; the government has prevented us from working in the system, blocked our access. The courts for years have enshrined abortion as the one sacred right of American life. Congress won't act, and the politicians have all left us. You can go to jail for simply protesting. And if you look at some of the bills in Congress now, even expressing our views is going to be a crime. Writing a letter to the editor will be called inciting violence. And on top of it all, the president is out to crush every pro-life group in the country. They're acting like we're the Ku Klux Klan."

"We may as well *be* the Klan, according to the public opinion polls," John interrupted.

Then Alex turned to Daniel. "You remember what Levitz just wrote? When a government stifles legal dissent, it invites violence. He's right."

Daniel rolled his eyes upward as if carefully weighing the point, then spoke deliberately. "I'll admit that this government has lost its moral authority," he said. "The White House is acting like a police state. And people out there are loving it. But I have to read Romans 13 literally. Government wields the sword for our good. I don't like it any better than you do. And I realize these guys care only about polls and elections and shutting up those who disagree. Okay, it's getting a lot harder to honor those in authority, but that's what the Bible says to do."

"So what do we do?" Alex asked, egging his brother on toward the natural conclusion of his reasoning.

"Well, the church has to act as the conscience of society. God knows no one else will. We have to resist."

"We have been resisting," said Lance, playing off Alex to make sure Daniel kept going.

"I know," Daniel said. "And when we break the law to make our protest public—like Gideon's Torch—we should pay the consequences and go to jail. Our guys in New York were all committed to that. Maybe the four of us belong there too. We knew about it." He paused. "We've had it easy on our end."

They were all silent for a few moments. Then Daniel continued thoughtfully. "But now I wonder if future generations will judge us," he said, "like the church in Germany in the '30s. It was silent. We haven't been silent, but maybe we haven't done everything that we should do." He rubbed his eyes.

"Proportionate response," said Jenkins. He knew his friend well. The phrase from Augustine clicked in Daniel's brain.

"I know," Daniel responded automatically. "Right. Just war theory says you use the reasonable force necessary to counter the evil. But only the minimum."

"Oh, great!" Lance said. "This isn't Sunday morning. You don't need to preach. This isn't theory. I've been in wars, just and unjust. I know how much force you need in order to survive.

"But we aren't talking about our own survival," Lance pressed on. "We're talking about thousands and then millions of unborn babies. The regeneration centers are like the slave ships, bringing in helpless people about to be tortured. They're like the trains bringing the Jews to Auschwitz. We can't just stand by with our little cardboard protest signs anymore."

Daniel stared at Lance. His comparisons caught in Daniel's throat. *Maybe it's not that complicated after all,* he thought. *We've tried everything within the system, and they just keep delivering up helpless people to the slaughter. So we try to stop them.*

He looked at Alex, who was making a road in the sand, just like he used to when they were boys. Daniel realized that over the past year or two he had tended to dismiss his brother more often than not: too impetuous, not well-read or well-reasoned enough. *Maybe there's a certain wisdom to such simplicity,* he thought.

And it didn't take much to understand that there were two sets of rules being applied. For years, abortion protesters had had to answer to a different standard than, say, animal rights protesters.

In Maryland a few years earlier, a group of PETA activists had thrown vials of their own blood on the sidewalk and blockaded the entrance to the building housing the animal labs at Bethesda's National Institutes of Health. They had gotten a free-for-all of media attention, appearances on the *Today* show, a thirty-day sentence in jail—suspended—and a $500 fine.

The same week a group of pro-lifers at the Planned Parenthood clinic at the corner of Sixteenth and L in downtown Washington had stood in the rain, quietly praying as the clinic opened. A ten-year-old girl with them had strayed into the legal "bubble zone" in front of the clinic entrance. Her mother, trying to retrieve her daughter, had gotten into a shouting match with the pro-choicers, been arrested, thrown into jail, and fined $10,000. The story—eighteen lines—appeared on page three of the *Post*'s Metro section.

Daniel had visited the woman when she was released to her home. She was pale and shaken, her arm still blistered from where a group of aggressive inmates in her cellblock had burned her with cigarettes before the guards had dragged them off her.

Her husband had stood with his back to Daniel, looking out the window. "There is no justice," he had said quietly, though his shoulders were shaking with anger. "We have no recourse. They've stripped us of dignity, they're mocking God's law, and no one cares." Daniel had nodded awkwardly, unsure of what to say or do. He felt impotent, a pastor offering nothing but carrion comfort.

Six months later, the man had been arrested in Bethesda, an explosive device in the trunk of his car and a map with a penciled circle around the home of the doctor who performed abortions at the Planned Parenthood clinic. He was in prison now, and his wife and child were living with her parents. Daniel had written the man a letter. He had gotten back only a rambling note, ending with the old quote from Edmund Burke: "All that is necessary for the triumph of evil is for good men to do nothing."

DANIEL STARED into the darkening ocean and sighed. He felt like he was slipping out with the tide.

"But wait. I still say—we mustn't fall into the tactics of the other side," he said suddenly. "You don't overcome evil with evil. You overcome their evil with good."

"I've been thinking about that," said Jenkins. "It's true. But we're not talking about defending ourselves, or about aggression. We're talking about defending the defenseless. For their good, we choose to break a lesser law. A lesser evil, for a greater good. We need to respond with a proportionate response. Some kind of surgical strike."

Alex couldn't help himself. "That's what we've been saying for months now," he exploded, though he kept his voice low. "We take the obvious target. The first regeneration center. I've got a munitions expert who'll help us. This is not a public relations campaign. This is practical. The center is due to open in the fall. We're not talking about taking people out, though getting rid of a few dozen of these doctors who do the D and X wouldn't be a bad idea. We're talking about a *building*.

"And once that building is open, at least a hundred babies a week will die there. If we take it out, that saves five thousand babies in a year. That might not sound like much, but it makes a difference—particularly to those five thousand babies. Oskar Schindler saved twelve hundred Jews; today their children's children's children play on the streets of Jerusalem."

Daniel sighed again. He had seen *Schindler's List* three times when the film had come out a few years earlier. Its images burned into his brain, particularly the ending, in which art and reality had merged and the Schindler Jews—the actual people whose lives had been saved, along with the actors—had walked in droves, topping the crest of a green hill in Jerusalem, wrinkled old men and women, their eyes full of life, their faces full of dignity, bringing flowers to the grave of Oskar Schindler.

Daniel thought about Schindler. He was a flawed man, but a man compelled by conscience to do what he could do. He hadn't sat around and debated the fine points of civil disobedience. He hadn't circulated petitions. The death trains were moving too quickly. He had acted.

Daniel looked out at the ocean again. It was dark now, and the waves seemed louder as they crashed into the cool sand. Alex and Lance and John were vague shapes in the darkness.

Daniel shook his head. "I'm sorry," he said. "I can't be part of something like that." He felt very tired. "But I can't tell you what to do. We all have to follow our own consciences. But don't do anything that hurts anyone."

Alex knew when not to push his brother further. He and Lance stood up together, picking up the pizza box, the trash bag, and their Coke cans.

"You coming?" Jenkins asked when Daniel didn't move.

"No, you all go on back to the house. I'm going to stay here for a while," Daniel said. "I need to pray."

41

IN WHAT had become his usual morning ritual, James Jones flipped open the *Fairfax Journal*. His wife had teased him that he was going to leave her as soon as he found who or what he was looking for in the personal ads. He had responded that he was just checking up on her to make sure she wasn't advertising for a younger man. Across the breakfast table, Justin, home from college, just grinned at his parents and attacked a huge plate of bacon and eggs.

It was in the fourth column, under the "Men Seeking Men" section. "Black man seeks same for discreet, explosive, good times."

Jones looked at it again, slowly, to make sure, took another swallow of coffee, and looked over at Justin. "I'll take you to the office this morning, son," he said. "Then I've got to go on a little errand in Arlington."

ACCORDING TO the upper-left-hand corner of the front page of today's *Washington Post*, sunset was due at 8:06. As the shadows lengthened at the site of the nearly completed regeneration center, the crowds of commuters at the George Washington University Metro stop began to thin. Every booth at Sam's Deli was full. At the GW library, summer students settled into their study carrels. In the hospital, groups of doctors and interns had just concluded their nightly rounds.

Lance Thompson turned right onto Twenty-third Street off Washington Circle and slowly drew near to the regeneration center in the van he had rented. He was calm, composed, and dangerously quiet as he examined his target.

The center's first floor was lit, like a model home beckoning buyers. The second floor was dark, except for a few dull glows that looked like security lighting and the lighted glass walkway that arched over Twenty-third Street, connecting the center with the hospital. Its decorative glasswork made it look like a high-tech amusement park tunnel. According to the blueprints Lance had studied, the center was secured from the walkway by an electronic door that could only be opened by a keycard, and a checkpoint that would later be manned by a guard.

Where's Alex? he wondered. Their plan depended on split-second timing. He would take the van under the building, and Alex would have the getaway car ready for their exit. They'd ditch it somewhere at the airport and get the 9:30 flight to Miami, then go on to Costa Rica. He had their fake passports, tickets, and everything else they needed.

Relieved, Lance saw Alex's brown Toyota edging up behind him in the rearview mirror. Then he watched as a police car whizzed past, made a U-turn at the next traffic light, and came back by, siren blaring. *Maybe the National Guard just shot somebody else*, Lance thought. Well, at least the cops weren't hanging around here at the moment. Good thing.

IN THE George Washington University Hospital's Tandy Pavilion, a theaterlike arena within the hospital that was used for teaching sessions, press conferences, and the like, the private cocktail reception was in full swing.

The regeneration center wasn't due to open for three more weeks, when there would be a major ribbon-cutting ceremony, speeches, and a big splash of media coverage. Tonight's event, however, smaller and absolutely private, with no reporters present, represented the real power base behind the center's creation: key AIDS activists from around the country and a few wealthy supporters whose names would grace the main wings of the center; they had kicked in big dollars to the private foundation piggybacking the center's federal funding. The center's senior staff were there as well, along with a few key guests from Capitol Hill.

The center's executive director, Dr. Barbara LaMar, had taken the group of thirty or so for a tour of the new building. Then they had returned to the Tandy Pavilion, where caterers had set up an open bar and waiters strolled with silver platters of hors d'oeuvres. There LaMar had delivered remarks, as had the chairman of the fund-raising matching campaign.

Congressman Peter Meyer had concluded the formal program, ending his short speech with the well-known personal odyssey of his own family and their struggle with AIDS.

"As many of you know," he said, "my wife was one of three siblings. She worshiped her oldest brother—his life, in fact, inspired her own decision to pursue public service. Doug's term in the Peace Corps, his bold campaign to save the rain forest, his tireless efforts for anti-bigotry legislation against those who would incite an atmosphere of hate and fear of diversity are shining examples of his ongoing contributions to society.

"Many of you know my wife, and April wanted me to express to you her regret at not being able to be with us tonight. But her decision to pursue law and her subsequent career on the bench came directly from the example of her brother's tireless dedication to justice and the service of others.

"We will never forget the pain of Doug's HIV diagnosis, nor the false hopes raised by AZT and other medications. We will never recover from the pain of watching April's brother wither, week by week, into a pale shadow. The loss of bodily functions, the loss of hope, the loss of life itself. Yet Doug died with dignity, the entire family by his side.

"Tonight, however, we gather with new hope, for perhaps our long national nightmare is almost over. Just around the corner is a whole new beginning, a new dawn when out of life new life can spring, when the sacrifice of women willing to exercise their reproductive rights for the good of others can bring about a new birth of hope for us all."

Meyer's unctuous speaking style was relieved by his striking good looks. He had not had much use for his wife's brother while he was alive, but in death Doug had served him well, providing an anecdotal verity and emotion to his otherwise predictable language. That emotion had resonated well with voters, and, it turned out, with people who held the purse strings for the "regen cen," as he liked to call it.

The alliance with the center had also helped Meyer's re-election campaign the past fall. He had faced a tough race and had needed as much television air time as possible to put his handsome face and resonant voice directly into voters' living rooms. That was expensive, but he had found that raising money for the center had put him in touch with celebrities and liberal corporate heads who didn't mind spilling a few extra thousand into his private coffer in exchange for political and legislative favors.

Another advantage of his association with the center was that it had brought him into contact with Barbara LaMar for the first time. He had heard about her long before he met her; the former NIH administrator and new head of the regeneration center was known in Washington circles as a tough, bright, sexy powerbroker. Meyer liked that trinity in a woman. His wife was tough and bright, but she failed decidedly in the third area. Barbara LaMar had it all.

Meyer finished his speech with the request that they all observe a moment of silence for the AIDS victims of the past and a moment of hope for those who would be saved in the future. He had found that that moment of spirituality worked well with audiences—even somewhat cynical ones like this small, powerful group. When the silence ended, most people made their way to the bar for fresh drinks, and the silver platters of smoked salmon and sushi circulated again.

Meyer popped a cube of fish in his mouth and drained the Chivas the bartender had just poured him. Even as he chatted most sincerely with one of the center's wealthiest benefactors, he watched Barbara LaMar working her way through the crowd, nodding, smiling, calculating, and, it seemed, making a bead right toward him. He smiled and ordered another Chivas. It was only 9:30, and April would be working very late tonight. Perhaps he wouldn't get home until late himself.

AT 9:30, in the regeneration center's security control room, Justin Jones flipped the center's automated security alarm—the one that rang automatically at the nearest D.C. police station—to its off position.

James Jones, sitting at the control panel at his company's offices, saw the center's monitor glow, meaning electronic security was down at the facility. His heart pounded. *Please, Justin, just get yourself outta there in time*, he thought.

LANCE LOOKED at his watch. By now Justin would have deactivated the automatic electronic surveillance. And traffic was light. He drove slowly to the center's entrance and slid the passcard Justin had given him into the front-gate monitor.

The electric gate slid open silently, and Lance drove through, down the curving drive past the central drop-off area and around the back of the building toward the underground parking garage. There, he inserted a second computer-coded card into the monitor standing like a small sentry outside the big double-bay doors to the garage. There was a rumble, and the huge doors rolled upward.

The garage was empty and dark except for the twin beams of the van's headlights. Lance drove toward the center of the garage, near the entrances to the elevators, and parked the van next to one of the huge, concrete, load-bearing pillars of the regeneration center.

JUSTIN JONES, making his rounds on the first floor, heard the rumble of the garage doors and looked at his watch. Lance was right on time.

LANCE OPENED the van door to shed some light, then went around to the back to deal with the job at hand. Most of his work had been done in advance; now it was just a matter of positioning the fuse igniter, then pulling its metal ring.

The van's two rear seats had been removed, and in the shell where they had been were now ten tidy stacks of military-issue explosive—seven hundred pounds of dense stickes of off-white material wrapped in olive-colored saran wrap and stored in army haversacks. Lance prepared to prime one of the sticks in the bottom layer of the explosives so the explosion, when it came, would go straight up.

He pulled what looked like a pair of pliers from his pocket, opened the tool, and pierced one of the sticks of c-4, rotating slowly to create a narrow hole. He slid the time fuse into the hollow blasting cap, then crimped its neck and secured the blasting cap in the c-4, unrolling a length of black electrician's tape and taping the deadly package so the device wouldn't fall out of the explosive. When the thing blew, in roughly five minutes, a spark would spit from the igniter into the concave end of the blasting cap, which would in turn create a shaped charge, focusing the explosion in a bubble that would shatter the regeneration center's floors right up through the building and on out the roof. An immense, voracious fireball would incinerate just about everything in the facility, including, Lance thought with satisfaction, the operating suites above his head.

He brushed his hands lightly against one another. He knew the c-4's deadly potential, but he moved deliberately and without panic. It was one of the easiest explosives in the world to work with; in fact, you could even set it on fire, and it would burn, but it would not detonate. In order to blow, it needed the small shock of the blasting cap. And in just a few more minutes, it would have it.

BARBARA LAMAR and Peter Meyer sat in the front row of the Tandy Pavilion, slouched a little in the padded blue leather seats. Barbara had taken off her red-linen jacket; underneath it she was wearing a thin, soft, cream-colored blouse with satin buttons. She had also kicked off her black heels. Peter had abandoned his jacket as well, loosened his tie, and they were near the bottom of the bottle of Chivas they had lifted from the bar just before the caterers packed up and left.

Peter twirled his short glass, expecting by habit to hear the clink of cubes. He had forgotten they were out of ice.

"So why didn't you stay with him?" he asked. They had gotten off on a tangent about travels in Europe and had figured out that they had both spent the same summer in Italy, years ago.

"It would have screwed up everything," she said. "I was just starting medical school. That summer in Europe was a last fling before I settled down for the long haul. It was a great affair and he would have left his wife for me, but I couldn't really see staying in Florence. What would I have done over the years? Get fat eating pasta and gelato? I needed something a little more fulfilling than being the armpiece of some rich Italian count. I'm sure he just got bald and died anyway."

"Your tenderness knows no bounds," said Peter.

"I'm as tender as you are, Congressman," she said sarcastically. "Why don't you show me your soft underbelly?"

"It's not my best feature," Peter said.

"I've been thinking about your features," she said, leaning toward him slightly. "None of them are too bad."

He liked her directness. He looked around the big empty room. Not exactly a private place for two public figures.

"Listen," she said, reading his mind. "I've got a private office already set up over in the center. It wasn't on the public tour earlier, but I think I can arrange a private showing. It's a little more comfortable than this."

"Is anyone over there?" he asked.

"In three weeks there will be a veritable army over there," she said, stumbling ever so slightly over the word veritable. "We've spared no expense on security. With those crazies out there, I wouldn't be surprised at anything, once the center's up and running. But right now all we've got is electronic surveillance, an electrified fence, and a lonely security guard making regular rounds."

"How lonely is he?" Peter asked.

"Not as lonely as you are," she responded. "So wouldn't you like to see it?"

"See what?" he said.

"My office!" she laughed. She picked up the bottle of Chivas and dropped it into her large Armani leather bag on the floor. It sloshed a little.

Peter Meyer laughed too and stood up, pulling her to her feet. "Yes, Dr. LaMar," he said. "I'd like to see it very much."

IN THE EMPTY, echoing underground garage, Lance breathed again. He had checked the device three times. It was right, and now the alarm was set. The thing would blow in four more minutes.

Lance turned and trotted across the expanse of the garage, exiting through the doorway to the right of the big doors. He walked briskly up the curving driveway, along the sidewalk, and then used Justin's security card to open the gate at the side entrance to the center. He hoped Justin was getting out according to plan.

The brown Toyota slowed next to the curb. He looked in, and saw that Alex looked like he was about to explode. His eyes were wide, and he was drumming the wheel wildly with his fingers.

I shouldn't have brought him in here, Lance thought. *I should have known he couldn't take it.*

He ran around the front of the car and opened the driver's side door. "Move over," he said.

"I'm supposed to drive," Alex hissed at him.

"I know, but trust me, man," Lance said calmly, noting the seconds ticking by on his watch. "I'll drive."

Alex started to protest, then shut up and scooted across the vinyl seat. Lance got in, started to accelerate, and saw that the traffic light on I Street had turned red.

As they waited for the light, both looked back toward the regeneration center. It looked just as it had when they arrived. The first floor was lit, the second dark except for the glass walkway connecting the center to the hospital. Lance turned back to watch the traffic light, and Alex made a choking sound. Lance looked back again. Two figures were strolling through the lighted walkway.

"No!" Alex said.

"They can't get in," said Lance. "It's locked. They'll just turn around."

The traffic light turned green.

"Pull over!" Alex shouted. Lance eased over to the curb.

Inside the glass tunnel, the figures stopped at the door. One had a big satchel; it was a woman. She reached in her bag and fumbled for something. The man leaned over her, wobbling slightly.

"No! No!" Alex cried again.

Lance looked at his watch. Thirty seconds. "We gotta go," he said.

THE MAN and woman had turned the big purse upside down and were rummaging through its scattered contents on the floor. As they did so, in the dark on the other side of the door, where no one could see him, Justin Jones was panicking. He had seen the man and woman on the security monitor on his side of the door. They weren't supposed to be there. How was he going to get out? He'd lost track of time, but he figured he still had a minute or so. Enough time to get to another exit. He turned and sprinted down the dark hallway in the opposite direction.

DOWN IN THE street, Alex watched as the woman in the walkway stood, triumphantly waving a card of some sort in her hand.

"What do we do?" he quavered.

"There's no time to go back," Lance said. "Just think of this as war, 'cause that's what it is. And in war, this kind of stuff happens."

"But we can't just let them get blown up!" Alex cried.

"There's no time," Lance shouted, the tension finally breaking through in his voice. "We've got to get out of here!"

He pulled away from the curb, but the traffic light was red again.

A police cruiser pulled up on the opposite side of the intersection and sat facing them, waiting for the light. A thin woman with a huge dog waited on the corner. Lance gritted his teeth, counting the seconds. Up in the glass walkway, the woman unsteadily tried to jam the card into a slot near the secured entrance into the regeneration center.

Just then Alex lost it. Lance saw it coming, but not fast enough. He popped down the automatic locks on the car, but Alex had already yanked up on his door handle and was out and running back toward the center, arms flailing.

Lance jerked the car into park and jumped out to get his friend. His brain counted down, even as he ran...three, two, one...

The flash was huge, the sound crashing down on top of them. Alex was thrown to the pavement. Lance, tripping, falling, got to him a second later and grabbed him under the armpits, dragging him back toward the car.

As he did so, he could sense, rather than see, the floors of the center thundering down on one another, crashing into the parking garage...tons of cement tumbling into the ground...shards of glass flying everywhere...screaming people on the street...smoke...flames...

Lance threw open the car door and thrust Alex onto the front seat. He was mumbling, and blood was streaming from his head. Lance scrambled around the car, into the driver's seat. He sent the Toyota hurtling away from the curb.

The last thing he saw as he screeched away was the D.C. policeman, out of his car, screaming into his radio, his face a mask of horror.

42

BERNIE FELT it before he heard it, a shiver running along the heavy wooden bar, just enough to make the golden fluid in his glass swirl slightly. Then, within seconds, came an enormous jarring thump, like a fist slamming on the bar.

As the rumble echoed in the summer night, people at the bar looked quizzically at one another. A few at tables near the door walked out onto the sidewalk, then shook their heads. Nothing in sight.

Bernie's first thought was the White House. Pointing at the television above the bar, tuned to a Cubs and Cardinals game on ESPN, he shouted at Henry, "Flip to Channel 5!"

The Fox network was first on with the late news at 10:00, so their news team, already set up at the studio, might know something. But the regular programming was still just blathering on. Bernie grabbed his portable phone out of his attaché case and dialed 456–1414.

Almost instantly he heard the familiar voice. "White House."

"Bernie O'Keefe just checking in, Mary. Everything okay?"

"Yes sir. We didn't page you, did we?"

356

"No, no, but give me W-16. Thank you."

The Secret Service duty officer answered on the first ring and quickly assured Bernie that everything was secure at 1600 Pennsylvania Avenue. But after volunteering to call the police and find out what was happening, he put Bernie on hold. While he waited for what seemed like minutes before the agent returned to the line, Bernie felt uncharacteristically uneasy.

"It's bad, sir. An explosion of some sort at GW Hospital. The police say a real big blast—looks like a whole wing is gone."

"What wing?"

"The regeneration center, whatever that is. Apparently something new, sir."

"Okay, okay, thanks. No, wait a minute. Call the president and inform him. Tell him I'm on my way back."

Bernie dropped a twenty on the bar and headed for the street, annoyed at himself for letting his driver go back to the motor pool. He didn't like the limousine sitting in front of Kelly's and had assumed he'd have plenty of time to call it back. No time now, though. He'd have to hail a cab.

The sidewalks were packed with people, and the traffic on M Street was bumper to bumper, the usual carnival atmosphere on a summer night in Georgetown. No cabs. Bernie turned right out of Kelly's front door and ran along the crowded sidewalk, jostling people along the way.

At the corner of Wisconsin and M, in front of Nathan's, a couple was just getting out of a yellow cab. Bernie ran toward the taxi, his arms waving, tie flapping. "The White House! This is an emergency!" he shouted. Bernie grabbed the door and jumped into the cab. "The White House!" he repeated.

Traffic was horrible. It took almost twenty minutes to get there. But finally Bernie was being escorted by Agent Ferguson up the main stairway in the executive mansion. The agent knocked on the door of the Lincoln sitting room and they heard the president growl impatiently, "Come in, come in."

Whitney Griswold's tie was loose and he was pacing, hands behind his back, a furious expression on his face. On the ottoman in front of his chair was an open briefing book which Bernie recognized as being from the National Security Council. The rebel government in Nigeria was creating huge problems, withholding oil shipments to Europe; prices were soaring, and the Germans were particularly upset.

"Bernie, they've done it now. Off come the gloves. All the way. Time to knock heads. We've been too easy, soft in fact. They're misreading us if they think they can do this. Blowing up a building ten blocks from the White House! Do we have no intelligence in this government? What in heaven's name are we spending thirty-two billion dollars for?"

Bernie had not heard Griswold this upset in a long time. There was a half-finished drink on the table next to his reading glasses. He was not a happy drinker.

Griswold didn't wait for Bernie's answer, since he knew there wasn't one.

"Bernie, call the Pentagon. If we need more troops, let's get 'em. And get on Gineen and Frizzell. I've already talked to Frizzell—told him to kick butt, get those agents out from behind their desks and on the streets. I want those responsible nailed." He turned toward Bernie and pointed. "You understand me? Cordon off this city. Roadblocks. I don't give a rip about all the pussy-footing civil liberties types. Just get 'em. You understand? Get them!"

The president was sizzling, and Bernie realized it was more than the scotch talking. Griswold was taking this as an armed assault. Revolution.

"I'll take care of it, Mr. President," Bernie said. "Don't worry about this. You concentrate on the important things—Nigeria."

Griswold nodded. "Okay, Bernie, you take care of it." He forced a half smile.

BERNIE WENT to his desk, where for the next several hours he was in almost continuous communication with the bureau, local police, and the attorney general, except for the interruptions from Griswold, who called every thirty minutes. The last call was at

1:00 A.M., when Bernie could tell he had almost calmed down enough to sleep.

At 2:00 A.M., Bernie called for his car. He needed some rest as well. He stopped in the washroom on his way to the elevator and then threw two Xanax in his mouth. One, he had discovered, didn't do enough.

"Yeah, I'll take care of it," he muttered, shaking his head. "Some job."

43

Beads of sweat clotted Lance Thompson's lined forehead as he gripped the steering wheel and propelled the car away from the city. Alex slumped in the front seat next to him, moaning, bleeding steadily into the red, sodden wad of paper towels he was holding against the back of his head. It was clear they couldn't make the 9:30 flight to Miami; Alex's head was bleeding too much for them to even think about getting onto a commercial airplane. So they'd have to get to Frank Doggett's and put plan B into effect. But first he had to get Alex stitched up. He knew where he could go for that.

It was a miracle, Lance thought, that they hadn't been challenged. Even as the screams of sirens echoed all over the city, they had careened away from Foggy Bottom, onto Constitution Avenue, and west on Route 66, toward the suburbs.

He tuned the radio to WTOP, the all-news station, as the first breathless reports of the bombing came over the air. "A scene of total devastation," the reporter said, obviously relying on reports coming out over the police radio. "Police and fire personnel are searching the area for casualties. They are also reporting that witnesses saw a brown four-door Toyota sedan near the scene just prior to the bombing…"

Lance bit his lip and glanced in the rearview mirror as he exited from Route 66 and made his way toward Falls Church and Daniel Seaton's neighborhood. He turned off the lights as he pulled into the Seatons' driveway, then drove around Mary's mulched flowerbeds at the side of the house and into the grassy backyard. He killed the engine.

Lance ran up three steps to the back door and rapped a few times, then swung it open. The Seatons never locked their doors until they went to bed.

Mary whirled around from the kitchen stove. The kettle was whistling; she was brewing tea.

"Lance! What's going on?"

Daniel rushed through the arched doorway from the living room. The television was on, and Lance could hear snatches of the news reports.

"What have you done?" Daniel stammered, ashen and trembling. "Where's Alex?"

Lance flicked his eyes toward the backyard. "He'll be okay," he said. "Got caught in the flash. We need some bandages. Maybe Mary can sew him up, and then we need to get out of here."

Daniel ran out the back door, and Mary froze, staring at Lance, then turned and ran upstairs. She was back seconds later, a plastic box full of medical supplies in her hands.

Outside, Daniel flung the car door open. His brother's dark hair was thick with blood, and his face was smeared with blood where he had wiped his eyes and forehead with the back of his sleeve. He was conscious, but barely coherent. Daniel ripped a handkerchief out of his jeans pocket and dabbed his brother's face. "Alex!" he cried. "I'm here!"

Alex groaned and looked at his brother. "We did it," he said. "We took it out. I saw it fall. Fire in the night. The walls came tumblin' down."

Daniel looked around the car. The vinyl seats were smeared

with blood. *Stupid! Stupid!* he thought. *How did I let them get to this point?*

Mary rushed down the back steps from the kitchen with her medical kit, Lance behind her.

"Alex!" she said. "Let me help you." She caressed his face lightly with her hands, looked into his eyes, felt around his head, and probed the injury. It was a long, slightly curved laceration, an eight-inch slice in the back of his scalp.

"What happened?" she said.

"There was a flash," said Alex. "It knocked me down. I woke up in the car with Lance."

"Concussion, isn't it?" Lance asked Mary.

"I think so," she said. "And he's got a long cut in his scalp; it's pretty deep, I think. But head wounds always bleed like this. Help me get him to the kitchen table. You can't leave here till I sew this up, or he's going to have problems later."

"Just patch him up and get us out of here," Lance said. He and Daniel hoisted Alex up the stairs to the back door.

Daniel closed the kitchen curtains while Mary positioned Alex in a chair facing the table, head forward on his arms. She swabbed his head wound with peroxide and saline solution then popped the plastic off a new Bic razor and quickly, evenly shaved the hair from around the gash. From her kit she took a 10-cc syringe, armed it with a 24-gauge needle, and injected lidocaine into the skin adjacent to the wound.

Alex moaned.

"That will deaden the area," Mary said, placing a comforting hand on his shoulder. "I'll have you fixed up in just a minute."

"Who're you calling?" Daniel asked.

Mary looked up. Lance had pulled a cellular phone from his pants pocket. He jerked his eyes toward the Seatons' kitchen phone. "It's tapped," he said. "I've gotta set something up."

He punched in a number, said simply, "B as in boy," and hung up.

In Leesburg, Frank Doggett sighed heavily and prepared for Plan B.

MARY OPENED a small box, pulled out a curved needle, threaded it with a small skein of 5-0 silk that she had stuck in her uniform pocket just last week after she had assisted Dr. Fortney when he stitched up a toddler who had fallen off a playground swing. She had never sutured a wound herself.

Pretend it's counted cross-stitch, she told herself as she plunged the needle into the thin skin of Alex's scalp. The gash was long, but there was no time for small, neat stitches. She tied off the knots and kept going, pulling the wound closed with ten long running stitches. It wasn't a great job, but at least the wound was closed. It would probably heal all right. And Alex's hair would grow back and cover the ugly scar it would become.

Mary smeared Neosporin over the bumpy, stitched cut, then stuck two 4 by 4 bandages over the mess, securing them with several lengths of silk tape. It wasn't exactly plastic surgery, but it would do.

"He's probably got a concussion," she told Lance. "But he should be okay." She thrust two sample bottles of Ceclor into his hand. "These are antibiotics. Make him take two with lots of water every four hours."

"We've got to get out of here," Lance said, pocketing the vials.

"Look," said Daniel, who had hovered and paced while Mary sewed his brother's scalp. "Where are you going? You're not gonna be able to get away. The FBI, the National Guard, the ATF—everybody is mobilizing. The news reports are already talking about a brown Toyota with Virginia plates. Give yourselves up! You've done what you wanted. You took out the center. Thank God no one was killed."

Alex moaned and began to say something, but Lance cut in. "We don't give ourselves up," he exclaimed. "They'll kill us—one way or another—if we do. I've had a plan for months. We have people in place. We can wait this thing out."

Daniel looked at Alex. Mary was talking gently to him now, the way she talked to the children when they were sick. He was looking up at her in the vulnerable, trusting way he had looked up at their mother when they were young. Daniel knew his brother wouldn't last a minute in prison. If he didn't get himself killed first. Lance was probably right. He was trapped.

"Okay," he said. "This isn't right, but you've got to get out of here. God forgive us." He plunged his hand in his jeans pocket and fumbled as he pulled a key off his key ring. "Take my car. Just get out of here."

"Thanks, brother," Lance said.

"You take care of my brother," said Daniel.

He leaned down and put his hands on Alex's shoulders. Mary had wiped Alex's face clean, but the fresh white bandage on his head was already oozing red again. Lance would have to redress the wound when they got wherever they were going.

Mary had fresh bandages in one hand and a big tumbler of orange juice in the other. She handed the gauze to Lance and held the glass against Alex's lips, popping two white tablets on his swollen tongue. "Drink this," she said. Alex tipped his head back like a child and swallowed.

"Alex," Daniel said. "It's time to go with Lance now. Be careful."

He and Lance lifted Alex from the chair, half-carrying him from the kitchen and down the steps. Lance backed the Seatons' white Honda out of the garage, and Daniel gently lowered Alex into the front seat. He pulled the seat belt around him, clicking it into place. "Be careful," he said again. "You know I love you."

Alex looked up at his brother, still dazed. "I'm sorry," he said. "I didn't mean to."

The Honda backed out of the driveway, no lights on, paused, and then roared down the quiet street. The last thing David saw, by the dim street light, was Alex, staring straight ahead.

AS LANCE and Alex drew closer to Doggett's Garage, they both slipped into a state of mind that was somewhere past fear.

Lance was back in Baghdad. There, discovery by the authorities would have meant death, and he had thrived on the thrill of eluding them. He felt the same way now. So he kept his foot steady on the accelerator, eating up the dark miles along Route 7 west by staying within the speed limit, using his signals, and behaving like a model driver. He had seen a police car or two in the distance, but the fragmented news reports weren't yet talking about a white four-door Honda sedan. No roadblocks yet. *We're gonna make it,* he thought.

Alex was in a world of his own. He watched the dark trees rush by in the night, silent, reliving over and over the brilliant flash of the huge fireball, the flying glass, the crash of concrete. Like the end of the world. He still clutched Daniel's handkerchief, wadded and bloodstained, tight in his hand.

When the white Honda pulled into Doggett's Garage in Leesburg, Frank Doggett was ready. Lance jumped out of the driver's seat and into the back; Frank slid behind the steering wheel and swung the car toward Godfrey Field, Leesburg's small municipal airport. The Honda had been in Doggett's driveway for less than fifteen seconds.

At Godfrey, Frank used his keycard to enter the unmanned front security gate. Though the airport was usually quiet at this hour, it was not unusual for private pilots and businessmen to take off at odd hours of the night. Freedom from conventional airline schedules was one of the privileges of private plane ownership.

The Honda crept silently into hangar number two. Frank cut off the engine, and he and Lance jumped out of the car. They guided Alex toward Frank's plane, a Cessna 172. Alex could walk, but he was disoriented—cooperative when they gave him instructions, but unable to focus on the situation unfolding around them.

"The blast knocked his head into the pavement," Lance said quietly to Frank. "But he'll be okay."

The Cessna, built in 1962, had nearly eight thousand hours of flying time on her and was on her fourth engine. The brown seats were cracked, their foamy lining showing between the splits in the leather. The paint, inside and out, was worn, the instrument panels cracked in a few places. It could carry four people, two seats in the front and two in the back. Lance didn't want Alex near the controls, so he strapped him into the right-rear seat.

The two men pushed the chocks away from the three wheels

and rolled the small plane out to the taxiway. Frank handed Lance a tiny flashlight and a hand-held Global Positioning System.

"It's all programmed," said Frank. "You stay low, don't fly over the mountains; you're going in between 'em. We don't want you popping up on radar screens if we can help it. I've put in your course; just trust this thing. Don't deviate from the coordinates."

Lance tucked the flashlight under his arm, took the satellite positioning device and the flashlight in his left hand and shook Frank's with his right. Then he swung up into the pilot's seat on the left and shone the tiny light on the control panel. He had flown small surveillance aircraft in the Special Forces; he was familiar enough with the design of the Cessna.

He pulled the knob regulating the plane's fuel mixture, opening it all the way and pumping the throttle several times. Gas flowed into the carburetor. Then he turned the battery switch on, kicking in the plane's electrical system, and pumped the throttle again. He knew Frank had been out here earlier this afternoon, double-checking everything, just in case they had to go to plan B; though the engine was cold, it was priming well.

Lance turned the key to start the engine then looked out the window and down through the struts supporting the wing. He nodded at Frank and saluted. "We'll see you in Costa Rica," Lance called, "if all goes well. Good luck!" Frank nodded, and Lance turned away for a moment to check on Alex. When he looked back, Frank was gone.

The little plane shook and sputtered. The four-cylinder, 145-horsepower engine was screwed on rubber mounts, but they weren't absorbing the shock. The plane's body popped and cracked, rocked and rolled. In the backseat, in spite of his lethargy, Alex's eyes were wide.

"Just relax and stay calm," Lance said. "We're gonna be fine."

Frank was an old pilot of the cowboy school; it didn't surprise Lance that his plane wasn't exactly a smooth ride. But it would get them where they needed to go.

He taxied toward the main runway. The lights were off, but there was enough glow from the moon and the pinkish haze of the distant lights of Washington and Tyson's Corner that he could make out contours and direction. The runway was five thousand feet long, and the little Cessna needed only about eight hundred of those feet to get up.

Lance pushed the knob all the way in. Full throttle, to the fire wall. Due north. He didn't want to get any closer to Dulles Airport, just ten miles to the south. He eased his feet off the brakes and began to roll down the runway, bouncing and jostling as the plane gained speed. The hangars on one side and the woods on the other whooshed by; inside the tiny cockpit, the roaring of the engine and the moaning and creaking of the structure precluded any conversation with Alex, who wasn't talking anyway. At seventy miles per hour, Lance pulled back on the wheel slightly; the wheels lifted, and the small plane was airborne. He did not turn on the transponder, the device at the bottom of the aircraft that would emit an identifying signal for traffic controllers.

Lance exhaled, loving the familiar rush of the plane's transition from ground to air, the freedom of the wind rushing by and the horizon beckoning ahead. At one thousand feet, he banked northwest toward Martinsburg. The landing gear was stationary, so he didn't need to worry about retraction; he made the fuel mixture leaner, but kept the rpms at about twenty-six hundred in order to keep the speed as fast as possible.

They were still below fifteen hundred feet, at the range that air traffic controllers didn't even need to hear from him; local jet traffic came in at five thousand feet.

AT THE Washington Air Traffic Control center in Leesburg, controller Jerry Leach sat at his Raytheon radar console, sipping from his old "Ollie for Senate" coffee mug. In the northwest quadrant of his 360-degree black screen, a green blip appeared. It was not a commercial airliner, just a small plane heading out of Godfrey and not in the Dulles traffic area. Not that there were many flights coming in or out of Dulles at this hour.

Leach paused for a moment, then flicked his radio switch to the frequency private pilots in the area used most frequently.

"Aircraft off Godfrey Field, please identify yourself," he said.

He waited a few moments, drained some more coffee from his cup, and passed a US Air flight bound for Pittsburgh off to the air traffic controllers at the Cleveland center.

It was quiet. Usually he listened to the radio late at night, but his wife, Holly, had gotten a new set of promotional tapes for the vitamin sales distributorship she had started in their home. He had the cassette player plugged in, ready to go, with tape number one: "Be Well, Breathe Well, Sell Well." Holly thought that after Jerry's retirement the vitamin business might provide some income on the side. As long as she was excited about it, he was willing to go along.

No response from the little plane. That wasn't unusual. Sometimes the private pilots forgot to turn their transponders on or ignored the radio contact with Leesburg if they were headed toward West Virginia. Late-night private planes didn't follow the same technical strictures that bound the commercial pilots, and Jerry didn't blame them. If he was flying late, he probably wouldn't bother with all the bureaucracy either.

Anyway, the plane was small and slow and heading toward Martinsburg. He decided not to worry about it. He took another swig of coffee and hit the tape player's play button.

ALEX'S MOMENTARY feeling of comfort from Mary's care was long gone. He stared out of the plane's windows in terror. The blue-black ridges of West Virginia were nearing; the plane was too low to go over them, and it was too dark to go between them. His stomach had been clenched ever since the explosion; now the nausea rose into his throat. He leaned forward toward the front seat, bile in his mouth.

Lance looked back for a second. "Don't do it!" he shouted, reaching back and pushing Alex's face to the side. Alex's stomach heaved, and the bitter citrus of the orange juice splashed all over the empty seat next to him.

He wiped his mouth with Daniel's handkerchief and put his head down as near to his knees as he could get it in the tiny space, so he couldn't see.

Lance looked at the dim outline of the mountains. He, too, was disoriented. It had been awhile since he'd flown, but he knew he couldn't trust what he saw. He looked down at the GPS Frank had given him. Arrows on either side of a center line would flash, telling you to adjust to the left or right; when the arrows didn't show, you were right on course. Good thing they'd had Doggett; he had planned this alternate escape as carefully as if it was the primary plan. Doggett had actually flown the route himself in the daylight, weaving through the mountain passes, entering in the correct GPS locations at each point.

Location A-1 was the first, A-2 would be the big turn south, and the others would take them all the way to the destination—ten station readings in all. He could fly blind if he trusted Doggett and this little box with its bleeping light. He did.

According to the chart, the first ridge was twenty-two hundred feet away. Lance knew if he climbed a couple of thousand feet he could clear the ridges easily. But he had no idea if the FBI had by now launched an all-points bulletin or if the FAA had been alerted. He didn't know what was going on. It had been over two hours since the explosion; anything was possible. So he would stay low, trust Doggett's GPS calculations, and wind his way between the mountains out of radar range. It would be pretty hairy, he thought.

Alex still had his head down. His eyes were throbbing, his mouth was sour, his head ached horribly. In his mind was a picture from a movie he had seen years earlier. *Sweet Dreams.* The story of country singer Patsy Cline, who, with her entire band, had died in a small-plane crash.

The climactic scene kept replaying itself in Alex's mind: Cline and her friends had been laughing; then, suddenly, the plane broke through a cloud and they saw the sheer rock face of the mountain looming before them. Then the impact: The small plane burst into flames. Then silence.

Just like tonight, thought Alex. *The explosion, the flames, the fire-ball...then the silence.*

LANCE FELT the familiar rush in his gut. He looked down at the GPS. The right arrow was flashing; he moved the wheel ever so gently to the left. Coming up on A-1. No radar was going to pick him up here between the mountains. He peered out to the side; it was black out there, but in the darkness he could still sense vague shapes whooshing by in the night. He realized these were pine trees—and they were higher than he was. He was annoyed to see that his hands were trembling. But no arrows were showing. He breathed easier.

Minutes later, he came to point A-2. He rose, banked left, just south of Martinsburg, he figured, and then dropped below twelve hundred feet; they were now in the quiet well of the Shenandoah Valley. He couldn't see, but the GPS was clicking off the points. He was right on course and should be approaching the mowed field where, if Frank had called them in time, friends would be waiting.

The Cessna dropped. Alex still had his head down. For the past half-hour he had been moaning about explosions, *Sweet Dreams*, Gideon's Torch...Lance had ignored him. He opened the fuel mixture, slowly lowered the flaps, and dropped toward the field he could not see. The GPS, A-8, told him it was there, and Lance had learned long ago that equipment was usually more trustworthy than people. Alex was proof of that.

Then he saw them: two tiny, faint lights, below and ahead in the darkness. It was unbelievable. They were there! The green light marking where he needed to touch down, the red one where he needed to stop.

He decreased his speed, the needle on the speedometer drop-ping alarmingly...100, 90, 80, 70, 60 ...The little plane would stall around 50. At 60 he flared the Cessna's nose up slightly and let her stall. He had done it a thousand times, but not recently.

But Frank's old plane responded to his touch. He dropped to what he thought was about a foot or two off the ground; no way of telling, really. The speed was still 60 when the plane banged hard against the ground. Lance flew up against the ceiling of the cock-pit, and Alex screamed in pain as his head hit the wall. They jostled and hurtled down the expanse of field, plunging and jerking into ruts and running straight toward the second little light in the darkness. Lance held his breath and held on, his thoughts too blurred for prayer. Alex clutched his oozing head and moaned.

The Cessna rolled to a stop, and Lance exhaled, exhilarated. He released his seat belt, opened the tiny door, and leaped to the ground. Ned Keener was running toward him, his flashlight already off. Together they pulled Alex from the plane; then Lance climbed back up and taxied the plane toward the crumbling wooden barn at the end of the field. Ken Jordan had opened the big double doors and was shining his light so Lance could see. He pulled the Cessna into the far corner of the barn where a huge mound of hay bales stood waiting.

Lance jumped down, grasped Jordan's hand, and then ran toward Keener's waiting truck. Alex was already in the middle of the front bench seat, leaning against Ned. Lance climbed in and shut the door, and seconds later they were slowly jostling across the field, heading toward the cabin in the hills.

44

CAMOUFLAGE-CLAD troops with M-16s stood at barricades erected at Washington Circle, Twenty-second Street, and G Street, creating an armed perimeter around George Washington University Hospital and the remains of the regeneration center. Hundreds of students and other area residents stood at the checkpoints, watching the small army of earthmovers, troops, and armored equipment passing through.

The east end of what had been the regeneration center was now a huge mound of jagged, smoking concrete blocks. Metal rods protruded from the moundlike spears. On the west end, there was still some shape to the collapsed structure, with concrete pillars thrusting in the air like smokestacks; the walkway to the hospital was smashed, part of it still dangling in the air.

Giant searchlights suspended from cranes illuminated the entire area as rescue crews began ripping through the deadly mound in search of life. Ambulances, trucks, and army personnel carriers lined the block.

An unshaven Anthony Frizzell arrived at the FBI's command-control trailer just before dawn. He let out a low whistle as he surveyed the damage.

"A real pro. Yes sir, this took a real pro. Army demo man is my guess," he mumbled. Toby Hunter nodded his head, as he did whenever his boss spoke.

Frizzell strode into the trailer where four agents sat at small desks, computers clattering. "Okay, give me everything you know," he barked.

The agents knew what that meant: though members of the press were being held half a block back from the bomb site, the networks would be ravenous for live reports for their 7:00 A.M. broadcasts. If they had anything good, Frizzell would be ready for those morning news shows interviews. If there was nothing promising, someone else would do them.

Toby handed Frizzell a small black sack from which the director extracted a mirror and an electric razor.

"Excuse me," Frizzell said to one agent as he leaned past him to plug it in.

Over the buzz of the razor, the agents gave their report. A bystander had given the FBI a description of a car seen leaving the scene after the explosion; it corroborated what the D.C. policeman had seen. Despite checkpoints around the city and officers patrolling the major arteries, however, the car had not been located.

"I already know that," Frizzell snapped, shaving his right cheek.

The agents continued. There were still no leads, but the bureau and local police were "fine-combing" the area. The perpetrators would never be able to escape the net. In an hour or two, bureau operations would print out a complete list of potential suspects. Agents would "visit" them, and it would be fairly quick work to determine who could not be accounted for. The director stopped shaving. Toby knew what this meant. Someone else would brief the media.

But the most alarming news involved persons not yet accounted for who might have been victims of the bombing. Congressman Peter Meyer had last been seen by a member of the hospital cleaning crew heading toward the glass walkway connecting the hospital to the regeneration center. His wife had informed agents that her husband had not yet arrived home.

Frizzell rolled his eyes. What else was new?

And, said the agents, Dr. Barbara LaMar was also missing.

ABOUT 5:00 A.M, a rescue worker found in the collapsed walkway part of a human hand, blackened and shredded by the blast. Two fingers were wholly intact, with long nails that had been painted with enamel, probably once red.

By 6:00, more remains had been discovered. No definitive IDs yet, but preliminary reports suggested that the blast might have claimed at least three victims, most likely Meyer, LaMar, and the security guard on duty at the center.

Frizzell called Emily Gineen, who called Bernie O'Keefe. He was groggy but alert enough to groan loudly at the grim news—news that was certain to inflame Whitney Griswold. Now, on his watch, a congressman had been killed.

Frizzell was not pleased either. Not because of any personal love for Meyer; Congress would be better off without him. But unless the bureau got the bombers within, say, a week, Frizzell thought, his job would be on the line. No time to mess around.

"Assemble the press at the west corner of Twentieth Street," he ordered. Then he turned to Toby. "Have the agent in charge of D.C.—Duffy—brief them. Short, sweet, to the point. Assure them the bureau will get those responsible. 'The director has ordered a nationwide manhunt,' et cetera, et cetera—you know what to tell them, Toby. Get to it."

Seconds later, the red phone rang, the direct line from the bureau's command center. It was the assistant director of operations.

"Good news, Chief," he told Frizzell. "Informant has finally checked in. It's Lance Thompson—the black guy we've been worried about, ex-Special Forces—and Alex Seaton. We've got an 'all points' out on these two. We'll get 'em."

"You listen to me," Frizzell interrupted. "Get those guys and get them now. Shake every one of their buddies loose. Somebody knows where they're hiding. Use whatever force you need. Just get 'em."

DANIEL SEATON sat at the kitchen table, drinking another cup of coffee. It all seemed like a bad dream, but his aching eyes and jumpy stomach attested to the realities of the night. After Alex and Lance had sped away into the darkness, he and Mary had sponged Alex's blood off their kitchen table, put away the medical supplies, and drunk a cup of tea while they figured out what to do next. There weren't any answers. In the end, Mary had collapsed into bed, exhausted.

Daniel had gone into each of his children's bedrooms, tenderly tucking the covers around Abigail, Dan, and Mark, and marveling, as always, at their absolute, trusting abandon as they slept, their small, warm bodies sprawled freely in their beds. He bent and kissed Abby, and she rustled for a moment, half-awake.

"Daddy, where's Kensington?" she asked. Daniel reached under the comforter and pulled out the well-worn brown plush bear. "He's right here, honey," he said. "You go back to sleep."

Now, just before seven o'clock, the children were still sleeping as he downed three extra-strength Tylenol with his third cup of coffee. Mary was downstairs again, and the two of them moved into the living room and flicked on the *Today* show.

It's ironic, Daniel thought. *I'm tuning in to national television to see if my brother made it out of town. How did it come to this?*

The camera zoomed in on Rockefeller Center, and anchor Rick Smith's voice was more somber than usual as he led with the morning's headlines.

"A huge explosion engulfed the soon-to-be-opened regeneration center in Washington, D.C., late last night, totally destroying the building," he announced. "The structure, which was due to open in September, was thought to be empty at the time of the explosion. But as investigators sifted through the rubble early this morning, they discovered two victims killed in the blast. These have now been identified as the center's executive director, Dr.

Barbara LaMar, and Congressman Peter Meyer. The building's security guard is still missing. Federal investigators are moving quickly to apprehend suspects. For more on this tragic story, we'll go live now to…"

"Oh, no!" Mary gasped, clutching her hands to her face.

Daniel felt as if someone had kicked him in the stomach, and tears stung the back of his eyes. *How could this have happened? Lance and Alex didn't say anything about anyone being in the building…why would a congressman be there at night?* His thoughts swirled, and he reached out for Mary. They huddled on the sofa, holding on to each other like children.

Suddenly, the doorbell rang. Daniel jumped, first worrying out of habit that it would wake the children, then moved toward the door with an awful sense of foreboding. He opened the door and saw four somber men standing on their small front porch.

"Good morning," said one of the men in the center. "I'm Carl Pratt, FBI." He flipped open a wallet and dangled a laminated card where Daniel could see it. "Are you Daniel Seaton?"

Daniel nodded, his throat dry. "Come in," he croaked. Mary was standing behind him, her hand on his shoulder. "This is my wife, Mary." He held open the screen door awkwardly, and Pratt and one of the men entered the living room. The other two men stayed on the front porch, like sentries.

"Please sit down," Mary said, gesturing toward the sofa. It was amazing, she thought, how social conventions still took over, even in the midst of chaos.

"Thank you," said Pratt. "We have a few questions for you, and they will necessitate your coming with us. Both of you."

"What about our children?" Mary asked. "They're sleeping upstairs."

"I'd suggest you call a neighbor or family member, ma'am. We'll need you for several hours."

Just then Daniel heard a familiar thump on the stairs and looked up to the landing. Abigail sat on the top stair, her hair tousled and Kensington Bear clutched under one arm.

"What's happening, Daddy?" she said.

Before Daniel could answer, there was a rap on the front door and one of the agents stuck his head in to address Pratt.

"Sir, we've found something in the garage we think you ought to see."

AFTER THE attorney general's call with the news from Frizzell, Bernie O'Keefe put the phone back in its cradle and rubbed both hands over his aching forehead. He must wake up, he thought. A congressman dead. He fumbled for the clock. 6:15. In fifteen minutes, Griswold would be on his infernal contraption in the White House catacombs. He had to get the information to him before he saw it on the 7:00 news.

Bernie stumbled only once on his way to the bathroom, when he almost tripped on his bathrobe wadded up on the floor. The throbbing over his eyes was intense; it seemed to have gotten much worse lately. Two ibuprofen and one Xanax would gently ease him back to the world of the living.

The hot shower helped too, and with surprising speed, he was dressed and downstairs in his library, waiting for his limousine, which he had summoned to come early. This library could be such a handsome room, he thought distractedly, if he could ever unpack. Every wall was floor-to-ceiling bookshelves and paneling. He ran his hand over the open-grained oak. It felt strong, reassuring.

Then he turned and faced the bay windows that looked out over the front yard, a small patch of grass boxed by a Victorian iron fence. He imagined what this room had been like when the man who sold it to him, a lawyer, lived here. Full of wonderful rich books, a great place to think about cases and arguments.

Bernie checked his watch. 6:50. Thank goodness Griswold was so predictably punctual; he picked up the direct line to the White House switchboard and asked for the president. Bernie figured he would just about be stepping out of the shower after his workout and Juan would bring him the phone.

Two minutes later Griswold came on the line. "Hey, Bernie, I'm dripping wet. What's up now?"

Your blood pressure is about to be, Bernie thought. He briefed the president in his most matter-of-fact voice.

Griswold instructed him to be in the Oval Office with Robbie at 8:00 sharp and to have the attorney general on stand-by. He sounded calm and deliberate. But Bernie knew this was not a good sign. When Griswold was really angry, he spoke more slowly in a voice lower than normal, carefully measuring words, carefully showing that he was absolutely in control.

AT 7:59, Bernie arrived at the staff entrance of the Oval Office, with Robbie a second or two behind him. They were nodded in by the Secret Service agent.

Bernie was surprised to see Griswold in shirt sleeves—uncharacteristic informality for this office. His face seemed somewhat flushed, as it often was after exercise, but he looked warmer than usual. Bernie knew his old friend well. Beneath the calm surface, he suspected, was a frothing caldron.

Griswold was reading the news summary but looked up, half-smiled, and motioned them into the straight-backed chairs on either side of the desk.

"Well, gentlemen, we have quite a situation on our hands. I assume you've gathered your thoughts as to what we should say. That's our first order of business, since Caroline tells me the press room is a madhouse; the animals there are all very restless in their cages. So, Robbie, you go first…"

"Yes sir. I'm of the opinion, Mr. President, that you need to be seen as in immediate and complete control. Reassure people that there is no cause for panic. I think you should come out to the press room at 10:00 and make a brief statement. We've already been assured the nets will carry it live."

Griswold's eyes pierced laserlike through Robbie, but his voice remained calm. "Let people know the president is right on top of things, is that it, Robbie?"

"Yes, sir. Caroline agrees, by the way."

"And I should explain," the president continued calmly, "how five thousand federal agents and ten thousand National Guardsmen could not keep some jackass terrorist from blowing sky-high a huge building built with millions of federal tax dollars not ten blocks from the White House, and then they threw in a congress-man for good measure. In control, did you say, Robbie? Who, may I ask, is in control of this government?"

"Well, sir, the polls tell us the people need—"

"No, no, I've thought this over. You're overexposing me, Robbie, and it's going to hurt my credibility. What about you, Bernie? You want to trot me out to the cameras as well, I sup-pose?"

Bernie was about to answer when to his relief Juan came in with a pot of coffee and three cups on a silver tray. At the same moment, the intercom rang.

"No one is to interrupt here." Griswold was plainly irritated. "I told Susan...yes...oh, yes, yes, ... yes dear..."

Griswold stood and turned to look out the window while he listened to the only person who could interrupt matters of state, his wife.

"Yes, dear, I agree with the Secret Service. Tell Elizabeth she shouldn't go...Is that so? Are they sure?"

As he began to pace, the phone cord slid under the saucer. Robbie saw it happening but couldn't move fast enough. With a snapping motion, the cord flipped the coffee and china into the air, and they crashed down on the desktop. Griswold jumped at the crash and the fact that hot coffee had splattered all over his back.

"Ahhhhhh," he screamed into the phone. "No, no, Anne, I'm fine. Just spilled my coffee."

Bernie was out of his chair immediately, rescuing brown-stained papers on the president's desk. Griswold was leaning over the desk when Robbie came around behind him and starting rubbing his handkerchief on the president's backside, blotting the coffee that had stained the seat of his tan, worsted suit pants. Griswold, startled, swung around and almost knocked Robbie over. Juan came running with towels and clutched the Nigerian briefing book marked "President's Eyes Only." Griswold, still try-ing to talk to his wife, grunted, "I'll take that."

The whole scene was enough to test even the sturdiest person's self-control. Griswold, Bernie could see, was about to lose his.

He hung up the phone. "My wife just told me that the bureau has identified the bombers—came over ABC a few minutes ago. Good thing Anne was watching television. Otherwise, I suppose, I would never have known. And my daughter is being told she can't go to school because the Secret Service thinks it is unsafe. Imagine that."

Griswold scowled, cursing as he sat down, then bolted upright again. "Seat's wet." He stared at Robbie and Bernie for a moment, then called for his valet. "Juan. Bring in a banana, no three bananas." Bernie and Robbie exchanged glances.

"If we're going to preside over a banana republic, we might as well eat bananas." Griswold laughed loudly.

"Bernie," Griswold stood behind his desk chair, pointing. "No more excuses. I want these guys. Get 'em. You tell Gineen and Frizzell that their jobs are on the line here. I want them to get these killers and get them fast. Twenty-four hours. No excuses."

"Yes sir," Bernie replied quickly. He had never seen Griswold this uptight, not even the time he thought Anne was on to one of his weeknight dalliances in New Haven. The stress was clearly affecting him.

"You see, Bernie, this is war. There are people determined to destroy this presidency. We are under attack, and blood is flowing. Their blood must flow too."

Bernie shouldn't have said anything, but he couldn't resist. "We are not at war with our own people, for heaven's sake. We're talking about a few criminals here, sir."

"What do you want, men with AK-47s running through the streets? That would be cleaner and easier. This is guerilla warfare—harder to fight, but it's warfare. Don't think it's not, Bernie."

"And Robbie," Griswold turned to his chief of staff coldly, "this president is not going to that press room. Why don't you go and face the lions in there? Do I have to do everything around here myself?"

Griswold shook his head, clutched his hands behind his back, and walked toward the french doors leading to the rose garden. The summer sun streamed into the room. For a moment he was silent, as if deep in thought. Robbie and Bernie sat quietly. Then Bernie spoke.

"Well, sir, every president has moments like this. It's an awesome weight on your shoulders. No one knows."

"That's it, Bernie. That's certainly it. No one knows. What a mess. And these terrorists—they're trying to destroy us. We have to stiffen up." He was pacing once more. "Nobody knows," he said. It seemed like minutes before he spun around and walked toward his desk.

"Well, gentlemen, it's clear then. Caroline will brief the press with the latest information. Advise them that the president is fully informed and in constant touch with the attorney general...that we will enforce the law to the fullest...and oh, yes, some nice words about Peter Meyer...now there's a challenge for you," Griswold chuckled. "What can we say? 'Crooked as a corkscrew, so we'll screw him into the ground at Arlington Cemetery.'" The three men laughed shallowly.

"And, somebody, please make sure Caroline explains that I'm in meetings regarding Nigeria. Does anyone realize what a madman we're dealing with in General Haoud? Holding Europe hostage, that's what he's doing. Crazy people in Nigeria and on the streets of Washington. No difference. The president has to be firm...anything else?"

Griswold grinned as his two aides nodded and headed for the door.

Robbie walked straight to the press room to give Caroline her instructions. His head still throbbing, Bernie was relieved just to be in the corridor.

He stopped for a moment and stared into the Roosevelt room, serene and quiet. He felt rotten; and now, for the first time, he was worried about his friend.

Bernie looked at the massive painting of Teddy Roosevelt charging the hill at San Juan. *Presidents had power then*, he thought. *The nation was small. Cohesive. Presidents could really lead back then.*

You couldn't do that anymore. People thought the president, the government, had so much power, but it was all smoke and mirrors, Bernie said to himself. Oh, you could make laws and issue statements and tell people you were going to enforce the law, but you couldn't do anything about chaos in the streets—let alone influence what people talked about over their breakfast tables in the morning. And it was those tens of millions of little decisions that ordinary people made that determined the habits and dispositions and decisions that defined a nation.

So what's the use? he thought, then caught himself. He couldn't afford to fall into another downward spell this morning. He'd better get another pill when he got to his office.

"COULD YOU pass me one of those jelly doughnuts?" Paul Vincent asked. He was sitting on his desk at the *Washington Post*, a cellular phone cradled on one shoulder; he was on hold, waiting for a friend who worked in George Washington Hospital's pathology department. "Raspberry, not the grape."

Jeanne Jasper fished a fat doughnut out of the white cardboard box and handed it to him on a paper napkin. They were both a little punchy; neither had gotten much sleep last night. The entire newsroom had scrambled madly to get the bombing on the front page of the final edition, but facts had been sketchy. Today they could start playing the story out with as many gory details as possible.

"Meyer's wife didn't even realize he was missing," Jeanne said to Paul, biting into her second doughnut and spurting red jelly onto her napkin. "Evidently it wasn't too unusual for him to stay out rather late. Like all night. Pressing congressional business, you know."

"Well, if he was pressing with Barbara LaMar, he wasn't the first," Paul said. "She's pressed half of Capitol Hill."

"Now, let's not exaggerate," said Jeanne. "She was a woman of principle. She only engaged in public relations with people who held purse strings."

"Barry's checking into the pathology reports," Paul said, nodding toward the phone perched on his shoulder. "They're still doing tests at the morgue, but it looks like LaMar and Meyer were both pretty pickled by the time of the explosion. Their blood alcohols were over the top. They were feeling no pain."

"That's good," Jeanne said. "From what I gather, there wasn't much of them left."

"Nope. But it's too bad for Meyer. He's going to get dissected all over the place. We were already starting to poke around into some of his campaign financing. Seems like his relationship with the regeneration center and some of its backers was ever so slightly incestuous."

"It'll be a great story," Jeanne said, popping the last bite of doughnut into her mouth. "It's got it all. Sex. Violence. Mysterious terrorists. Washington powerbrokers. Murky financial wheeling and dealing. And a mourning widow who just happens to be a federal judge."

45

THE DAY after the bombing, FBI teams rapped on the front doors of anti-abortion activists in Pensacola, Wichita, Chicago, Minneapolis, Tacoma, Portland, and Los Angeles. Some of those targeted had been involved with civil disobedience activities in the past; others were simply contributors to mainstream groups such as Americans United for Life and the National Right to Life.

In most cases, agents found their quarry at their breakfast tables, groggily listening to news of the bombing; many were bundled off for interrogation in their pajamas. Plain-clothes personnel stayed behind to search activists' homes, dredging up everything from computer files to study notes in people's Bibles.

Meanwhile, local phone company records had been requested, bank records subpoenaed, passports seized, and neighbors questioned about suspicious meetings or behavior. Nearly a hundred people were taken in for questioning.

In Falls Church, Virginia, agents were absolutely tight-lipped with the media regarding the arrest of Daniel Seaton and the search of his home. Mary Seaton had been detained for six hours then released to care for her children; Daniel was now being held without bail at the Arlington County Jail.

Amy O'Neil, Mark Demmers, and several other Networkers were questioned for hours by the FBI. After determining they knew nothing about the bombing, agents released them. Amy returned to her congressional office to find her desk cleaned out and her personal possessions in a cardboard box by the door. The congressman would not see her.

Shaken, Amy called her parents in California; her mother flew to Washington the next day to help her pack her things and come back home.

In Leesburg, agents discovered Daniel Seaton's white Honda in Frank Doggett's garage, but Frank and Ida Doggett were nowhere to be found. All-points bulletins had been issued for Lance Thompson and Alex Seaton as well as the Doggetts, and their pictures were being shown on special news bulletins and hourly newscasts.

At the site of the explosion, agents continued sifting through the rubble of the regeneration center, reading the telltale residue. Twelve hours after the blast, the experts—many of them veterans of the World Trade Center bombing investigation—knew roughly the make of the van that had housed the explosives, the approximate amount of explosives used, and the fact that the blast had been caused by military-issue C-4, a high explosive with medium- to high-range brisance favored by the army.

Agents were dispatched to investigate army installations on the East Coast, starting with those within a day's drive of Washington.

Friday, June 5
Arlington County Jail

Mary Seaton sat nervously at the cubicle in the visiting room, perched on the edge of an orange plastic chair. She had been patted down by a female officer and scanned with a hand-held metal detector before she entered the main part of the jail. Now she had nothing with her but her driver's license in her jeans-skirt pocket and a crayoned sign the children had made for their father. She wasn't allowed to give it to Daniel, she had been told, but she would be permitted to hold it up to the glass partition separating them.

She looked up at the big clock on the cinder-block wall, angrily coveting the minutes ticking by; she would have only ten minutes' visiting time, and they still hadn't even brought him out from the cell. Then she heard the far door on the prisoners' side of the partition opening; a bulky officer held it open while Daniel shuffled through awkwardly.

Standing up so she could peer over the waist-high counter in her cubicle, she could see that his legs were manacled, each ankle wound with a thick circlet of steel and bound together on a three-foot length of chain. He wore an ill-fitting, bright-orange, one-piece jumpsuit. The suit and the manacles made him look like every piece of television footage she had ever seen of serial killers. It was unbelievable.

I mustn't let him see me angry, Mary thought. *There's time for that later. I need to be absolutely positive, so I don't add to the struggles he's already going through.*

Mary smiled brightly and stood as Daniel shuffled toward her. She stretched both of her arms wide, as if to hug him, then sat down while the guard assisted him into the plastic seat on the other side of the glass.

Daniel nodded toward her, and they simultaneously picked up the black telephones hanging on the partition wall. She knew she had to keep the conversation as ordinary as possible; the guards were watching them carefully, and agents were probably listening in on the telephone connection.

"Daniel, I love you so much! Are you all right?" she whispered into the phone, willing warmth and encouragement into his ear.

He smiled, looking at her carefully and taking in her dark shining hair, her steady gray eyes, the color in her cheeks. "I'm fine," he said. "I'll never complain about your cooking again, though. You are an absolute Julia Child compared to the chefs who concoct my prison cuisine."

She laughed. "Thanks for the encouragement."

"How are the children doing?" he asked quietly.

"They're doing fine," she said quickly. "They miss you, and they keep asking when Daddy is coming home. I keep telling them that it will be soon, that Daddy has done nothing wrong."

He raised his eyebrows, and she kept going.

"They drew you this picture. The officers wouldn't let me give it to you, but can you see it?" She held the drawing up to the glass, which had thin gray wires woven between its double thickness.

Daniel smiled as he looked at the crayoned field of green, the gray castle—their conception of the jail, he assumed—and the bright yellow-and-orange butterflies escaping near the top turret window.

"Tell them it's beautiful," he said. "I can see they all worked very hard on it."

Mary hesitated. "Otherwise, things are pretty quiet at home without you. There's not much to tell. We haven't heard anything from anyone...people from the church have been really kind, though, bringing meals over and helping with the kids—stuff like that."

Daniel watched her eyes. So Alex was still out there somewhere. He cleared his throat. "Please tell everyone hello. Tell them I'm doing fine, and I hope I'll be home soon—as soon as these gentlemen decide they've extended their hospitality to me long enough." He nodded toward the officers standing against the wall.

He reached his hand up to the glass, and Mary put her right hand up as well, so they were palm to palm, separated by the wall of glass. "I love you so much," he said.

"I love you too," said Mary. "Please don't worry about us; we're doing fine. We pray for you all the time, and we know you'll be home soon."

Friday, June 5
The National Cathedral

Judge April Meyer took a deep breath to compose herself as the long black limousine pulled into the circular drive in front of the National Cathedral. Her chin-length dark hair was streaked with gray, and deep lines etched her cheeks and forehead. In her black knee-length suit she looked as severe as she did in her usual black calf-length robes. But today she didn't have on the tortoise-shell half-glasses she usually wore on the bench. And though she had taken more care than usual with her hair and makeup, she looked exactly how she felt: exhausted, embarrassed, and angry.

It was one thing for Peter to betray their marriage in private. But for him to go out like this, drunk on his butt with a bottom-feeder like Barbara LaMar...it was absolutely humiliating, and she had no recourse. Before, she could just hide in her work, ignore it, get on with her own life...but now their private lives were all over the front pages. It hurt.

She took her sunglasses out of her purse, put them on, lifted her chin, and swung out of the limo. Her younger brother, John, and her mother were with her. John took her elbow to escort her up the warm white steps to the cathedral's magnificent center doorway. The limo behind them had pulled up as well; in it were Peter's parents and his two brothers, clones of her husband in looks and attitude. She would rather not deal with them today if she could help it.

Mourners on either side cleared a path for her. Looking slightly to the left and right behind her dark glasses, she could see people's faces. Some looked sorry for her. A few wore small, tucked-in smiles, the catty look she had seen so many times at cocktail parties when Peter was off somewhere in a corner with the hostess or some other man's wife. But most of the faces were reserved, respectful, lined with genuine shock. Whoever he had been in life, Peter had gone to a hideous death, his life blown away at the most casual, unexpected moment. It was everyone's nightmare.

The nightmare was evident, too, in the extraordinary security around the building. As they pulled up in front, she had noticed agents armed with automatic weapons. Metal detectors had been set up for all the mourners to pass through, and there were Secret Service personnel everywhere.

Just inside the door, waiting for her, was her escort, John Edward Stevenson, chief justice of the Supreme Court, his silver hair shining in the morning light. She took off her sunglasses, smiled at him, and took his arm.

As they moved forward, she felt an odd echo of her own wedding, when she had held her father's arm and walked the long aisle to meet Peter, so handsome, smiling, waiting for her by the altar. She looked down the immense path of marble before her. Peter was at the end of the huge cathedral, waiting for her again. Except this time he was in a long, burnished box, closed forever, hidden by huge sprays of yellow roses. Her steps faltered, and Edward patted her hand on his arm.

She looked up. The rose windows on the right side of the massive church flooded warm color on the stone pillars that marked her path toward the front. Magnificent strains of Bach floated from the organ pipes, echoing off the vaulted roof.

Suddenly there was a slight commotion at the front. With so many people pressed into the rows of wooden chairs on either side of the center aisle, it was hard to tell at first what was happening. Then she could see the Episcopal bishop of Washington waiting in the front. His head turned toward a swirl of Secret Service agents entering from the side, and in their midst she could see the tall form of J. Whitney Griswold.

The president moved to the front row, agents fanned out around him, and then he turned and smiled at her, holding out his hand as she moved toward the empty seat next to him and the first lady. Griswold smiled gently at her and embraced her quickly. April clasped the president's warm hand.

"How are you doing, April?" he asked quietly.

She paused and looked up into his blue eyes. "I don't know, Mr. President," she said.

"These are strange times," he said. "What happened to your husband is absolutely horrible, and Anne and I both want you to know you have our deepest sympathies."

The Bach prelude swelled to its final chords and the bishop

moved toward the pulpit. The television cameras, positioned next to the great pillars at the front, rolled as the service began.

Griswold leaned toward her again, and the cameras caught the image for the evening news: the president of the United States whispering encouragement to the grieving widow.

"You have my word," he told her in a low voice, "we are doing everything in our power to obliterate the animals who did this."

46

ALEX SEATON gingerly touched the back of his head. Little bristles were sprouting where Mary had shaved him. They were immensely irritating. Lance had changed his bandage several times since they had arrived at the little mountain cabin, but now they had run out of bandages, and Lance had told him the air on his wound would be good for him. "Just don't touch it!" he'd commanded, as if Alex was three years old. Alex had tried not to touch it, but the bumpy scab and prickly hairs felt so strange that his hand kept straying back there, as if his fingertips would help it heal.

The three days he and Lance had been in the cabin might as well have been three weeks. The cottage had a small front porch with a cord of firewood stacked near the door, a small living/dining room dominated by a large fireplace, a cramped kitchen with a door to the back, and two narrow bedrooms, one with a double bed, the other a single. Ken Jordan had been kind enough to stock the dressers with a few changes of clothing for each of them, and though the pants were too big and the legs too short for Alex, he cinched his belt tight and wore them up around his waist.

"You look like Jethro Clampett," Lance had told him.

There was also a bathroom with a shower and a medicine cabinet stocked with a few essentials—toothpaste, brushes, soap, shampoo. Old-fashioned braided-cotton rugs covered most of the floors, except in the kitchen, and there were several plaid easy chairs in the living room, along with large woven baskets stuffed with dozens of back issues of *Field and Stream* and *Popular Mechanics*. Mounted on the wall was a gun rack holding two 12-gauge over-and-under shotguns, a .30 caliber high-powered hunting rifle, and a smaller caliber rifle.

The place was certainly cozy enough, if you were here for a quiet weekend getaway. But it was beginning to drive Alex crazy. Neither he nor Lance had been outside since they were dropped off in the middle of the night after their hair-raising flight through the mountains. And after dark they dared not use the lamps, lest someone notice that the old cabin was inhabited.

The kitchen was stocked with cans of pork and beans, corned beef hash, green beans, corn, and, fortunately, a can opener. There was also an industrial-size box of peanut butter crackers and a case of Coke. Aside from that, they had the metallic-tasting tap water, an old green teakettle, and some dusty Red Rose tea bags. Alex longed for a pitcher of orange juice.

The time passed slowly.

For his part, Lance had settled into his soldier routine. He did pushups three times a day on the living room floor, ran in place, and had read almost every magazine in the cabin already, sitting erect in one of the easy chairs, absorbing them as if preparing for an exam. At night he paced the cabin like a sentry, checking doors, adjusting curtains, staring out into the darkness beyond the windows. Alex didn't know when he slept.

Alex himself slept a lot. Maybe it was the concussion; or perhaps it was an automatic response to the confinement. His dreams were consistent and strange: replays of the explosion, the quick visit at his brother's house, the plane escape. He kept Daniel's handkerchief underneath his pillow. It was a blood-stained mess, but it felt like a physical link with his brother and the faraway world of normal life.

Their only connection to the outside world was a radio, and they left it on all day. The news reports were full of the bombing investigation, the search for the perpetrators, and the arrest of dozens of suspected conspirators. They knew Daniel's car had been found at Doggett's Garage, but it sounded like Frank and Ida had slipped through the net somehow. Hopefully they had made it to Costa Rica.

They knew, too, that Mary had been questioned and released. And they knew that Daniel was in the Arlington County Jail, held under highest security. Alex stared into the empty fireplace, wondering how Daniel felt, how the other inmates and guards were treating him, and thinking about how much he must miss his family.

If it hadn't been for his injury, Alex thought, they would never have had to involve Mary and Daniel. They would have made the 9:30 flight to Miami and caught the next morning's flight to Costa Rica with the phony passports from an old friend of Doggett's in Baton Rouge. They even had backup fake passports, and the eyeglasses, scissors, a Clairol hair-coloring kit, and other materials necessary to alter their appearances accordingly.

Unknown to Alex, Lance also had two military-issue handguns and ammunition, along with several thousand dollars folded into the compartment in the thick belt around his waist.

Now, on the third afternoon after the bombing, they were sitting in the kitchen, listening to the little radio. Thank goodness they had electricity, Alex thought. He dipped his tea bag into one of the mugs he had found in the cabinet. The brownish water was faintly tea-flavored. Trying to conserve, he had already used the bag three times.

"Don't touch your head!" Lance shouted suddenly. Alex jumped, and tea sloshed on the old wooden table.

"Sorry," he said. "I can't help it."

"You can help it. If you break open those stitches, you'll be sorry."

Alex fished the bag from his weak tea, then turned the volume up a little on the radio. "Congressman Peter Meyer has been laid to rest following services at the National Cathedral...

"Turn it down!" Lance hissed at him, grabbing the radio away. "You don't seem to understand what's going on here. No one must hear us, no one must see us, no one must know we're here, or we could end up in prison for a very long time—if not death row. You think you feel penned up in here? Just think about what prison is like!"

"I have been," Alex said, spilling his tea again as he raised the cup to his lips. "How can I not think about it? Daniel is sitting in prison right now. Because of us."

"He's not in prison. He's in jail. There's a difference."

Lance looked at Alex's thin, pale face. He never should have been on this mission. James had been right. A long time ago he had warned Lance. "Just use military men," he'd said. "You can't expect a civilian to be able to handle a special op like this." Alex was falling apart in front of him, looking to Lance for every move, totally dependent, thinking too much, missing too much, shaking too much.

Well, it adds to the challenge, he thought. *People are working on it, and if we can get out of here, we're doing all right.*

Alex broke into his thoughts. "It's our fault," he said again. "Daniel never wanted it to come to this. He got frustrated, but he never wanted violence. And we didn't mean for anyone to get killed. But now he's sitting there getting questioned every day about things he doesn't know anything about."

"That's good," Lance broke in.

"Why are you so cold?" Alex exploded. "This isn't Vietnam or Iraq or some military mission. This is my brother!"

"Look," Lance said. "I can't expect you to understand, but you've broken the first rule of military engagement. You've gotten personally involved because somebody in your family is hurting. Don't you remember everything you were saying a month ago? This is war! You said it didn't matter if you were killed; we had to take out the regeneration center. We had to save babies from execution. And we did it!

"So get hold of yourself. Daniel is a grown man. He can take care of himself. He doesn't know anything. They'll have to release him eventually. Don't worry about him. Right now we've got to concentrate on hanging tight here and then getting ourselves away from the heat. It's all going to be fine."

Alex stared at him, biting his lip. He reached up and probed the back of his head again then looked at his watch. Four o'clock. Time for news on the hour. Time to hear how his brother was doing.

47

THE DAY after the bombing, Emily announced that there would be a crisis management team meeting at 7:00 every morning. This morning, FBI Director Frizzell had done most of the talking as the assistant attorney general for the criminal division, Frizzell's two operational directors, the head of the office of legal counsel, Paul Clarkson, and Emily listened.

Frizzell always managed to project an air of authority. Part of it was his dress—the trademark blue pinstripe suit, heavily starched white shirt, bright silk tie, and pocket handkerchief to match. And part of it was the intensity of his mannerisms and expression, in spite of the fact that today he had little new information to impart.

When he had completed his briefing, Emily thanked him, then addressed the group. "I need not remind you that bringing these guilty parties to justice is the very highest priority of this government." Her voice sounded tired and, Paul thought, she seemed distracted.

"Thank you, gentlemen," she said with a slight wave as she assembled her notes. The group left, but Paul remained.

"Are you all right, Emily?" he asked.

"Of course. Why would you ask?" she snapped, then immediately caught herself. "Yes, just fine. I'm sorry, Paul, I just haven't had much sleep."

"The FBI will find them. Don't worry. Frizzell will make sure of that. His whole career's at stake."

"No, no, it's not that. I'm sure they will. But what's happening to this country? There's such anger and hatred and fury. The newscasters are foaming at the mouth. People on the streets are mad. It's so ugly out there."

Emily was standing behind her chair at the end of the massive table. Paul knew she had an 8:00 meeting scheduled, and she didn't look in any mood for long philosophical discussions. But he thought it worth a try.

"I think we're going at it all wrong, Emily. The answer isn't troops and cops; it's making people believe that the system works. I know I sound like a broken record, but it's a moral problem. People don't know what to believe in—or even what's appropriate."

"Appropriate? Bombing? Don't give me that stuff, Paul," she cut him off, her eyes cold. "Don't stand there and tell me moral values, or lack of them, even excuse or justify this kind of thing. We're talking about people blowing up hospitals, killing people. This is anarchy—revolution. And if we don't stamp it out, this society will come apart." She paused, took a breath. "And that's what these people really want—these anti-abortion terrorists. Your people, right? They want to bring the government down. Admit it."

Before he could reply, she shook her head. "I'm sorry, Paul. That wasn't fair. I'm beat. And I shouldn't take it out on you. I just don't understand what's going on. What moves these people? I'm serious."

"Emily, don't apologize. Sometimes I think you're the one person in this government who has her head screwed on right. This is very bad stuff. But you, of all people, need to see why."

"Okay, then," she sighed. "Go ahead."

"Right now there's tremendous frustration out there. People just don't think the system works. They don't believe the political elite—that's people like us, inside the Beltway—that we hear them or care. And without the confidence of the people, democracy just doesn't work. Our system depends on the consent of the governed. It's a fragile thing."

"I know, Paul. I used to lecture on this at Harvard...the Social Contract. I'm well aware, but—"

"I know you are, Emily, but the contract has been broken. Look at it through the eyes of ordinary people out there. A majority of voters in Cincinnati pass an anti-pornography statute. Majority will. And a judge overrules them. Twenty-three states pass term limits. The Court says no. Same thing in Washington State. People pass a referendum outlawing assisted suicide. Judge overrules it, citing *Casey v. Planned Parenthood...*" Paul paused, half-smiling.

"You needn't be cute," she said defensively. "That's mine. I'm proud of it. It's a matter of liberty."

"Maybe. But think how ordinary citizens see it. They thought their vote counted—that they made the laws, that they decided how they were going to live together—and along comes some judge or bureaucrat who says he knows better. The people get squeezed. They feel they're not part of things. And they get angry. And that's what you're seeing."

"Maybe. Some judges have gone too far. But it doesn't justify this." Emily tapped vigorously on the briefing memo she was clutching. "This is violent revolution."

"Of course not. But when people feel the system isn't working, when all the political doors have been slammed in their faces and they know babies are being killed, it pushes them over the edge," Paul said. "I'm not justifying violence, Emily. But you have to understand the way they think. And that's why troops and cops and tanks only push them further."

Emily shook her head, more in despair than disagreement. She looked tired, vulnerable, her cheeks pale.

"What we've got to do is let people have some room to vent their feelings; we have to let them know we understand, that we hear them, that their government works. You're the one person who can do something. Griswold and his gang, they'll never see this."

Emily smiled wanly. She knew when she was being flattered. It felt good. Then she nodded again. "But the system does work, Paul."

"Are you sure, Emily?"

Outside the windows they heard the sudden shriek of sirens as several police cars raced by on the street below. Emily sighed and shook her head.

Friday, June 5
FBI Headquarters

"Yes sir," FBI dispatcher John Pascoe said to Toby Hunter. "The calls came in within a few minutes of each other. Maybe the weather is clearing people's minds out there in Virginia."

Hunter grinned. The humidity had dropped overnight, and it was a clear, bright June day, rare in muggy Washington. He and Director Frizzell had had no doubts they'd crack this case, but it certainly helped to finally have some specific leads. The white Honda and the Seatons' home had yielded nothing in terms of specific clues as to where they should concentrate the search for Alex Seaton and Lance Thompson.

He scrawled some notes on the pad in front of them. "So tell me about the call from the FAA guy."

"Name's Jerry Leach," the dispatcher responded. "He called first thing this morning. Said that he's worked at the FAA Leesburg facility for twenty-two years and doesn't usually think much about unidentified small aircraft in the area of Godfrey Field; a lot of pilots there seem to take off at odd hours without many formalities.

"So on the night of the bombing, at 22:15 hours, he noted an unidentified radar presence on the screen. Small plane. He radioed a request for ID, but the pilot didn't respond. Leach didn't think much of it at the time, but he didn't know about the bombing yet.

Then, he figured, since the bureau hadn't located the perpetrators yet, maybe the radar blip was something to report. So I was getting ready to send that up to you, sir, and then the second call came in.

"This one was a guy down in Warren County, near Front Royal. Stonewall J. Dinkins. These people still fly Confederate flags from their barns. Anyway, Dinkins owns a well-drilling business and has a hundred acres of apple orchards on the side. He's a real piece of work. Seems he and wife Loretta were sleepin' the other night and Loretta woke up and started punchin' him in the belly. Evidently his belly is rather ample or that's not too unusual, 'cause he just keeps sleepin'; but then Loretta starts pullin' his hair and tellin' him she hears a plane comin' in real low."

Toby Hunter grinned again, though he was tapping his pen impatiently on the desk. The dispatcher was doing pretty well laying on the accent.

"Okay, Mr. Pascoe, so then what?"

"So Loretta's havin' a tizzy, Dinkins tells me, because she had read about a plane crashin' into a house in New York a month or so ago, and she jumps out of the bed and is lookin' out the windows, but she can't see anything 'cause it's dark. Then they both hear the plane comin' lower, lower, lower, and then the motor sounds like it's about to stall, according to Dinkins, and then it cuts out. And they're still alive, their house is still there, they still can't see anything, and he's tired, so he just tells Loretta to hop back into bed, that it's probably just some boys playin' around with their daddy's plane. That's what he said. Then Loretta takes a snort of Jack Daniels to calm her nerves and they both go back to sleep.

"He said it was a little before midnight. He and Loretta go to bed early; they were sound asleep by then. And he wasn't gonna call, but Loretta's been readin' about the bombing in the papers and kept buggin' him to call. So he did."

"Sounds like Loretta's not someone to mess with," said Toby Hunter.

"You got it, sir," the dispatcher replied.

WITHIN THE HOUR, a swarm of FBI agents descended in Leesburg. Jerry Leach, interviewed at home, repeated what he had told the dispatcher.

A search of Frank Doggett's records revealed his ownership of an old Cessna 172, and agents made their way to Godfrey Field, where the nervous airport manager escorted them to hangar number two. Doggett's plane was gone, but agents sealed off the area and called in a team of forensic technicians. The technicians picked up several bags of evidence—most notably, several small splotches of dried blood on the hangar floor near where the plane would have been parked.

Meanwhile, at FBI headquarters downtown, a team of agents gathered around a long conference room table, looking over a detailed Virginia state map. Using a large compass, Special Agent McCrane drew a red circle passing through part of West Virginia, the Shenandoah valley, and the Blue Ridge mountains.

"The Cessna's tank holds forty-two gallons of fuel," he said to the men around him. Their shirt sleeves were rolled up, their suit jackets off, and their weapons draped under their armpits and around their shoulders in leather holsters.

"Leach must have spotted the plane on radar just after takeoff, heading north toward Martinsburg. The Dinkinses heard the plane right here." He marked an X about midway between Front Royal and Winchester.

"So, gentlemen, I think this makes it fairly straightforward for all of us. They've got a few days on us, but they can't have gotten too far without a lot of help, and we can shake that down. I want teams here, here, here, and here." He jabbed the map again, this time with a green pen.

"Command center will be set up in White Post. I want two SWAT team companies, and we've requisitioned a regiment of army Rangers to lend a hand. We'll search every barn, every house, every cabin, every field, every outhouse, every apple tree. We will bring these boys in, and we will consider them armed and extremely dangerous. If they can blow up a building in downtown

Washington, they have resources and weapons on hand. They've already killed three people, including a United States congressman.

"Any questions?"

48

Saturday, June 6

"FBI'S ON OUR trail," Lance said to Alex as he came out of the bathroom. "I just heard it on the radio. 'Unnamed officials confirm that a tip from the FAA has concentrated their search along the Virginia/West Virginia border.'"

"I guess we don't have a plan C, do we?" Alex asked, sighing and walking slowly into the living room.

"I'm working on it."

"Well, I'm going to take a nap," Alex said. "I'm exhausted, and it's not like there's anything we can do here. Have you ever thought about just giving ourselves up?"

"We didn't come this far to give ourselves up," Lance said quietly. "Why are you sleeping so much? It's not good for you."

"You're not getting any sleep at all. You're pacing all night long. That's not good for you either. You're wound so tight you don't even sound like yourself anymore."

Lance let that pass. "Look," he said. "The radio says the FBI has launched a full-scale search, concentrating in Martinsburg. That gives us some time; they won't get this far south for a while. We need to get to Ken and Ned before the FBI does. Tonight, after dark. They can give us a car, and maybe we can get through, just keep moving south, get to Miami."

THE BLACK government car looked incongruous, parked slightly askew on the freshly mowed farm field. In his gray windowpane tropical wool suit and shiny wing tips, Toby Hunter looked equally out of place. A piece of hay clung to his right sock, and he leaned down to brush it away then shielded his eyes from the sun as he straightened up and looked at the barn.

"Good work, men," he said. "You make working for the United States government a pleasure."

The SWAT personnel and a small cluster of Rangers lifted their eyebrows at that but cleared a path leading toward the barn. Its big, red double doors were propped open with piles of cinder blocks; inside, straw and hay were strewn everywhere. And in the far corner, the little Cessna rested like a baby bird in the nest, its wings still partially covered with hay, its tail bearing the ID number they were looking for.

"Good work," Hunter said again. "If we could just find our friend Mr. Doggett, he would be so delighted to hear that his plane has been safely located."

An assistant with a cellular phone trailed behind Hunter, and he turned toward her. "Patti, keep the media thing going. Get our guys in Martinsburg to leak that there's a promising find up there. A gun, or two changes of clothing, or something. We just need a little more time down here, I think, and I'd like our friends in hiding to feel like we're not as close as we are. I'm sure they're listening to the radio."

"Yes sir," said Patti.

Hunter saluted the Rangers and the SWAT team leader. "Go ahead and pick the plane apart," he said. "I want fingerprints, blood samples, whatever we'll need when this thing comes to court. And let's pay a visit to the man who owns this barn."

ALEX LEANED over the small bathroom sink, plastic gloves on his hands. His hair, under a cap of clear plastic, was smeared with light brownish-gold goup. "'Loving Care,'" he said to Lance. "'Covers the gray'... 'ash blond'...I never thought it would come to this. It'd be funny if it wasn't so awful."

Lance felt slightly encouraged. Alex was still acting like an automaton, but at least he was doing what Lance told him. And having a plan in place had given him a small burst of energy. Maybe once he got out of the cabin he'd be all right. But before then, they had to alter their appearances as much as possible. Then they'd wait for darkness, make their way to Jordan's house, get his car, and head south. Lance had the guns and ammunition in an old suitcase he had found under the bed—ready, just in case.

"You're doing a good job," Lance said. "Rub just a little more into your eyebrows. Once you've got these glasses and a baseball cap on, you won't even look like the same person. And once we get clear of Virginia, we can even stop and get you some pants that fit."

Alex obediently smeared goop into his brows. "The directions say to leave it on for about half an hour," he said. "I'll just sit in here so I don't get this stuff on Ken's furniture." He flipped the toilet lid down and perched on the edge. "Could you get me a magazine?"

"Sure," said Lance. "*Field and Stream* okay?"

"That's great," said Alex. "Maybe you could bring the radio in here, too."

"Why, yes sir. And would you like a cup of cappuccino and a slice of apple pie with that?"

Alex's eyes widened for a second until he realized Lance was kidding. "Don't torture me," he said.

"I won't," Lance said. "You wouldn't last a minute under real torture anyway."

AT THE White Post command center, Patti Ward looked up at Toby Hunter.

"Ken Jordan works in Front Royal," she said. "He sells insurance in a little storefront office on Main Street downtown. His secretary says he usually goes home right at five unless he's out on the road. Today he had an appointment in Winchester at four o'clock. He told her he'd go straight home after that."

ALEX LOOKED in the mirror. It was incredible. He really did look different. He tried the glasses on again. Maybe it was his imagination, but he looked more nondescript now. Less noticeable.

Lance wasn't less noticeable, but he looked different too. He had shaved his entire head, then carefully glued a short mustache to his upper lip. He looked forbidding and streetwise.

Alex moved into the kitchen, where Lance was heating some beans. They planned to eat early, then wait for darkness. The radio was on, low. It was almost 6:00; Alex sat down to listen to the news on the hour.

"Mutual News," the announcer said. "Federal investigators report no breakthrough developments in their search for the terrorists who bombed Washington's regeneration center three days ago. Though Rev. Daniel Seaton has been in custody for almost four days, he has shed no new light on the bombing.

"And today, as Seaton's wife, Mary, visited her husband in the Arlington County Jail, she was accosted by a self-described militant AIDS activist who said that the destruction of the regeneration center had signed his death warrant. A man named Hugh Ripken approached Mrs. Seaton as she prepared to enter the jail and doused her with a vial of what he said was HIV-contaminated human blood. Mrs. Seaton was shaken but unharmed by the incident..."

"Oh, man!" Alex moaned. "It just gets worse and worse. Mary didn't do anything. Daniel didn't do anything. We did it, and they're the ones taking the heat for it all. I should be there, in jail, instead of Daniel, not sitting here getting ready to run away."

"You're not there. We have to deal with the situation we're in," Lance said calmly, continuing to stir the beans on the stove though his hand tightened in anger on the wooden spoon. "We've just got to get ourselves out of here."

"When will that be?" Alex shouted, jumping to his feet. "This is never going to end. I'll never see them again."

"Quiet!" Lance turned and grabbed Alex by the arm, wrenching him back into his chair. Lance spoke through clenched teeth. "Listen to me and get a grip on yourself. We are going to get out of here as soon as it gets dark. We are going to get a car. We are going to get to Miami. If you ever want to see your brother and Mary again, you do everything I say exactly when I say it. There's no other way."

Alex just sat at the table, holding his arm where Lance had wrenched it. Lance looked so different, so sinister, with his head shaved and the dark mustache positioned above his lip.

"I'm sorry," he said meekly. "Maybe I'll just take a nap for an hour or so, if that's all right."

Lance nodded. "You can eat later. You'll need your sleep, anyway. I can't drive the whole way."

Alex headed back toward the small bedroom, rubbing the back of his head. Lance looked at his watch, then at the shadows of the trees outside. The sun was sinking, and they were just beginning to lengthen.

AN EIGHT-MAN SWAT team, heavily armed, lay in the tall grass and bushes around Ken Jordan's small garage. They nudged one another as Jordan's pickup topped the small hill on the approach to his property, raising a cloud of reddish dust as he turned onto the long, unpaved road leading to his house.

The team leader spoke very quietly into his radio. "Subject is on his way."

ALEX'S HEAD throbbed as he lay on the old bed. He was asleep but thought he was awake, back in Falls Church. He and Mary were eating apple pie at the kitchen table. "I'm sorry," he was telling her. "It's okay," she said. "Did you know that there weren't really any people in the building? It was just a dream. No one was hurt."

Then the doorbell rang, and Mary and Alex went to answer it together. Daniel stood on the front porch. "It's all over," he said. "They set me free!" Then there was the sound of running feet, and Abigail was scampering down the stairs, running toward her dad...

The running feet sounded heavy. Alex started, then realized where he was. The feet were Lance's, running back and forth from room to room. What was happening?

LANCE HAD been staring out between the drawn curtains of the front window. *If I could just get some sleep, I'd be okay*, he was thinking. But he couldn't sleep. Not until they were well on their way to Florida. It was just like a special op; the mind had to overcome the body's weakness and do the undoable ...

Then he saw them. Six of them. Four in green fatigues and two in black jumpsuits. They were coming up the gravel road from Jordan's house, and if he was seeing right, they had semiautomatics in their arms. The way they were coming meant two things: There must be more of them in the woods, and Ken Jordan must already have been arrested.

Lance whirled from the window and back toward his bedroom. He split open the old clasps on the suitcase and shoved a loaded weapon in both of his big front pockets. Then he ran back to the living room and ripped open the gun rack on the wall. Two nights ago, while Alex was sleeping, he had carefully oiled and loaded each weapon. They were in good shape.

He ran to the back door, through the kitchen, and looked out into the thick woods in the back. In the shadows from the trees, he saw more shadows; the blurry shapes of men stealthily approaching the cabin. He bit his lip; they were surrounded.

He ran to the front door again, his mind racing through options. There weren't any good ones. He thought of the men in the rear, and his mind slipped off its tracks; he was back in the narrow alleys of Baghdad, caught in the web of Revolutionary

Guards. They had approached in the same way, picking their way from point to point until they were almost upon him.

The Iraqis had been careful, but they had seemed arrogant, as if they knew they had this renegade black American in their grasp. They had been less insolent when he blew them all away... Now Lance thought he saw that same arrogance on the white faces out the front window. The SWAT teams were just sauntering up the road in their bulletproof vests, cautious but confident, as if he was just a boy, like Alex.

Lance bit the inside of his cheeks so hard that blood filled his mouth. He wasn't going to let them take him. He took the high-powered rifle and prepared to break the window and take aim.

"No!" Alex screamed, charging out of the bedroom. He clutched his brother's blood-stained handkerchief in his hand and lurched toward the door like a crazy person.

"Get out of here," Lance screamed back. "Get back in the bedroom! It's too late! It's all over!"

"No!" Alex screamed again, throwing himself toward the front door.

Lance used the gun stock to push him to the floor. "Get back in the bedroom!"

Alex scrambled backward on all fours, like a crab, then suddenly rolled and catapulted himself toward the kitchen.

Lance pulled the .38 from his right pocket. He snapped it up like a gunfighter and pulled the trigger, firing over Alex's head. There was a loud explosion, and Alex shrieked as he slipped on the linoleum floor; he scrabbled desperately with his fingers at the back lock.

"No!" Lance shouted, the rifle in one hand and the .38 in the other. He rounded the corner just as Alex wrenched the door open and ran down the two back steps, screaming and waving his arms, the handkerchief trailing off his right hand like a dingy flag. "No!"

It all happened within five seconds.

Alex sprinted toward the woods, focusing on one army Ranger in the distance, not even seeing the SWAT men who had dropped to a firing position on the ground, weapons trained on him. As Alex ran, waving the handkerchief, Lance blew out the glass on the kitchen window.

There was a deafening blast, and the man in front of Alex dropped to the ground like a dead squirrel. Then there was another explosion from the men on the ground, and crashing thunder from the cabin, and Alex suddenly realized that he wasn't running anymore. He was on the ground, and the sound of gunfire was all around him, deafening, the ground shaking like the end of the world...and then the sounds grew fainter, fainter, and he realized the pine needles around him were wet and sticky and warm, and he felt cold...and then he felt nothing at all.

49

"**R**EVEREND SEATON?**"** the guard called. Daniel Seaton was still huddled on his cot, face down, shoulders shaking. He had been that way for hours.

"Go away," Seaton responded, his voice husky and thick. "Please go away."

Thomas Chambers peered through the cell bars a moment longer then shrugged and turned away. Nothing he could do. But he felt for the man. Daniel Seaton was a nice guy, even if his brother had been a crackpot.

Thomas knew what it felt like to lose a brother, though. His own little bro had been gunned down three years earlier, popped off execution style by a rival druggie down on Fourteenth and R. It hurt to lose a brother, even a bad one. He patted the bars for a moment then turned away. He'd see if he could find some coffee for the reverend.

DANIEL'S THIN pillowcase was wet, and his head ached. He turned on his side and swung his feet to the floor, then sat there, head down and cradled in his hands. His thoughts swirled, the same ones over and over.

Stupid, stupid. It was my fault. He didn't know any better, and I let it all go on and on until it came to this. I should have known. I kept hoping things would somehow get better.

"It is your fault," his conscience echoed, kicking in like a prosecutor. "You just let it go. You assumed that things would get better? Since when does good come out of bad? Alex and Lance were out of control, and you knew it."

He got up slowly and made his way to the far end of his cell, ten feet from the bars, staring at the wall.

"It was my fault!" he shouted, anger surging inside of him and taking control. Suddenly he lashed out, slamming his fists on the concrete, beating the wall again and again, until the sharp pain in his hands and the blood on his knuckles made him stop. He staggered unsteadily back to his bunk.

I shouldn't have let him get so involved with Lance, Daniel moaned to himself. He clutched the pillow so tightly that his raw hands trembled. Blood splotched the sheets. For the first time he felt thankful that his parents weren't alive so they didn't have to feel what he was feeling. He tried to pray, but his mind was too scrambled. *Forgive me,* was all he could manage. *Forgive me.*

THOMAS CHAMBERS gingerly approached the cell again, a Styrofoam cup of coffee sloshing in his big hand. Reverend Seaton was curled on the bed in a ball. He was saying something out loud, and Thomas leaned near the bars to hear.

"My brother," Daniel Seaton sobbed. "My little brother!"

THE BLACK government car idled outside the two-story brick condo in Reston. In the bedroom, Jennifer Barrett zipped shut a hanging bag and a small suitcase; the agent waiting in the living room had already carried down the rest of her things. Later other agents would pay off her lease, scrub the apartment of fingerprints and any other identifying information, and leave it as she had found it when she began the assignment. Her higher-ups had determined that her usefulness within the Network movement was over. She'd have a short break then be prepared to testify at the trials to come—and then another assignment.

I wouldn't mind a drug case, she thought. Infiltrating narcotics smugglers was extremely dangerous, but at least with the druggies she knew what she was dealing with. These religious terrorists were something else. She'd been briefed to expect a cult rallying around one charismatic figure; the FBI had taken as its models the cases of Jim Jones, David Koresh, and even the Swiss extremist leader of the Order of the Solar Temple.

Jennifer had been a natural for the assignment. Having grown up attending church twice every Sunday, and every Wednesday night for seventeen years, she knew not only the religious jargon, but a fair amount about the way these people tended to think.

But the cult model had been all wrong, she thought. She had found Daniel Seaton a self-effacing though vigorous personality. The women in the movement had not been a gaggle of mindless groupies but had distinct personalities and views of their own. The men had listened to her ideas. Their prayers and practices had been similar to the home she grew up in, but their attitudes had been markedly different. For the most part, they had treated her with real warmth and compassion; in some ways it hadn't been a hard assignment at all.

On the other hand, she'd had a job to do, and even if most of these people were rather likeable, not at all like the caricatures for which the bureau had briefed her, they still had their dangerous elements.

Alex Seaton: classic case of someone whose passions overcame his reason. Her stomach turned when she thought of all her lunches and afternoon runs with him. His touch had reminded her of those thin, tentative, yet invasive young men she had met during her freshmen year at Bob Jones, before she woke up, escaped, and started a new life far away from the strictures of fundamentalism. And Lance Thompson: another classic case. A veteran who had gotten unhinged somewhere in the midst of enemy fire. She was sorry she'd had to deceive the women, but such men needed to be exposed and stopped. Absolutely.

Jennifer called to the agent in the living room. "Could you carry these suitcases down? I want to get the potted palm. I brought it from home."

She hoisted the palm and hugged the big plastic planter with both arms as her eyes swept the room one last time for any personal items.

Well, it's over, she thought. *I did it.* But there wasn't the sense of accomplishment and closure that she usually felt when she finished a job. Just a dull sense that there was something she'd missed.

50

AIR FORCE ONE touched down precisely at 5:00 P.M. and taxied to its berth at Andrews Air Force Base. The giant walkway was wheeled up to the front door, and within seconds, the president, who had that day spoken to the Chicago Economic Club, appeared in the doorway. Immediately behind him were Harvey Robbins, the secretary of treasury, and the secretary of commerce. Blue-uniformed air force officers snapped salutes, which Griswold returned with a casual nod.

He waved quickly to the press pool assembled to the side of the ramp, stopped at the bottom of the steps to wave to the small crowd clustered behind the chain-link fence, and then, with Robbie walking two steps behind, was passed quickly from the air force to the marines.

Marine One was less than a hundred feet away, its door open and red carpet unfurled. A marine in dress blues with white gloves saluted smartly as Griswold, Robbie, two Secret Service agents, and the president's doctor climbed inside.

Air Force One had glided gracefully onto the runway; *Marine One*, its engines groaning noisily, lifted slowly straight up forty feet in the air in direct defiance of the laws of gravity, jerked its nose downward, turned to starboard, and shot across the taxiways.

On board, the president sat in his leather-padded chair on the port side. Robbie sat facing him across a desk folded out under the large window, taking notes as Griswold issued rapid-fire instructions about the upcoming state dinner for the king of Spain and the agenda for the cabinet meeting. In spite of the helicopter's plush padding and heavy insulation, the engines were deafening. Robbie could barely hear the president, and the desk table was vibrating so badly, his notes were almost illegible.

"And Robbie, we didn't have a chance on the plane to talk about the Seaton case. Poor George Norton—I thought he'd never shut up. You'd think the Commerce Department was the only agency in the government. If I heard once more about his plans for a new digital oceanographic survey, I thought I'd get up and push him out the cabin door—right at thirty thousand feet."

"He was the same way at Brown," Griswold continued. "Insufferable when he got involved in something—thought everybody ought to be as excited as he was...still, he's a good secretary, don't you think?"

"Yes, sir, the business community thinks he walks on water," Robbie smiled.

"Well, I don't know if he walks on it, but he certainly carries water for them. They ought to like him. He sucks right up to them. Not too much though, do you think?"

"No, sir, he handles it well."

"And we want to keep him happy. He raised a ton of money in the campaign. And next time he'll be scooping it in with both hands."

"Yes sir, he's very important," Robbie nodded.

"So we'll give him a chance to prove how brilliant he is—at least as long as it isn't too often . . . Now, Robbie, the regeneration center bombing. The polls still showing the same thing?"

"Yes sir, numbers rising."

"People want capital punishment, right?"

"Seventy-eight percent think those who did it should be

executed. They believe Daniel Seaton was responsible for the bombing," Robbie chuckled.

"What do people say that you talk to? What are our friends saying, Robbie?"

"The same thing, sir. The only thing that will settle this country down right now is to nail these people. Lock 'em up. Execute Seaton."

"And do you agree?"

"Yes sir, you've got to restore public confidence, Mr. President. You were elected to do this. And these people are directly challenging the office of the president. You do it for the sake of the country and for the sake of protecting the integrity of this office."

"Now listen, Robbie," Griswold leaned across the table, "when we land, you get hold of O'Keefe. Tell him 'no ifs, ands, or buts, no fine points in the law books.' I want Bernie to understand how important it is for us to get Seaton. I mean all the way. Every statute we can use, every way we can tie him into a conspiracy. Go the whole way. You understand?" The president sat back in his chair. Then he turned to stare out the window.

"Absolutely, sir. It will be done." Robbie sensed the president's anger. Griswold seldom showed rage; it was part of his stoic Yankee reserve not to show strong emotion. But Robbie could tell.

"Execute this man Seaton. Yes, he must be executed," Griswold muttered, his words barely audible over the whine of the engines and the thump of the spinning blades. He continued to stare at the river as the chopper crossed over the Fourteenth Street Bridge and swept alongside the Jefferson Memorial. Near the Reflecting Pool, the pilot banked sharply to the north.

"It's merciful to them. Of course most people don't understand. They never do. But that hijacking of the American Airlines flight in Miami two years ago. You remember that, Robbie?" Griswold turned and looked at his assistant, who nodded.

"Well, that bureau marksman did the right thing. Shot to kill. Brought the guy down with one shot between the eyes. That was right, Robbie. People like that are better off dead. It's the natural way societies have of weeding out dangerous influences. Right?" The president did not wait for a reply. "And it's the same with this crowd. I mean these people are really crazy, don't you think, Robbie?"

"Yes sir, they are obviously unbalanced. Probably have a death wish."

"Well, we'll take care of that." Griswold arched his eyebrows and smiled faintly.

ROBBINS PHONED O'Keefe in his office immediately after the chopper landed. Bernie was not pleased with the curt orders.

"Look, Robbie, you take care of the schedule and the polls and parading the president around, and keeping the state dinners straight—don't get yourself into this. Justice has to work its course. This is a very sensitive business."

"I'm just relaying the orders of the president who, the last time I checked the Constitution, had the oversight of faithful execution of the laws of the United States."

"Yeah, yeah, that's all well and good, but we're talking about a highly charged, emotional atmosphere here, and the justice system can't be played with. Any sign of prejudice or political pressure, and you'll mess up this case. Leave this one to the pros, Robbie."

"The president said you'd cite cases and throw the law books at him."

"Well, he's right. But it's for his protection and for the country's."

"Remember, Bernie, the president has to look at the big picture. There are some grave issues at stake here—public confidence that he's got to have in order to handle problems in Nigeria and Europe and the Middle East. You won't find anything like that in your law books. We're dealing with the balance of peace in the world. Just take care of it, Bernie."

"'Take care of it.' Yeah, I understand." Bernie hung up the phone, chucked his glasses on the desk, and turned in his chair to stare out at the south lawn behind him. He sighed deeply.

ROB KNIGHT had known Daniel Seaton for several years. Rob's sister and her husband were members of his church. And while

Rob was well-known to the Washington pro-life community for his defense of pro-lifers who had trespassed on clinic property or been arrested for blocking access to the clinics, he had certainly never expected to represent Daniel Seaton in a court of law.

Knight was a tall, thin man who never stopped moving; he was always beating his fingers on a table, tapping his feet, pacing about the room. He was in his mid-thirties but looked younger, and when he wasn't in court, he usually wore jeans and casual cotton shirts rather than the power suits of the Washington legal elite. His sandy-brown hair hung over his collar in the back, and he wore a pair of gold wire-rim glasses that he ripped on and off as the spirit moved.

Rob loved a good challenge, and his friend's situation certainly presented one. But he didn't want Daniel to take him on with any rosy illusions.

Right now he was pacing, at least as much as the confines of the jail conference room would allow. By contrast, Daniel Seaton sat unmoving, quiet, hands folded, docilely watching him roam the room. Daniel's short time in jail had already accentuated his introspective demeanor, making him seem passive and emotionless. Rob was worried about that.

"Rob," Daniel said, "I want you to represent me. I know you haven't exactly been doing this kind of case...I know I could find somebody more high-profile; all kinds of lawyers out there would salivate at the publicity this case will bring...but I want you. I want someone who thinks the way I think, somebody who's going to bring the same moral perspective into the courtroom. That's more important to me than your legal experience."

Rob stopped and leaned over one of the orange-plastic chairs, draping his elbows on the back, turning his glasses in his hands.

"I'll do anything to help you, Daniel," he said. "This thing is a nightmare, and I want to help. But I want to be sure that you get the kind of representation you deserve. I don't think you realize how serious this is."

Daniel looked down. "Look, I've lost my brother, I'm locked up away from my family, I'm in jail with the wildest group of characters you'd ever want to meet, and, yes, I do understand that the government wants to burn me at the stake. I know I need help. But I don't want some flashy hired gun. I want you."

Rob jumped back up, put his glasses on, and started pacing again while Daniel continued.

"I don't want to sound naive, but I can't imagine that it's going to be that bad. I didn't do what they're charging me with; I wasn't part of any conspiracy to blow up the regeneration center, I had nothing to do with the deaths of the congressman and the others. I've always preached nonviolence. We can get dozens of people to testify to my character... All I did was bandage Alex's head and let him go on his way. I realize that was wrong in the eyes of the prosecutors, but what would *anyone* do if their brother came to them with his scalp sliced open?"

Rob ripped his glasses off again and rubbed his eyes, hard, with his hand. Controlling himself, he sank down in the chair opposite Daniel.

"This is exactly what I am worried about," he said. "You are naive. It is *not* simple. We are dealing here with a situation where the public is absolutely screaming for your blood. The perpetrators of a terrorist bombing in the heart of Washington are now dead. The one other member of the conspiracy alive is John Jenkins, but the government doesn't care about him. I'll tell you what will happen. They'll offer him a plea bargain he can't refuse, and he'll say anything the prosecutor tells him to. It'll be your neck to save his skin. At the U.S. attorney's office they're already talking.

"Listen, Daniel, they want you. Bad. They are going to bring down every ounce of energy and venom and expertise they have to convict you. Remember the scapegoat? Very biblical, right? You are about to become one, in a big way."

"Well, at least I'm not pleading guilty," Daniel said. "At first, I thought that was the right thing to do. You've talked me out of that. I'm guilty of a few things here, and I know what they are, and I've asked God to forgive me for them. I've repented of what I did wrong. But I'm not guilty of what they're accusing me of."

Rob pulled out a thick sheaf of legal papers.

"Think about your charges. Murder…including the killing of a congressman. It's murder in the first degree because the perpetrators of this crime had reasonable cause to believe the building might have people in it; so the crime was done with malice aforethought, willful, deliberate, malicious, premeditated. Explosion… knowledge that the circumstances existed to cause the death or bodily injury to any person, or substantial damage to property. Conspiracy to commit a crime of violence. Aiding and abetting these crimes. And, of course, accessory after the fact.

"And the thing is, if Alex and Lance were alive, the government would offer you a deal. They'd want information, and they'd go light on you."

"I would never testify against my brother," Daniel said.

"The prosecutors would find a way to make you feel like it wasn't ratting—that you were offering up truthful testimony to the government rather than concealing the facts. And I know you. You would have to tell the truth to those in authority, as much as you knew."

"That's just it. I didn't, I don't, know anything!"

"Well, it's moot," Rob said. "Alex and Lance are gone, so it's all gonna fall on you. What the government will do is, in effect, try Alex and Lance in absentia for the bombing, the deaths of Meyer and LaMar and Justin Jones, and the destruction of the center… then they'll tie you into aiding the execution of these crimes and harboring and helping them after the fact.

"Accessory after the fact wouldn't be so bad. They couldn't nail you for much; that is, if five years isn't considered much. But what the 'aiding and abetting' and conspiracy charges mean is that you will be, in the eyes of the law, equally culpable as the perpetrators of these crimes.

"And when it comes down, who's the jury going to believe? This isn't a jury of your peers; this will be a motley crew of District of Columbia residents who will find great pleasure in convicting a naive white guy from the suburbs."

Daniel sputtered, but Rob kept talking through clenched teeth.

"And if you're found guilty, you will receive the same penalties Alex and Lance would have if they were convicted, which they would have been in a heartbeat. There's no death penalty in D.C., unless they try to pull this under one of the crazy federal statutes. There you can get the chair for killing a poultry inspector. And they might try. They gave it to Paul Hill, remember?

"Anyway, the least you are looking at it is between twenty years and life in prison. Not much difference. And the federal sentencing guidelines mean that that sentence is absolute. The judge has no discretion to mitigate it because of your unblemished record or your family life or your pastorate or your rugged good looks—"

"But I'm not guilty!" Daniel protested. For the first time he seemed agitated. "The jury will have to believe me."

"Listen, Daniel. That jury will never hear from you. As I see it right now, I'll never put you on the stand. Our best chance is to let the government stew in its own juice. They can't corroborate their facts—"

"But—"

"But nothing. You need to understand one thing. From here on out, I'm in charge. I run the case. That's the way it is. The lawyer calls the shots. Otherwise you can get somebody else."

Rob could see that Daniel wanted to object, and he kept going to drive his point home.

"This isn't *Perry Mason* or *Matlock*...no one is going to jump up in the courtroom at the last minute and confess and you'll go free, a hero. This is the real thing, and it's going to be nasty."

51

Friday, June 19

PAUL CLARKSON stretched his aching legs and looked out over his backyard. The grass needed mowing and was a little dry; he'd need to remind Paul Jr. to stick with his yard work. But the cascading mounds of pink and white impatiens edging the flower beds were full and bright, the mulch was fresh...things looked pretty good on the whole, he thought.

He had slept in a bit this morning, and now he and June were having their coffee on the back deck. It felt strange to be sitting here at 7:30 on a weekday morning, but he was going to take June to a doctor's appointment at 9:00. He had told Emily that he would be coming in to the office late. His wife's health came first this morning, and the two of them were enjoying an unusual few minutes of quiet.

The *Washington Post* lay spread out on the round glass table under the green-striped patio umbrella. Paul had usually digested the news, editorial, business, and federal sections by this hour, but today he couldn't get past the story that began on page one: "Senator Langer Announces Retirement: Mississippi Statesman Cites Poor Health, Fatigue."

"He didn't even call to tell me," Paul said.

June sighed and watched a mockingbird chase interlopers away from the Bradford pear tree adjacent to the deck. "You need to call him, Paul. He needs you now more than ever."

"He's hung in there all these years; he's been through all kinds of attacks," Paul said. "But this thing really cut him to the quick. I hope Bernie O'Keefe realizes what he's done."

"He'd have to have a conscience to do that," June said dryly. "I don't think Bernie O'Keefe has a conscience."

52

BERNIE LIFTED his briefcase onto his desk, ready to pack it in for the day. *If only this bag could talk,* he thought, running his hands over the supple, golden-brown leather worn to a smooth patina. What tales it could tell. Stories of long hours in the most exalted courtrooms of Boston, Washington, and New York. Journeys on the backseats of limousines or in the overhead racks on sleek jets, including *Air Force One.*

A surge of nostalgia swept through him, and he looked over at the huge, white, beautifully calligraphied parchment that hung behind his desk: "J. Whitney Griswold, President of the United States of America to Bernard Jerome O'Keefe…Reposing special trust and confidence in your integrity, prudence, and ability, I do hereby appoint you Counsel to the President of the United States of America." His commission. The most coveted possession in Washington.

Then he shook his head; he didn't need any more play on his emotions today. He began stuffing files and papers into the soft-sided case that opened at the top and easily held, along with his files, extra shirts, shaving gear, even a laptop. He knew he wouldn't read any of this stuff tonight; he just needed the security of having it. Then he shut the bag, headed through the door, and into the outer office, trying to decide whether to go home or stop at Kelly's. It was already nearly 8:00 P.M.; he and Barbara had put in a long, brutal day. Stopping at Kelly's would probably help.

He was still stewing over the message Clarkson had sent by e-mail, chastising him for his part in bringing down "a good and decent man, a man who wanted nothing more than to serve his country." The charge had stung because it was true. Langer had flinched in battle, then covered it up. So what? Who knew what he'd have done with Vietnamese crawling all over him and shells exploding.

"Bernie...Bernie...are you all right?"

The words jolted him. He looked down and saw his hand on the knob to the outer door. He had walked right past Barbara—his secretary and faithful friend who had mothered him for the past twelve years. He hadn't even looked at her, let alone said good night.

"I'm sorry, Barbara," he said. "I'm fine. Never better. A rough day, you know, but you can't keep the sons of the old sod down for long," he said with an Irish brogue and a broad grin.

But it was a lie. An hour earlier he had felt the familiar sinking feeling in his chest and stomach, the sensation that everything was senseless...the awful, inexorable feeling of deep despair.

When he felt it coming, Bernie had taken a double dose of the pills Dr. Nikkels had prescribed, and they had stabilized things a little, though he still had difficulty getting energy into his legs. His brain was giving the commands, but his joints and muscles were ignoring them. Insubordination.

Nikkels had told him to call if he began slipping into what he had called the dark tunnel. Bernie needed professional attention at once during such periods, the doctor had warned. But Bernie never liked to ask anyone for help; he could handle things himself. He had the scars to prove it.

Besides, he usually disdained psychiatrists, at least in public, even though he liked and needed Nikkels in private. "A lot of them are quacks," he'd once told a colleague after calling a psychiatrist as an expert witness. The doctor's testimony had succeeded in getting off one of Bernie's most celebrated defendants, a man Bernie knew perfectly well to be guilty. He also knew that the doctor would say anything he wanted him to for a price. He'd had little respect for psychiatry since then—until he hit the black tunnel five years ago. Then it was Nikkels—almost as much as Marilyn—who had pulled him through it.

KELLY'S EASILY WON the tug-of-war, and by 8:15 Bernie was at his favorite spot at the bar. Maybe it wasn't going to end up such a bad day after all. Tonight there was even an empty stool.

Henry greeted him warmly and was starting to pour his usual when Bernie stopped him. "Henry, tonight I need a Bud Lite—nice and cold."

The bartender stared. He'd never seen Bernie O'Keefe drink anything but scotch, always Dewars and always on the rocks. "Bud Lite, draft?"

"Yup," Bernie grinned. "A little change."

Dr. Nikkels had been insistent. "Remember, Bernie, absolutely no alcohol while you're on this medication." But a beer wouldn't hurt, Bernie reasoned. The slight alcohol content would wash right out before it could do any harm. Besides, beer was made for the Irish, their national tonic. No one ever saw a depressed Irishman.

Bernie downed almost half of the first mug in one swallow, then rested both elbows on the bar as the familiar, comforting sensation coursed through his body; he could feel muscles relaxing and his mind clearing. He wasn't really responsible for Langer, he reassured himself; somebody would have exposed the guy. He was living a lie after all; it wasn't as if they had made something up about him. Simply the truth coming out. Mr. Military Hero had been impaled on his own spear. That's life—justice actually.

Whitney Griswold was another matter, though. Bernie gulped down the rest of the beer and rapped the mug on the bar for a refill.

Probably Whit's just blowing off steam, Bernie told himself. *But I want no part in executing a criminal defendant.*

Memories of his deep-seated opposition to capital punishment filtered through his mind, starting back when he was a kid at Sacred Heart and had argued passionately against the topic in debate: too many innocent men wrongly convicted, and no real deterrent to crime. Later, a professor at Boston College, Father Sheehan, had tutored Bernie in moral philosophy and drilled into him the anti-capital-punishment arguments at a philosophical level. His study of capital cases at Yale only deepened his commitment. Now the president of the United States wanted to take Seaton and hang him, just to appease public anger.

Bernie shook his head. What had his old friend come to? Where was the noble Yankee gentleman called to the highest ideals of service to others? Corrupted, that's where, and Bernie was being corrupted right along with him. No decency or truth, or tolerance, for that matter, in their administration. He swallowed deeply. He'd have to find a way to back Whit off, make him listen, regain their balance.

Bernie finished the second mug and beckoned to Henry. Thank goodness for malt and hops and the Irish. It was the first time he'd felt alive all day. He even found himself cracking jokes with the bartender in between swigs from the third mug. The cold liquid soothed his throat, a pleasant contrast with the warm flush he felt in his cheeks. His limbs felt lighter, buoyed by an unseen force. *Ah, the relief.*

"Fill it up again, Henry," Bernie said. "I'll be right back." He headed for the men's room, a familiar-enough route. Around the bar it was...no, not that side. He made two false turns, then found the hallway, his legs a little rubbery.

BACK AT THE BAR, Henry was waiting with the fourth round. "You sure you want another?" he asked sternly.

Bernie reached out. "Of course. You ever seen me drunk, Henry? I've never in my life lost control."

"You aren't walking too straight, Bernie." Henry was scowling.

"Give me that glass. No Irishman quits with two beers," Bernie grinned.

"This is number four."

"It's only beer, Henry."

"Last one." Henry handed it over cautiously, then smiled. "Well, with all the pressures you got, guess I can't blame you."

Bernie nodded, wiping the foam from his lips.

"Hope you guys are going to nail that maniac Seaton." Henry scowled again.

"If he's guilty we will." There was a coolness in Bernie's voice now.

"Guilty? Of course he's guilty. These are bad guys, Bernie. Oughtta fry 'em."

"Yeah, I know." Bernie stared into his beer. Why should Robbie bother with all those expensive pollsters? Just come into Kelly's and ask Henry. Fry Seaton. Sure. Why not? Who gives a rip? Guilty or not. What's one sacrificial lamb anyway? Griswold's got it right. He knows.

At that moment, as the toxin level in Bernie's blood rose, the uninhibited, almost giddy feeling began to fade. For just an instant he felt a touch of nausea, though it quickly passed; but he could sense the tunnel, that he was nearing it, about to enter its vacuum. The awful thing about the tunnel was that there was no way out, and the walls closed in.

"Thanks, Henry. I'll see you. I'm going to take a walk." Bernie slid a bill out of his wallet, then slid off the stool, bumping hard into the man on his left, and walked unsteadily to the front entrance.

"Bernie, you sure you're okay?" Henry called after him.

Bernie turned back for a moment. "Of course," he said, then saluted and went out the door.

OUTSIDE HE TOOK several deep breaths and looked around, absorbing the sights and sounds of the warm summer night. Spanish music floated over from an outdoor cafe, a man was selling bouquets of fresh red roses on the street, and couples strolled past him arm in arm.

Bernie had already decided not to call for his car; he would walk home. He had done it twice before and enjoyed it. So he turned left out of Kelly's front door, listing slightly to the right under the weight of the overstuffed briefcase swinging at his side.

He waited at the light then nearly tripped on the curb as he crossed M and headed up Thirty-fourth Street, walking quickly up the small hill, enjoying the exercise. *Just like the old days*, he thought. When he was on the BC football team he could drink half the night and still play hard the next afternoon, hurling his muscular body at opposing players, grinding them into the ground. Those were great days. Carefree days.

Hey, he thought. He was only four blocks from Georgetown University. Why not walk through the campus? There'd be summer students there, maybe even some pretty ones. It was such a beautiful night. Maybe he could walk away from the tunnel.

N Street dead-ended into the university at Thirty-first Street. Bernie climbed several flights of steps up to the main level of the campus, which, like most older, eastern, urban schools, was an eclectic mix of Victorian, Gothic, and Colonial architecture surrounding rectangles of green. To his left he saw book-laden students streaming in and out of what was obviously the library. In front and to the right of him was Healy Hall, Georgetown's distinctive landmark, a gray Gothic structure with narrow spires soaring into the night sky.

Awash in memories, Bernie drifted past the library, stopping to admire the collection of whiskey bottles some party-loving student had lined in his dormitory window, fondly remembering his own undergrad days. Another window held a lighted neon "Lite on Tap" sign. The campus was serene, though, a few students sitting on benches talking quietly. The lampposts that lighted the path seemed to flicker in the gentle breeze.

Bernie staggered right and made his way up a brick walkway bordered by beds of ivy and boxwood hedges and eventually came to a central square hidden behind Healy. This was evidently the heart of the campus. If it weren't for the jets roaring overhead on their landing approach down the Potomac River to National Airport, Bernie could have imagined himself transported back into the nineteenth century.

At the center of the square was a charming brick building with curved steps leading to its entrance. Two students were sitting on the steps, talking loud enough for him to hear, something about some Jesuit retreat or something. They looked up at him quizzically. As he walked closer, he realized this was the chapel, and he walked up the three steps to read the signs posted on the board. Several masses were scheduled, he noted, the last one at 10:15 P.M.

Bernie looked at his watch—9:40. He always joked about being a three-Sundays-a-month Catholic, but that was stretching it. More like once every few months, and only then when Marilyn absolutely insisted. In fact, he hadn't been to Mass at all since he'd come to Washington.

Church held no meaning for him anymore, if it ever had. Church was the nuns who used to whack his knuckles at Sacred Heart, or the priests who droned on in Latin when he was a kid—even when they'd switched to English, he couldn't under-stand them. Church was his mother holding him by the scruff of the neck and scrubbing his face on Sunday morning; it was his brief time as an altar boy before the priest discharged him—to his father's horror—for laughing during Mass; it was his father locking him in his room. Church was rules and pain.

The two students left, and Bernie stood alone on the front steps watching the bubbling fountain in the middle of the green and the towers behind, stretching straight and narrow into the night sky. His head throbbed; though the air and exercise had helped, the tunnel was not far away. He could sense its nearness in the cramped feeling that gripped his chest and stomach. He took several deep breaths and sighed.

Then he felt an odd prompting to go into the chapel. *Why?* He chuckled to himself. Here he was, Bernie O'Keefe, one of the most powerful men in the United States, clutching a bag full of sensitive government papers, standing on the steps of a chapel in the middle of a campus full of twenty-year-old summer-school students. But he was also feeling wretched and angry, maybe even frightened. He couldn't sort out the jumble of emotions raging inside.

Bernie turned and went through the doors. He was struck immediately by the inviting warmth and informality of the large room. Not a cold, sterile cathedral—more like a library. There were blond wooden chairs with worn red cushions, linked in rows, with red-leather kneeling pads under each one. Wooden beams arched across the white-plaster ceiling, all bathed in soft light from the sconces on the walls.

The altar was a simple table with candles on either end. Behind it was a piano, and to the right the most unusual crucifix he had ever seen. At least eight feet high, made of gray iron with a silvery statue of Christ impaled on it. It was starkly compelling, and Bernie found himself slowing walking toward it. At the second row, by reflex, he genuflected and slid into a chair, putting the briefcase down at his side. He bowed his head.

If only it were all true. But even if there were a God, what would He care about someone like a Bernie O'Keefe and these clutching demons, he thought. The indictments began to sear his mind like hot irons.

Bernie O'Keefe, you are a wretched husband. Marilyn left you and with good reason. Even if she didn't know about the other women—and she probably did—she knew you cared only about yourself. Not about her, not about the kids.

And you have been a total failure as a father, never even getting to one of Matt's games last fall. Not one. You don't know your kids, and your kids certainly don't know you. *Failure.* It stung.

You put your whole life on the line for Whitney Griswold, a pompous ass who has used you and will discard you like a used Kleenex if it suits him. That is, if his whole government doesn't collapse in a heap first. The army in the streets and chaos in the country—nice work for only six months in office.

And now, to top it all off, you've destroyed a decent man's career and are about to try to get the death penalty for another.

Surely any good God would banish such a man to the lowest

reaches of hell. Bernie's chest was heaving with huge sighs. He thought he might break into tears.

"If I can help in any way, I'd like to," said a voice, and Bernie felt a hand rest lightly on his shoulder for a moment. At first he thought he was imagining it, probably losing his mind by now anyway. Then he slowly looked up into the face of a man with penetrating deep-blue eyes.

"No, no," Bernie said. "Just thinking through some things."

He was startled by the man's directness, but that attracted him as well. He'd always liked straight shooters. The man was dressed in a white polo shirt and khaki pants. Over his arm were some white sheets. *Maybe a choir robe*, Bernie thought.

"I'm just fine." Bernie said, his defense mechanism back at work. "Just needed a little space. You know how it is. Are you a graduate student here?"

"No." The man stuck out his hand. "I'm Bob Garrison."

"Oh, well, good to meet you." Bernie shook his hand.

"And you are?"

"Bernie."

"I noticed you staring at the crucifix, Bernie. Interesting, isn't it? I do the same thing myself all the time."

"I've never seen one quite like it. Do you know who the artist was?"

"Oh, someone pretty well-known, actually. But the significance is what you see in it. A lot of people see themselves. Crucified, suffering, death to self. I see myself in it often," the man said as he stared at the cross. "And, of course, I see Christ, suffering for us."

The man, probably in his early thirties, was handsome, but it was his smile and his air of confidence that were so compelling. As he talked, he threw his head back slightly and ran his hand through the spears of light brown-hair that had fallen over his forehead.

"You're a Christian, are you, Bernie?"

"I was raised Catholic."

"That wasn't what I asked," the man said. "Do you believe?"

"I don't know." Bernie shook his head. "Right now I don't know what I believe."

"It's all right. You can find answers here. Something's really bothering you, isn't it?"

Bernie paused. "Well, you could say I've been through some things. Who are you, anyway, if you don't mind my asking? Campus thought police?" He grinned at his own stupid joke.

"Oh, I'm sorry. Of course. I'm Father Bob Garrison. I'll be celebrating Mass here in a few minutes."

"But you're so—"

"Casual?" The priest chuckled. "Well, this is a campus, you know. I've just come from a student Bible study."

Bernie nodded. A priest leading a Bible study?

"But don't worry, I'll be dressed properly." He held the white robe and chasuble up before him and smiled. "See? I turn into a priest at 10:15."

Bernie smiled.

"Why don't you stay, Bernie?" Garrison looked at him directly again.

There was a long moment of silence.

"No, thank you," Bernie replied. "I just came in here to sort some things out, clear my head, get a load off."

"Well, you're carrying a heavy load. I can see that. Christ said that His burdens are light. Why not take Him at His word?" The priest pointed toward the cross. "The Lamb of God who takes away the sins of the world."

"Father, I haven't been to confession in ten years." Bernie put his hand up, palm outward. "And you don't have time to listen. We'd be here all night and into some time next week."

"I have all the time you'd need—but it's not a matter of time, is it?"

Bernie suddenly felt trapped. "I'll be honest, Father. I used to believe . . . I guess. But I'm afraid I'm a long way from where you are."

"No, you aren't. You're here. And you're not here by accident, you know. Something, or I should say Someone, compelled you to come here. All you have to do is receive—"

"No," Bernie broke in. He couldn't believe that God had somehow compelled him, after a day like this, to end up in this chapel talking to this priest. God must have other things on His mind. "I just came here by accident. It's a beautiful evening. I wanted to walk around. I was curious about the chapel."

The priest simply smiled.

Bernie could feel the beads of sweat on his forehead. He was torn. The priests he had known were never like this kind, yet strong young man. He wanted to cry out, "Yes, I'm here! Help me! I'm going down the tubes!" But he was Bernie O'Keefe, successful and important and in no position to open his messed-up life to some obscure priest on a college campus. What if it ever got out?

"Look, Father, I can't say I believe if I don't. Most religious people are hypocrites anyway. They don't really believe, I mean way down deep inside."

"Ah, yes," the priest laughed. "We all have doubts and we all fall short. I suggest you come, join us for Mass. You'll probably feel right at home."

Then he stopped and looked at Bernie, hard. "Listen," he said. "You must believe so you can understand, and when you understand, you will believe."

Bernie stared, trying to sort through the words. He couldn't make sense of them.

"Thank you, Father. I think I'll just sit here and think it through."

"Great. Stay through the Mass, and then we'll talk more. Let me buy you a cup of coffee down the street. But stay. Whether you realize it or not, you've come here because God has brought you. Stay and meet Him. Celebrate with me." Father Bob locked eyes with him for a moment then turned and went through a door in the back of the chapel into the sacristy.

A few minutes later, as the pianist began playing, he reappeared in a flowing white robe with a light stole draped over his shoulders, on it a green-and-gold embroidered cross. He moved slowly now, deliberately, his hands together, palm to palm. His face was peaceful, composed.

Bernie looked around. A few dozen people had slipped in while he and the priest had been talking. An odd mix: a few older people, some faculty types, a street person, and a surprising number of students. And also, squirming in discomfort, the counsel to the president of the United States.

FATHER BOB GARRISON looked at his troubled visitor several times during the liturgy. The man's bloodshot eyes were fixed on him, and the priest almost felt distracted: Where had he seen this man before? He read the familiar words, but as he did so, his heart swelled and hurt for the silent soul before him.

He held up the silver chalice, saying softly to the people and himself the amazing words of Christ: "This is the cup of My blood, the blood of the new and everlasting covenant. It will be shed for you and all so that sins may be forgiven. Do this in memory of Me."

He looked at the crucifix. In memory of Christ, yet celebrating with the risen Christ even now, alive and present this warm summer night. He smiled and looked back at the people who were acknowledging: "Christ has died, Christ is risen, Christ will come again."

His eyes stopped where the man had been sitting. The chair was empty.

HOME. Sort of. Bernie entered his library and rubbed his open palms over the oak paneling. So rugged and enduring. This room with oak everywhere reminded him of the first law office he'd clerked for, one of the last of the big firms to remain in an old turn-of-the-century, granite-faced building in downtown Boston, the kind that still had elevators with steel-meshed doors and worn black-and-white marble-tiled corridors. Lawyers today chose mahogany or rosewood or sleek, exotic furniture; but in those days, when lawyers were lawyers, not smooth-talking technocrats, it was oak and big desks and overstuffed leather.

If only he had a chance to unpack, he'd make something of this room, he thought for the umpteenth time, something solid and stable. "Which I could use right now," he startled himself, saying it aloud into the silence. Something like he had felt in that chapel—a feeling he hadn't had in a long while.

Bernie pushed his briefcase under the desk, chucked his coat onto a large packing crate, and kicked off his tasseled loafers. The walk home had tired him, and he slumped into the big black-leather desk chair, the one his partners had given him when he left the firm.

Yes, there was something about that chapel. Bernie rubbed his eyes, even as the images passed through his mind. The crucifix was so striking. The aluminum stark, yet in the figure was all the agony and passion it represented, that good and decent and innocent man being executed to satisfy the anger of the mob.

Nothing has really changed in two thousand years, Bernie thought. We'll kill today to satisfy the mob. Even a decent man like Griswold will—and without blinking an eye.

But could it be true? he wondered. Did Jesus really die for others? The priest had spoken of Him with such familiarity. And he had looked right into Bernie as if he knew him—and loved him anyway. The priest had seemed...so good, so decent, so kind, and yet strong. Not a patsy. Not beholden to anyone. Bernie hadn't met anyone like him since he'd been in Washington.

And why should he have? Think of those buttheads in the government...Robbie, the cold, calculating vampire who probably slept in a refrigerated vault. Frizzell, just a gutter-fighter. Many of those jokers on the Hill would turn in their own mothers to get elected, not to mention the little power-mongers who strutted around the corridors of the White House, and their junior clones-in-training, the beaver patrol. And then there was Griswold himself . . . Bernie tried to remember back to how they had first become friends. Why? Maybe he'd never really known the man, or maybe he'd changed. Could Washington have done this to him—or worse, was it something in him?

Probably all of us are the same, Bernie thought. So prideful and powerful and self-assured on the outside, rotten and whimpering within.

Bernie didn't like being so honest. But how could he ever face his law partners who had sent him off to save the republic? He thought of their admiring, envious grins, their strong hands clapping him on the back. He shook his head, staring at the empty bookshelves. All those grand dreams and plans, unraveling now, he thought. The country is in absolute turmoil, we have how many more years of this to go, and our administration is crumbling. An absolute failure. *I can never go back.*

The images rolled in his mind, tossing his emotions. One moment he felt better, lifted with a surge of hope; the next he crashed in despair, dashed to the sand. His head hurt worse than it had in a long time. The beers had worn off, and the darkness was still there. His limbs felt heavy, his mouth was dry, his vision slightly blurred, and that awful, sinking sensation was back in his abdomen.

Bernie got up quickly and walked down the hallway to the kitchen where he took an unopened bottle from the twelve neatly stacked on the pantry shelf. General Dewars was there to serve. Then, tucking the bottle under one arm, he filled a glass with ice. He returned to the front of the house, checked the security system, then turned back into his library, stepping over a pile of mail on the floor.

Bernie never used a shot glass, boasting that he could measure two ounces exactly with his eye. Maybe once that was true, but the two ounces looked suspiciously like four as he filled the tumbler three-quarters full and sat down again at his desk.

Dr. Nikkels had also warned him to beware of the signs of alcoholism, and lying about how much he drank was the first sign. The next was when he felt he had to have a drink. Bernie told the doc that never happened, but that was a lie too. The truth was that Bernie refused to believe he was addicted or ever could be. Yet tonight he watched his hand tremble as he lifted the glass and took several swallows.

If only it were true. Bernie couldn't shake off that thought, nor could he clear his mind of the image of the cross or the appealing expression on the priest's face. "The Lamb of God who takes away the sins of the world," the man had said. Something else came back to Bernie, something from childhood. "Seek and ye shall find." Could it be true? If only...

It was less than a minute before the familiar relief returned, starting with the warm sensation in his stomach, and he suddenly remembered he hadn't eaten since lunch. Then came the numbing of his nerve endings and a sudden release of tension.

Dr. Nikkels had warned him against even one drink when he was taking Xanax or lithium; it would release inhibitions faster than normal, he said, and there would be no resistance to the second, third, and fourth drinks. On top of the drugs, that amount of alcohol could almost shut down the central nervous system and possibly be lethal.

But it had been six hours since the last pill, Bernie thought. The beer hadn't killed him, and anyway, how he felt now was such a relief that it was worth it, no matter what.

Bernie leaned back in his chair, breathed in deeply, and massaged his temples. The pain was easing but not the images. He should have stayed for the Eucharist. "The blood of Christ, shed for you and for all, that sins may be forgiven." Memories of childhood, his first confirmation, his mother's hug. He felt a moistening in his eyes.

Whoa! Get yourself together, O'Keefe, he commanded. Annoyed, he took out his handkerchief and dried his eyes. Maybe he could call the priest.

The phone book, a huge gray-and-yellow volume, was on the floor. With some effort he found a listing for Georgetown University.

An operator picked up on the second ring. "Georgetown University."

"May I have the chapel, please?"

"Is this a joke?"

"No, no. Connect me to the chapel. I don't know the name."

"You mean Dahlgren?"

"I don't know. Is there more than one?"

"Look, sir, it's nearly midnight. I'm sorry. I can't connect you with the chaplaincy services until office hours tomorrow morning."

"This is an emergency. I need to find Father Bob."

"Do you know his last name? I can look in the directory if he lives on campus."

Bernie stopped. He thought. He could not remember the priest's last name.

"Sir?"

Bernie gently put the receiver down and wiped his eyes dry. He finished his drink and poured another generous portion.

Bernie had always thought of himself as one of the more fortunate people in life. He had been either lucky enough, or smart enough, to seize the moment as the winds of fate blew past, finding his destiny by being clever enough to recognize the opportunity and take it.

Had he just missed such a moment?

Within a few minutes the second drink was gone, and Bernie poured a third. All inhibitions removed now, he experienced a momentary euphoria. But only momentary. The surge of alcohol in Bernie's blood, coupled with the residue of Xanax, was dramatically depressing the functions of his central nervous system, which acts as a command center for the body. Its signals exert control of every nerve and muscle, including the automatic functions of the lungs and heart. As the signals dim and the body begins shutting down, fatigue and ennui set in.

"So what," he muttered aloud. "So what. Nobody cares about me. Mr. Big Shot Lawyer. Hah! Oh sure, they all look up to Bernie, the president's right-hand man. And what happens? The whole blasted country is up in arms. Cops, National Guard, FBI. People shooting each other. And we're going to end up throwing the Constitution down the tubes... Hah! What would Professor Friedman think of me now, his prize student in constitutional law!...

"It doesn't matter." Bernie was crying uncontrollably but made no attempt to dry his eyes. He was breathing harder, and the head-throbbing returned with a vengeance.

"And Marilyn. What a hero she's hung around with all these years. She's right. I've failed her and failed the kids," he sobbed.

All the veneer and bluster were stripped away, and what Bernie saw revolted him. He hated himself.

Then an alien thought fought its way through the fog of his memory. *Paul Clarkson.* He once offered to help me. He's a religious guy. Sort of like that priest tonight . . . Father what's-his-name. Maybe I could talk to him.

"Hah!" As quickly as the thought came, he dismissed it as ridiculously funny. He had destroyed Clarkson's hero. Imagine calling him at midnight. "Excuse me. Could you tell me how this religion thing works?"

Bernie laughed, almost hysterically. "He'd slam the phone in my ear. No, I'd do that to him; he probably wouldn't do that to me. That's the difference between us . . .

"I've got his number somewhere," he exclaimed, pulling his wallet from his hip pocket. It was jammed full with money, receipts, scraps of paper with expense information, dry cleaning tickets. He tore the money out and started through the wads of paper. He took two big gulps, finishing his third drink, frantically pulling paper out of his wallet, balling up piece after piece and throwing them on the floor.

He flung the wallet to the corner of the desk. The paper was not there.

He checked his watch. Moving toward midnight. The White House operator could find Clarkson; she'd get anyone, anytime. No, the Secret Service might be monitoring the phones, as they did randomly. He didn't want them nosing into anything.

It didn't matter anyway, he thought; the darkness was here . . . the tunnel . . . waiting to swallow him. He swallowed another drink, but the alcohol only intensified his feelings of rejection . . . aloneness . . . hopelessness . . . danger.

I can't do it, he thought. *Nobody cares . . . and why should they?* His self-loathing was almost overwhelming.

The answer suddenly seemed clear. He reached for a sheet of paper from the center drawer of the desk. He scrawled some words on it, folded it neatly, and laid his pen on top of it.

He took another quick shot of the Dewars, then reached into

the bottom drawer of his desk, behind a thick file folder. His hand closed around the cold blue metal of the Smith and Wesson .38 caliber revolver the Secret Service had issued him for emergency security at home.

Suddenly he felt a surge of confidence, an odd assurance that he was in charge again. He could get out of this on his terms.

He was breathing hard, but the tears had stopped.

There is a way out of the tunnel, he thought. He could control it.

He loaded one soft-nosed bullet into the chamber and snapped the cylinder shut.

Then, holding the gun with both hands, he placed the barrel in his mouth and pulled the trigger.

53

Late Tuesday, June 23
The White House

WHITNEY GRISWOLD'S long form was draped over a spindly nineteenth-century chair in the Lincoln sitting room. It was almost midnight and he was alone. A Secret Service agent stood outside the door and others were down the hall, but here in this room he was alone. Alone with his thoughts as the nightmare day drew to a close.

After the news broke about Bernie's suicide, the media had been absolutely out of control, and his own shock had been so great that he couldn't rally the strength to even issue a statement. This was a scenario he and Bernie had never anticipated.

He wasn't even sure who to be. The tough president, striding into the press room, assertive and confident? The competent president, announcing a plan of action that others might follow? The grieving-but-in-control president, issuing poignant statements of condolence and comfort?

In the end, Caroline Atwater had simply put out a terse announcement that the Griswolds were mourning the loss of their close friend in private...and now J. Whitney Griswold was simply the wounded president, sitting in an uncomfortable chair and reading, over and over, the copy of the note Bernie had left for him. The Secret Service had confiscated the original from Bernie's desk, but the photocopy was cruelly clear.

The president was drinking Dewars. It felt like the right thing to do, in memory of Bernie, but it also felt exactly wrong without his old friend slouched on the sofa opposite him, red-faced and enthusiastically trading barbs, relishing their successes, laughing at something some pompous bureaucrat had done, brainstorming their next political victory.

The shots of Dewars weren't helping. His mind felt as clear as ever, the pain still there like a razor. How could Bernie be gone? He had clapped Bernie on the back just hours ago, telling him to buck up, things were going to be all right. He couldn't be gone.

Griswold looked down at the single sheet of paper in his hand. It had come in a White House envelope marked "For the President's Eyes Only," and he vaguely hoped the staff had honored that plea for privacy.

On it, scrawled in the bold handwriting he had known so well for more than twenty years, was but a single sentence: "Whit, I'm not going to be able to take care of this one for you. —B"

54

ANNE GRISWOLD and Marilyn O'Keefe had never been soul mates. But as her limousine headed toward the O'Keefe's Georgetown home, Anne realized that the years of their husbands' friendship had bound them together more closely than she'd thought.

Anne rarely did anything apart from a carefully considered strategic plan, but she had simply felt compelled to visit Marilyn. The younger O'Keefe children were being cared for by their aunt, and now Marilyn was at the house with her oldest son, Matt, and her parents, going through things, planning Bernie's funeral, doing whatever one does after a shock like that.

I hope she has some Valium or something, Anne thought. *There's just no way to cope with something like this otherwise.*

Secret Service personnel had restricted other cars from parking on the narrow Georgetown street around the O'Keefe townhouse, so Anne's limo was able to pull right up in front. Marilyn must have been watching from the window because the front door opened just as Anne got to the top step.

"Come on in," Marilyn said.

Anne stepped into the foyer. One of her agents stayed on the front porch; the other stepped discretely into the living room. The two women paused for a second, then hugged.

"I'm so sorry," Anne said. "I don't know what to say."

"I don't know either," Marilyn said. "Let's go in the kitchen. My parents are upstairs packing boxes for me. I can't face that just yet."

Anne couldn't help glancing toward the library that Bernie had used as his study. The doors were shut; she could only imagine what it had looked like when they found him.

"Would you like some tea?" Marilyn asked. She gestured toward the tiled counter, piled with gift baskets, flowers, and tins. "The neighbors have been bringing food. There's some wonderful apple bread here."

"Thank you, a cup of tea would be nice," said Anne.

Marilyn looked thin and exhausted. When they were younger, the fullness in her face had disguised the sharpness of her features, but now Anne could see deep lines etched around her eyes, the thin skin stretched tight over her cheekbones, the sharp line of her narrow lips. *How did we get so old?* Anne wondered vaguely.

"I don't know what to say," she said again. "We had no idea Bernie was so depressed."

Marilyn looked up from the teakettle. "How could you not?" she asked. "I don't mean to be rude, but you knew we were separated. Whitney must have known how much Bernie was drinking..."

Anne felt a flush of irritation. "Whitney is very busy. He has a thousand things on his mind every day. Everything's top priority. He's the president! How could he know what Bernie was doing after he left the office?"

"I'm sorry," said Marilyn. "It's just that we all should have known. There were plenty of clues, and we didn't pick up on them. I just knew that I'd had it; I needed to get my children into a normal lifestyle... how could he have done this?"

Anne picked up her tea cup. "I don't know." This visit was going badly; after all, she needed to comfort Marilyn, not get into some blame exchange. A phrase from the California spiritualist whose book was on the best-seller list popped into her mind.

"They say that when someone takes his own life, it's actually a great catharsis," she said. "Maybe Bernie's inner pain was so great that this was the only way out. He had the courage to recognize his choice and take it, and now he's at peace. And I'm sure his life energy is with you and the children now, but now he's free of all his pain... It was his choice, his right."

Marilyn stared at Anne, her face harsh. "His right? What about my children's right to a father? You don't really believe that garbage, do you?"

Anne looked into her tea cup. "I don't know what to believe," she said with rare candor. "I just want you to feel better."

EMILY GINEEN slumped in the leather chair behind her office desk, alternately twirling a Flair fine-point pen between her fingers and dabbing her nose with a Kleenex. Paul Clarkson sat opposite her in the blue wing chair facing the desk, sipping a cup of coffee.

Usually their Justice Department schedule did not allow time for slumping, but a flu bug and laryngitis had caused Emily to cancel her plans for the day, a speech at the University of Virginia. *Just as well*, she thought. The idea of giving a speech on the pursuit of justice while her mind was reeling with the news of Bernie O'Keefe's suicide seemed more than she could handle.

She sneezed, dabbed her nose, and popped another menthol eucalyptus lozenge into her mouth.

"Did you know Bernie was so depressed?" she whispered.

"Bernie and I weren't exactly confidants," Paul said.

"Maybe I've been insulated all my life, but I've never known anybody who committed suicide," said Emily. "Why would he do this? There had to be some terrible thing in his life, some deep dark secret we knew nothing about, something he just couldn't deal with. But what a tragedy. He had so much going for him, so many opportunities ahead. He's... he was... much smarter than the president."

"Maybe he was so smart he saw he was running out of options," Paul said.

"What do you mean?"

Paul paused a moment. "People like Bernie are on the fast track. They make a lot of compromises. Bernie had a conscience—we all do, even if we bury it sometimes. Maybe he just got tired...and it's not like he could just drown out his conscience and stay drunk all the time."

Emily stared at Paul. She had never heard him sound so harsh. "That sounds so self-righteous," she said bluntly. "I know you're a straight arrow, but you can't tell me you've never done anything to offend your conscience."

"Of course I have, Emily. Every day. But I know there's an answer. That's the heart of Christianity. Christ died for my sins so I can be forgiven. So I can go on. So I can know that life has meaning. I couldn't go on without that."

"Yeah, but not everyone has it put together like you do, Paul," she croaked. "You've got a wonderful family and a good profession and your faith gives you comfort. If Bernie's whole life was falling apart, and on top of that he had all of Griswold's problems on his shoulders...I guess that's enough to make anyone depressed—even without any dirty little secrets."

"Don't you think I was depressed when this happened to me?" Paul asked, gesturing toward his legs. "I was depressed when we lost our first baby at three months. I'm like anyone else—I get depressed. But your state of mind isn't dependent on what you have or don't have. It depends on who you are."

"If anybody had self-confidence, it was Bernie," Emily whispered, coughing into her Kleenex.

"I don't mean confidence in oneself," Paul said. "I mean confidence in something outside oneself. The self-confident person has the biggest problem of all. When he looks at himself and doesn't like what he sees, if that's where his confidence is, he's done. No, there's got to be something beyond ourselves that we have confidence, or faith, in; otherwise we'd all commit suicide."

"Bernie was a Catholic," Emily said. "He had faith in God."

"I don't just mean believing that God exists. I mean a personal faith, the kind that—"

"I know about that," Emily interrupted. "I walked the aisle when I was a kid. Every summer I'd give my life to Jesus again at Bible camp. I'm born again. Just like most of the American public."

"No, I'm not talking about the clichés. I mean down deep—a real commitment. One you'd stake your life on," Paul replied.

"That sounds so sanctimonious," Emily rasped, "as if you have the corner on truth, and anyone who doesn't phrase things just the way you do is out in the cold. Or out in the heat, going to hell."

"I'm sorry," Paul said. He hated conversations like this. "I'm not judging anyone. But I believe that Christ is God; that He gave His life for me, and so my life is not my own. It belongs to Him. And that shapes my beliefs about everything else."

"You make it sound so simple." Emily snapped her fingers. "Come on, Paul, faith is fine, but life is more complicated than that."

"No, Emily, when you think about it, there are only three logical choices in life. The first is to accept the Truth. It's not easy, but it is what gives life meaning. The second choice is to reject the Truth, to believe life has no meaning; and so you do the only honest thing—you get it over with. You put a gun in your mouth. Remember what Camus said, if God is dead, the only philosophical question is suicide.

"Or," he continued, "you can avoid the question altogether and just keep yourself anesthetized with booze or TV or sex or power. But if you don't keep yourself distracted all the time, if you get involved in the contradictions of life and try to struggle with them, you eventually go nuts. That's it, three options: life, death or madness."

Paul paused. He could see that Emily was listening, processing, the way he had seen her evaluate dozens of briefings during the months they had worked together. He knew he couldn't argue his faith as if it was a legal case; certainly faith was logical, but it couldn't be boxed. If Emily was going to understand, he thought, it would have to come from more than any clever arguments he might make.

"Listen," he said. "Bernie's suicide is a terrible shock. It's a nightmare for his family and for this administration. We don't know what he went through at the end. We're just left to deal with what he did. And we need to pull ourselves together now. You'll need to be there for the president. He'll be leaning more on you now, so the country needs you to be strong. And the first thing we need to do is work on your cold. Can I get you some hot tea?"

Emily nodded, glad to get him out of the room for a moment. As Paul limped out the door, she sighed. What he had said made sense, but it also scared her. It reminded her of those smug Christians she had known in her youth, that Sunday school world where emotion ruled over reason and anything deemed too hard to figure out intellectually was simply glossed over as a matter of faith.

But Paul wasn't like that, she had to admit. He wasn't smug. Everything she had ever seen him do spoke of dedication, commitment, excellence, even humor. He had served her, and this administration, well. He hadn't nagged or bugged anyone in the office about his faith. He was different. And he was consistent.

There was a tap on the door, and then it bumped open. Paul leaned on his cane with one hand and in the other he had a big mug of steaming tea balanced on a small plate, with a white napkin and two fat wedges of yellow lemon on it.

"Where in the world did you find that?" she asked.

Paul grinned and shrugged. "The Lord provides," he teased.

Emily grinned back. "I'm sure He does," she said. "I'll think about what you said. But right now we need to get back to work."

Thursday, June 25

The motorcade slowly pulled away from the cemetery gravesite. The private service earlier had been in the Catholic Church in Wellesley Hills, a Victorian-era, stone structure filled with mourners for Bernie O'Keefe. The crowds outside had been held back by the Wellesley police under the watchful eye of the Secret Service.

A strong northwest front had moved through the night before. Even in June there were occasional cold days in New England—

and this was one. As the president's limousine passed through the cemetery gates, a few pieces of paper scuttled across the narrow road, then swirled in a sudden gust of wind.

In the back of the heavy, black limousine, the Griswolds said nothing, but sat closer together than usual. Anne reached out to take Whitney's hand. It was cold. He had refused to wear a coat.

The graveside ceremony had been rather brief. At the end they had left Bernie's coffin next to the rectangular hole in the earth, and Whitney had escorted Marilyn and the children to their car. Then Anne had watched as he turned to look back at the coffin, resting on the pulleys that would lower it into the grave. His face showed nothing as he turned, silently put his hand under her elbow, and escorted her to their own car.

Now, as the motorcade turned onto the main road, Whitney stared out the window at the cemetery and the old parish church next to it. And then the bells began to toll.

55

Thursday, July 16

DANIEL SEATON stood beside Rob Knight as the judge strode through the door of U.S. District Court room number six, his black robes swirling around him. The words of the bailiff were still ringing in Daniel's ears: "Oyez, oyez. The U.S. District Court for the District of Columbia is now in session, the Honorable Randolph Green, presiding. All persons having business before this court will please rise . . ."

Rob Knight looked at the table to the left. There were six lawyers from the U.S. attorney's office flanking the U.S. attorney himself, Sam Gilquist. *Press hound*, he thought. The U.S. attorney rarely appeared in court, and certainly never for a simple arraignment.

Judge Green sat down, and the lawyers, clerks, stenographers, and rows of spectators—mostly press who had clamored for credentials—did the same thing. Except for the rustling of the bodies, the room was quiet as the judge sat staring sternly at a sheaf of papers. Known for his no-frills style, this was a judge who had little patience with the self-indulgent rhetorical excesses of bombastic attorneys; he ran a tight ship.

Green's wife had been killed three years earlier, when, under the influence of alcohol, she had collided head-on with a teenaged driver on his way home from high school band practice. Judge Green rarely spoke about the horrible incident, but his staff and those who appeared in his courtroom had found that the experience had softened the once-stringent technocrat. Since the accident, he had shown more compassion for the human lives touched by the strictures of the law. Some might say his justice had been tempered with mercy.

Now the judge smiled and nodded toward the prosecution's table. "Ah, I see the government is represented this morning by its senior counsel. We welcome you to our courtroom, Mr. Gilquist. And the defendant is represented by his counsel, Mr. . . . ah, yes, Knight—good to see you also."

The lawyers and Daniel rose and moved a few steps forward. Daniel had lost so much weight that his suit hung limply, but he was grateful for it; Rob had arranged with the U.S. attorney's office for him to change from his orange jumper into his regular suit in a holding cell just outside of the courtroom. It was the first time he had been out of prison garb since his arrest.

He was struck by how sterile the court seemed. Just a big cube-shaped room with light paneled walls. The furniture was austere, upscale government issue. It all seemed cold and clinical, like an operating room, and he was the body now being wheeled in.

It was difficult for him to follow what was happening. The judged fired questions at the prosecutor about the grand jury and the papers that had been prepared. Rob interjected some comments and asked about motions. Then the docket clerk walked forward and began to read very stiffly and dramatically: "The United States of America versus Daniel Seaton . . ."

That hurt. He loved his country, always had. And now here it was, the United States against him, as if he had betrayed her.

Rob had agreed to waive the reading of the indictment, but the prosecutor had insisted, so the clerk droned through it. Daniel knew he was being charged with everything in the book, from aiding and abetting the destruction of the regeneration center, to homicide of a U.S. congressman, a doctor, and a security guard, to conspiracy, to accessory after the fact. It was written like a verdict, like all of these things had been proven. It was a good thing Rob was gripping his arm; he needed steadying.

As the clerk cited each statute—18 USC Section 831, 18 USC Section 841, 18 USC Section 371, 18 USC Section 3, 18 USC Section 351—Daniel winced. It was like salt in a wound. He thought he heard Mary sobbing somewhere behind him.

"How does the defendant plead?" the judged peered down after the indictment was read. Rob nudged Daniel, who spoke clearly, "Not guilty, Your Honor."

Then the haranguing began. The lawyers sparred over preliminary hearings, scheduling of motions. Judge Green kept interrupting. There was an extended argument over the time for the trial, the prosecutors arguing for sixty days. Rob, knowing the government wanted the trial while passions were highly charged, was balking.

Finally Judge Green hit the gavel. Barring unforeseen delays, he pronounced, the case would begin in ninety days. He whacked the gavel again and stood up, walking off the platform to the side door. There was a loud buzzing in the courtroom as people broke into conversations.

Rob turned to him and said only, "Okay. Round one is over. It's just technical. The indictment."

Then two armed marshals grasped Daniel firmly under each elbow and began moving him toward the side door to the right. He almost stumbled trying to see Mary. She was looking straight at him, her eyes steady, smiling, nodding her head slightly, willing him her love and support and strength.

"It'll be all right," she mouthed toward him through the confusion. "We love you!"

Wednesday, July 22

Harvey Robbins took no responsibility more seriously than the plotting and protection of Whitney Griswold's schedule. To that end, each night he mapped out the next day for the president, minute by minute, like a theatrical script. Then he would attach file cards for every event—crib sheets for the president, who had grown totally dependent on the technique.

And Griswold was very good at it. Before a meeting he would glance at the cards, memorize them quickly, and then sound wonderfully spontaneous and informed with his visitor.

Robbie remembered the time when Max Wendell, an old Nixon aide, now CEO of a major international conglomerate, whom Griswold had made chairman of a commission to study Head Start programs, came into the office to present an interim report on the commission's work. Wendell's wife was with him. The two had not been back to the White House for several years, and Wendell was obviously moved as he walked into the Oval Office. Griswold greeted him warmly and walked him around the room, explaining each change that he had made and what had been in its place when Nixon had sat at the same desk so many years before.

Then Griswold stopped, put one hand on the older man's shoulder, and recited four paragraphs from Nixon's first inaugural address. He didn't miss a word. Wendell listened raptly.

"I was, of course, just a youngster at the time," said Griswold, "but it made an impression on me that has remained to this day. Those words were so filled with vision and passion... They gave me the inspiration to pursue a career in politics. Those words are part of the reason that I'm standing here today as president of the United States."

Wendell nodded. His wife dabbed a tear from her eye. Robbie smiled slightly. Griswold had followed his instructions to the letter.

But now Robbie was frustrated. In the weeks since Bernie's death, Griswold had been uncontrollable. He ignored the program sheets, couldn't or wouldn't bother to memorize the cards, got consistently behind schedule, something neither he nor Robbie would have tolerated in the past.

And by ignoring his briefing materials, he had made some substantial gaffes. He had given a framed picture of the White

House—one of the gifts, like the boxed cuff links, that he often gave important visitors—to a leader of a Native American tribe, suggesting it would look good on his tepee wall. Another time he told the muscular dystrophy poster girl how much his daughter, Elizabeth, liked to play basketball.

Much of the time the president simply seemed detached and disengaged, just going through the motions. Robbie had even talked to the White House physician, who said these were normal reactions to deep grief and that they would pass in time.

But now Robbie was sitting in his office, waiting for Griswold's call to start a senior staff meeting, a meeting Griswold himself had requested to set out their legislative agenda before Congress adjourned in August. It was 8:55, already ten minutes late, utterly unlike the president. Busy people were cooling their heels, and the entire day was getting backed up.

Robbie tapped his pencil on his desk impatiently. He had nothing to read at the moment because he had arrived this morning at 7:00, as usual, to clean every memorandum off his desk. It was a strict discipline—the only way, he believed, to stay ahead of things. And the 8:00 senior staff meeting had adjourned at 8:30 promptly, as scheduled; and he'd signed off on every action paper for the day.

Just as his irritation was increasing, his secretary buzzed over the intercom. "The president is ready."

"Good thing," he mumbled, tucking his black, leather-bound folder under his arm and bounding out of the chair.

GRISWOLD WAS SEATED behind his desk, writing. He looked up just long enough to wave the staff in. Six men and one woman took their regular seats around his desk.

Forbes Carlton, a lanky, angular man whom Bernie had, under some pressure from Griswold, appointed his deputy, sat in what had been Bernie O'Keefe's regular chair. Griswold had pushed Carlton, a Harvard graduate and partner in Dewey Ballantine in New York, only because his father and Griswold's father were best friends and polo partners. It was the one favor Griswold's father had asked.

But the president felt some irritation as he looked up and saw the studious Carlton, his lips tightly pursed as if he had just eaten a dill pickle and a shock of brown hair dangling over his forehead, staring at him through thick lenses and, of all things, sitting in Bernie's seat.

"Well, good morning," Griswold smiled, putting the cap on his pen and straightening up in his chair.

"Good morning, Mr. President," came the chorus.

"Robbie will first review very briefly my schedule for the next ten days so you'll know what we are working with here." Griswold nodded at Robbie, who reviewed in detail upcoming commitments. Griswold grimaced. Something every minute, it seemed, and worst of all, no time for Camp David on the weekend.

"Now let's look at each legislative agenda; that is, what we must accomplish before the distinguished members of Congress go home for August—and what a wonderful day that will be," he grinned. "National Security first, General."

Maloney had only one item, the Gatt III Treaty, but it was assured passage, with a vote coming within the week.

Each senior staffer followed with options and requests for the president—a call to a key fence-sitting congresswoman, a public works project awarded for another. Robbie was pleased. The staff was well prepared and organized, and, most important, Griswold seemed to be tracking with them.

Robbie checked his watch—thirteen minutes left. They might even recover lost time and keep the day on schedule, particularly important today because every minute was planned until lunch when Griswold would eat his cottage cheese and apples, then take his daily twenty-minute nap. From 2:00 until 6:00 was tightly scheduled with key representatives and senators, one after another, most of it arm-twisting on the crime bill—and important.

Griswold had been listening to John Parker, former congressman from Pennsylvania and now the legislative liaison chief. The president was taking notes and, without looking up, nodded toward Carlton. "All right, Bernie, clean this up for us...oh." The president jerked his head up, looking angry and startled. "Oh, my, I'm sorry...go ahead, Carlton, I mean Forbes."

Robbie thought Griswold's complexion looked unusually sallow, and his face seemed creased and sharp. His eyes never met Carlton's—although that might have been partly because Carlton was reading a very bureaucratic and lengthy explanation of the effort by liberal members in the Appropriations Committee to cut off funds for the National Guard. Having failed to override the Declaration of Emergency on the floor, they were now working a back-door approach. As Robbie watched, he could see Griswold's impatience grow.

"Oh, forget it, Carlton. Forget it. Those jackasses will never get it out of committee. Don't waste your time with it." Griswold made a great sweeping motion with his hand as if to dispense with the entire Congress—and maybe Forbes Carlton at the same time.

But Carlton persisted. "But, Mr. President, sir, there could be a basis to argue under—"

"Oh, put it in their ear, Carlton...I mean Forbes...it's drivel. They're like little red ants, and you can just step on them. As a matter of fact, you should go up to the Hill and moon them." But Griswold wasn't laughing. He was scowling, and Caroline Atwater looked startled. "You know what I mean. That's what they deserve."

Robbie made an effort to get things back on track. "Well, that's a good morning's work. I'll put the action sheets together, have them in your office in an hour." But Griswold wasn't finished.

"What you've got to learn, Carlton, or Forbes, whatever—I had a friend at Brown named Carlton—is not to let the little people get under your skin." Griswold had an almost sickly grin on his face, an expression Robbie had only seen once or twice—when the president was very upset.

"So don't give them the time of day. There are people out there who want to take down the presidency. We've got to defend this office...all of you. You need to understand that. But no one does really, I suppose..." Griswold suddenly turned reflective. "Nobody understands, nobody."

Then he turned away, stood up, and walked to the table behind his desk, and slowly began rearranging the pictures of his family.

Everyone sat silently. They weren't dismissed, and the president might be thinking some great thought. So they sat uncomfortably for what seemed a full two minutes before Griswold turned back and faced them. He still had that odd grin on his face.

"Yes, Carlton. That's fine. Good work. Now the Seaton case. I'll need a full report. By tonight. I want you to tell me in detail what is going on. I'm a lawyer; I understand it. You are not to let Justice drag their feet. They do that, you know. You'll find out. All of them are the same. They just don't see the big picture. Most people don't. Never do. Well, let's get to work…"

The senior aides all nodded, filing out one by one. The president remained standing behind his desk, smiling faintly and gripping a picture of his daughter.

PRISON LIFE both mocks and mirrors the human condition. The soul is stuck, thwarted, wings beating against the bars of the cage, sick, pacing, alone, and sad. The walls close in, assaulting the spirit. The mind longs for a fresh scent, a flower, a glimpse of blue sky above.

And yet for some, the mind and body embrace the rigid constraints of life in the box. Some inmates abandon themselves altogether, sleeping up to twenty hours a day, lost in the nether world of dreams beyond the wall. Others come to so rely on the quarantine of choice that they begin to depend upon it. They are told when and what to eat, when to sleep, when to shower, when to exercise; upon release, the free world seems overwhelming in its dazzling array of options. Most ex-prisoners commit new crimes. They just cannot deal with life outside the box.

Daniel Seaton's confinement had not yet progressed to the monotony of the full-fledged prison experience. Though he chafed at the routine, he'd had regular visits from Mary and the few friends who were allowed in. Mary's parents had come from Florida for an extended visit, and her mother was now staying at the house, helping with the children.

And he spent many hours with Rob Knight in the special

visiting room set aside for attorneys. These meetings were often painful and at cross-purposes. They kept going over the same ground, exhaustively, and Rob seemed to be looking to Daniel for ideas about how to cross-examine the government's witnesses, especially John Jenkins...Daniel had no idea. And Rob was jubilant that he was forcing delays in the government's case while Daniel simply wanted it all over.

But the days were all right—except for the ceaseless noise: the clanging of steel, blaring of radios, and inmates shouting at the guards and one another. It was the nights Daniel dreaded. Even though the cellblocks were finally quiet, in the dark he was alone with the ghosts of his thoughts about Alex and the sick sense of shame. He re-examined his motives; he anguished again and again. He had not meant to do evil, but he had been naive. And evil had been the result.

Over and over again he saw Alex at his kitchen table on the night of the bombing, bowing his head while Mary stitched his scalp. He thought of the mad rush away in the night and imagined the chaos that had followed. The FBI hadn't revealed much about how Alex and Lance had died, but he had pieced the scene together in his mind. All he could think of was Alex as a child, Alex leaping the waves at Rehoboth Beach when they were young, Alex's rising anger in the pro-life cause, escalating to the point where his rage had overrun his reason.

For his part, Daniel realized that he had been like Alex. Not that passion had overtaken him; he wasn't that sort of person. He had allowed himself to be overcome—to slide, inch by inch, into the sin of despair. He had given up, relinquished the battle. Back at Rehoboth Beach, when he sat on the sand with Alex and the others and had, in essence, let them go, he had done so because he had lost hope. He realized he had come to believe, ever so unconsciously, that the only way left to stop the regeneration centers was the path of violence. Just as long as he didn't really know what was happening. He had compromised, vaguely assenting to ugly means in order to achieve the godly end he so desired. He had passed off his personal responsibility, he had lost hope, and the bars now penning him in seemed a fair price to pay for that sin. Alex's death did not.

Daniel had not been allowed to go to his brother's funeral, a small and private affair attended by Mary and the children, Mary's parents, and a few members of their church. The police had provided security for the family and kept the media at a distance, but they hadn't been able to shield Mary from the taunts and threats she received each day when she visited the jail.

Daniel marveled at his wife's strength; she seemed to take it all with such dignity, even when things got ugly. When she had been splattered with blood by the AIDS protester, her response had defused the situation. Ira Levitz had written about it in his newspaper column—something about grace quenching rage—and it seemed there had been a wave of sympathy for her since.

Not so for Daniel. If his wife was now perceived as a good woman drawn under the influence of a crazed cult of extremists, according to the papers, he was still the villain, the mastermind of a conspiracy that had now taken the lives of five people.

In the jail, though, he wasn't seen that way. Most of the inmates knew well the pitfalls of blood ties and betrayal; they knew how an innocent man could get caught in a legal vise that could pull him all the way down. And most of them operated by the convict code of ethics: Those who would have marked Daniel for death if he was accused of child molestation didn't find killing a congressman a particularly heinous crime.

"Way to go," one old guy with vacant, watery blue eyes had whispered to Daniel in the shower room. "Blow 'em all up! That's the only way things'll ever change."

In the world of the haves and the have-nots, where life's inequities were chalked up to a "crooked system," where the rich got rich and the poor got poorer, none of the cons had particular sympathy for the likes of Peter Meyer and Barbara LaMar. Whether Daniel had anything to do with the bombing or not.

And Daniel's attitude toward them didn't hurt either. He had found that the parishioners to whom he was now called had common enough needs. Car thieves, drug dealers, burglars, muggers, drunks, and illegal aliens—they all needed someone to listen. He tried to hear the needs behind their words, to gently expose the flaws in their thinking: They were all innocent, even the man who admitted he had shot his wife in a drunken rage.

Daniel began to realize that he hadn't listened, really listened, to Alex. And though Alex was no longer with him, these men were.

56

A S AUTUMN FELL into winter, the atmosphere in Washington felt as bleak as the frigid breezes. At George Washington Hospital, the windows broken by the bomb blast had been replaced, but the site of the regeneration center was still cordoned off. On the wooden fence that had been erected around it, someone had spray-painted, "death to the anti-choice hypocrites." Officials removed the graffiti on six separate occasions, but by the next morning, the message was always there again. Eventually they just left it.

Every day, news reports brought more grisly headlines. Some of the violence, like the graffiti, was directed against anyone perceived to be a "religious extremist" or connected with the Seaton case. In Virginia, someone left a dead lamb on the Seatons' front porch. In St. Louis, a group of homosexual activists conducted a march outside a Presbyterian church hosting a prayer meeting; later, hundreds of condoms filled with mayonnaise were found scattered throughout the church's Sunday school classrooms. In Minneapolis, three nuns sitting on a bench in front of a doctor's office were harassed and spat upon.

Most of the violence was random. But it was also rampant.

On October 31, the annual Halloween parade in Georgetown evolved into a full-blown riot. As usual, the police had cordoned off the main thoroughfare for the parade; in deference to the curfew, they had mandated that the streets be emptied by 10:00 P.M. By 9:00, the crowd had swelled to several thousand at the corner of Wisconsin Avenue and M Street, milling around the gold-domed Riggs Bank on the corner and down the hill toward the Potomac River, where the waterfront restaurants were doing a desultory business; most of the Halloweeners didn't have the money or interest to be good customers, and the usual business-and-government clientele stayed away, put off by the devils and the undead.

With good reason. At 9:30, chaos erupted at the corner of Wisconsin and M when a gang of teenagers dressed as Hell's Angels started harassing a group dressed as SS officers. A witch and a werewolf who'd had too much to drink got into the act and joined in the obscenities raining down on the Nazis. A local TV crew, taping an interview with a vampire, turned its cameras to cover the scene.

People started pushing and shoving, and even as two D.C. police officers on the sidelines started to move through the crowd toward the fight, one of the Nazi officers pulled out a real gun from under his uniform and started firing into the cluster of Hell's Angels.

People ran in every direction, but they were hemmed in by the mass of bodies, and so many were so drunk that they stumbled to the pavement and were trampled...and as the policemen closed in on the shooter, with another officer on the side barking into his radio for National Guard backup, the dark night turned into a nightmare. So many in the crowd were smeared with fake blood, made up as ghouls, that as the ambulances started arriving, it was difficult to discern whose wounds were real and who should be treated first.

In the end, armored personnel carriers bristling with machine guns rolled down M Street, and more than seventy-five people were taken to local hospitals, with a final body count of three dead.

Washington was not the only site of civil unrest. In Chicago, an arsonist torched three of the apartment blocks in the Cabrini-Green housing project. Fifteen residents died, mostly young children. Since government housing and social services agencies were already stretched beyond their limits, there was nowhere for the survivors to go.

After the most recent earthquake in L.A., 6.8 on the Richter, riots erupted in the south central sector of the city, chalked up to allegations that rescue units had responded quicker to wealthier sections of the city.

In New York, a freak storm in early December knocked out electrical power for seven hundred thousand people. The governor declared a state of emergency within half an hour of the outage, but in spite of armed federal troops patrolling the streets of Manhattan, looters broke into Fifth Avenue's most exclusive half-mile. Merchants later reported $60 million worth of damage and lost merchandise.

"HAPPY HOLIDAYS," Emily Gineen said grimly to Paul Clarkson. Government employees had been restricted from saying "Merry Christmas" for several years now, but the generic holiday greeting still didn't feel natural to Emily. She sighed; in five minutes they needed to adjourn to the conference room for the AG's annual "winter celebration"—what used to be known as the office Christmas party. Her two secretaries' desks were lined with tinsel, and there was a holly garland on the fireplace in Emily's office, but she felt anything but festive.

"I hate parties," she said to Paul. "I particularly hate parties where I have to personally greet and mingle with 150 of my closest professional friends. Isn't there some national emergency just about to break that will necessitate a quick trip to the White House? I *don't* want to go to this party."

"I think we've had enough national emergencies to do us for quite a while," said Paul. "I can't ever remember a time like these past months."

"It's like the whole country is in a horrible mood," Emily said, turning to stare out of her fifth-floor window to the wet, gray scene below. "You'd think things would be coming together. We've clamped down like never before, we've got troops on the streets and a policeman on every corner, just about, and—the crime rate continues to *climb*. That's why I can't go into this party and smile and pretend everything is all right in the halls of justice. Everything is not all right."

"No, it isn't," Paul said. "And what we're doing is not going to fix it.

Emily frowned.

"You and I have talked about this. When people lose their inner restraints—conscience . . . religion—you have to keep putting more and more outer restraints on them. They get more and more frustrated. And you end up with troops and tanks in the streets."

"You make it sound so simplistic, Paul."

Paul shrugged. "Lord Acton had it right. You've seen that quote on my office wall. 'The greater the strength of duty'—and he meant *religious* duty—'the greater the liberty.'

"If people aren't moved by a sense of religious responsibility, something above themselves, then the only way you can restrain or control their behavior is by fear. The more fear, the less freedom. That's what's happening."

There was an awkward silence for a moment, then Emily turned from the window to face him. "Thank you so much for that encouraging word," she said, adjusting the cuffs of her blouse and buttoning her double-breasted red jacket. "Perhaps you'd like to deliver a short speech at the party?"

"I'm sorry," Paul said. "I shouldn't be adding to the mood here. Things will probably get better after Christmas and after Daniel Seaton's trial. Let's hope so—until it's over, people aren't going to settle down. They've made him into the biggest national villain since Saddam Hussein. It's ridiculous."

But Emily wasn't listening. She had switched gears, and Paul watched her as she leaned over her desk, intently studying the typed list of those who would be attending the party as if it were a legal brief. She had a remarkable ability to compartmentalize. Right now, if duty called for her to shove aside personal feelings and host a party, then she would do it. And by the time she entered the conference room, Paul knew she would be greeting people right and left, never stumbling over a name, charming and gracious and witty. She was amazing.

She looked up and grinned at him, connecting again for half a second. "Okay," she said. "Let's get in there and have a good time, even if democracy as we know it is heading right down the tubes."

She strode to the door, flung it open, and moved briskly toward the conference room, where people were already milling about, balancing punch cups and plates of smoked salmon and crackers. "Rodney!" Paul heard her exclaim warmly to someone whose name she would not have remembered five minutes earlier. "It's so good to see you here!"

57

Thursday, January 7

A S T H E N E W Y E A R began, a pass to the Seaton trial was the hottest ticket in Washington. Thanks to Rob Knight's legal machinations, the trial had been delayed several times, but by the first week in January, he could hold it off no longer.

On Thursday morning, January 7, crowds began to gather behind cordoned areas on the street leading up to the steps on the United States Courthouse, the sand-colored fortress sprawling across the corner of Constitution Avenue and Third Street NW in downtown Washington. Despite the slushy sidewalks and plowed piles of dirty snow, there was almost a festive atmosphere. Vendors were soon sold out of hot coffee and bagels. Others hawked T-shirts. Television cameras zoomed in on the array of posters and placards. "Abort Seaton," read one. "Pro-life Hypocrites Deserve Justice—Gay and Lesbian Alliance," said another. And there was the usual, terse, "Fry him!"

Daniel Seaton escaped the maddened crowd; at 7:00 A.M., marshals had driven him in an armored wagon through the garage entrance to the courthouse. Since then he had been pacing a six-by-nine holding cell in the basement.

Mary Seaton was not so fortunate. Following Rob and surrounded by friends from church, she braved the gauntlet at 9:30.
There was a clamor from the crowd, and uniformed officers
formed a human barrier in front of the police sawhorses.

Rob, weighed down with fat briefcases and legal folders,
pushed past the camera crews hanging over the barricades near
the main door. Mary picked up a folder he dropped and followed
him through the door.

Every seat in the courtroom had been assigned. Family and
friends were in the first two rows on the right side behind the
defense table; the media, along with the courtroom artists down
front, occupied most of the left-side seats. Behind the family, seats
were reserved for government officials, researchers, some graduate
students, and even representatives of the diplomatic corps. Tickets
had been handled by the chief judge's office with the same care as
if it were a state occasion.

AT PRECISELY 10:00 A.M., the bailiff announced the court in
session. The room hushed, and Judge Randolph Green entered
from the door to the left of his desk. He pulled his black robe
together and walked solemnly to his seat.

Rob Knight and Assistant U.S. Attorney Jack Barnes moved
toward the bench as Judge Green asked, "Are we ready to call for
a jury?"

Fifty potential jurors were in the pool, and the first two days of
the trial were occupied with winnowing them down to the twelve
jurors and six alternates who would ultimately hear the case. Rob
Knight knew that in the District of Columbia the majority of the
jurors would be black, probably suspicious of any white suburban-
ite. On the plus side, of course, he only needed one dissenting vote
to hang a jury, and he could count on the odds that at least one of
the African Americans on the jury would likely be a member of an
inner-city Baptist church.

But Jack Barnes had done his best to winnow out anyone with
religious inclinations. Counsel couldn't ask a juror's religion, of
course, but he fished around; one potential juror who admitted

listening to WAVA, the Christian radio station, was quickly dropped.

The jury was impaneled by Friday evening. Seven women and five men. Ten blacks, one white, one Asian. Four worked for government agencies, two were unemployed, one was a schoolteacher.

BY MONDAY, the court was ready for opening statements. Judge Green looked over his immense desk and down to Jack Barnes and Rob Knight. "I don't want to hear any inferences or advocacy in these statements," he said. "Stick to the facts you can prove, gentlemen. Thank you."

Jack Barnes was a tall, handsome man, smooth and deferential in his approach, a political player who knew how to grease the wheels of the system. He strode slowly to the counsels' podium.

"Your Honor," he said in a deep, confident voice, "ladies and gentlemen of the jury. We come to this court of law to see to it that justice is done—justice in the face of a most extraordinary assault on our system of justice itself.

"We will demonstrate to the court that Mr. Seaton—though no doubt before his involvement in this plot a decent and well-intentioned man—was part of an insidious conspiracy attacking the very foundations of our American democracy and our national order.

"This case involves a conspiracy by people, including the defendant, who held themselves above the law. They violated not only the civil rights of those they slaughtered by means of deadly, overwhelming force, but also in so doing they violated the peace of mind of every American... for if religious extremists can strike down a federal officer, a congressman, in the heart of our nation's capital, how then can Americans trust in the safety of their streets across the nation?"

Rob Knight, scratching notes on a yellow pad, whipped off his glasses and rubbed his eyes. He had known it would be like this. But now the drama of the courtroom—the clerk taking down every word, those same words hanging in the air for a moment, then digested by the media and the jury—suddenly felt over-whelming. Rob's stomach turned over, and he clenched and unclenched his hands, then his jaw, trying to relieve the tension. The prosecutor was making it sound like Daniel had personally pulled the trigger and killed one of the Founding Fathers.

"It is too late for the other conspirators," Barnes continued, "the perpetrators of this bombing, murder, and mayhem to stand before us in this court of law and be held accountable for their crimes. But the proceedings of this court will signal that this nation will not tolerate Mr. Seaton or others like him setting themselves up according to what they call a higher law but which is, in fact, a law unto themselves.

"The government will prove that these men, including the defendant, did knowingly and willfully plan to bomb the regeneration center in Washington, D.C., a place designed, ironically enough, to save lives." Barnes looked disdainfully toward Daniel and then proceeded to outline his case: Alex Seaton and Lance Thompson, with the aid of the other named co-conspirators, including John Jenkins and Daniel Seaton, did plan for the destruction of the center, plant and detonate the explosives, and take the lives of Congressman Peter Meyer, Dr. Barbara LaMar, and security guard Justin Jones.

Barnes continued, clinically, "Said defendant did aid and abet the perpetrators by providing medical help after the bombing, failing to tell the authorities of their whereabouts and assisting in their escape."

The outline was clear, Rob noted with a sigh. The government would take weeks proving the bombing, the deaths, all of the horrors, just to get to two points of fact: whether Daniel had foreknowledge and whether he assisted, with an overt act, in the bombing.

On both counts the evidence was shaky and circumstantial. Inferences would have to be drawn. But would the jurors see how narrow it was? He'd have to rely on the judge to keep instructing them.

Barnes moved slowly away from the podium and walked toward the rail behind which the jurors were seated in two rows. He leaned on the rail and smiled.

"Ladies and gentlemen, you know, as I do, that our country began as a place where liberty-loving people found freedom to practice their particular beliefs.

"Today it is a place brimming with the diversity of such beliefs, a place where people must be allowed not only their freedom to choose their own way, but the freedom to live their lives without the interference of those who believe they have the corner on what they call 'absolute truth.'

"In this anti-choice movement, this group on trial, we see those who would impose their particular beliefs, by means of violence, on others. This trial allows us the opportunity to assert that America is still a place of liberty and freedom."

Rob Knight looked down at the floor, tapping his feet. Next to him, Daniel seemed unmoved by the sweeping charges coming down.

"The anti-choice movement has a very dangerous wing," Barnes continued, "an extremist and fractured faction within it that will stop at nothing to accomplish its goals. Daniel Seaton is the leader of such a faction.

"Murder itself is not off-limits to these so-called 'pro-lifers.' They, and anarchy-minded extremists like them, must be sent a message. This trial constitutes a powerful means to not only convict Daniel Seaton of the crimes for which he is guilty but also to send that message.

"Thank you."

Barnes, who had started his speech in an understated style, had by now come to a crescendo. He concluded by looking directly into the faces of the jurors, establishing the sort of intense eye contact that made it clear to everyone in the courtroom that the fate of the nation and the future of democracy itself hung on the twelve men and women in the jury box.

It seemed that everyone in the crowded room exhaled at once, and Rob Knight got slowly to his feet. He didn't want to be dependent on notes, so he had memorized most of his statement as if it were a part in a theatrical production. He would improvise a bit now, leaning on his instinct that many of the people in the jury box were probably suspicious of someone too smooth. That was, in fact, the reason he had worn an old suit—not that he had any new ones—a plain tie, and, to his wife's consternation, a pair of brown suede oxfords that he usually wore on Saturday mornings to do errands.

"Why those shoes?" Lisa had said when he left the house that morning. "They look so unprofessional."

"That's exactly the point," he had told her as he kissed her and headed out the front door. "Those government lawyers will look like big money, big guns; they'll have on their power ties and every hair in place. Barnes has probably already put on his pancake makeup for the TV cameras. I need to look like a real guy, not some corporate attorney."

He groaned as he spilled a few drops of coffee from his travel mug onto his pants and tried ineffectually to scrub them with a napkin that still had bagel crumbs on it. "I've gotta get out of here," he said. "Pray for me!"

Lisa rolled her eyes. "Of course I will . . . you'll need it!" she shouted cheerfully. "I'll be watching you on the news—let's hope the cameras don't pan down and show your shoes!"

But in spite of her teasing, his wife knew him well. Earlier that morning she had told him, "Just be careful. Don't get too worked up. Don't get too dramatic. Don't overplay your hand. The other side will be very careful; you have to watch out that you don't get carried away by the passion of the moment. You do that sometimes, you know."

Don't get carried away, Rob reminded himself now. He had already decided not to bother contesting Alex and Lance's culpability; no need to expend energy on that or use up any of the jurors' goodwill fighting about the deceased perpetrators. Just set Daniel apart from them—and create reasonable doubt in the minds of the jurors.

"Your honor, Mr. Barnes, and ladies and gentlemen of the

jury," Rob said, nodding to the government's attorneys and then focusing his attention on the people in the jury box.

"Mr. Barnes has spoken to you from the government's perspective. He speaks for dozens and dozens of attorneys, an army of legal minds who have carefully constructed and crafted a case to make you believe that Pastor Daniel Seaton is the evil mastermind behind an entire chain of events designed to bring democracy itself crumbling down around us.

"Mr. Barnes has postulated and inferred and obfuscated and conjectured so much that it is difficult to clearly focus on the facts. Let me speak plainly. He is doing that because the government does not have a case against Daniel Seaton.

"Here is the matter at hand. We are here to consider the innocence or guilt of Pastor Seaton. We cannot try his younger brother, Alex; Alex Seaton is dead. But if we could try Alex, we would have an entirely different case before us.

"Daniel Seaton does not contest the horror of the events that Alex Seaton and Lance Thompson set in motion. Daniel is not some kind of religious zealot. He is like you, and me, and every American who grieves with the families of those who were killed. He decries the destruction of property, the wanton violence of the bombing, the events of the night of last June 3.

"And what the evidence will demonstrate is that Daniel Seaton was in no way responsible. He is no terrorist. He is the pastor of a small church. He has always preached nonviolence to his congregation. He has always lived a productive, peaceful life with his wife, his children, his neighbors. He put himself through seminary as a carpenter; he continues to work hard and live simply. And he has spent far more time helping others, working with the hungry, the homeless, the hurting, with sufferers of AIDS—real people with real needs—than he has engaging in political debates. He has been steadfastly pro-life in the truest sense of the word, helping people live their lives in peace and dignity.

"As this trial proceeds, however, you will see that the prosecution would desperately like to punish *someone* for the bombing of the regeneration center and the deaths of Congressman Meyer, Dr. LaMar, and Justin Jones. The leaders of the government are angry, and their attorneys are desperate. So they have seized upon Pastor Seaton, whose chief connection with these crimes is the fact that his brother committed them.

"I would submit to you that if we have come to the point in America where a person can be tried for a crime committed by his brother, then perhaps Mr. Barnes is right, and our democratic system of justice *is* in jeopardy."

Rob was jarred by the crashing of the gavel. "Mr. Knight, let me gently remind you that arguments will come later. Stick to the evidence you will establish, sir. There will be time later for inferences." Green spoke gently, like an instructor in a beginners' class.

Rob tried to show no reaction. "Of course, Your Honor," he smiled. "I was simply responding to Mr. Barnes."

Rob continued, but with less passion in his voice. "Ladies and gentlemen of the jury, we will demonstrate that Daniel Seaton is no extremist, no terrorist. He is not a bomber and a murderer and a conspirator.

"Of course, we will not contest that Daniel Seaton is guilty of one thing. He is guilty of loving his younger brother. And when his brother came to him in the night, bruised and bleeding, he helped him. He bandaged him. He washed his face with a damp towel and gave him a glass of orange juice.

"Who among us would not do the same for our brother or sister? The evidence will be clear: Daniel Seaton did not know what his brother had just been involved in...he knew only that he was hurting. He ministered to his brother's pain. This is not a heinous crime. Yet because they cannot convict Alex Seaton, the government and its armies of attorneys want their pound of flesh. So they want to take a decent, kind human being and destroy his life, just to make a point. You must not allow them to do that.

"Thank you."

Rob turned and returned to the table. His lower back was killing him; he had been holding the muscles contracted, clenched, in his concentration to make his points to the jury. It was a relief to sit down. As he took his seat, he noticed that Daniel was looking at him with an expression he couldn't quite read.

DURING THE lunch break many spectators stayed in their seats, afraid they might lose them. But Ira Levitz left the courtroom and headed for Constitution Avenue. He had been trying to take a brisk walk every day at lunchtime; his doctor had told him some fresh air and moving his legs vigorously were the least he could do to combat the cigar smoking, the inactivity behind the computer screen, and the big lunches at his favorite restaurants.

Ira chewed his unlit cigar as he walked, his overcoat flapping behind him in the winter wind. There was no way the government was going to convict Seaton, unless they had some major surprise ahead. They just didn't have the evidence, and the conspiracy charge seemed absolutely ridiculous, the type of inept legal action more reminiscent of Communist courts of the 1960s than of the U.S. government in the 1990s.

He sighed. The picture fit, though: tanks on the streets and trumped-up charges in the courts.

BEGINNING WITH the second day of testimony, the forensics experts were on the stand.

"Yes," a specialist named Lynn Mickey said in a strong voice. "This is the photograph taken at the scene of the bombing. It's hard to recognize what one is looking at, but this is the wreckage near the hospital entrance leading to the regeneration center."

Using a pointer, Jack Barnes indicated the center left of the large, blown-up photograph displayed on the easel at the front of the courtroom. "And would you be kind enough to tell us what this is?"

Dr. Mickey cleared his throat. "Human remains in a bombing of this type are almost always unrecognizable as having been human. This photo indicates a mass of blood and tissue, here, and a general area of fragments and matter, here, that were the largest single identifiable remains of the deceased."

Just like an abortion, Daniel Seaton couldn't help thinking.

"Dr. Mickey, were you able to reassemble the bodies of Congressman Meyer and Dr. LaMar?" asked Barnes.

"Yes, after combing the area, including the street below the walkway, where quite a bit was found actually, we were able to make positive identification."

"What was the cause of death?"

"Death would have been instantaneous. The body would be hit first by the concussive blast, then by shrapnel—that is, the glass and other debris. But the acoustic injuries from the blast would kill the victim instantly, tearing apart the lungs and arteries. Although it might not be of any comfort to the families of the deceased, I would add that the victims of this bombing did not suffer. It was too quick."

"Would an explosion of this type have been survivable, Dr. Mickey?"

"There are always cases that defy the odds, so I hesitate to call something absolutely unsurvivable. But an explosion of this type, in a relatively small building of this type, would almost inevitably lead to the deaths of anyone in the building. Particularly in the walkway."

"Thank you, Dr. Mickey. Your witness, Mr. Knight."

"Thank you. We have no questions, Your Honor."

A RATHER LOQUACIOUS demolitions expert named John Spout was next on the stand.

"Commander Spout, how many bombing sites have you examined?" asked Jack Barnes.

The lieutenant commander, a massive, square man in his late forties with a tanned, lined face and bright blue eyes, sat erect in the witness chair.

"Over the years it would be hard to say, but I would say I have been on site for at least twenty-five post-explosive incidents."

"Have you also had experience with planting explosives?"

"Oh, yes. I've had extensive experience in military demolitions—be glad to outline that for you, sir."

"There's no need for that at this point, Commander. We're interested right now in the forensics of the regeneration center blast."

"Yes sir." Spout cleared his throat. "All explosives leave some form of residue after they've been exploded," he said. "The residue is like a fingerprint almost...with the right chemistry you can determine its origin. Even to the point of international origin, if the explosives didn't come from this country.

"You can also tell the rate of detonation—and the higher that is, the more shattering effect it has. We call it brisance—that's the French word for the breaking or shattering effect of the sudden release of energy. Another defining characteristic is the nitrogen level. All explosives have a high concentration of complex nitrogen molecules; if you can determine the types, by analyzing the residue, you can also determine what kind of high explosives were used."

Spout gushed forth for some time regarding rates of detonation, plastic explosives, and the like.

Rob Knight sat and doodled. All of this was simply dragging the case out. It didn't matter. Everyone knew these guys blew the place sky high.

Spout surmised that Alex and Lance must have filled a van with between seven hundred and one thousand pounds of military-issue C-4 explosive, rigged it with a non-electric timer, pulled the fuse igniter, then skedaddled out of the parking garage.

Fine, thought Rob. Point was, *Daniel* was on trial here. But, of course, the government was going to great lengths to paint the horrors of the bombing; they'd also go to great lengths to establish a conspiracy. Rob shifted uncomfortably in his chair.

Spout kept spouting. As the time went by and the courtroom got warmer, Rob noted one juror's head bobbing. The temptation to snooze was strong. Now the judge was cutting in.

"Counselor," Judge Green addressed Jack Barnes. "This testimony regarding the explosives, is, of course, quite interesting, but how much do you need to establish here? Where are you going, may I ask? No aspersions on your testimony, of course, Commander."

"Your Honor, this expert will demonstrate the ease, if you will, with which this building was exploded. How, in fact, any amateur—or anyone familiar with standard military-issue explosives—could do it, which the government believes is important to its proof."

"Well," said Green dryly. "I would hope the government would not advertise it as being so easy, or you'll have every aggrieved lawyer coming in here with haversacks full of C-4."

The courtroom erupted in laughter. The jury woke up.

"I'll let you go until 4:30, Counselor. Then this court will recess."

"Thank you, sir."

Jack Barnes prodded his witness, and eventually came down to his final question. "In your expert opinion, sir, would it take a high degree of professional expertise to set up a bomb like the one that destroyed the regeneration center?"

"That's just it," said Spout firmly. "It's not that difficult. Anyone with a little military explosives training could do this in a heartbeat. C-4 is one of the easiest explosives in the world to work with. All someone would need is a little bit of knowledge, a lot of explosives, and a little chutzpa."

"Thank you, Commander. Your witness, Mr. Knight."

Rob stood. "We have no questions, your honor."

The jury was nodding, whether in understanding or in relief was anyone's guess. Judge Green dismissed his court. It had been a long day.

REPORTS REGARDING Spout's testimony headlined the evening news. Since federal courts allowed no TV cameras in the courtroom, the trial itself was not televised. But its progress was duly reported, day after day, with the networks breaking into scheduled programming throughout the day if anything juicy came up.

After the trial each afternoon, Daniel was returned to the holding cell in the courthouse basement; there, he changed into his jail-issue orange jumper for transfer back to the Arlington jail. With processing and security, it was often 7:00 P.M. before he was back in his cell, and later if he and Rob met in the jail conference room to discuss the case.

THE NEXT DAY, the prosecution called Mabel Watkins to the stand. The small, slightly built woman with dark, graying hair stepped into the witness box and raised her right hand to take the oath. She wore a navy blue suit, severely cut, with a white blouse and sensible, low-heeled pumps. Her only concession to jewelry was the round gold National Association of University Librarians pin on her lapel; her only concession to makeup was some startling red lipstick slashed haphazardly across her thin, pursed lips. She wore a pair of half-glasses on a thin cord around her neck.

"Please state your name and occupation, Ms. Watkins."

"Mabel Watkins. I'm a librarian at the George Washington University main library. I've worked there for twenty-three years and seven months."

"Could you please tell the court what you witnessed on the night of last June 3?"

"Yes, I can. It's my regular practice to walk my dog each night before I go to bed. I feel safe as long as I stay in my neighborhood; everyone knows Fifi."

I bet Fifi is a miniature black poodle who looks just like the dog version of Mabel Watkins, Rob Knight thought as he drummed his fingers on the table.

"What kind of dog is Fifi, Ms. Watkins?" Jack Barnes asked solicitously.

"Fifi is a Great Dane."

Well, I missed that one, Rob said to himself.

"My brother gave her to me five years ago," Mabel Watkins continued. "He was worried about me living alone in the city. I've never had any trouble since I've had Fifi."

"So please continue," said Jack Barnes. "You and Fifi walk each evening."

"Yes, we do. I have her on a leash, of course, and I carry a pooper scooper and a plastic bag. The city is pretty strict about these things."

"Yes, it is," said Jack Barnes, grinning for a moment as a chuckle went through the courtroom. "A good thing, too. Well, please tell us, if you would, what happened as you walked Fifi near the university hospital."

"Certainly. I had just rounded the corner across the street from the building that was under construction, the regeneration center."

"So you were directly across the street from the regeneration center?"

"Yes. I looked at my watch; we were right on schedule. Fifi had relieved herself, and I had put her waste into a trash can on the corner of Twenty-third and I Streets. I was standing there for a moment, waiting for the light to turn, and then all of the sudden, Fifi started acting very strangely."

"Strangely?"

"The only thing I can compare it to is how she acts during a thunderstorm. She was pacing back and forth, whining, pulling on the leash, her ears pricked up. She was upset, and I didn't know why. I looked around. There was no one nearby. Then I looked across the street, and there was a car next to the curb with its motor running, and two men acting strangely."

"What did these men look like? And, if you could, please tell us what you mean when you say they were acting strangely," Jack Barnes said.

"Well, one was tall and thin; he was Caucasian. Then the other man was shorter but stockier, heavier looking. He was African American. I could see them because of the streetlights. The thin man was running toward the center; the other man seemed to be chasing after him. They were shouting, but I couldn't really hear what they were saying. Then Fifi pulled on the leash again, and I looked down at her, and then I looked up at the men again, and suddenly there was the sound of a huge explosion, and a huge flash. I've never heard anything like it."

"Could you describe it for us the best you can, Ms. Watkins?"

"It was like a huge fireball. The flash was so bright in the night that it was like when a camera flashes in your eyes and you see red reflections afterward. I closed my eyes, of course, and then it was all confusing. The building was crashing down, there was black smoke, and fire, and the sound of shattering glass everywhere, and I fell down on my knees, hugging Fifi.

"When I looked up again a second later, still holding Fifi, there was smoke everywhere, and fire, but I saw the two men again. The bigger one was dragging the tall man under his armpits, pulling him toward the car on the curb. Then he pushed him in, got behind the wheel, and drove away. It was very strange. First all the noise of the explosion, and then this moment of silence...then crashing and screaming, and then sirens and horns and total chaos."

"It must have been terribly frightening," said Jack Barnes.

"It was horrible," Mabel Watkins said. "But I just thank the stars that Fifi was all right."

"Ms. Watkins, do you believe you could identify the two men you saw leaving the scene of the bombing?"

"Yes, I could."

Jack Barnes held up a large foam-backed posterboard with a blown-up photograph of Alex Seaton.

"That was the thin man I saw that night," Mabel Watkins said.

"And what about this man?" Jack Barnes asked, holding up a large photo of Lance Thompson.

"Yes, that was the African American, the larger man who dragged the other man away from the explosion."

"Thank you, Ms. Watkins. No further questions. Your witness."

Rob Knight stood up. He had anticipated casting a little reasonable doubt on Mabel Watkins's self-important testimony. He just hoped it worked.

"Ms. Watkins, you say you saw two men the night of the bombing?"

"That's correct."

"Let me understand. It was dark outside?"

"Yes, of course. But I could see by the light of the streetlights."

"And you were across the street, approximately thirty yards away from the car you say the men drove away in?"

"Yes, that's about right."

"You said that the explosion caused your eyes to see red flashes afterward?"

"Yes, like after someone takes your picture in the dark with a bright flash."

"So your eyesight was not, shall we say, at its optimum after the flash of the explosion?"

"Just for a moment, I guess, you could say that."

"And you have stated that the entire incident, from the time you noticed Fifi acting strangely until the time of the explosion and the car driving away, was just a few moments long?"

"Well, it seemed longer. A traumatic thing like that stretches out in time."

"I would suggest, Ms. Watkins, that the duress of that trauma might have affected both your eyesight, as you have stated, and your impressions, adversely. Can you be sure that these men you saw at a distance, in the dark, in the midst of a very traumatic incident, were the same men Mr. Barnes has so selectively shown you in these photographs?"

"Well, I have a very good memory," said Mabel Watkins defensively. Rob had gotten her where it hurt. "In fact, I have a photographic memory. I can read a printed page and practically memorize it, because I can see it in my mind's eye. That's why I love being a librarian."

"And you are saying that you can remember faces the way you remember the printed page?" Rob asked.

"Oh, yes. I never forget a face."

"That's certainly admirable," Rob said. "Let me ask you a question. Look at the second row on the left side of the courtroom. Do you see any faces you recognize there?"

Mabel Watkins took ninety seconds before she answered, carefully scanning each person on the row. "No, sir, there is no one there whom I have seen before."

Rob turned. "Ms. Watkins, I would beg to differ. My wife, Lisa, there in the red dress, second from the end of the row...Lisa came to your library and used her GW alumna card to check a book out from you last Tuesday, five days ago. In fact, she was wearing the same red dress she's wearing today. And you initialed her copying expense receipt for her. I have it right here."

CUTE, THOUGHT Ira Levitz. He liked Rob Knight, thought he was refreshingly spunky, even though Knight occasionally got too excited for his own good. It was okay this time to show off his stuff and play Perry Mason if it helped break the tedium. It really didn't matter anyway; everybody knew these guys blew up the center.

But Knight had better be careful, Ira thought. *He's the kind of person who could trip up if he doesn't watch out.*

THE FOLLOWING morning, the government called an army NCO named Bruce Pearson, who had cut a deal with prosecutors. Pearson had had responsibility for maintaining ammunition and demolitions security at Fort A. P. Hill, near Fredericksburg, Virginia, an hour's drive south of Washington. Since demolitions training was routinely conducted at Fort A. P. Hill, Pearson had, over a number of months, routinely checked out slightly more demolitions than needed for training exercises.

The standard C-4 explosives came in twenty-pound haversacks. Pearson had stockpiled the extra haversacks in which the pliable sticks of explosives were stored, slipping them out of the base regularly on days he knew he could breach security. The haversacks were fairly easy to conceal and came equipped with handy carrying straps, almost like a backpack, about twelve inches wide, four inches deep, fifteen inches high. Over the months, Pearson had managed to assemble a considerable amount of explosives, as well as non-electrical blasting caps, time fuses, and fuse igniters.

Pearson hadn't been part of the pro-life movement. Ideologically, he didn't care much about the fetal tissue issue. He had been well paid for his services. The final payment had been a thousand dollars, the week before the bombing, he said matter-of-factly. But the main reason he had gotten involved in the plot was out of loyalty to an old army buddy, Lance Thompson, who had set up the scheme and brought him into it.

Pearson would have died to save Lance; but now that his friend was gone, he owed no similar loyalty to anyone else involved in the case. When investigators started administering lie detector tests to all personnel with access to explosives, Pearson knew his time was short. He volunteered: his court martial for the lesser charge of misappropriation of government funds in exchange for his testimony.

Rob Knight didn't consider the Pearson testimony particularly compelling or relevant, one way or the other. But Jack Barnes took a long time establishing Lance's connection with the NCO. It seemed a psychological boost for the other side to convict a dead man. But Rob was focused on his client, alive and well, though pale, in the chair next to him.

BY THE twelfth day of the trial, Jack Barnes was questioning Jennifer Barrett.

"Ms. Barrett, you have told us that you had cause to observe Alex Seaton and Lance Thompson for a period of several months while you were part of the The Life Network group as an undercover federal agent. You have established that they planned the bombing of the regeneration center and were involved, as well, in the sabotage of the network news broadcast in order to air the anti-abortion video. Did you also have cause to observe Daniel Seaton during that same period of time?"

"Yes," said Jennifer Barrett. Her long legs were crossed and her hands folded in her lap. She was cool, dispassionate, and reserved on the witness stand. "I didn't see Daniel Seaton as much as I did his brother and Mr. Thompson, but I attended his church and saw him and his wife at least once a week, often more."

"In what circumstances would you see the Seatons?"

"The church was a small congregation. People tended to spend a lot of time together. They were like a little community. I became part of that community, so to speak, so I shared meals with the Seatons, and I worked with them on some of the church's outreach projects."

Jack Barnes chose not to pursue the image of shared suppers

and ministry to the poor and needy. "Did you ever discuss the issue of abortion with Daniel Seaton?"

"Yes, we talked about a number of issues over the months. We spoke about abortion a lot. We also talked about the harvesting of fetal brain tissue."

"What was Daniel Seaton's disposition about this issue?"

"Oh, he was extremely passionate about it. He said that the harvesting of fetal brain tissue represented the most grievous slaughter of the innocent since the Nazi Holocaust."

"Those are strong words, Ms. Barrett. Are you sure that you remember them correctly?"

"Yes. The comparison with the Nazi Holocaust stuck in my mind, particularly since I heard Alex Seaton say the same things, and that taking out the regeneration centers was the only way to stop the holocaust."

Rob jumped to his feet. "I object, Your Honor. The witness is volunteering a connection here that can only prejudice the jury. That proves nothing."

"Sustained. The jury will disregard the answer."

"Let me ask this, Ms. Barrett. Would you say that the Seaton brothers had similar views regarding the regeneration center?"

"Yes. I remember Daniel Seaton saying once that it was ironic that the president was spending all his time dealing with crises in Africa and Korea instead of focusing on the scourge of his own nation. He said the regeneration centers were immoral, that our leaders would one day be held to account for their carnage against defenseless human life."

Daniel Seaton, sitting at the defense table, bowed his head for a moment. He remembered saying that. He had said a thousand similar things, all in light of the coming judgment of God...not the judgment of taking matters into his own hands and bombing the center. But in court, stripped of its biblical context, his words sounded harsh, crazy, and violent. Exactly the way Jack Barnes wanted them to sound.

Jennifer Barrett's testimony, all in similar vein and all obviously well-rehearsed, went on for another hour. Rob Knight's cross-examination of her was disorganized but helped to defray the damaging picture she had painted.

"Ms. Barrett, it must have been hard to pretend to be something you are not, living with a group of unsuspecting people as if you were their friend, as if you shared their deepest-held beliefs, when in fact you were an informant for the federal government."

"I object, Your Honor. That's not a question. It's a statement," Jack Barnes called out.

"Mr. Knight, why don't you rephrase your question?" said Judge Green mildly.

"I'm sorry, Your Honor. Ms. Barrett, according to all concerned, you fit in remarkably well with Pastor Seaton's church. You knew all the old hymns. You 'talked the talk,' if you know what I mean. Do you have a Christian background?"

Jennifer Barrett raised her eyebrows but shrugged slightly. "I grew up in a fundamentalist religious home," she said.

Rob paused for a moment. "You told people in Pastor Seaton's church that your father was an insurance salesman. But a little checking reveals that your father was a minister. Isn't that true?"

"It's not uncommon to alter one's life details when one is undercover," Jennifer Barrett said. "Yes, my father was a minister."

"Did you get along with your father?"

Jack Barnes objected again, but Judge Green allowed the question.

"No, Mr. Knight, I didn't get along with my father. He was an abusive, rigid, cruel man. I left home when I was a teenager."

"Have you attended church regularly since, Ms. Barrett?"

"No, I have not." In spite of her training, Jennifer Barrett was getting angry. "The example of Christianity I grew up with wasn't exactly the type of thing I'd want to be part of ever again."

"So you are, shall we say, hostile toward conservative Christianity?"

"I wouldn't put it that way."

"Some might think, Ms. Barrett, that you were settling a score."

"I object, Your Honor."

"Sustained."

"Let me ask one last question. Were you chosen for this assignment to infiltrate Pastor Seaton's church, or did you volunteer?"

Jennifer Barrett looked down for a moment, then raised her chin just a little too high as she met the defense attorney's eyes. "I volunteered, Mr. Knight."

"Just so. Thank you, Ms. Barrett. No more questions."

ON SATURDAY NIGHT, Rob and Lisa had Mary Seaton over to their home for dinner. The previous day, the FBI men who had found the getaway vehicle in the Seatons' garage the morning after the bombing had testified. The court had also heard testimony from the agents who had found Daniel's car at Frank Doggett's house in Leesburg.

It had been the most direct testimony thus far tying Daniel to any aspect of the actual crime, and it was damaging. Rob, of course, had known it would come. But it was still circumstantial and after the fact. It did not tie Daniel to the bombing itself, a point Rob hammered home in his cross-examination.

Over linguine and sautéed chicken breasts, the Knights and Mary talked about other things for a while, chatting rather distractedly about the Seaton kids, the church, and a mutual friend who had just lost her husband to cancer. After dinner, Lisa carried the dishes into the kitchen, piled them up in the sink, and returned with three mugs of steaming coffee.

"How do you really think it's going?" Mary asked Rob quietly.

Rob swirled some milk into his coffee. "I get in trouble with Lisa if I seem too enthusiastic, but I would say that things are really going pretty well. Yesterday was a little squirrely, but unless the prosecutors have some ace up their sleeve that we don't know about, we're doing okay. The other side is intimidating—after all, it's 'The United States of America' versus Daniel Seaton. But they've got some big holes."

"What about the car thing?" Mary asked. "Looking back, I can't believe we were so naive, but Daniel did loan Alex our car.

We had no idea anyone had been hurt in the bombing. We were upset, Alex was hurt, we just wanted to help him. But he was a fugitive, and we helped him escape in a different car than the one the police were looking for...all of that is bound to look pretty bad to the jury."

"Not on the major charge, that Daniel was part of the bombing conspiracy. Remember, in order to convict, the jury has to believe beyond a reasonable doubt that Daniel is culpable, that he had guilty intent," said Rob. "They have to believe that Daniel was involved, that he was really part of an evil conspiracy and that he took some action—one act is what they would have to prove—to further the conspiracy.

"The prosecutors have hung a few little pieces of things out there, but nothing that really establishes guilty intent or aiding and abetting or conspiracy. Now, on the other front—accessory after the fact—that's where we're weak, but that's a much lighter charge."

Mary shook her head. She knew that "much lighter" charge still meant several years in prison for Daniel. But she smiled at Rob as she said, "There's just one thing. I do wish you'd let me testify. I mean, who knows Daniel better—and I *know* he wasn't part of this. Why not, Rob?"

"Mary, you know why. You'd be great on the stand—believable, articulate. But don't you see? I can't put you on and not put Daniel on. It would look like he was hiding behind Mama's skirts. It would be death with the jury."

"And you aren't putting Daniel on, for sure?"

"Not in a million years. They've got a real job to prove intent except from inference, and I'm going to impeach their witnesses. If I put him on the stand, Barnes eats him alive on cross-examination. He would get enough, I am positive, to put your husband away for good. No, no, no." Rob tapped hard on the table with his fingertips; the coffee cups jumped.

Mary smiled at Lisa and put her hand on Rob's arm. "Thank you for everything you're doing," she said. "My husband's life is in your hands. You've been such a good friend to us through all this. We trust you."

AS ROB LOOKED over the government's witness list, he thought that the only tough one ahead of them was John Jenkins, who, like Bruce Pearson, had made a deal with the prosecutors. Rob hadn't been worried about Pearson, but Jenkins might be a loose cannon. The government had evidently done a good job of scaring him.

AFTER THE bombing of the regeneration center, it had taken only a matter of hours for John Jenkins to make his decision. The FBI had interrogated him the next morning, and he was surprised by the degree of terror he felt. He hadn't even thought about how he would react once Alex and Lance really carried through with the bombing. Now he realized he certainly wasn't willing to give up his family, freedom, and business for the cause.

In spite of his fear, Jenkins had been composed enough to refuse to answer any of the agents' questions. Then, after they left, he'd called Dick Kingman, one of the hottest criminal lawyers in Washington. By that afternoon, Kingman had contacted Jack Barnes. It had taken only hours for Kingman to cut a deal with prosecutors, an arrangement that would, as Kingman put it indelicately, "save Jenkins's butt."

And indeed he had. Kingman got him a grant of full immunity in exchange for the testimony the government wanted. Jenkins, whose fear of prison had escalated with each passing day since the bombing, thought Kingman's retainer of $25,000 was eminently reasonable.

FROM THE moment Jenkins took the stand, Rob marveled at how well-coached he was. He had a pleasant smile, which he occasionally showed the jury. He scrupulously avoided eye contact with Daniel, even when he was asked to identify the defendant.

Barnes did not drag out the testimony but simply established Jenkins's clean record and admirable family life. Then, the jury's interest piqued, he moved in for the kill.

"On May 16 of last year, did you visit Rehoboth Beach, Delaware?"

"Yes sir."

"Who were you with?"

"Lance Thompson, Alex Seaton, and Daniel Seaton."

"What was the purpose of the trip?"

"Well, we needed some time to get away from Washington and relax. Also, to think about our next strategic move regarding the abortion industry."

"Whose idea was the trip?"

"It was Alex's, I guess, or Lance's. They thought it would be good for us to have some time alone. And they were worried too about security. We didn't feel it was safe to talk back in Washington. We knew the FBI was monitoring us. We just didn't know how."

"What did you discuss during the weekend?"

"Well, we talked about what had happened so far. We talked about people's response to the abortion video on television—that people didn't care. Alex and Lance argued very hard that we had to do more."

"Like what?"

"Specifically, to destroy the regeneration center."

Jenkins spoke so firmly, almost defiantly, that a murmur went through the courtroom.

"And why was Daniel Seaton included in this trip?"

"Alex said he couldn't do it, wouldn't, unless Daniel approved."

Now another murmur rippled through the court. Almost everyone could sense what was coming. Rob's stomach turned over. Daniel was just staring at John Jenkins as if he couldn't believe what was happening.

"Did Daniel know of the plans that were being discussed to bomb the regeneration center?"

"Certainly."

"Did he approve of these plans?"

"Not before we went to Rehoboth. No." John Jenkins looked straight at the jury. "But at Rehoboth he did."

A loud stir went through the courtroom, mostly from the press. Judge Green hit the gavel, calling for order. Some reporters slid through the back door, obviously to get the jump on the rest.

Barnes continued. "I'd like you to be specific. Exactly what did Daniel Seaton say?"

"There was a very spirited discussion. Alex and Lance were pressing for action—that is, to bomb the center. Daniel listened carefully, and then at the end of the discussion he told them that they would have to follow their consciences, that if they felt that was the right thing to do, they should."

"Are you saying, Mr. Jenkins, that he told them to go ahead?"

"Yes, he said there were no other options."

There was yet another stir, and this time one of the jurors exclaimed, "Jeez." Green hit the gavel again.

"Mr. Jenkins, were you with the others the entire time?" Barnes asked.

"I believe I was. I was part of every conversation. We left Daniel alone once at the beach. He said he wanted to pray. But I'm certain I heard everything said."

Barnes smiled, turned toward Rob Knight, who was furiously scribbling notes, and said, "Your witness."

Rob knew he couldn't immediately attack Jenkins's credibility. At that moment, the jury wouldn't even hear it. For two hours, Jenkins had been well-spoken, personal, reasonable, dispassionate.

Rob knew he had to slowly change the jury's perception, and then, at the end, move in to destroy him. This was absolutely crucial; the fate of his client would ultimately turn on whether the jury believed Jenkins. At least so he thought.

Rob took thirty minutes establishing the relationship of Jenkins and the others, how close they were, how much they trusted one another, trips they took together, prayer sessions together, meals shared . . . Throughout, Jenkins kept his pleasant disposition.

Jack Barnes, watching from the prosecution table, knew exactly what Knight was doing: putting all of the conspirators together, painting them with the same brush. Clever, he thought. It showed maturity on Knight's part that he wasn't jumping down Jenkins's throat.

Then Rob stopped pacing and stood directly in front of the witness.

"Mr. Jenkins," he said, "you have testified that Daniel Seaton was an adamant foe of the regeneration centers."

"Yes, that's true," said John Jenkins.

"That fact is well-known," Rob said. "Pastor Seaton hates the regeneration centers and what they are designed to do...that is, the harvesting of brain tissue from mature fetuses while they are still alive. Do you support the regeneration centers?"

"No, I do not."

"So you are against them?"

"That's correct."

"And you have made statements regarding your feelings about them? Again, there are a number of people who have heard you speak out against them."

"Yes, I've spoken about my feelings."

"It strikes me, Mr. Jenkins, that your testimony about Pastor Seaton's animosity toward the regeneration centers could apply equally toward yourself or any other individual who disagrees with the morality of cutting open the soft skulls of the unborn and suctioning out their brains. Yet you have gone further in your testimony against Pastor Seaton, a friend who has supported you in difficult times in your life. You have seemed to put all the responsibility on him."

John Jenkins's composure was fraying slightly. It was obvious that he was a man caught between his instinct for self-preservation and a fair degree of self-loathing for his own efforts to save himself.

"I've simply answered the questions," he said.

"Well, that's appropriate, Mr. Jenkins. But it seems to me that you are all equally involved—or not involved."

John Jenkins was silent.

"Did you favor the bombing of the regeneration center, Mr. Jenkins?"

"I didn't object."

"That's not my question. Did you favor it?"

"Yes, when I was asked my opinion, I did."

"Just like you say Daniel Seaton favored it, though I think you also said he was very reluctant."

"That's true." Jenkins looked rattled.

"And yet, Mr. Jenkins, you are not on trial. Would you explain to us why that is so?"

"I have been granted immunity, as the prosecutor said at the beginning."

"Of course, of course. I think we call it making a deal, do we not?"

"Your Honor, I object." Jack Barnes jumped to his feet. "This line of questioning is intended only to damage Mr. Jenkins before this jury. There's no question of fact here. The government has made it clear from the beginning that John Jenkins is a government witness who has been granted immunity—a standard practice in conspiracy cases."

Green stared down from the bench. "Now, Mr. Barnes, I understand your point, but I am going to allow counsel to pursue this line of questioning. It does, after all, go to the believability of the witness, a proper area for examination."

For the next ten minutes, Rob Knight performed masterfully. And Jenkins squirmed. Rob asked about briefing sessions with the prosecutors, whether they had suggested testimony, whether Jenkins's lawyer had made any offers at the time the deal was struck. Barnes objected frequently, to no avail. Jenkins consistently answered that while he had made a deal, everything he had said today was true.

During much of the questioning, Rob did not look at Jenkins. Instead, he positioned himself in front of the jury box and stood leaning against the jury rail. His tactic was to get the jury to identify with his questions.

"Mr. Jenkins," Rob said finally, after a long pause, "I have no further questions. And I am sure you don't either because you know the oath you have taken today is one made not only in this court but before God. You understand, I am sure?"

Jenkins sat staring, saying nothing, his face now ashen.

The government rested its case. The court adjourned, to resume in the morning.

58

RANDOLPH GREEN had begun his career as a sole practitioner hanging around the courthouse waiting for some judge to assign him a case. Anything to pay the bills. Though he was now the Honorable Judge Green, he had not forgotten what it was like to work alone and scrounge for evidence, comb through law books, and sometimes improvise in court. The judge had therefore agreed to Rob's request to use his conference room for preparation time with the defendant. It would be a particular help during the presentation of the defense, sparing Rob the drive to the Arlington County Jail and all the security hassles there.

The afternoon after the prosecution rested, marshals led Daniel into the judge's chambers to a large rectangular room with a window at one end, floor-to-ceiling bookshelves on either side, and a huge conference table in the center. The marshals guarded both entrances, nervous only about the window, although it would trigger an alarm if opened.

As Rob and Daniel faced each other across the table, Rob was grinning, his leg bouncing incessantly under the table. "Well, let me sum it up, Daniel." he began. "First, we've made it through with no surprises. That's very good. Most lawsuits that get lost do so because of surprises.

"Second, Jenkins hurt us, but it's only a surface wound. His credibility was pretty badly damaged on cross. I think I did as well as I could—"

"Rob, you did a great job." Daniel smiled reassuringly.

"Well, good enough, I hope. But the big thing is that there is no overt act. Even if the jury believes you gave them your permission, agreed with their plan—and I don't think they will—but even if they do, that isn't an *act* furthering the conspiracy. They can't get you on aiding and abetting without an act. Like handing them the bomb or something. Or, actually, any little thing before the crime.

"On that score," Rob continued, "they've come up empty-handed. In fact, in the morning I intend to move for a directed verdict. That is, ask the judge to direct the jury to find you 'not guilty.'

"Now, don't get your hopes up. There's only one chance in a hundred—judges don't like to take cases away from the jury. But this judge just might. And at least I'm going to let everybody know that the government hasn't made the case. I can plant some doubts.

"But whatever happens on that motion, there's always the accessory after the fact. There we don't look so good. But even if we lose that, remember, the maximum is five years. Not good, but it's not life."

Daniel was standing, stretching his legs. "So then we go with our defense, right?"

Rob began to list witnesses and what each would say to establish Daniel's good character, his consistent position against violence, the sermons he preached about obeying the law, work he had done with local government officials indicating his respect for the political process. Rob had seven witnesses planned, five of whom were members of the church and two local government officials in Falls Church.

Daniel walked toward the window while Rob was outlining the defense and jotting notes on a pad. Not much of a view, just an inside courtyard, but better than three walls of concrete and bars in prison. He was staring distantly, showing no emotion; in fact, Rob wondered if he was listening. It was understandable. After the shock of the bombing, Alex's death, his own arrest and imprisonment, now this ordeal, he was probably numb.

"Rob," Daniel said quietly, turning to look at him.

Something in his voice made Rob put down his pen. "What is it?" he asked.

"I've been thinking a lot over the past few days. You're not going to like this, I know, but I feel convicted that I have to take the stand."

"No way," said Rob. "We've been through that before." He picked up his pen again.

"I mean it. I've got to take the stand," said Daniel.

"Why?" Rob looked at Daniel carefully, then jumped up and walked over toward him. "Why?"

"When you lie on a prison cot at night, you think a lot," Daniel said. "I've thought so much about Alex, about this whole mess. I've missed my children, I've died inside wanting to be next to my wife. But the main thing that has happened to me is that I've realized that all this is so much fluff. Chaff. I can't put the earthly things above the heavenly things. What would it profit me to win this case but lose my own soul? . . . So I have to do what is absolutely right according to my conscience."

"What are you talking about?" Rob said, his voice shaking.

"I have to testify. I have to tell this court what I did and said. Honestly face the charges and answer. And I am innocent, at least as you explain it, but I will leave that to the justice of the court."

"What are you talking about?" Rob said again. "Have you gotten some Messianic complex going here? Have you gone nuts?"

"No. You and I both know the truth. I did some things wrong—and I'm willing to face those. But I sure didn't bomb the regeneration center, and I didn't agree to anybody else bombing it. The jury will believe me.

"Besides, remember how all this began, Rob. We wanted to expose the horrors of abortion. That's why I started The Life Network in the first place. So maybe this could be the greatest opportunity yet. There's much I can say that could affect the conscience of this court. I think."

"You're insane. I think I can have you certified and put away. Don't you realize Barnes will tear you apart on cross-examination? He'll take every little thing you say innocently and make it sound guilty. The only hope they have of winning this case will be if you take the stand, and there's no way I'm handing that to them on a silver platter. And if you're convicted, we won't have a chance of appeal, because you did it to yourself. There's no need to do this!"

Daniel looked at him with a trace of anger. "You can't tell me there's no need if I'm sensing a conviction from God that there is a need! You can't dictate my conscience!"

Rob beat his hands on the conference table. "I'm your attorney! I'm your friend! You can't do this! I'll quit, and you'll have no defense at all!"

"Look," Daniel said, his calm demeanor returning, "you are my friend. So you won't quit. And besides, you're my attorney—and you can't quit unless I perjure myself. I looked that up in the jail library. And perjury is exactly what I won't be doing."

Rob was holding the sides of his head. "Okay, tell me again why you want to do this. I understand about your conscience. But why is your conscience affected?"

"I really started thinking about how I needed to testify after Jenkins was on the stand today," Daniel said.

"That lying weasel?"

"Well, he was afraid, and he made a deal. That's his problem. But I have to testify now."

"Why?"

"He was right about one thing," Daniel said. "I told them they had to follow their conscience. And now I have to follow mine. I have to say exactly what happened as I know it. I can't run away from this."

OVER THE next four days, Rob Knight produced each of his witnesses. Their answers could not have been better if he had scripted them. Barnes made only a perfunctory cross-examination, knowing that this would, in the end, have little influence on the case.

Rob had waited until the last moment to announce that he was calling the defendant as a witness. He had hoped, right down to the end, that he could persuade Daniel that it was utterly rash, but Daniel was resolute.

The morning he announced that Daniel Seaton would be the defense's final witness, Jack Barnes struggled to keep the smile off his face. Members of the press murmured to one another and grabbed their notebooks. Green had to pound the gavel several times to restore order.

TWELVE BLOCKS away at the Justice Department, where Emily Gineen was presiding over a senior staff meeting, one of her office interns brought her a note reporting the latest development from the courthouse.

Emily interrupted the assistant attorney general for administration's report.

"Ladies and gentlemen, you are, of course, all following the events in Judge Green's court in the matter of Daniel Seaton. You might wish to know that the defense has just announced that Seaton will testify in his own behalf."

There were gasps around the table.

The assistant attorney general for the criminal division interjected, "I knew it. It's another case like Paul Hill. He's got a death wish."

Emily sat back in her chair and looked pensive. "I don't know. I don't know," she muttered. "I simply do not understand this man."

DANIEL'S TESTIMONY went better than Rob had expected. He concentrated on Daniel's view of nonviolence, his lack of involvement in meetings with Lance and Alex, and his view of the evils of abortion and why he felt that the general nonviolent activities were so essential.

Barnes objected several times on the grounds of irrelevancy, but Green was not about to curtail anything the defendant wanted to say in his own defense. Each objection was overruled.

Rob felt he actually made some headway in the case by pointing out the childhood relationship between the two brothers and Daniel's history of protecting Alex; this just might help on the lesser charges.

When Rob announced that he had finished his questioning, Judge Green recessed court for the day. They would resume at 10:00 the next morning, he said, with cross-examination of Daniel Seaton.

Back in the judge's conference room, Rob acknowledged that Daniel had helped his cause.

"But tomorrow, Daniel, you're in for the most brutal day of your life, and I want you prepared. So right now I'm going to ask you every difficult question I can think of. Remember, on Barnes's cross, he'll try to lead you down the primrose path with yes and no answers. Answer fully, but only answer the question he asks. Never volunteer. Stay on the point."

For the next four hours, Rob paced the room, his tie loosened, shirt sleeves rolled up. He was as brutal as he knew Jack Barnes would be. But Daniel stood up to the assault so well that when Rob finished, he walked around the table, helped Daniel up out of the chair, and threw his arms around him.

"There's just one thing left," Rob said, looking into Daniel's reddened eyes. Both men were exhausted.

"What's that?" Daniel asked.

"Pray."

THREE FLOORS below in the prosecutor's chambers, Jack Barnes sat alone in his office going through volumes of transcripts of Daniel Seaton's sermons and writings—material he had never expected to have the pleasure of asking the defendant about.

It was 11:00 that night when he finally flipped off his office light and started down the long corridor. He noticed the lights on and some noise coming from the third office down on the right.

He went to the door, knocked, and swung it open. Inside, six of his assistants and two paralegals were sitting around a small table in shirt sleeves, laughing and joking. On the center of the table were two bottles of champagne.

"Get that out of here immediately," Barnes scolded furiously.

"Sorry, Chief," one of the young lawyers responded, "but this is a night to celebrate."

"No," Barnes snapped. "Prosecutors don't celebrate. We don't seek victories, only justice . . . and we don't have that yet. We still have a lot of work to do."

THE SILENCE in the courtroom was almost unnerving as Daniel Seaton took the stand. He was wearing a dark-blue suit that showed up his prison pallor, a bright tie that Mary had selected, and he seemed relaxed as he took his oath.

Jack Barnes began with basic questions to put the defendant at ease and draw him out. Then came the questions Rob Knight had dreaded.

"Reverend Seaton, you have been adamant in your anti-abortion views for quite some time, have you not?"

"That's true. Since I became a Christian in high school."

"You have testified that you do not support violence as a means of protesting abortion, that homicide is never justifiable in the cause of saving the unborn."

"That's true," Daniel said.

"But have you, in fact, supported the rather radical notion that revolution is justifiable in certain situations?"

Daniel, concentrating hard, didn't see what Jack Barnes was getting at, but Rob Knight could see it coming.

"Well, that's a rather complicated question. I think that in certain conditions, revolution could be warranted. I would have to apply just war criteria to evaluate such conditions. But revolution would only be a last resort after all other forms of civil disobedience have failed."

"Have you not written on this matter of revolution and civil disobedience, Mr. Seaton?"

"I could have…"

"Allow me to refresh your memory with these words: 'There are two realms, and Caesar is not to usurp that which belongs to God. When a government violates the law that is higher than its own, God's law, it exceeds its legitimate authority. When a government destroys life and order, rather than protecting and establishing them, the church must resist. In such cases Christians must rise up against godless leaders.'"

"I think I wrote that a long time ago," said Daniel. "You're taking it out of context."

"I have here also the tape of a sermon you delivered eleven months ago. In it you say that 'governments are established by God, but the Christian must discern when it is time to resist godless leaders who forfeit their authority by ruling contrary to the higher law, God's law'… Do you believe there are two sets of laws, Mr. Seaton?"

"That's a theological question," Daniel said.

"Still within the prosecutor's power to ask you. Please answer," Judge Green leaned across his desk.

"Yes, I believe there are two laws. There is man's law—that is, the legal codes we all live by, ranging from everything from the law that we must wear seat belts to the laws prohibiting murder. In many cases, man's law complies with God's law; it reflects God's law as it was handed down on Mount Sinai in the Old Testament account. But in some cases, man's law violates God's law; I believe that the Supreme Court decision that opened the doors to legal abortion all those years ago is a prime example. It was an immoral decision because it sanctioned violation of the sixth commandment, 'Thou shalt not kill.'"

"So you have taught your congregation that when push comes to shove, God's law is supreme?"

"I'm not quite sure what you mean by that. When man's law conflicts with God's law, the Christian's higher allegiance is to the law of God."

Jack Barnes switched gears again.

"In your writings and sermons you have referred repeatedly to 'ungodly leaders.' How would you define an ungodly leader?"

"One who flagrantly defies and disdains the laws of God."

"Do you believe that President Griswold is an ungodly leader?"

"Well, I don't know the condition of his heart."

"You seem to be avoiding the question. Have you not said from the pulpit that Whitney Griswold was ungodly?"

"I may have, not as a political statement, but in the sense that nothing in President Griswold's public policy record would indicate to me that he considers God the ultimate authority."

"So you have, in fact, called President Griswold an ungodly leader?"

"Yes, I suppose I have."

"Let's see," said Jack Barnes. "We have covered my questions about your thoughts about revolution and civil disobedience, and your thoughts about what you call a higher law that requires you to disobey civil law, and your analysis of President Griswold... let me ask you if you recognize another piece of writing."

Rob Knight felt sick. It was impossible for ordinary citizens to put theological truths in context. Still, Barnes was only dealing with state of mind, not action.

"This is from an article you wrote, I believe, a year and a half ago, for a conservative journal, but I understand that you never sent it in for publication." Barnes paused and then read from the photocopy John Jenkins had given him. "I quote:

> We must read the writing on the blood-soaked walls of our nation. An individual who takes the lives of the defenseless has no defense; he brings judgment upon himself. A nation that devours its young digests its own future. A leader that allows lambs to be led to the slaughter will be held responsible.
>
> It appears that our nation is no longer content merely to spill the blood of the unborn, but will now begin, in large numbers, to extract the brains of the near-born. The regeneration centers represent, in fact, the new Holocaust of our own day, the killing centers where the slaughter of the innocents will be accelerated to new heights of horror. We can only pray that our

new administration, whichever one it is, will turn while there is still time, before judgment comes upon it, and us.

"Do you recognize those words?"

"Yes, I think I may have engaged in some rhetorical excess."

Jack Barnes took a sheaf of paper off the prosecution table and held it up before the judge. "Your Honor, I would like to call for prosecution exhibit number 3-A a copy of the open letter sent to President Griswold on January 24 of last year and published in the *Washington Post*. Would you, Reverend Seaton, read the first two paragraphs?"

Daniel read the beginning of the open letter sent to Griswold in the wake of the Fargo shooting. With a few small alterations, the wording was exactly the same as Daniel Seaton's unpublished article.

There was a gasp in the courtroom. Mary Seaton, sitting in the front row, clenched her hands so tightly that her fingernails dug into her palms.

Daniel paused, trying to regain his equilibrium. "So what is your question? I didn't write the letter to President Griswold. I was as surprised as anyone else when I saw it in the paper."

"It's odd, though, Mr. Seaton," said Jack Barnes smoothly. "I find it hard to believe that the exact same language is a coincidence. Do you?"

"Alex sometimes looked to me for ideas," said Daniel. He paused and looked down at his hands for a moment trying to recover. "Perhaps someone lifted some of the language from my article. I don't think Alex did it," he continued. "But I certainly did not write that letter to President Griswold."

"Did you at any time discuss the bombing of an abortion facility with your brother?"

"Certainly. Since the 1980s we've talked about it a lot. That's when clinic bombings first started happening. Everyone talked about them. But I consistently opposed it."

"What about more recently?"

"Yes, I think we've talked about the issue in recent times."

Rob was surprised. This was the first time he had heard Daniel shade an answer, even slightly.

"Mr. Seaton," Jack Barnes said loudly, "did your brother at any time discuss with you the possibility of bombing the regeneration center? Mr. Jenkins has testified that he did at Rehoboth on May 16 and 17 of last year."

Daniel took a deep breath. "Yes, Mr. Jenkins was correct. Alex did discuss it with me."

There was a loud murmur in the courtroom.

"And what did you say?"

"You need to understand the context, Mr. Barnes." Daniel's voice shook with emotion. "It was an intense conversation. We were all very frustrated, absolutely sick about unborn children being killed and harvested—"

Barnes cut in. "What did you tell your brother?"

"I told him that he had to follow his conscience."

"Did you think your brother capable of such violence?"

Daniel paused. He had reviewed all this in his mind, but was he sure? He thought about the look in Alex's eyes when the abortionist was shot in North Dakota. He thought about the glow on his brother's face when he had talked about taking down the regeneration center.

"Yes," he said tiredly, "to be absolutely truthful, I believed Alex to be capable of blowing up the center."

"And yet you did not warn the authorities, Mr. Seaton? Even though you have preached that one must respect and obey the governing authorities?"

"No, I did not."

"Thank you, Reverend Seaton. I have no further questions, Your Honor."

Judge Green started to nod, then Barnes cut in. "Oh, no, I'm sorry, Your Honor, I have just one more question, if I may?"

"Go ahead, Mr. Barnes," said the judge.

"Mr. Seaton," Jack Barnes said deliberately, "how much money did you give your brother, Alex, in the week before the bombing?"

Rob was out of his chair almost before Barnes had finished asking the question. "I object, Your Honor. There was no matter of this sort raised on direct."

Green rolled his eyes upward, thought a moment, and then said, "The objection is premature. I'd like to see what the prosecutor has in mind. Overruled."

"I'll repeat the question, Mr. Seaton," Jack Barnes said. "How much money did you give your brother in the week before the regeneration center was bombed?"

"I'm not sure," he replied. "I was in the habit of giving Alex money often. He was in the construction business, you know; his income went up and down. He always paid me back eventually."

"That's understandable, Reverend Seaton. But just tell us what you gave him in the week prior to the bombing of the regeneration center."

"I don't recall..."

Rob Knight had his head bent over the table, muttering to himself. *Don't remember, don't remember. Oh, please God, don't let him remember.*

"Well, wait," Daniel said slowly. "I think I'd have to check to be sure, but I believe I gave Alex money right around that time."

"How much money, Reverend Seaton?" Jack Barnes asked.

"I remember now," Daniel said. Alex said he needed some cash, and I was busy with other things so I didn't think much about it. I borrowed it from Melissa Brett for him. It was a thousand dollars."

A gasp went through the court. One of the jurors, apparently sympathetic, exclaimed, "Oh, no." Jack Barnes looked at the jury, shaking his head as if saddened by this news while Green pounded the gavel to restore order.

Barnes then turned to the judge. "We have no further questions, Your Honor."

IN THE judge's chambers, Rob Knight was furious. "You should have told me...you should have told me," he exclaimed.

Daniel looked hurt. "It never occurred to me. Rob, you've got to believe me. I gave Alex money all the time. He was always in trouble, and he always paid it back. I didn't even remember until Barnes prodded me about it."

"But you knew. You should have known. Pearson already testified that his last payment for the explosives was a thousand dollars. Didn't you remember? Don't you see? This is an overt act."

Daniel said nothing.

Rob shook his head. "I don't think anything I can say will make any difference. But I'll do my best."

THREE FLOORS below, Jack Barnes walked into his office, followed by his assistants. He was laughing. "Break out that champagne after all," he said.

They all laughed, but one young attorney looked puzzled. "I didn't see any reference to money in any of the papers we all went through. I mean, there was one thing about Alex borrowing money from Daniel all the time... but how did you know he gave him money before the bombing?"

"I didn't," Barnes grinned. "Just a hunch. I got lucky. Very lucky."

THE PROSECUTION'S closing arguments went quickly. Jack Barnes simply reviewed the evidence: The conspiracy for the bombing was established, and each of the conspirators, including those now dead, had played their own role. Daniel Seaton's role was clear. He knew in advance of the bombing, encouraged his brother, gave him the thousand dollars needed to finish paying for the explosives, knew full well what it was being used for, then provided the escape vehicle. He was just as responsible as those who had rigged the bomb and set it off.

"Your deliberations," Barnes told the jury, "carry great weight. Not only is the fate of a man at stake, but so is the fate of justice in this nation.

"By finding Daniel Seaton guilty, you will send a message to all Americans that this remains a nation under the rule of law, that those who take the law into their own hands—for whatever reason, matters of conscience or otherwise—must nonetheless pay the price under that law. I trust each one of you to uphold the laws of this nation." He met each juror's eyes, then turned and walked back to his seat.

Rob Knight's closing arguments went much longer. He had not gotten much sleep, and though he had knocked himself out to pull it all together, he felt conscious that he was truly on the defensive, now forced to answer charges and suspicions that hadn't even been in the jury members' minds when he made his opening arguments. He felt like he was going around and around, desperate, circling back on his own rabbit trails. Then, finally, he closed.

"Again, ladies and gentlemen of the jury, please don't let the passion of the moment, the current atmosphere around us, cloud your reason. The prosecution has shown no compelling evidence that Daniel Seaton is a murderer and a conspirator; they have dredged up old papers and chance comments that mean nothing.

"Surely you know in your hearts from Mr. Seaton's own testimony that any involvement he had with the events cited in this case were wholly innocent, compelled by his love for his brother. Mr. Seaton believes enough in a system of justice that he testified before you, knowing you would have the wisdom to discern his innocence."

Rob walked back to the rail in front of the jury box and leaned on it. "Ladies and gentlemen, you have in your hands the fate of a good and decent, caring human being whose principal failing, as happens so often in history with noble figures, is that he cared too much. He cared too much for his congregation, for unborn babies, for his brother. If he stands convicted of anything, it is of zeal for what is right and just and truthful."

Rob walked back to his seat, feeling weak in the knees, his back stabbing him in the usual place. Lisa was looking at him, her brows knitted; Mary Seaton had a similar look on her face.

But Daniel seemed buoyed by some invisible force. He put his arm around Rob's shoulder. "Thank you, Rob," he said. "We've done our part. Now let them do theirs."

AFTER JUDGE GREEN had charged the jury and dismissed them to deliberate, he allowed Rob to take both Daniel and Mary into the conference room.

"The longer they're out, the better for us," Rob grinned, trying to encourage them.

Less than two hours later, the jury sent the message that they had reached a verdict.

As the jurors filed back into their box, their demeanor gave Rob no cause for hope. No encouraging smiles at his client. Each juror was looking straight ahead.

Daniel seemed oblivious. He just watched the bailiff bring the white piece of paper to the judge. Judge Green read it, then nodded. The white piece of paper then traveled back to the foreman of the jury. The foreman, a portly black man in his mid-fifties, cleared his throat.

"As to count one, the charge of conspiracy, we the jury find the defendant guilty as charged."

There was a huge gasp in the courtroom and then a muffled cry from the first row. The murmur continued as the foreman continued reading.

"As to count two, aiding and abetting in the act of homicide, we find the defendant guilty as charged."

Rob Knight closed his eyes. He couldn't watch. He knew every other count would be the same, and the words "guilty, guilty, guilty" echoed in his head. He had his arm around Daniel and turned toward his client with a look of absolute agony. Daniel had his lips pressed together, and he was looking back toward Mary, straining to connect with her.

But when he turned back to Rob, his eyes were clear. "It's all right, Rob," he whispered. "It's the court's will, and the Lord's will. My conscience is clear. I told the truth."

Judge Randolph Green banged his gavel. "Thank you," he said to the jury. "You are dismissed. Sentence will be pronounced in three weeks. This court is adjourned."

59

A S PAUL CLARKSON entered the attorney general's office, Emily Gineen was behind her big desk, her suit jacket off, focused on a thick pile of papers. She looked up and smiled, gesturing Paul toward his usual chair.

"I've been looking at the Seaton trial transcripts," she said, "trying to understand why this guy did what he did. I talked with Jack Barnes, and he is one grateful prosecutor. He's probably never prayed before in his life, but he's been thanking the Man Upstairs ever since Seaton took the stand. He said it was like the guy had a death wish."

"Well," Paul said, "I've seen defendants give up before, just throw in the towel and plead guilty. This wasn't like that; he didn't have a death wish. From what I've heard, evidently he had gone over it all in his mind, and he wanted to make sure that the court knew every detail of the whole story. Just the facts...judge for yourself. No spin."

Emily nodded. "I don't mean to offend, but I had assumed Seaton was a religious wacko until all this happened. But reading the transcript, he sounds like a decent person. He sounds too smart to get sucked into something this stupid. I don't know why, but I'd like to meet him. His sentence is pretty well determined by the federal guidelines, but the government still has to make its recommendation to the judge. And this is such a high-profile case, Barnes wants us to concur. But he wants the full extent of the guidelines; and I want to be sure that's right. I want to know more about what kind of person Seaton really is, what makes him tick."

Paul, in his shirt sleeves, ran his hand through his hair. "Why?" he said. "You know what we have to do—demand the maximum. If it gets out in the media that the attorney general met with Daniel Seaton..." He let out a low whistle. "People aren't in a pretty mood about this thing."

"On this one, I just have to follow my gut," she said. "I'm not sure what it is, but I need to meet him face to face. We'll keep it quiet, and if it is leaked, well, I would think the press would appreciate a hands-on attorney general. Out of the ivory tower and into the prison—it makes a nice spin, don't you think?"

Paul raised his eyebrows. "No, but I'll get it set up," he said. Then he smiled slightly. "And I'll go with you. You might need an interpreter."

AS IT worked out, Paul was able to keep the visit quiet. The Arlington County sheriff, Burt Kloster, was a friend and a member of Paul's church; he arranged the extraordinary clandestine meeting between the attorney general and the convicted felon. It was no small feat; Seaton was probably the most publicized defendant since O. J. Simpson.

Emily and Paul, traveling in Paul's old Volvo, arrived at the jail's back entrance at 6:00 P.M. The sheriff and an aide met them and escorted them quietly through narrow cinder-block hallways to the sheriff's inner office, where, in deference to protocol, both were frisked with a hand-held metal detector and Emily had her handbag searched.

Emily accepted a Styrofoam cup of weak coffee from the

sheriff's secretary. It tasted as if it had been brewed from old socks, but it was something to hold on to. She hadn't been in a correctional facility for more than a decade.

It's shocking, she thought. *Here I am, the senior criminal justice administrator in the nation, and I haven't even set foot in one of these institutions. More than a million and a half people in prisons across the country, and I haven't been near one for ten years.*

It was the smell that took her back. Years ago, as a young prosecutor, she had visited a few miserable jails to take depositions from defendants. They had all smelled this way—a muddled but distinctive mixture of close stuffy air, unwashed bodies, unbrushed teeth, unwashed hair...

But the smell took her back even further, to something she hadn't thought about or even remembered for years. As a teenager, she had loved to sing—and she, at fourteen, had also had a crush on a sixteen-year-old named Will Sizeman, one of the few boys who could sing bass. So she had joined her Baptist church's youth choir. That Easter, the choir had accepted an invitation to sing at a nearby prison's sunrise service. It was a minimum-security institution for women, so the youth group was allowed in; Emily's parents had encouraged her to go, to broaden her horizons.

She didn't remember much about the prison itself. Except for the razor-wire fences, it had looked like a drab college campus. The service had been held in the cinder-block chapel. After the choir had arranged themselves on rickety risers at the front, the inmates had filed in, filling most of the small chapel.

The inmates had responded warmly. They had clapped after each song, and on some numbers had sung along with the choir; all in all, it had been a surprisingly pleasant experience, except that the place had been stuffy and smelled bad. But what Emily now remembered, for the first time in years, was the reaction of one woman as they did their closing song, the traditional Easter anthem, "He Lives."

Emily was singing her part, watching the women and the choir director at the same time, and also thinking about Will Sizeman on the back row behind her, wondering if they would sit together on the bus on the way home. Then, when they got to the chorus, suddenly this big black woman on the front row stood up, hands swaying in the air, singing along with them.

"He lives!" she was shouting. "He lives! Christ Jesus lives today!" She was weeping, tears running down her face and dripping onto her wrinkled smock.

Emily had stopped singing, aching with adolescent embarrassment at the open display of emotion. *Why is she crying?* Emily had wondered.

THE SOUND of shuffling footsteps in the corridor brought her back to the present. The door to the outer office opened, and an officer entered, then another escorted Daniel Seaton into the room. His legs were shackled, and his wrists cuffed in front of him. His prison jumpsuit hung on his tall frame, and his face was gaunt. There were pale, fleshy puffs under his eyes, and his hair stood up in little spikes in the back, courtesy of the jail barber. His lush mustache had been shaved off before the trial, but some photos the newspapers had been using for months had showed him with the mustache. He certainly didn't look like the robust, stocky man she had seen in the newspapers.

"Reverend Seaton," Sheriff Kloster said, "we weren't able to tell you the nature of this special visit until you arrived in my office, and we would ask that you yourself keep this matter confidential as well. The attorney general asked to meet with you personally, and while this is highly unusual, we of course honored her wishes."

Emily stepped forward. "Good evening, Mr. Seaton," she said, feeling awkward because she couldn't shake his hand as she normally would. "I'm Emily Gineen, and this is the associate attorney general, Paul Clarkson. Thank you for meeting with us."

Daniel extended his shackled hands toward her. "I'm honored to meet you, Mrs. Gineen," he said. "I must say, when they told me I had a special visitor, I was hoping it was my wife. But in her absence, it is a great pleasure to make your acquaintance...and yours, too, sir," he said to Paul.

Surprised, Emily smiled. "I'm told that your wife is a very courageous woman," she said.

"That she is," Daniel said. "I never realized how amazing she is until all this happened."

"Well, that's what I would like to talk with you about, Mr. Seaton," Emily said. " 'All this.' " She took charge. "And I'd like to ask you gentlemen," she nodded to Paul, the sheriff, and the officer next to Daniel, "if you would excuse us, so we might talk in privacy."

Paul jerked his head, and the sheriff started to protest, but Emily cut them off. "Sheriff, as you know, I have brought no picks or files to assist Mr. Seaton in an escape. Perhaps he and I could adjourn to your office, and you could stand by here in the anteroom. Have some coffee. Maybe you and Paul can talk about church business. This officer can also stand by, and we will leave the door open, so you can be assured that everything will be all right."

Paul looked at Emily carefully, then he and the sheriff nodded.

Emily and Daniel walked slowly to the sheriff's inner office, where she gestured toward two vinyl chairs next to the file cabinets. He sank awkwardly into one, and she took the other.

"We don't have much time, so I want to speak with you as directly as possible, Mr. Seaton," she said, leaning forward in her chair. "I sense from your statements at your trial that you are a direct person as well. As you probably know, the U.S. attorney makes a sentencing recommendation to the judge in your case about the range within the federal guidelines. Normally that would be handled by others, but I wanted to get directly involved in your situation, because I want to understand what is at the heart of it."

Emily shifted in her chair. Daniel was sitting slightly bowed but looked directly into her eyes while she spoke.

"The crimes for which you have been convicted have struck an exposed nerve with the American public. Understandably. They have done great damage. They have contributed to, if not created, a dangerously ugly mood in our nation. Terrorism always does. And yet in your court statements I found you to be a man of reason and some civility. We are not retrying your case right now. But I want to know: What were you trying to accomplish with The Life Network group?"

Daniel waited a moment, as if expecting her to say more, then took a breath. "First, I want to say that I fully accept the judgment of the court. I had no intention to cause anyone's death or any damage to property, but I inadvertently allowed others to pursue a path that led to those ends."

"I understand that," Emily interrupted. "I'm asking something more basic than that. Why did all this get started?"

"I started The Life Network because I believe that abortion kills unborn human life. We've fought that for decades now. But I knew that as soon as the regeneration centers opened, the demand for fetal tissue would increase dramatically. I knew that the immorality of abortion would be compounded and multiplied even further.

"But the public was being led down a rosy path: The centers were to be our new national hope—lifesaving facilities for AIDS sufferers...but they are, in fact, killing facilities for the defenseless. I had to shine a light on them, expose the evil. I could not see any difference between them and the extermination camps of Nazi Germany. Can you?"

"Abortion is a constitutional right," Emily said. "These matters have been settled in the courts for years. It is legal. Millions of Americans find it personally acceptable. Those who don't, don't have to have one. It's a matter of personal choice."

"With all due respect, Mrs. Gineen, if we're going to engage in a political argument, we might as well save our breath and you can go somewhere where the coffee is better," Daniel said. "You asked why I did what I did. Because abortion—and the harvesting of live fetal tissue, which I notice you didn't mention—may be legal according to human law, but it is wrong according to God's law."

"Laws are based on the will of the people," said Emily.

"Cultures change. America is not a theocracy; our laws don't come from the Old Testament Jewish code."

"I agree with you. We can't impose God's law, even though some people say that we want to. But the Christian has to work in the democratic system, trying to influence the process, so that human laws conform to God's character. And God hates the murder of the defenseless. He is the ultimate Judge. And God doesn't change, no matter how much we change."

Emily refrained from rolling her eyes, but she found herself absolutely frustrated, the same way she felt sometimes in arguments with her husband...impossible to resolve, no way out. Why can't relational conflicts be like legal arguments, both sides present their case and then the judge rules? She paused in her thinking. The analogy felt uncomfortably like where Daniel's language was leading.

"Look," she said. "You're right; we don't want to argue political issues here. So let's argue theological ones. How can you purport to know the mind of God? How do you know what God thinks about a particular issue? There are plenty of clergy who disagree with you about abortion. Do you have the corner on truth?"

Daniel looked down at his manacled hands. "Please forgive me if I sounded self-righteous," he said. "Being in jail has caused me to realize how weak I am. I've made terrible mistakes. And I'm paying for them. But it's also made me realize more deeply than I've ever known that God does not make mistakes. God is God. He has spoken. His word is Truth."

"What do you mean?" Emily said bluntly. " It sounds so presumptuous, almost arrogant. How can you be so sure—how can you even know there *is* truth?"

"First of all, because you asked that question," Daniel responded. "Something in you causes you to ask it. We have a mind, a consciousness...there is something, some ultimate reality, and the mind and soul are restless for it."

Emily frowned. "But even if there is some ultimate reality, one can't know it with certainty."

"Ah," said Daniel, "but that's the search. Look at the order of the universe. Think about its physical realities." He lifted his manacled arms high and let them drop; the chains rattled. "Gravity is a physical law; without support, anything will fall. Every time. If there are known physical laws, why would we even suggest that there aren't known moral laws? Certain behavior produces certain predictable consequences. Every time. And if there are physical and moral laws, there has to be a Lawgiver. That's what I mean by ultimate reality. It is God."

"I've always believed in God," Emily said defensively. "He set things in motion. He made people able to discover the truths about things on their own—"

"But a Christian believes Jesus," Daniel interrupted, not even conscious he was doing so. "Jesus said 'I am *the* Truth.' He holds together the universe—all that we know and can understand flows from Him. I know it's hard to take, but it's the only certainty we have. We call what we see around us the 'real life,' as if life was nothing but buses and budgets and newspaper headlines. But how many times have you experienced the fact that the real is the unseen? Do you have children?"

His abrupt question startled her. "Yes," she said.

"So do I," he said. "I love them. My love for them is real—I would die for them—but you can't see my love. You can just see its effects. And it is there whether you accept it or not. Or let me think of another example...

"Maybe you've been sailing at night. We used to do that when I was a kid, my dad and Alex and me, and we would sleep on the boat..." He paused and looked away for a moment, then swallowed. "But there would be times on moonless nights when you couldn't see ten yards ahead of the boat. There was a light positioned at the top of our mast, but if we had tried to navigate from our own light, which was moving with us, that would have been no help. So my dad would navigate by the stars. Fixed points, shining out in the darkness above a spinning world.

"Now, if the stars moved, or if I believed the stars were in one place and you believed they were in another and we were both supposed to be right, how could anyone navigate? Truth has to be fixed in order for us to know how to live. In order for it to be truth. God is real. Certain. Even though we can't see Him, we see the effects of His presence. Like the wind. And one day we *will* see Him. Face to face."

Emily felt a tightening in her throat. Daniel's homey analogies made intellectual sense, but they also stirred something in her imagination that hadn't been touched since she was a small girl. A longing for a fixed point above a world spinning out of control. A warm hand on her shoulder in the cold. A light on a dark path. She wished it were true. She longed for it to be true.

"I would like to believe with that kind of certainty," she said slowly, feeling very tired. "But I don't know how. It can't be true."

"If it weren't true," he said. "I wouldn't be sitting here in jail with handcuffs on. I'd be at home with my family, because I would have lied in court faster than anything you ever saw."

"You wouldn't have had to lie," Emily said, her legal demeanor returning. "You didn't have to take the stand."

"But that's just it," Daniel said. "I got myself into this. And once I did, I couldn't lie to get out. Maybe I might have been cleared by the earthly judge. But I would have done wrong in the eyes of the heavenly Judge."

TWENTY MINUTES later, Emily and Daniel emerged from the office. Paul and the sheriff stood up, looking puzzled. They had heard the constant buzz of voices but hadn't been able to hear any of the conversation.

As the officers escorted Daniel out the anteroom door, Emily whispered something to the sheriff. He nodded, and followed the group out the door.

Paul looked at Emily. "Well? How was it? What did he say?"

Emily opened her purse and took out a roll of mints, offering one to Paul. He shook his head.

"He said what you said before," she told Paul. "Same message. Different messenger."

Paul looked at her sharply.

"I've asked Sheriff Kloster to arrange for a car to take me back to the office," Emily said, peeling off a mint and putting it in her mouth. "You go on home. It's late."

"What—"

"Paul, I'll see you tomorrow," Emily said with unusual abruptness. "Thank you for setting this up. Good night."

60

D ANIEL SEATON'S sentencing was, like his trial, a huge
media event. Though the federal sentencing guidelines had
little flexibility, they allowed for a range, and so the courtroom
was crowded with reporters waiting to hear Judge Randolph
Green's pronouncement—as well as the Seatons' friends and
parishioners, who had been praying for some sort of miracle.

Daniel himself had prayed for one. He had felt peaceful ever
since he had testified, in spite of the outcome. But he also could
not help but hope that God would somehow deliver him back to
his family. At one point he had even found himself praying the
prayer of Gethsemane: "If You are willing, Lord, remove this cup
from me; yet not my will, but Yours be done"—and then he had
felt ashamed. He wasn't exactly going to the cross.

So on the morning of February 22, Daniel sat as peacefully as
any man could who was awaiting a decision that might take most
of the rest of his life away. Beside him was Rob Knight. Jack
Barnes and his team sat across from them. The courtroom was
hushed, expectant, when the door opened and the judge entered
the room.

Daniel and Rob approached the bench and stood as Judge Green began to address them. He was to the point, but surprisingly personal.

"I am not ordinarily an angry man," the judge said in even, measured tones. "But I have been for some time enraged to find myself in the ironic position of being an alleged agent of justice, and yet having, in some cases, to dispense gross injustice. This is, I fear, such an occasion.

"Rev. Daniel Seaton, as I read the probation officer's report, you are a good and decent man. The history of your life has been previously unblemished, without so much as a parking ticket on record. You give every evidence of having been a productive and exemplary citizen, and you have consistently helped others in a way we can all admire.

"Yet you made a serious mistake. You became involved in the violent business of the tragically misguided effort to expose and stop the regeneration center, so you have been found guilty by a jury of your peers—on rather circumstantial evidence, I might add. I must abide by that decision; it is the way our system has worked since the beginnings of this nation.

"But in the matter of determining punishment for Reverend Seaton," the judge continued, looking out at the packed courtroom, "I have little discretion. I am not allowed to exercise the very justice of my office in considering the nature of the crimes, the likelihood of future danger to society, nor the commendable history of the defendant. Instead, because of the rubber-stamp nature of the federal sentencing 'guidelines,' as they are called…" Green spat out the words. "I must, against my will, judgment, and discernment, issue push-button, mechanical 'justice.' It is the judgment of the court that the defendant, Daniel John Seaton, be hereby committed to the custody of the Bureau of Prisons, to serve not less than twenty years."

He leaned down and spoke directly to Daniel. "I am very sorry, Mr. Seaton. May God go with you."

Then the gavel fell.

61

Tuesday, March 8

"B UT, MR. PRESIDENT, sir, it doesn't seem appropriate for Daniel Seaton to be in Newton," Emily Gineen said into her office phone. Usually she did whatever the president wanted when he wanted it. But Whitney Griswold was being utterly unreasonable. "He's not a threat to others, and we've got to get him into a safer institution. Newton is one of the most violent prisons in the country."

"Seaton is a terrorist!" Griswold shouted into Emily's ear.

He's really losing it, she thought—a thought that had confronted her with unsettling frequency in recent encounters with the man.

"He blew up a building, killed people, and he belongs in maximum security, not in some cushy institution," Griswold continued. "People out there want him locked up. They'd want him in the electric chair if we could do it. I will not tolerate a person like him anywhere but in Newton...and Emily, if I hear about any more quiet moves on your part to put him in a different prison, it will raise very serious questions in my mind. I am not going to have the authority of this office undermined by my own attorney general. Do you understand?"

Emily had been gripping the phone so hard that it was hot. She forced herself to unclench, took a breath, and said, "Yes, Mr. President. I understand you." She hung up, restraining her desire to smash the receiver down.

I understand you, Mr. President, she repeated to herself. *You hate bigots and zealots? Well, you've become the very thing you hate most.*

RISING ABOVE the rolling hills and flat farmlands south of Philadelphia and north of Wilmington is a medieval fortress little-known to the outside world, but notorious within the netherworld of the federal institutions of corrections. Named for a colonel who died defending his post in an Indian uprising, Fort Newton traces its origins to the early 1700s, when it was an out-post for the embattled colonists who settled there. Since then, many more men have died within its bounds.

The Indians burned the wooden fort to the ground, but it was reclaimed and rebuilt by the colonists. Some years later it served as a holding facility for those found guilty of criminal offenses in the brutal environment of pre-Revolutionary America. Prisons, as such, had not yet made their debut, but early chronicles of the fort detail an execution held there in 1758: the offender was disem-boweled, then his entrails thrown upon a fire while he was still conscious enough to watch; he was then decapitated and his body quartered. The offense: horse stealing.

The first American prisons were established in Pennsylvania in 1790 and in New York two decades later, championed by Quakers and others who believed that, given a place of solitude and enforced reflection, a criminal would contemplate his sins and penitently seek to reform his errant ways. Hence the felicitous language of "penitentiaries" and "reformatories"—myths that endured, in spite of the reality that those early humanitarian experiments failed miserably. Many offenders did not quietly reform; instead, the solitude, inactivity, and despair drove them utterly insane.

Yet the fantasy of rehabilitation behind prison walls persisted, and by the late twentieth century, America's "correctional" facilities hosted a million and a half offenders of every degree. The expensive, unwieldy system, a behemoth of government ineptitude, had succeeded only in evolving into a huge tax burden and a separate society with its own language, values, and code of conduct for the culture's most violent.

Ironically, the inmates who complied with the official system were the most likely to be victimized, and the prisoners who ruled this upside-down world were the absolute rabble of a vicious society.

By the time Daniel Seaton arrived at its gates, Newton had become a federal concrete fortress encircled by hundred-year-old thirty-five-foot-tall stone walls. Gun towers that were even taller bulged out from the walls at each corner of the fifteen-acre compound. Approached from the narrow highway that led toward it, Newton looked like a gray, medieval citadel, rising like a nightmare in the middle of pleasant farmlands.

Inside, six wings—concrete corridors lined with barred cells—jutted off from the main prison. One wing housed the most dangerous inmates, allowed out of their cells only an hour each day. Another housed protective custody, the no-man's land where snitches, child molesters, and other vulnerable prisoners sought the dubious protection of solitary confinement. Other wings housed the crazies, the druggies, and the gangs, and there was one open dormitory in which inmates deemed less dangerous slept in gray rows of bunks. Even there, though, stabbings were frequent. On average, there was a serious assault every week at Newton.

Between the spokes of the main structure and the wall was an exercise yard, a gray, forbidding place without grass. In the past, inmates had used the turf to conceal weapons: shanks made from scissors, sharpened shards of metal snapped from cots, shivs made from wooden dowels inlaid with pieces of metal slowly ground to a cutting edge by furtive, endless scraping on the concrete floor. When the guards found such weapons, they always marveled that men of such volatile, murderous impulses possessed the patience it took to make a prison knife. After many such weapons were found hidden in the grass, prison officials had poured a huge slab of concrete that lapped to the very edges of the towering walls. The slab made the yard blistering hot in the humid Maryland summers and dismally gray and cold in wintertime. And the prisoners found other places to hide their weapons.

But even though it was a concrete plateau rimmed by walls of stone, walking the yard was a coveted privilege that relieved the endless, mind-numbing tedium of prison life. There the prisoners could at least breathe relatively fresh air and see the sky.

Monday, March 14

This was the world to which Daniel Seaton arrived, shackled and chained, on a gray prison bus. As the bus topped a small rise on the ribbon of highway slicing the cornfields and he saw the dark stronghold with its immense walls, his stomach had tightened.

Nothing in his experience had prepared him for life in a maximum-security institution. He had tried to mentally prepare himself. He had resolved to relinquish, as best he could, any holds on life beyond the walls. He realized that living for his family's visits could drive him to despair, so he would live one day at a time, meeting the challenges and troubles as they came. *God is with me*, he told himself over and over.

He shared a two-man cell with a lifer named Don who painted and wrote odd, Zenlike poetry. Twenty years ago, Don had killed his ex-wife and her fiancé with a mail bomb disguised as a wedding present. Don was quiet, reflective, and a little bit crazy, but he kept out of Daniel's face and occasionally enlightened him with bits of wisdom about prison life.

For his part, Daniel read his Bible furiously, focusing in particular on Paul's letters, relishing the kinship of incarceration, a link he had never expected to share with the great apostle. If Paul had survived prison—that is, until he was executed, Daniel thought wryly—then he could do the same. God was with him.

A FAIR NUMBER of D.C. drug-gang members were incarcerated at Newton. Though the gangs had been popping off one another with great regularity for years, there seemed to be an endless supply of young men rising up in the drug ranks to take their places.

With each generation, the loss of conscience had grown greater, until the young men in their late teens and early twenties now at Newton made no distinction between right and wrong and knew only violence as a means to prove their manhood. They were a pitiless lot, and many of them were housed on Daniel Seaton's wing. From there they ran a busy clandestine smuggling operation within the prison, where drugs and other contraband were astonishingly plentiful.

One officer who had looked the other way for them a few times was now driving a champagne-colored Lexus. Another, who had thrown three of them into solitary confinement when he had found drugs on them after visits from their old ladies, had been surrounded one morning and stabbed repeatedly with homemade prison knives. He had recovered, but had been forced to retire on disability, having lost the use of his right arm.

IN THE MIDST of all this, Daniel prayed vehemently to keep his expectations and emotions at a stable level. He got involved with the chaplaincy program, one of the various educational and work opportunities offered to inmates, depending on security clearance, and found a small but vigorous Christian community. There was a chapel meeting once a week with volunteers from the outside, and against his best efforts, Daniel found himself living for that Thursday night Bible study and Mary's weekly visits on Saturdays.

On her last visit, Mary had told him, a little breathlessly, that she had received a phone call from the attorney general herself, woman to woman, telling Mary that she was thinking about a way that she just might be able to get Daniel moved. He would be farther from home but in a federal institution with a less-violent reputation, one that housed mostly white-collar criminals.

"Keep this absolutely quiet," Mary had said. "Mrs. Gineen said she was thinking about doing something fairly radical to get you out. I don't know quite what she meant."

Daniel had tried to thrust that particular hope to the back of his mind...but despite his most vigorous efforts, it became a lifeline for him through the cold, damp days of March.

Thursday, April 14

It happened on a Thursday evening.

That morning a busload of new inmates had arrived, and, as always, the older cons had looked over the young guys stepping uncertainly into their cell blocks. Some inmates were welcomed with backslapping and shouts, as if it were a big, happy family reunion.

"Been waitin' for you, man," the shout came down as one muscular new arrival with a shaved head entered the wing. "What's the word on the street?"

Others entered the blocks with less confidence. New inmates, or "fish," were vulnerable; most would have to align themselves with a group for protection in order to survive. Some new prisoners found that the price for protection was their own bodies; some became prison prostitutes or the property of older inmates, called "jockers" or "wolves." Young or physically weak inmates were particularly vulnerable. In the all-male environment of prison, many otherwise heterosexual prisoners met their sexual needs with "queens"—gay inmates who adopted a feminine role—or by preying on "punks," weak inmates who performed sexual acts in order to stay alive.

So it was that a stream of catcalls and whistles greeted a slender, smooth-faced boy named Terrence Watson. Watson was borderline retarded, one of six children, who had no idea who his father was. One summer night, his seventeenth birthday, he had drunk a bottle of MD 20-20 with a sixteen-year-old friend then decided to rob a small Korean grocery store on Capitol Hill, armed with handguns they had "borrowed" from the sixteen-year-old's older brother.

The boys had gotten angry when the clerk had locked the register and reached for the police alarm button, then panicked when a second clerk burst out of the storeroom in the back of the shop. They had wildly sprayed the two men with gunfire then fled on foot. Police had found them hiding in the scraggly bushes of Lincoln Park.

The two clerks had died, and now Terrence Watson, who still didn't quite know why he had done what he did, was looking at a life sentence in Newton Federal Correctional Institution.

Watson's eyes were wide with fright as he looked over the dark rows of barred cells. Calls filtered toward him.

"Hey there, darlin', I want some of that."

"Need a place to sleep tonight, sweetheart?"

Daniel Seaton, who had drawn the job of cleaning the walkways of his cell block, kept swabbing the concrete floor with a fat gray mop, but inside he was burning with disgust.

That evening, as Daniel was on his way to the chapel for the Bible study, he turned a corner and found three inmates surrounding the new kid. He recognized the three as members of one of D.C.'s drug gangs; Don had pointed them out to him during his first week at Newton. Two were huge men; they had been convicted of murdering five members of a rival gang in just one night of drive-by shootings and execution-style murders. They were bodyguards, of a sort, to the third, a convicted murderer named Shaqqar Redding, who had a reputation as the mastermind behind some of D.C.'s dirtiest drug business. It was Redding who was harassing the kid.

"You gonna need some protection while you here, sweet boy," he was saying. "What's your name?"

"Terrence W-w-watson," the kid stuttered.

"My friends and me, here, we'll be glad to take care of you, Terrence," said Redding. "We hear you like to drink sweet wine, and we've got a little something you might enjoy."

"I dunno," said Terrence. "I got to get to my cell. I don't wanna mess up on my first day."

"We'll take care of you," the older man said smoothly, laying his hand on the boy's arm. "You just come with us. We got a little time before the next count. You won't mess up."

Daniel's stomach pitched with fear, but he stepped forward.

"Why don't you leave him alone?" he said mildly. "He's just a kid."

The three men turned slowly, deliberately, toward Daniel.

"It's the preacher," the bigger bodyguard said to Redding.

Shaqqar Redding looked Daniel over, his grip tightening on Terrence Watson's thin arm.

"You might want to just mind your own business," Redding said with exaggerated courtesy. "This doesn't involve you."

For a flicker of a second, Daniel agreed. The cardinal rule, every halfway friendly inmate had told him ever since he had arrived at Newton, was "Don't get involved." Period. Stay to yourself, see nothing, hear nothing, say nothing, and maybe nothing will happen to you.

He looked at the kid again. The boy's eyes were wide. The bigger man's fingers pressed deeper into his arm. He looked at Daniel, wincing a little bit.

Daniel took a deep breath and looked both ways down the corridor. He could see an officer about a hundred feet away, rounding a corner, heading slowly in their direction.

"Listen," he said again, "why don't you just leave him alone? Give him a break. Think of him as your younger brother."

Redding's muscles tightened in his jaw, and as he turned fully toward Daniel, Daniel saw his eyes for the first time in the fluorescent light. His pupils were tiny pinpoints. Daniel realized belatedly that the man was high on something, probably smuggled amphetamines.

Redding looked at his lieutenants, then shrugged and dropped Terrence Watson's arm. "Sure," he said to Daniel. "Fine. We'll just leave him alone. Come on, boys."

Daniel exhaled, not sure what to think. The two bodyguards clustered around Redding for a moment as he turned and began to walk away, and Terrence looked at Daniel questioningly. Then, suddenly, Redding whirled around, his right hand clenched tight in a fist. Extending from the fist was a six-inch narrow blade with a needlelike point on the end.

The stiletto caught Daniel in the upper left chest and pierced his heart. The muscle continued to pump for a moment, tearing itself further with each beat, and blood flooded Daniel's chest cavity even though the small hole in his shirt barely bled.

Daniel looked down at himself in disbelief for just a moment, then sank to his knees on the concrete. The three men walked rapidly in the opposite direction. Terrence Watson stared down for a moment, not even sure what had happened—he had seen only the fist, not the stiletto. Then he began to scrabble away as well, following the three, who by now had vanished around a corner.

The officer, in the distance, had seen only a clump of inmates talking, then saw one of them pitch to the ground. He ripped his radio off his belt and called for backup, then ran toward the fallen inmate.

Daniel Seaton lay in a heap, facedown on the cold concrete floor. The officer turned him over and saw the small red tear in his shirt. A slender river of blood ran out of his mouth, but his eyes were already fixed and dimming. He was dead.

62

EMILY GINEEN pressed her forehead against the cool glass of her library window, looking out into the dark night, seeing nothing but the faint shadow of her own reflection. She felt sick.

The kids were in bed, and she had been sitting at her desk, sipping a mug of tea and working her way through a stack of papers, when the call came. She was alone; there was no one to confirm that the ghastly call had really happened, so she found herself actually checking reality again.

Yes, she thought slowly, the phone had rung; Mort Cranston, head of the Bureau of Prisons, had told her tersely that Daniel Seaton had been murdered at Newton earlier tonight. There were several suspects, but details were sketchy at the moment. They would find out more and call her back in the morning with a full briefing. She looked at her scribbled notes on the pad next to the phone. It hadn't been a dream.

She looked at her watch. She dreaded the 11:00 news, but the media might have a detail or two about Daniel's death that Cranston had not. She had to watch. Then she would call Frederick. Then Paul. And maybe Mary Seaton.

Monday, April 18

Four days later, Emily was back at her desk, the doors to her office shut, Paul Clarkson sitting opposite her. She had canceled all appointments for the afternoon and blocked an hour of time with him. No calls except the White House, she'd told her secretary, absolutely no interruptions.

"I went to see Mary Seaton late last night," Emily told Paul. "I drove myself, got there after her children were in bed, after the media had left for the night."

Paul nodded. Emily looked terrible. She was as tailored and crisp as ever, but there were deep circles under her eyes and her face was pale, tired, older.

"She's an incredible woman," Emily continued. "I wanted to tell her myself about Terrence Watson's testimony about the situation surrounding Daniel's death. I wanted to tell her that I felt responsible for that situation. He probably should not have been convicted in the first place—well, that was out of our hands—but he never should have been sent to Newton. This administration has created such an ugly atmosphere, Paul. It was like Daniel was a scapegoat for all that. People were hungry for blood, and they got it.

"I wanted to understand how Mary was dealing with everything that has happened," she said. "I didn't comfort her much; it was almost like she was a priest, and I was there for confession. Once we got started, I couldn't stop talking."

Paul nodded again. Emily had been coming apart at the edges ever since the news about Daniel's murder. She hadn't been herself. He could almost—but not quite—imagine the torrent of words that must have confronted Mary Seaton.

"I told her that Watson said Daniel was trying to keep the other guys from hurting him. He said it all happened so fast, but it was like Daniel turned their attention away from him and toward himself. He was protecting him. And they killed him."

She looked down while she said this, then looked up again at Paul. "Watson has been in protective custody since he talked to the officers. I've given the order for him to be moved this afternoon to another institution. I am not repeating the same mistake that happened with Daniel Seaton.

"I have also given quite a lot of thought and consideration to the other matter I want to share with you," she said, speaking more like her usual self. "I've prepared a letter to the president—typed it up myself early this morning. It is my formal resignation from the office of attorney general."

She slid a single sheet of paper across the desk toward Paul. He read it quickly.

"This is a draft, I trust?" he asked, catching her by surprise.

"Why?" she asked, teasing for a moment. "Did I spell something wrong?"

"Something bigger than that. Why are you doing this?"

"For the first time in my life, I have absolutely had it. I'm a fixer by nature. Usually I can see how to make a situation better, how to win...but not this time. This time I see no way out but out. I've been thinking about it a lot. From the very beginning—actually, from even before the inauguration, when that abortionist was shot—this administration has missed the boat.

"I shouldn't have expected the president to really be able to see it; I realize he's not a particularly discerning person when it comes to moral issues. Far from it. But I should have seen it. It was like I had blinders on. At every step, in response to every crisis, we made policy without any understanding of human nature or the moral issues. You made some good points along the way, but I guess I wasn't really listening. Until the last few months.

"Now I look back, and everything is one huge mess. The most powerful government on earth, and we are running on fumes. Over at the White House, the president has turned into an automaton. Ever since Bernie's death. He doesn't know what to do next unless some pollster tells him it'll be popular. This is not the type of work I signed on to do."

She paused to take a breath.

Paul inhaled deeply, gathering his thoughts. He was exhausted, too. He hadn't slept much the past few nights. But he also hadn't realized what a toll recent events had taken on Emily. Ever since she met with Daniel Seaton in the jail, she had pulled back from him a little, in subtle ways. They still had a great working relationship, but it was as if she had become more private with her personal assessments. Now they were spilling out in a flood.

"Emily. Please reconsider," he said. "If you resign, what in the world will Whitney Griswold do? You've said it yourself: The administration is in a shambles; the cabinet is on autopilot—"

She broke in. "You told me before, right after Bernie's death, that people have three choices. They accept Christ as the Truth, they reject Him, or they go insane. You tell me what you think will happen to Whitney Griswold."

Paul stared at her. "Wait a minute," he said. "We were talking about your resignation. Where did that come from?"

"Look," she said. "I'm sorry. I guess I am jumping around a bit. I haven't slept much. One thing at a time. What did you want to say about my resignation?"

"You can't pull out," he said bluntly. "This government needs you. Some of the problems we have right now have come because the government—actually, I should say the people who make up the government—have not understood some basic principles. A government can't govern wisely unless it's made up of people of virtue. Government is not some mega-nanny or huge computer technocracy. It has to be the means by which justice is maintained for the people. For that to happen, it needs people within it who understand right and wrong, people who determine to restrain evil and promote good within the populace at large. People who have the confidence of the governed.

"If you leave your post in this government, Emily, who will do that? The person who takes your place? Not very likely."

"Unless it was you," Emily broke in.

Paul stopped for a moment. That thought had never entered his mind. "Are you kidding?" he asked. "They would never even consider me. I'm here because of a horse trade with Langer, remember?"

Emily raised her eyebrows. Her private conversation with Senator Langer about Paul's appointment seemed like a hundred years ago. It had made her so angry at the time. She couldn't quite remember why.

"I've thought about resigning a dozen times over the past few months," Paul said. "I've been tremendously frustrated. But I've felt like I had to stay, to be a Christian influence where it's desperately needed. Any government, but particularly this administration, needs people who recognize moral standards in positions of influence, Emily." He paused for a moment, fumbling for words. "And even though you don't call yourself a Christian in the same way I do, you need to be at your post as well."

"How do you know I don't call myself a Christian the same way you do?" Emily said. "Isn't that a little bit presumptuous?"

Paul waved his hands. "You know by now I don't mean to offend. We've had that conversation before. I just didn't want to label you in a way that you've told me in the past you don't appreciate. You've said you don't consider yourself one of those 'wild, extremist born-againers.'"

Emily grinned at him, looking for the first time in days like her old self, but still a little different. "Well, maybe I've become one."

"What do you mean?" Paul said, thoroughly confused by the course of the entire conversation.

"I'm still not an extremist. And I still don't like labels. But I've been realizing something ever since I talked to Daniel Seaton. It's like I've been remembering something I knew once but had forgotten. The remembrance of things past, something half-known but buried like a dream, a longing for something permanent, fixed, absolute, something that I once hoped existed, but for which I had lost hope.

"But when I talked to Mary Seaton last night, it all came together for me. I can't put it into religious terminology for you, but it's like what Daniel Seaton said, and something you said earlier: You either believe that Jesus is the Truth, or you don't. Well, I believe it."

63

IN RESPONSE to the Orwellian events around them, the president's advisors had taken a decidedly Norman Rockwellian turn, studding Whitney Griswold's schedule with all kinds of old-fashioned, cheerfully contrived pieces of vintage political Americana.

The president had appeared at the outdoor wedding of his brother-in-law's niece, grinning and dancing with the blushing bride, a relative he had last seen when was she was six and missing two front teeth. He could still barely remember her name.

He had dedicated a new track on the D.C.-to-New York Metroliner run, cutting a fat red, white, and blue ribbon and then boarding the train, waving and chatting casually, yet presidentially, with a select crop of commuters.

He had taken a group of underprivileged children to the circus, muttering under his breath to his aides the entire time about the stupid acts, the dirty animals, and the obnoxious vendors with their sticky cotton candy and hot dogs. But he had still managed to grin and point to the elephants, laughing with the big-eyed kids. That night, at the White House, he had drunk more than usual.

Some of the photo ops were more substantive: meetings with

foreign leaders in the rose garden, convening a conference on crime with experts from around the country, chairing Cabinet meetings. In such settings, J. Whitney Griswold's tall, graceful demeanor appeared utterly presidential, and the pictures looked good on the evening news and in the papers. Robbie was beginning to hope that maybe, just maybe, their string of bad luck was over.

In late April, Griswold visited Washington, D.C.'s Woodrow Wilson High School for an assembly. The school gymnasium had been transformed into a town-meeting setting, with the less trustworthy elements of the student population arrayed on bleachers. A handpicked group of several dozen students sat in folding chairs on the newly polished gym floor in a semicircle around the president.

Secret Service personnel patroled the building, which had been sealed off. Everyone had passed through metal detectors; everyone had submitted to extensive searches of their persons and book bags. Along with the students, the gym was crowded with members of the print and television media.

Things got off to a decent start. The president had been briefed thoroughly, and the day's topic, "Rights and Responsibilities of the Coming Generation," actually yielded an interesting discussion. The students brought screened questions for the president on higher education, the quest for democracy in central Africa, yet another baseball strike, and his own decision to pursue a law career while he was in high school.

Then a sixteen-year-old named Vidalia Perkins stood up. Vidalia was an honors student chosen to ask a key question about healthcare reform for the inner city, a centerpiece of the president's legislative package on its way to Congress. She walked to the standing microphone and bent it down toward her face. The slip of paper with her question typed on it was in her hand, but she didn't refer to it. *Good poise*, Whitney Griswold thought as she looked him directly in the eye.

"Mr. President," Vidalia said, clearing her throat and stumbling for a second, then regaining her composure. "My name is Vidalia Perkins, and I had a question about healthcare all planned for you, but there's something else on my mind. May I ask you that instead?"

The news cameras turned toward Whitney Griswold, and he nodded smoothly. "Sure, Vidalia," he said. "You go right ahead."

The reporters' recorders and video cameras picked up every word.

"Well," Vidalia said, "I've seen a lot of my friends die here in the city. They've gotten into trouble with drugs. My girlfriend killed herself last week. She left me a note that said she just couldn't go on. I know you had somebody on your staff who killed himself, and I've been wondering how you dealt with it. I mean, what's the point? What kind of hope can you give people in my generation? Many of us feel like there just doesn't seem to be any meaning to life..."

She trailed off, and the president's easy smile took on the look of an animal frozen in a truck's approaching headlights. He quickly assumed a brow-furrowed look of compassion.

"That's a great question, Vidalia," he said, stalling for a moment. "Bright young people like you have asked that in every generation. I'm really sorry about your friend; I know how much it hurts to lose a friend. Believe me." He shook his head in obvious pain. "But even when the going gets tough, those of us who are tough have to just keep going. It's kids like you who make the future bright for the rest of us...and this government is pledged to do all we can to create a society in which you can have hope and opportunity. Together we can do that. Look at the programs like our voluntary service and youth corps.

"As you get involved in things like this, you'll feel good about yourself—you know, get in touch with your feelings and realize who you are. That's it. Because when you feel good, when you have high self-esteem, then you'll help others."

TWO DAYS LATER, Ira Levitz's column blistered the editorial page of the *Washington Post*.

"Feel good?" A bottle of cheap wine can make you feel good. If this is the best response the leader of the free world can offer a questioning teenager, we are in far more trouble than any of us ever realized.

The problem is, President Griswold not only missed the answer, he didn't even understand the question. Vidalia Perkins was speaking for a generation of young people who are far smarter than we give them credit, a generation that has seen the situation in America and found it wanting.

I would suggest, in response to Ms. Perkins's question about untimely death and the meaning of life, that perhaps there is far more to be found in the death of convicted conspirator Daniel Seaton than in the death of presidential counsel Bernie O'Keefe.

By all accounts, O'Keefe struggled with a growing sense of despair. Many of us have faced that same black void, and my sympathies are with the man in his last, tortured moments, as well as with his family, left behind to deal with his loss. But his death took place in a vacuum. What meaning can one derive from it? "Don't do this"? Why not?

By contrast, I can't help but take the rather unpopular view of admiring Daniel Seaton. Seaton's naiveté hooked him into a conspiracy that took him, unjustly in my opinion, to the pit of one of our worst federal correctional facilities. There, Seaton died defending a young, handicapped inmate from the depraved designs of a group of criminals. In essence, Daniel Seaton gave his life for another. Never mind that the man for whom he died was a convicted murderer, an impaired young man who will never see free society again.

Seaton died defending someone weaker than himself. O'Keefe died escaping from himself.

There is a lesson for Vidalia Perkins—and all of us—in Mr. Seaton's death. The "meaning to life," as Ms. Perkins put it, is to be found more in the ancient notion of giving oneself for others than in the modern concept of feeling good about oneself. If this president ever knew that fact, he has forgotten it.

Perhaps, through the death of a good man in the nexus of evil, we will begin to find that the moral malaise of the past year can begin to be purged. Perhaps, when the despair goes deep enough, something within us responds, saying "this far, and no farther."

Perhaps, as we confront the mayhem, we are compelled to return to the hope of permanent truths long abandoned. Perhaps we are compelled to look to something beyond ourselves...

LEVITZ LEFT THAT LAST SENTENCE of his piece unfinished. He couldn't think of a time, ever in his life, when he had concluded a column with an ellipsis, but this time it felt wrong to end with a declarative summation. No, better, just this once, to leave it open...

BY THE MIDDLE of June, as summer officially arrived, there were small signs of change in the warm, fragrant air.

The hydrangea was flowering in Mary Seaton's garden just a few days after she received a surprising phone call from Jennifer Barrett, who expressed her condolences and asked if she might visit. Soon after, Mary also received an ebullient letter from Amy, who had married the youth pastor at her parents' church in California. She was expecting twins. In Mississippi, Byron Langer, who was preparing to open a law office after the elections and the end of his Senate term, presided over the first birthday party of his sixth grandchild.

In North Dakota, a young woman named Sherry Sullivan, a long-time friend of Alex Seaton, turned herself in for the murder of Dr. Ann Sloan and implicated two others in the conspiracy. Meanwhile, the FBI pursued a tip that Frank Doggett had been sighted in a small village forty miles from San José, Costa Rica.

John Jenkins and his family moved from Washington to Southern California. Anne Griswold resigned four of her board memberships and made plans for an extended summer stay at Martha's Vineyard.

Hal Humsler became the manager of a video rental store in Spartanburg, South Carolina, and always remembered to take his medication. Reginald Warner completed his community service sentence and prepared to enter Columbia University's media communications program.

Influenced by his friendship with Father Bob Garrison, Marilyn O'Keefe's eldest son, Matt, made plans to go to Georgetown University, where attendance at Mass and student-led prayer meetings had been so high that even the *Washington Post* had sent a reporter to cover the story.

Rob and Lisa Knight welcomed a baby boy into their family. They named him Daniel.

And, pressured by his own Justice Department, J. Whitney Griswold withdrew the National Guard from the streets of several of the nation's major cities. Ironically, statistics showed a slight drop in the crime rate in those cities the following month. To the surprise of many, a move was begun in the Congress to block the regeneration centers. Though it fell short of a majority, sponsors promised a renewed effort. Shortly after, an ABC News poll found a significant shift in public sentiment, with the majority of respondents *opposing* the centers. And a *Newsweek* national poll found an unexpected slight upturn in people's confidence regarding the future for the nation.

ON JULY 4, Attorney General Emily Gineen hosted a catered picnic at her home for her staff and their families. After feasting on grilled chicken, hamburgers, pasta salad, watermelon, and double-chocolate brownies, Paul Clarkson packed his family and a few leftover balloons into their Volvo. Before he swung into the driver's seat, Paul paused to shake Emily's hand.

"Thanks so much, Emily. This was the best idea anybody at Justice has had in a long time. Everyone has been saying what a boost it's been."

Emily grinned. "It's good to get away from the office and stop and appreciate one another now and then. Thanks for all your help." She leaned down and waved through the window. "Bye, June. See you Sunday."

64

Saturday morning, July 9

THE SUN was barely above the horizon, a blazing orange ball shooting its fiery glow across the churning ocean. A glorious moment, and Whitney Griswold breathed deeply of the fresh, salty air, enraptured by the splendor of the setting. A brisk southwest breeze was raking the waters just off Martha's Vineyard. He could see across Nantucket Sound to the shoreline of Cape Cod. A great day for sailing.

Yessir, perfect sailing, thought Griswold, and he was ready for it, dressed in khaki slacks and a blue turtleneck sweater. Draped over his left arm was a dark blue windbreaker with the presidential seal embroidered over the left breast. The windbreaker was a standard White House perk for senior staff—but only Griswold, of course, had "The President" embroidered over the seal.

The President. Griswold smiled to himself. *Yes, indeed.* He used to stand right on this spot as a kid and think of his destiny, the greatness he knew he would attain. He lifted his foot onto the thick rail that surrounded the enormous veranda running across the front and around the side of his cedar-shingled Starbuck Point home. Then, with folded arms, he leaned forward on his raised knee and looked across the generous green lawn that stretched level, then sloped gently down to the ocean. Perhaps this evening the family would play croquet at sunset, just like they used to years ago.

Griswold took in huge gulps of the salt air and exhaled slowly. The doctor had told him that deep breathing was not only good for tension but for cleansing the oxygen in one's body. Gazing into the distance, he could see small boats already pushing into the waves across the harbor on the other island, Chappaquiddick. He sipped his coffee—made with six scoops for eight cups of water, just the way he liked it—and checked his watch. 7:45. In fifteen minutes the launch would take him to his boat, the *Sea Hawk*.

Oh, how he'd longed for this moment for months; to be here and on the water. It would give him a fresh perspective. He needed that, with only four months to the mid-term elections.

Not even two years in office, he thought, and already it had aged him. He breathed deeply again as he ran his right hand over the deep creases in his cheeks. In the mirror this morning, while he was shaving, he'd noticed how hollow his eyes looked, dark and a bit sunken.

He had been too idealistic. He'd had such high hopes when he became president, such noble ideals about public service. But his dreams had been shattered by that assassin's bullet in Fargo, splintered even before his inauguration. It had been downhill ever since. He'd had to use force to suppress attacks on legitimate authority. It was his duty. But the more he applied force, the more the terrorists fought back. It was like fighting a guerrilla war, and the guerrilla always had the advantage.

Terrorism. Violence poisoning our society. Upsetting our balance as a nation. Griswold clenched his fists, breathing harder, faster. Crime and ugliness rampant. And now look at us! The National Guard in the streets...people angry and fearful. Whatever became of the American dream? *Whatever became of my dream?*

Why had all this happened? No doubt it's the fault of radicals who want to bring down our system, he thought angrily. *Like the Seaton brothers—dangerous men, better off dead.*

But then there are some signs things may be turning around, he thought. Just maybe. Robbie says attitudes are different, a little more peaceful since that sanctimonious Daniel Seaton was killed. The polls show it; 60 percent still say America is on the wrong track, but a few months ago it was 80 percent. And whatever happens in the short run, this will all be put in perspective by historians. Remember, Lincoln wasn't popular during the Civil War. Historians are always more charitable. Look at Nixon. Still, we have to get through the November elections.

But people will give us high marks in foreign policy, he thought. No thanks to the State Department, that striped-pants, little-pinky, tea-set crowd. Griswold sipped his coffee and breathed in more of the fresh morning air. Yes, the public would give him credit for the tax cut too; Wall Street certainly liked it. And the Fed—his buddy Roger, now chairman, was coming through—loosening money just in time before the elections. Just like he'd asked him to do. The trade negotiation was good for business, and the crime bill should make people feel safer.

If only the jackasses in the press would give us half a break. They don't want to, of course—that's the problem. They're only happy when they're tearing someone down. A rotten lot—like the rest of the critics. Doesn't matter whether it's the Congress—that slimy, self-seeking bunch of hypocrites—or the lobbyists sucking around sniping at everything you do. Problem is, they're all in the bleachers watching. Only the man in the arena, sweat streaming down his face, bloodied but unbowed, only he understands. That's where the real honor is, not on the sidelines. Teddy Roosevelt understood when he wrote those words. Only the man in the arena.

He smashed his fist into his palm. "We'll show them," he muttered.

But today all that didn't matter. What counts is this twenty-mile-an-hour wind right out of the southwest, he thought, lifting his face to taste the salt breeze. A perfect day to sail. He checked his watch again—five minutes to go—and began to pace the long veranda, past the big wooden rockers with the fresh white cushions tied over the seats and backs. This grand old home, its white trim and balustrades shining against the weathered cedar shingles, was a proud place. For eighty years it had stood with its jaw set against the fiercest nor'easters Mother Nature hurled its way; like the man in the arena, it was unbowed, its honor unsullied. That's the real measure of character: to stand against the best they could hurl at you and keep going. Chin up. Thirty-two percent approval in the polls—so what? They're not in the arena.

Anne, wearing a blue-and-green rugby-striped sweater and white shorts, came through the screen door with Elizabeth and Robert following behind. Like his father, Robert loved the water and was dressed for sailing; Elizabeth was still in her Mickey Mouse nightshirt.

"You sure you ladies won't come?" Griswold said, putting one arm around Anne and drawing her close. "It's a great day to sail."

"No," said Anne. "I've got a tennis game this morning, and Elizabeth's going into town with the Tate girls."

With his other arm he drew Elizabeth to his side, kissing her on the cheek.

"Whitney, please be careful today. Watch the rocks at West Chop," Anne frowned.

"Really now, Anne. I've sailed that point a hundred, no, two hundred times," he grinned.

"I know, dear, but concentrate on your sailing. You've been very ... well, forgetful lately, Whit."

"Nonsense." He put his index finger to her lips. "Just a lot on my mind, you know. But today Robert and I will sail. That's all I'm going to think about."

"The launch is ready, sir," Captain Slattery, the president's naval aide, announced from the foot of the six wide steps leading to the huge oceanfront lawn. He was carrying two bags. One was "the football," the brown bag that contained the code cards for launching a nuclear strike—an anachronism in the post-Cold War world, Griswold had thought, but the military insisted. With terrorists and rogue nations like North Korea, the world was still an uncertain place. In the other bag was the battery-powered communications equipment, a direct satellite uplink courtesy of the army signal corps, enabling him to talk to anyone, anywhere in the world, at any time, almost instantaneously. His doctor along with two Secret Service agents and navy enlisted personnel would be waiting at the launch.

Two other agents, wires from their earpieces threaded under their dark windbreakers, were stationed on the fence line at both corners of the property. They watched as Griswold, Robert, and Sullivan walked down to the pier and the launch.

The chief boatswain's mate saluted as Griswold stepped aboard the forty-five-foot, high-powered vessel. The navy called it an admiral's barge, a fiberglass boat accented with generous amounts of mahogany. In the center was an enclosed cabin with bulletproof glass windows. On the bow were two men, their submachine guns held just below the gunwales, and two others were stationed in the stern.

The boat's engines were throbbing as Griswold stepped into the cabin after returning the boatswain's salute and waving to the lieutenant at the wheel. Its lines cast off, the boat pulled gently from the dock; then its engines roared as it turned northeast to begin the swing around Starbuck Point and then south into Edgartown harbor. Griswold came out of the cabin once the boat was under way, his hair blowing straight back in the wind.

Before he was president he used to have to walk down North Water Street past the Daggard House, then into a narrow street leading to the harbor and the yacht club launch that would take him out to his boat. He missed the sights and sounds and smells of Edgartown harbor. But security was a big consideration, and the navy made it so easy; he could be under way fifteen minutes after leaving his front porch.

As the launch threaded its way into the harbor, Griswold watched the current surging out. A good sign. It would be going with him when he sailed out of the harbor.

He glanced ahead at the two navy patrol boats clearing their way through the harbor; on shore he could see the armed marines. Griswold felt uncomfortable disrupting the tranquil life of Martha's Vineyard. He knew the locals resented it, even though he was a hometown boy, so to speak—but the tourists and shop-keepers loved it.

The *Sea Hawk* came into view, its gleaming black hull looking sleek and graceful at its mooring. Shrewd fellow, his grandfather, to have laid a cast-iron mushroom in the late 1920s right in the choicest mooring spot in this harbor. The *Sea Hawk*, a forty-three-foot wooden ketch, was twenty-three years old but lovingly maintained, its mahogany and brightwork polished and its rails covered with varnish so thick you could see your reflection in them. It had the best pedigree in the harbor, designed by Sparkman and Stephens and built at the Hinkley yard in Southwest Harbor, Maine, the finest yacht craftsmen in the world.

The launch pulled alongside and Whitney scrambled aboard, followed by Robert, Captain Slattery, the doctor, and two Secret Service agents wearing thick sunglasses. Two boatswain's mates who would help crew, along with Lieutenant Coughlin, a communications specialist, were already on board. So was Jeff Springer, a Boston investment banker and an old sailing friend of the president's from boyhood.

Jeff grinned and saluted loosely, and Griswold slammed him on the back. "Great day, huh, Jeff. We'll make the old girl fly today."

Griswold went directly to the cockpit and unfastened the lines holding the boom; then he nodded to Jeff, who went to the base of the main mast and began pulling on the halyard, slowly hoisting the main as Griswold held the boat into the wind.

He grinned as the giant sail fluttered in the breeze. Less proficient or more cautious sorts would motor off the buoy and out of the harbor before setting sail. But the tides were right, so he'd sail off like any good old salt should do. He didn't even turn on the engine, though he noticed one of the boatswain's mates was standing near the switch.

"Secure this," he said, handing the line to Robert after he'd pulled in the mainsheet. Then he turned the helm hard to starboard, and a puff of wind filled the sail just as Jeff, now on the bow, released the mooring.

"Perfect timing," Griswold yelled, grinning triumphantly.

The *Sea Hawk* sliced through the blue water as other boaters cheered. So did a small cluster of people standing on a nearby pier, held back by a wide rope stretched in front of them.

Jeff and Robert unfurled the jib as they glided north, and a cheer went up from another cluster of townsfolk standing on Memorial Wharf. Griswold glanced to the left and waved. A quaint picture it was, the town of Edgartown with its gray, cedar-shingled, colonial buildings decorated with white trim, a church steeple or two, some gingerbread decoration on a few of the buildings, piers, and docks lined along the water. Boats everywhere.

Griswold felt a sudden exhilaration. Home. His harbor. His beloved boat. The salt air. He was positively giddy.

The *Sea Hawk*, jib and main full, began to heel as they left the harbor headed for Marker 8. A puff of wind raised spray, the cold salt water smarting Griswold's cheeks.

At Marker 8 Griswold brought the boat around to a port tack.

"Let it out, son," he shouted, and Robert released the main-sheet, letting the boom way out so that the sail could catch the full breeze coming off the port stern quarter. The boat began to pick up speed, gradually reaching eight knots.

Griswold grinned broadly as he set the course past West Chop, a point of land dotted with homes owned over the years by celebrities like Mike Wallace and Carly Simon, and then took a straight 330-degree bearing, right for Woods Hole. With the wind like this, they'd be there in an hour and a half, and from there through the narrow cut off Nonamesset Island into Buzzards Bay.

JEFF OPENED a beer for himself and asked Griswold if he wanted a Coke; he knew his friend never drank while sailing. The president nodded and smiled.

Jeff thought Whit was unusually quiet today. He'd said nothing other than to call for sail changes. But Jeff waited for him to initiate any conversation, out of deference to the position his friend now held.

Finally Griswold turned to him and said, "Great day."

"Yes, it is," Jeff answered. And then for another twenty minutes Griswold said nothing. He simply gripped the wheel with an almost childlike smile on his face, seemingly unaware of anything or anyone around him.

Finally Jeff could hold back no longer. He had to break the silence.

"Wonderful, isn't it, Whit?"

"What?" Griswold looked startled, then quickly recovered. "Yes, beautiful, beautiful, nothing like it."

"You're quiet today. Everything okay?" Jeff said.

"Just fine, just fine," Griswold grinned. "You know, the great thing about this boat is that the captain controls it. It's right here in my hands." He gripped the wheel and continued to stare straight ahead.

"You turn to the right, it responds. To the left...there, see." He jerked the wheel. "Maybe the only thing left in life that a person can control."

"You need to do this more often, Whit. Get away from Washington."

"And how. You know, Bernie, it's a sick town."

Jeff bit his tongue. Better not correct him; he knew Whitney was still haunted by the suicide of his old friend.

"Positively sick. Full of power-mad people who want to destroy us—the presidency. But we're not going to let those no-good...oh, sorry, Jeff...hard to shake it all off. Yes, this is wonderful, the greatest pleasure I have. Here, Robert, take the helm. Hold this course. We're two miles off Woods Hole."

Robert bounded up to the wheel, and Jeff sat back, relieved.

"This is like old times," Jeff chuckled.

"Sure is." The president pushed up his sleeves and sat back on the cockpit seat, but he still looked somewhat distant.

"Steady on course, Son," Griswold commanded, staring straight ahead, the breeze blowing his hair in all directions.

They were a mile off Woods Hole, headed for the entrance to Buzzards Bay, when the water darkened ahead.

"Looks like the wind's picking up," Jeff said. "Maybe we should reef the main."

Griswold didn't respond.

"Dad!" Robert said, "I think we've got too much sail up."

Griswold was still staring into space. Jeff and Robert looked at each other, uncertain what to do.

Then, just as Jeff stood up to dig out the reefing lines, they hit the first gust and the boat heeled sharply, digging the starboard rail into the water.

"Dad!" Robert yelled, and as Jeff and Griswold were thrown against each other, the president finally snapped out of his daze.

But even after they'd pulled in some sail and Griswold was back at the wheel again, Jeff still couldn't make eye contact with the man.

The pressures must be awful, he thought to himself.

"A beautiful sound, isn't it?" Griswold asked suddenly.

"What?" Jeff asked. "The waves?"

"No, no. The bells, Bernie, the church bells. Must be coming from Falmouth." The president brushed the hair out of his eyes, staring straight ahead.

"I don't hear any church bells, Whit. Can't be. This is Saturday. Maybe it's a bell buoy."

"No, no. Church bells. Listen, clear as can be, and beautiful."

"I don't hear them either, Dad." Robert said, glancing at his father.

"Of course you do," Griswold snapped, finally looking at them, first at his son and then at Jeff with steely eyes and an expression so intense it made Jeff shiver.

"Whit, are you all right?"

"Ah, yes," Griswold sighed. "Bells, beautiful bells. Hear them ring."

ACKNOWLEDGMENTS

We are profoundly grateful to a number of people who have so graciously helped to make this book possible.

We owe heartfelt thanks to: Grace McCrane and Nancy Niemeyer, administrative support; Kim Robbins and Roberto Rivera, as well as Jean Epley and Gordon Barnes, research help; Bessie Cool, interview transcriptions; Emily Murray, Scott Sforza, and Kathy Doyle, ABC News; Ed Wright, Harry Mahon, and their colleague, satellite communications information; Lyn Mickley, the National Institutes of Health; Captain John Sandoz, explosives expertise; Rob Showers, Gammon and Grange, legal help; Father Bob Tabbert; Ted Collins, piloting expertise; Dr. Joseph Spano and Dr. Paul Hoehner, medical information; Nat Belz, *World* magazine.

We appreciate Steve and Sandy Smallman, Wallace and Cynthia Zellmer, General William Maloney, and Dr. Gary Pileggi for taking the time to give critiques of an early draft of the manuscript. Chuck is grateful to Dick and Dottie McPherson and Jack and Ruth Eckerd for the creative time spent in their guest houses. And Ellen extends hearty thanks to Jan O'Kelley, Jan Pascoe, Mildred Santilli, and Norma Vaughn for their kind help with baby-sitting.

Thank you to our faithful, fearless editor, and long-time friend, Judith Markham.

And, as always, we thank our spouses, Patty Colson and Lee Vaughn, for their steadfast love, support, and patience.

ABOUT THE AUTHORS

CHARLES COLSON writes from his rich, unique experiences as a Washington insider who served as a chief Senate assistant on Capitol Hill, and as counsel to President Richard Nixon. He is the recipient of the 1993 Templeton Prize for Progress in Religion, a highly regarded speaker and columnist, and the founder and chairman of Prison Fellowship Ministries. Mr. Colson has authored numerous best-selling books, including *Born Again, The Body* (with Ellen Santilli Vaughn), *Why America Doesn't Work*, (with Jack Eckerd), and *A Dangerous Grace* (with Nancy R. Pearcey).

ELLEN SANTILLI VAUGHN, a talented, accomplished writer in her own right and former vice-president of executive communications for Prison Fellowship, has worked with Charles Colson since 1980, collaborating with him on seven previous books. A Washington D.C. native, she, too, is intimately familiar with the capital city settings of *Gideon's Torch*. Ms. Vaughn earned a bachelor's degree from the University of Richmond and a master's from Georgetown University.